WILD
THORN

Other Fiction by William Hoffman

WILD
THORN

William Hoffman

HarperCollins*Publishers*

WILD THORN Copyright © 2002 by William Hoffman. All rights reserved. Printed in the United States of America. No part of this book may be used or reproduced in any manner whatsoever without written permission except in the case of brief quotations embodied in critical articles and reviews. For information, address HarperCollins Publishers Inc., 10 East 53rd Street, New York, NY 10022.

HarperCollins books may be purchased for educational, business, or sales promotional use. For information, please write: Special Markets Department, HarperCollins Publishers Inc., 10 East 53rd Street, New York, NY 10022.

FIRST EDITION

Printed on acid-free paper

Library of Congress Cataloging-in-Publication Data is available upon request.

ISBN 0-06-019798-6

02 03 04 05 06 ❖ RRD 10 9 8 7 6 5 4 3 2 1

For Emilie Jacobson

Each draws to his best-loved.

—VIRGIL

WILD
THORN

ONE

I lay face up under a night sky not unbounded by space but starless, looming, and closing in as if to make its weight known to me. A random wind carried a restless message and disturbed the sage and swishing buffalo grass of the Great Plains. The wind stirred smoke from our campfire that had shrunk to embers and caused them to come alive with a convulsed red pulsing. The two hobbled horses moved like phantoms through the dark as they searched for graze. A shallow creek flowed over rocks rubbed so many centuries by the relentless water that they had lost all edges and become transformed to smooth configurations of rounds and oblongs. The pitiful, wavering cry of a lone coyote rose off a low bluff and seemed to give voice not just to its own loneliness and longings but also the world's.

The wind aroused scents of the plains and more—the sea of grass, the soil's acrid thirst from lack of rain, and memory if memory could have an essence. The miles I, Charley LeBlanc, had traveled had provided no escape from broken images of loss that invaded and drifted through my mind. There was no fleeing anything, only rickety evasions created to deceive the self.

In shifting scenes played against the murky night, I pictured another time, another place—not mountains like the craggy giants of western Montana or the glacial summits that held skullcaps of snow long into summer and beyond, but elevations forested and tamed that pushed up a measly three or four thousand feet, what the natives hereabouts would consider little more than buttes. The mountains of southern West Virginia weren't gnawed upon by erosion as in the Badlands or kin to the jagged peaks of the Rockies but would this time of year be uncurling moistly green and yielding reluctantly to spring. Beneath them ran not strata of copper, silver, and gold but of low-sulfur coal produced by millennia of the past when luxuriant swamp vegetation decayed and became compacted to petrifaction under the earth's overburden till finally transformed into black diamonds—both the blessing and curse of what in part was a forlorn and desperate land.

I thought of this Montana's wind blowing across the plains, traveling and twisting its way to and among those puny mountains, maybe disturbing the red oaks, the shelly-bark hickories, the papaws, the sycamores, and ruffling their new leaves. The wind would find the gorge the Wilderness River had cut, a torrent of water raging not south or east, but north, up from Carolina to join the Bluestone, the Greenbrier, the Gauley to become the Kanawha, which in turn junctioned with the swollen mighty Ohio.

I pictured a trail that had almost disappeared under sodden leaf falls from mountain hardwoods of generations beyond count as well as recalled the pull against my pants' legs of hip-high growths of snagging hawthorn and stunted honey locusts. The river more than a thousand feet below broke against boulders as large as elephant herds that'd gathered to drink at their evening watering hole.

I augured up in my mind rusted, broken machinery lying among tangles of gleaming poison ivy and ashen wild grass that had somehow found root among crushed coal of a fallen tipple. Wheelless buggies lay overturned, crows flew squawking from crossbeams of wireless power poles, and kudzu had reclaimed beehive coke ovens and reshaped this once half-domesticated land to its own smooth draping. Beside the river the board-and-batten houses of the abandoned camp faced each other windowless across an unpaved company street. As the moist cold of the mountain's shadows filled the gorge, I found partial shelter and refuge in a water-rotted, half-collapsed Jenny Lind— cabins named, my father had told me, after and in honor of the world's most famous opera star, called in her day the Swedish Nightingale. I cleaned out a fireplace and levered off strips of the house's siding to stomp for kindling. From the street I picked up coal where lumps lay scattered among thistles and jimson weed.

Stretched out on the spongy floorboards, I listened to the horned owl's dirgelike love song, a dog barking, a lynx's shriek, the death squeal of a rabbit, the crashing course of the Wilderness River, and the bugled tattoo of a railroad engine's horn, which sounded the plaint of lonely men everywhere. The muted clack of its wheels became lost in the river's din.

An alien sound wakened me—the spaced crunching of boots upon cinders. With the opened blade of my Old Pal pocketknife clenched in my teeth, I crawled to the crumbling porch and peered out among the line of ghostly houses. A shape passed, no hungry grizzly or roaming cougar such as might have been on a hunt here in Montana, but a figure moving upright and not so much walking as seeming to glide as if detached from this earth. The shape vanished among dark gaps between houses, then reappeared like a pilgrim in a ceremonial procession—a moon-silvered form flowing slowly through the night to become reabsorbed by its blackness.

The dog continued to bark, insects throbbed on the mountain's slope, and a whippoorwill sang abruptly and was answered by another more distant. Could any of those sounds have been the language of Esmeralda? If she yet walked the earth, she would not speak the tongue of women but that of creatures of the glens and forests. Did she roaming among the cliffs still hear the thrashing of the river or the ravens' cries from the mountain crests?

For two years I'd been gone, yet in Montana found no release from memories that I tried but could not evade because they would not die.

"What?" Blackie asked. She lay zipped inside her padded sleeping bag laid out alongside mine, her head resting on a rolled poncho athwart the dip of her western saddle. The coyote's cry had quieted. For a moment a sliver of moon tore at clouds before they dragged at and captured it back.

"Guess I'm going," I said.

"What?" she asked again, rousing and rubbing at her eye.

"Back to Shawnee County."

"And you're the one who swore to hell he never would."

TWO

Except for Aunt Jessie Arbuckle, I'd never talked the truth about Esmeralda with anyone, not even Blackie. As she and I droned southeastward in the red Caddy Sedan de Ville bought her with insurance money left me by the woman I'd believed to be my mother, we listened to the radio and CDs, her favorite Willie Nelson, whose wayward, rusty voice carried the honest freight of hard living that both Blackie and I'd known from way back. Over the long run to expect anything else from the life given or inflicted upon you was a trap that set you up for a smash in the face and knockdown for the count.

From Chinook the interstates rolled through South Dakota, Iowa, Illinois, Indiana, Kentucky toward West Virginia. The hum and bump of the Caddy's radials over pavement merged with the music and became as much a part of us as the beat of blood. My body tuned itself to them, though I'd meant to escape forever wheels spinning over the asphalt and concrete fetters that bound the nation.

Blackie and I shared driving. I'd also given her the two-carat diamond ring that glittered while she steered. She wore it not over the third finger of her small weathered left hand but on her right. During the night as we pushed on, headlights of onrushing cars caught a glint in the long scar on her face that ran from her cheekbone to her chin. In public she wore eye patches from a collection she'd sewed—some pink, others polka-dotted or zebra-striped. Both the scar and loss of her eye resulted from a drunken bloody fight with the army sergeant who'd been her stud of a womanizing husband. She had severed his jugular with the jagged edge of a smashed fifth of Jack Daniel's bourbon and served a ten-year-sentence reduced to seven for good behavior at the Federal Prison for Women in Alderson.

I too had known the hole, mine Leavenworth, Kansas, not for killing, though I'd done that at the prison as well as in Nam, where for taking lives I'd received government permission and a soldier's pay.

Blackie's swarthy complexion traced back to coal country with its stew of nationalities—Italians, Poles, Slavs, Negroes, and Middle Europeans all drawn or lured into earning their beans by digging black diamonds among the West Virginia mountains during the early 1900s. She could call up little about her ancestry beyond her dead Spanish grandmother, while I was able to spiel off the LeBlanc branch of my family line all the way to French Huguenots of 1740, a recital my grandfather had required me to perform on occasions at his Bellerive plantation. Since I fled Tidewater, Virginia, I'd never again spoken those names. The other branch of my family tree had been axed and had no designation beyond Esmeralda.

Blackie had taken off for Montana with me in my army-surplus Jeep, and among the few things she'd carried along from The Pit, a roadhouse she'd owned that went broke, was her lever-action Winchester .30-30. At Chinook we had leased two hundred fifty acres seven miles northwest of the town where we meant to shake off our shoes the dust of the south as well as all shackles of the past.

For seven months, even during winter howlers that shut us in for weeks, we never laid a hand on each other. The night the buckskin mare Belle Madre dropped her foal by lantern light, we drank tequila to celebrate our firstborn and found ourselves touching like two people feeling their way around through the darkness of strange and alien space. Blackie shoved me away.

"You sure we ready for this?" she asked. She'd washed her black hair, which she let grow to waist length, and in the flicker of light from our fire she appeared made of fewer edges and a more womanly woman. Blowing snow beat the roof and windows of our cabin. Flakes driven by the wind made it down the chimney and gave up their lives in sizzles. Flames wavered on her face.

"Give it a try," I said.

Her good eye caught glimmers from the fire. The wholeness of the right side of her face and the long scar on the left caused shock to those who first met her—like looking at two different people instead of one. To me that physical division had become natural, and I wouldn't have wanted it different. Plus, to my way of seeing, scars of the body or the mind were survival badges. I trusted few people and remained particularly wary of men or women life had not wounded and marked.

"Okay, tomcat, your move," Blackie said as she unbelted her wool bathrobe.

We stripped down by firelight and fumbled around on the bed. I felt anxious because I'd not known a woman's body since the night following my release from Leavenworth and a steamy, drunken tumble with a Kansas City whore who stole my wallet and left me with the clap. I'd wanted many a woman since but learned for good and all that tits and wheels were nothing but trouble.

Yet in Montana my eyes had begun to take in and wander over Blackie's small, agile body that despite her toughness had lines and curves surprisingly feminine. I noted the grace of her hands when they served me at the table and caught glimpses of her strong thighs when she stood from her bath. We didn't exactly tear up the sheets that first time, but settled to each other and held on. From that night forward we'd slept in the same bed, though neither of us ever breathed the word *love*. Any talk about what we had might've ruined it.

•   •   •

I liked lying back in the seat and seeing her drive. She thought ahead, and to save tire rubber and pads never used the foot brake if she could avoid it. I dozed and at times watched the territory change from the cold, somber vastness of the western plains to domesticated land that seemed to squeeze and contract the farther we traveled east. With each span of distance, I became more uneasy—as if the diminishing countryside and expanse of cities were binding and constricting me.

We pushed that Caddy hard, got pulled by a trooper for speeding outside Cincinnati, and fined a hundred and twenty-five dollars. We stopped only for gas and to wash up and eat. When we drove through the second night into the Appalachians and reached Shawnee County, a morning mist the color of skim milk drifted and gathered in shifting pools along the vales. The secondary road wound upward among wet wooded new growth that covered scars of timbering and coal—lesions in the earth that if not healing were at least hiding. Rusted tracks from a broken headhouse descended and became lost among laurel of the slope. In another couple of years nature would have it all back except during the winters when the land had to show itself naked.

The Caddy climbed looping around the mountain and leveled out at the county seat's town limits. The metal sign read CLIFFSIDE, ELEV 3190. The sign still had a bullet hole in it, and likely no funds existed for repair or replacement. During its day, the early 1900s and up to a dozen years after World War II, Cliffside had been a twenty-four-hour-a-day roaring blast of new wealth and rowdy miners who as fast as they could take it in hand spent the dollars paid to them by the coal companies. When the rich seams thinned or became depleted, the town bled out, not quickly, but a slow hemorrhaging until it became what it was now, a near corpse.

Blackie and I passed neglected frame houses, some covered with artificial brick siding. Along General Lafayette Street closed shops and stores looked out from darkened empty windows. The three-story hotel named the Mountaineer Majestic, which in advertisements had bragged it offered a bath in every room, now stood deserted, its panes of glass broken or gone. Pigeon dung whitened the Chinese-style red roofing tiles of the Victorian courthouse. A "Vote for Byrd" sticker arrayed the barrel of the World-War-I French 75mm artillery piece, and the statue of a Confederate soldier forever trodding had lost half the bayonet blade of the rifle he carried. Only the aged white oak tree, responding to sun and warmth after a mountain winter, displayed any vestige of bygone glory.

When I stopped at the Shawnee Food Market, the shelves did not appear fully stocked. I bought a carton of Camels for Blackie and me and a tin of Copenhagen snuff as well as two pounds of lemon drops to carry to Aunt Jessie Arbuckle, who was no blood kin, though I called her aunt, as did most everyone else in the county. She'd dip the snuff and pay out the lemon drops a few at a time to Esmeralda. I also intended to leave money for Aunt Jessie to buy clothes or anything else Esmeralda might need.

Ancient, shrunken, her face rutted, Aunt Jessie gave off not only dignity, but also a self-sustaining independence that had once existed in these mountains among the natives prior to the inroad of out-landers the coalfields had drawn. Hers was the blood and pride of the wild, feuding Scotch-Irish who had been dominant before the arrival and final conquest of the mining companies and the seduction of the mountain people.

Aunt Jessie lived southwest of Cliffside, down a narrow mountain road riven by potholes, the edges broken into shards, the shoulders falling away steeply. On the way I slowed so Blackie could look at The Pit, the rollicking roadhouse she had once tried to operate. Only sections of the cinderblock foundation remained, and they had grown crops of briars and honeysuckle. All had been plundered, every board, screw, and nail carried away under cover of night to find new life in houses and sheds of those who had once been neighbors. In a wanting land nothing was wasted.

"Where'd I ever get the idea I could make a living out of that rat hole of a place?" Blackie asked. "Wasn't much left anyhow after you and Junior Bartow tore it up fighting."

"Only fighting I did was trying to get out alive," I said.

"Fighting's fighting," she said. "It don't care about who, what, where, when, or how."

We crossed the chipped one-lane concrete bridge over Persimmon Creek, a stream that ran fast and pure, its grassy underwater strands like long green hair stringing and waving in the current. Nothing had changed. The dirt road on the other side trailed up beside the flow before cutting away and zigzagging across the slope as if laid out by a drunk. The crookedness could've been intentional, a means to lessen the straight-up pull of this vertical land, a switchback demanded by gravity and laid by wagon wheels over uncounted years.

As I slowed before turning, the two-toned brown State Police patrol car swerved out onto the county road in front of us. I braked hard. The trooper stopped his Ford, backed beside the Caddy, and peered at me. I felt the old sickening fear rise like a submerged rotted log. My hands tightened on the wheel, and my foot edged toward the accelerator until the ruddy-faced trooper drove on without speaking, his tires throwing up bits of sod brought down from Aunt Jessie's.

"What'd the law be doing up there?" Blackie asked.

"Maybe checking on her or carrying a message," I said. "She's not got a phone."

"I know what she don't got," Blackie said.

I quieted and lengthened my breathing. You paid and are free, I told myself, yet once taken by the law and run through the gullet of its merciless machinery, a man never again felt really free, not even in the endless flat and open expanses of the Great Plains.

I steered up the wagon road. Sumac, laurel, and black haw covered the lower slope. We passed outcroppings of lichen-splotched limestone. The pitch of the land lessened to a bench of cleared fields and a farmstead bounded by split-rail fences of locust posts and chestnut rails—they, like Aunt Jessie, meant to last. The pasture held a lowing, cud-chewing Holstein. A run flowed down the mountain and into an entry beneath her plank springhouse. The cold water's swirling around jars and demijohns served as Aunt Jessie's refrigerator. She had no electricity and, like me, wanted none.

Her apple trees dropped white petals on the slanted orchard. The southern lee of the mountain protected the log cabin, which had a fieldstone chimney and cedar-shingle roof seasoned the color of slate. No smoke rose from that chimney, but Dominickers and guineas pecked around the yard. Where was Rattler, her dog, who usually came barking? And there was something else.

"What's he doing?" Blackie asked as we drew closer.

A man, a county mountie, walked backwards from the rear of the cabin. Dark brown stripes ran down the seams of his tan uniform. His badge, the leather of his belt, and his holster caught polished gleams of an emerging sun. He unrolled yellow tape from a spool toward the persimmon tree in front of the doorway and stopped to tear off an end. He wrapped the end twice around the trunk before tying a knot.

I stopped the car, switched off the ignition, and we stepped out. Blackie lifted the paper sack of Copenhagen and lemon drops off the seat. When the deputy saw us, he held out a hand palm upward as if stopping traffic. He laid the spool of tape on the ground before approaching.

"Far enough, this property off-limits," he called, a young man who looked as if he could've been out of high school not more than a year or two. He wore his tan trooper hat with a slight forward cant. The plastic nameplate pinned over his shirt pocket read HARP LESTER.

"Why?" Blackie asked, not kowtowing to the law but boldly and as if she had every right to know. Backing off was not her style, she a banty rooster of a woman ready to scratch and claw. Let her, I thought, do the talking. I hated my chest's tightness and the sweat forming under my armpits.

"This place undergoing a police investigation," the deputy said. "You not allowed up here."

I looked past him to a scythe lying on the ground alongside Aunt

Jessie's wooden bench placed beneath limbs of the persimmon tree. Beyond, the iron pot she used for making soap sat on a circular bed of smoke-blackened rocks. Her vegetable garden had been weeded. I remembered the wild sourwood honey and the hot and heavy biscuits she'd made and served me when I was on the run from the law. Again I wondered about Rattler.

"Where's Aunt Jessie?" Blackie asked.

"You kin?" the mountie asked. He had taken in Blackie's scar and white eye patch. She had become used to being stared at.

"We here to see her."

"Miss, you be having a hard time doing that, at least on this earth. Aunt Jessie was laid to rest the day before yesterday down at Mt. Olivet Baptist."

"Aunt Jessie's dead?"

"They usually dead when they plant them down at Mt. Olivet," the smart-ass mountie said.

"Don't talk to me that way, buddy," Blackie shot at him. "You got no respect for those in the grave?"

"I got respect. I seen too much of dying. Blood and guts spilled all over the highway. See them in my sleep."

"And Esmeralda?" I asked.

The deputy turned and gave me his who-the-hell-are-you-to-question-me expression. I made myself meet it.

"You all just get on to the sheriff if you got questions about Aunt Jessie and Esmeralda 'cause you sure can't come up here," he said. "Me, I got to finish taping and get rid of all these damn chickens."

"Foxes, coons, and lynxes'll do that," Blackie said and looked to me. I nodded. We walked back toward the car. The deputy had picked up the spool of tape to finish stringing it around the cabin.

"They all snotty," Blackie said. "They train them that way. Let's go see that thing around here they call a sheriff."

THREE

We headed back fast to Cliffside and pulled in at the curb alongside the courthouse, its faded red bricks grimy, its Chinese tile
roof and eaves a roost for pigeons who looked as if they too could've
used a hosing. Plenty of parking spaces among lines of rusting meters
installed when coal was selling and times good. An hour's parking cost
a dime. Blackie knew from the days she'd lived in Shawnee County
that the sheriff's office was in the basement.

She opened the Caddy's door, stepped out, and tightened the belt
of her Levi's. It had a Mexican silver buckle and a tumbleweed design
tooled into the leather. Tumbleweed suited us, could've been our coat
of arms. She leveled her pearl-gray Stetson. The heels of her western
boots struck hard on a sidewalk heaved up by the roots of the domi-
nating white oak tree. Even wearing boots and the hat, Blackie was a
shorty.

Aunt Jessie's spirit and strength of character had been a model for
Blackie and me. The grand old lady had tended her garden and milk
cow as well as cultivated a small patch of illegal tobacco to satisfy her
hankering to chew. She'd tossed scratch corn to her Dominickers and
guineas. Despite her age, she had survived the winters alone in her

snug kitchen, where she hung up dried vegetables as well as rabbits and squirrels she'd snared, skinned, and smoked. Snow might pile up as high as the windowsills, but her woodpile had lasted, and during the worst shriekers her chimney smoke had scented the area, a wisping flag of her survival and dominion snatched away but always revived.

She'd stood by me when it looked as if my time had run out for good and all. She'd also revealed to me the truth about Esmeralda, the wild woman who lived in the forests, burrows, or caves and snuck out nights around Cliffside, where people hung food for her in trees to keep wild dogs from eating it. Aunt Jessie had left Esmeralda not only food and warm clothes but also rationed out the lemon drops I sent money to provide.

Because the sheriff's office was underground and windowless, the place had the feel of a cavern. Light from buzzing fluorescent tubes along the ceiling didn't seem to reach all the corners. One nearly burned-out tube flickered and spat. I glimpsed the cellblock's black iron bars, and my genes cringed and urged me to make tracks. Blackie glanced at me. She touched my arm to keep me moving.

An elderly deputy stood at a table along the gray wall frying an egg in a skillet on a gas one-burner hot plate. His tan uniform shirt opened unbuttoned at the collar, his green twill pants sagged around his hips, and his smudged high-top basketball shoes were loosely tied around his bony ankles. He looked at us as if fretted by the interruption.

"Ain't had breakfast yet," he explained and flipped the egg into the hissing grease. He used a plastic spatula to splash more grease over the egg. He wasn't about to stop to deal with us. The weight of his badge fastened to a breast pocket caused it to droop. His .38 Police Special and handcuffs lay on the table beside the hot plate.

I glanced at curled men-wanted posters on the wall, the rotary-dial telephone, the out-of-date radio transmitter. The gun rack held a twelve-gauge shotgun and an M-1. A calendar from Beckley's Appalachian Bank pictured a ruffed grouse drumming on top a mossy log. The place smelled of grease and a moldy dampness.

"We come to ask about Aunt Jessie Arbuckle," Blackie said, stepping ahead of me.

"Aunt Jessie gone," the deputy said, slipping the spatula under the egg and setting it on a slice of white bread drawn from a sliced loaf. "Done give up the ghost and met her Maker."

"How'd that happen?"

"Well, she upped and died," the deputy said and bit down on the bread and egg. The runny yellow spread over his grainy tongue.

"We able to figure that," Blackie said. "Upped and died from what?"

"What you need to know for?" he asked as he chewed with slow methodical strokes of his jaw. His false teeth were too large for his mouth.

"We from out of town and went up to visit her at Persimmon Creek."

"You not from out of town. I recognized you soon as you come through that door. You Mildred Spurlock and used to run The Pit. You left this town without telling nobody nothing."

"I remember you too," Blackie said. "You a Lester and got this job 'cause you a cousin to the sheriff."

"A man got to put bread on his table," the deputy said. "You want to know about Aunt Jessie, you best talk to Basil."

He took a second bite of his sandwich as he shuffled toward a closed door, knocked, and entered. Still eating, he shut the door behind him.

"I know the sheriff," Blackie said. "Wish I didn't. Basil Lester. They held me here in this jail a spell. Basil'll kiss any ass that's got the shine of money on it. Tried to become a professional wrestler who fought under the name of Mountain Man. Didn't go very far and never made TV. His kinfolk keep him in office. Election Day they come down out the hollers like squirrels out the trees and vote him in."

The door opened, and the deputy shuffled out swallowing the last of the sandwich. He rubbed his hands as if washing them at a sink.

"Basil'll see you," he said, and stood aside.

Sheriff Basil Lester had been playing solitaire. The cards spread across his desk, and he didn't acknowledge us till he finished placing a black jack on a red queen. He was heavyset and muscular, though giving way to settling flesh. He appeared a dude, wearing not a uniform but a lightweight gray suit, white shirt, red tie, and white Panama hat. Deep-set eyes pushed up under dark bushy brows. He lowered his palms against his desk to stand as if being sparing of his energy and wishing to pay it out slowly.

"So there you are, Blackie," he said. "I figured you was gone for good."

"Basil, you putting on weight."

"Who ain't?" he asked. "Yeah, figured I'd seen the last of you. Whose this gent'man you got behind you?"

"Charley's my name," I said.

"That all? Most people got last names, least 'round here."

"He's a LeBlanc," Blackie said.

The sheriff ran his eyes over me as if I was a beef he considered buying at the livestock market.

"I remember talk of the High Moor LeBlancs when they ruled the roost in Shawnee County," the sheriff said. A large Masonic ring set with a ruby stone circled the third finger of his right hand. That ring was meant not only for display but also hitting, like brass knuckles. It was a weapon. "You the same blood?" he asked.

"He's Boss John's son," Blackie said.

Boss John was John Maupin LeBlanc III, my father, the man who had reopened the High Moor mines and restored the family fortune. He'd also hated me for being a living reminder of what he had done to Esmeralda and my knowledge of what he really was.

"Well now," the sheriff said. "I thought the LeBlancs had turned tail out of this county for good and all. Charley, huh? Let's see, I think I got it. You the one that's been in the government hotel and the law was chasing down in Virginia, am I right?"

"Chasing wrong," Blackie said. "He's been cleared."

Reluctantly I shook his meaty hand. Except for Blackie, I didn't like touching anybody. The sheriff's grip was strong and enveloping.

"You don't have to look at me so mean like," he said, again facing Blackie. "I wont the one who closed The Pit."

"Funny thing it was you at the door," she said. She stood with a knee bent, her left boot set at a right angle to the instep of the right.

"Just doing my job carrying out court orders."

"Well, I see you slick as a hog from that dirty work," Blackie said.

"Not so good, Blackie. Things going downhill around Cliffside. At one time I had me eight deputies. Now it's two, and I fought to keep those. This country's going back to briars and bobcats."

"But you still keeping kin on the payroll," she said. "And I guess you handing out pints of cheap liquor or five-dollar bills on Election Day."

Blackie would stand up to a buzz saw.

"Liquor's not cheap, and a man has to do what a man has to do," the sheriff said.

"But you done more of it than most."

"Forgive and forget, Blackie, that's my way of living. Now, are we having us a social hour here or you got business on your mind?"

The wall held a glossy picture of the sheriff and a black bear he'd shot. In the photo he knelt beside the bear and held the tip of a bolt-action rifle in the bear's mouth to pry it open and exhibit the teeth. The animal's eyes looked alive and startled. I knew something about bear hunters. They used relay teams of hounds to run the bears until they became so worn down they finally stopped and fought. The hounds swarmed howling, snarling, and biting over them. The men stood off with their rifles to enjoy the sport and make an easy kill.

"We been to Aunt Jessie's," Blackie said. "That deputy up there your boy?"

"No, Harp belongs to my brother Wesley."

"He was stringing tape and wouldn't tell us nothing. Told us to ask you. What I wonder is why couldn't he tell us himself?"

"Yeah, Aunt Jessie's gone to glory," the sheriff said and sat heavily. Another picture on the office wall showed him in red, white, and blue wrestling shorts. Dark curly hair covered his body. He was scowling and posed stepping forward and holding his brawny arms out wide as if about to grab an opponent and crush him.

"We already got that far," Blackie said.

"Just about everybody left in Shawnee County came to the funeral," the sheriff said as if he hadn't heard. "People I not seen in years. She was a fine woman, a good and godly one."

"We been knowing what kind of woman she was," Blackie said.

"You heard nothing about what happened?" the sheriff asked. He hadn't taken off his Panama hat. Neither had Blackie nor I our Stetsons.

"Just rode into town," Blackie said. "Drove out to her place and saw the tape."

"There's an investigation going on," the sheriff said as he fitted himself to his chair. He hadn't asked us to sit.

"We figured that. Concerning what?"

"Well, nobody's been seeing a lot of Aunt Jessie lately. 'Course we used to her staying up at her cabin by herself. During the winter we don't expect to hear nothing much from her. This spring she ain't come to town. The rural mail carrier stopped by up there to check on her and say howdy. Her dog Rattler and them chickens and guineas was around, but when he knocked on the door nobody answered. Wasn't locked, so he pushed it open and found Aunt Jessie lying on the floor dead."

The sheriff stopped and rubbed his nose, which appeared rubbery against the push of his finger joint.

"And?" Blackie asked.

"Our first thought was she just old and ailing and had give out, though she'd been tougher than a dozen of these modern women always hollering about their rights. She eighty-seven or more."

"What your second thought?" Blackie asked.

"I went up there to check and didn't see anything that indicated her dying might be anything more than natural. Looked like she'd fallen and hit her head on her hearthstone. Doc Bailey drove over from High Gap in Seneca County—we use him as our coroner since we don't have a doctor around anymore ourselves—and certified her death as natural. 'Course Doc's old too. Eyes gone bad. It was Bernard Duiguid that found the puncture in the back of her head." The sheriff faced me. "Bernard's our local one-and-only undertaker and knows enough to be a doctor if he took a notion to."

"What kind of puncture?" Blackie asked.

"Like she hit on something small and sharp. Maybe a heart attack or stroke felled her and she struck her head on a poker or andiron. Anyhow we didn't think much about it until we got word that Esmeralda had been seen up there. Mr. LeBlanc, you ever hear about our Esmeralda?"

"I've heard," I said.

"People around here used to think she brought us luck. Well, maybe her luck turned bad and run out. Cliffside's sure has."

"What about Esmeralda?" I asked.

"She been acting different lately. After Aunt Jessie's death people been hearing Esmeralda screaming in the woods and up on the cliffs. Rolled rocks down at a group of rafters running the river and was seen hurrying away from Aunt Jessie's cabin about the time Doc Bailey figured Aunt Jessie died. Esmeralda was toting a bundle. That's the report we got from an eyewitness. Now we trying to find Esmeralda. Might be something to it. Might not."

"You thinking she stole off Aunt Jessie?" Blackie asked.

"I'm not thinking. Just looking."

"What's the mail carrier's name?" I asked.

"Spears. Leroy Spears."

"Except for Lupi Fazio, Aunt Jessie was the only person around here Esmeralda ever trusted," Blackie said. "She wouldn't come close to nobody else."

"Blackie, I know all that."

"It's crazy thinking she'd do any hurt to Aunt Jessie."

"Yeah, well, so what's new is I sent my deputy to tape up her place and keep people away until we know what to do next. Can't afford to pay anybody to stay at her cabin full-time. No matter what, it'd be good for Esmeralda to get caught and taken care of by the state in a dry warm place."

He removed his Panama hat and carefully ran his hand over the top of his wavy coal-black hair so as not to disturb the deep furrows left by his comb.

"She don't belong in no dry warm state place," Blackie said.

"Matter of opinion," the sheriff said. "You going to be around here with us long, Mr. LeBlanc?"

"No longer than he has to," Blackie said.

"Got business?" the sheriff asked.

"That any of your business?" Blackie asked.

"Let's you and me make up, Blackie. I don't carry grudges."

"You could've helped me, Basil. You coulda gone on the line for me."

"Maybe I should have, and if it's so, I'm sorry. Anything I can do around here to make your stay easier, you let me know."

"Oh sure," she said. "Like you got a red carpet you can lay out."

"Key to fun city," the sheriff said, and his deep laugh dislodged phlegm. He swallowed it. "You all have yourselves a time now. You married?"

"Don't even try answering him," Blackie said.

The sheriff winked at me as I followed Blackie from the office. We left the courthouse and crossed down the walk to our parking space. A Jehovah's Witness had stuck a *Watchtower* tract under the Caddy's windshield wiper. I balled it up. Blackie was still angry, and anger made her draw taut.

"Basil never done nothing for anybody he couldn't get a dollar out of," she said.

"You pushed him pretty hard."

"And you stood there like you'd forgot how to talk."

She gave me directions to Mt. Olivet Church. East of Cliffside, it sat on a saddle of Battle Mountain, which'd had its timber cut off and appeared scalped. Only a few volunteer honey locust trees grew around Mt. Olivet except for a flourishing sugar maple that spread its shade. Though the front of the squat frame church had been recently painted white, the sides were flaking or bare to the boards, indicating a lack of maintenance money. The steeple still held a field bell.

Blackie opened the front door. Only city churches locked their doors. Inside were no stained-glass windows or sacred embellishments, not even a cross. All was clean, white, and austere except for the dark oak benches held together not with nails but wooden pegs. The seats of the benches had been honed to a shiny slickness by the generations of butts that had slid across them.

We walked around behind the church and opened the gate to the cemetery at the rear to move among the markers, many tilted and some so old the names and dates had been scoured off by wind and weather. Pioneers had been buried here, men who had known and hunted with Daniel Boone. We found the raw, turtleback earth over Aunt Jessie's grave identified at the head by a tag tied to a length of pipe pounded into the ground. Wilted blooms lay about, mostly wildflowers. The tag read:

JESSIE DOUGLAS ARBUCKLE

1912–1999

A GOOD WOMAN

LIES HERE

"I guess that goes on a tombstone," I said. "I'd like to pay for it."

"And clean up this graveyard," Blackie said. "It's bad neglected. I could plant some lilies and narcissus. Get that bag of lemon drops and leave them."

"Why?"

"Esmeralda's always watching and sees everything. She'll know where Aunt Jessie lies and find the lemon drops."

I walked to the car for the bag worried about what Esmeralda would do without Aunt Jessie. I set the lemon drops at the head of the grave and laid beside it a wild daisy I picked beside the fieldstone fence.

FOUR

"No way in this world Esmeralda would steal anything from Aunt Jessie," Blackie said as I drove toward her Cousin Ben Henshaw's house nine miles west of Cliffside. Blackie had explained Ben wasn't really blood kin but had been a friend of her father, who had died at High Moor. He still lay buried under the collapsed roof of a drift mine more than a mile back in the mountain that had become both his assassin and tombstone.

"If Esmeralda took anything off Aunt Jessie, Aunt Jessie would've wanted her to have it," Blackie said. "I don't like it, but they won't be able to lay hands on Esmeralda. She knows these hills better than any ten lawmen."

Sweet-smelling basswood and witch hazel trees flanked the county road. Alongside the pavement a branch ran fast and clear, its riffles trapping sunlight. A grouse flew up from the graveled shoulder and slanted into hemlock shadows. I tracked him with my eye as if I held my old L. C. Smith sixteen-gauge side-by-side, a habit that had stayed with me all these years whenever a game bird flushed. Out in Montana I shot pheasants and jackrabbits, but it was on bobwhite partridges in Tidewater Virginia I'd learned how to gun.

"Cousin Ben was always around for me during my bad days," Blackie said. "I didn't have nobody else. He sat ever' day through my trial, brought me food at the jail, wrote and came visiting during the years I served in the place. Talk about shooting game. He could put a bullet in a bat's eye. And he got himself a bunch of medals over in France."

Blackie had told me that Cousin Ben made his living as a school-bus driver, mechanic, carpenter, plumber, and farmer. He and Blackie still sent each other letters, his penciled on lined tablet paper of the kind used by children in grade schools, his printing as exact as an engineer's and suggesting no damn nonsense. He never wasted words.

Blackie was tough, a woman who had grown up hard, but she had a tender center, especially for the mountains around Shawnee County where she'd been born, reared, and led her life before we took up together and I talked her into riding along in my Jeep to Montana. I'd meant never to come back, but I'd catch Blackie staring out our cabin window when there was nothing to see but the sweep of a lifeless wind-whipped frozen land that seemed to have forgotten what the flowering and fragrance of spring could be. She hadn't really been looking out but into herself and memories of the mountains she left behind.

"Don't believe I'll ever be warm again," she'd say and pull a blanket purchased from Barney's Army Surplus around her shoulders despite the plentiful heat from the cabin's fireplace. The cold she felt she carried inside herself, and was connected to longing, not weather.

"Why couldn't I have took up with a man who wanted to live in Florida?" she'd ask. "Why a poor cold-blooded thing like you?"

I liked Montana and the long view across the glistening snow-glazed fields to the rise of ice-shiny Bighorn Mountain, which appeared untouched by man, his crap, and the hurt he could do. I liked not seeing people. Except for Blackie I'd had enough of people to last ten lifetimes and beyond if there was such a thing. Now and again I'd have enough even of her and needed to be alone. I bought a pair of Bausch & Lomb 7X35 binoculars to watch elk nose through snow in search of graze, camped out, shot and skinned mule deer, and tracked cougars. I liked the sky swept clean when the only sound heard was wind that had been filtered of all man's clamor by the long, unsoiled distance it had blown.

"You should've been a hermit," Blackie had said, and she was near right. I envied the mountain men who stayed out alone for years at a time. They died unseen, no one knowing how or where they'd fallen. No meaningless words spoken over their graves, if they had any. They give themselves back to the land like the animals that lived on it.

When I could avoid it, I never went into Chinook, small town though it was. If we needed provisions, Blackie took the list and drove the Ford-150 pickup to do the buying. Some nights I'd slip out and lie in the barn with the horses because I found it restful to hear them nicker and snatch hay from the bin. I'd picture mustangs galloping wild and free on the plains and sink to sleep hearing their hooves drumming the hard dusty ground.

Cousin Ben had located his place in a broad glen of Big Bear Mountain. A creek ran full through grass of his pasture. The house, Blackie told me, had started out as an aluminum trailer, around the central portion of which over the years he had framed additional rooms and added a front porch. At the rear he'd knocked together a henhouse and shed. He stored his firewood under an overhang just outside his back door. It used to be said that you could take the measure of a man by the size of his woodpile. If so, Ben was mighty, for his red oak logs cut to exact lengths reached high as the house's eaves.

He sat on his porch that had trumpet vine growing among trellises, a tall, gaunt man whose blue-eyed gaze seemed not to be just looking at you but also checking out what you were made of. When we shook, his hand felt lean, and I sensed a restrained strength. Blackie had told me that Ben had been a bachelor all his life, didn't drink, kept himself shaved, his clothes washed, and his house neat. Ruffled white curtains stitched on his own sewing machine hung at his windows.

"He loved a woman over in Mt. Hope," Blackie had said. "Turned him down for a miner who was a drunk and pitched her out a second-story window."

Blackie wasn't much given to showing affection, but she hugged Ben and kissed his cheek. He smiled as he looked down at her. She seemed a child standing beside him, and I caught a glimpse of the pretty young girl she had once been. I thought of her as I'd seen her our first spring in Montana when she stood beneath a cottonwood tree, her arms lifted, the silky white pollen drifting down and finding purchase in her long black hair.

"Well, you not got blown away by that wind," Ben said to her. "And looks like you're finding plenty to eat."

"I been missing you, Ben. We shoulda got married."

"I'm too old for a filly like you, gal. You'd a worn me out after one night in the bed. Now let's get your gear from the car."

He had to be in his seventies, yet he crossed off the porch with an erect military posture and insisted on helping us unload the Caddy even after I told him I needed none. When I opened the trunk, he lifted two bags from my hands to carry into the house, his stride long, unhurried, and exact. It would haul him a far distance without tiring.

"You all married yet?" he asked Blackie and me in the house. He knew about us living together from letters Blackie had written.

"In a way maybe," she said, and her eyes slid away from his.

"Maybe don't mean nothing. You stood before a preacher?"

"Standing before a preacher's not everything," she said.

"It is in this house. You get separate sleeping billets under my roof."

The bedroom he chose for her was on the east side of the house, mine on the west. Blackie and I wouldn't be able to reach each other without walking through the central section, which was the trailer, though its roof had been raised. Ben had furnished it with a sofa, two chairs, and a space heater. On a shelf he had set a lump of coal chipped into the likeness of President Franklin D. Roosevelt, who still remained among Appalachian people the next thing to God. The lump he'd coated with shellac. I saw no radio or TV set, but books lay stacked on both chairs.

"Not mine," he said. "I sign them out from the mobile library bus when it makes its monthly rounds. One thing the state government does right in these parts."

His kitchen had a Kalamazoo wood-burning cookstove and a round table covered by checked oilcloth. Only one chair at the table. The walls he'd left undecorated except for a 1903 Springfield bolt-action rifle that rested on a wooden rack. He had converted it to a sporting gun with a walnut stock he'd carved himself. The gun gave off the gleam of dutiful care.

I liked what I saw about Ben and his house. In Nam I'd devised a grading system for sizing up other grunts. It had three classifications: S#1, S#2, and NS#3. S#1s would shit their pants and run. S#2s would shit their pants but fight. NS#3s fought with tight assholes. The system worked pretty well for classifying men in civilian life. I wasn't quick to lay it on anybody till I'd seen him walk the brink, but even had I not heard from Blackie about his medals, I would've sensed the presence of an authentic NS#3 in Ben.

He cooked our dinner—thick slices of roast pork, mashed potatoes with floured brown gravy, and snap beans. For dessert he served strawberries picked fresh in his garden and covered by thick rich cream from his Guernsey cow. The strawberries had a natural sugar flavor you couldn't buy from any store. I wouldn't have minded a drink beforehand, but none had been offered.

"You folks look tired," Ben said and wouldn't let Blackie and me help with the dishes. "Get you some sleep."

We thanked him and left the table for our rooms. My bed was a cot that had an army blanket over the clean sheets stretched tight beneath. In the service Ben had learned how to square the corners. A fifty-cent piece dropped on the blanket would've bounced high. I picked up a small framed photograph from the bureau, a picture of a young girl of nine or ten wearing a white dress and hat. It had to be

Blackie. She held a bouquet of wildflowers, was laughing, and had no scar back then. Maybe dressed up for church.

Though Ben was right about my being tired, I didn't quickly descend to a deep sleep. During the days I lived at Bellerive, my father's home, I'd learned to sleep light. Later, in the jungle, I'd sensed movement in darkness and detected shifting shapes taking form out of it. I'd made them vanish by letting go with a full clip from my M-16. Even in civilian life, my radar rarely shut down.

Thoughts of Esmeralda again invaded my mind, faded, returned. She slipped into my consciousness as she might in the flesh have sneaked around the fringes of Cliffside from shadows of the forest. I imagined her stepping under blowing hemlocks to move silently through the night searching for the food or clothes left out for her. The legend had it that no dogs, no matter how vicious, ever barked at her.

I didn't own a watch but knew when I'd had enough sleep. I raised the window and lay listening to the sibilant flow of Ben's creek, the bewonks of frogs, the throb of crickets. Later those sounds quieted to a purr. I sat on the edge of the cot, smoked, and looked out to the moonlight shimmering over the orchard grass. A silhouette stepped out from under a sycamore tree. For a second I thought it might be Esmeralda, but, no, it was a deer proceeding delicately, its ears lifted, its shadow following it.

When I left the bed to go to the bathroom, I saw light under the kitchen door and looked in. Ben sat at the table. He remained erect even reading a book. He brought this one up to his eyes rather than bent forward to it. He squinted at me as if he'd forgotten my name or that we'd ever met.

"Coffee's in the pot," he said. A windup alarm clock ticked on the table. The time was twenty minutes before six. The mugs set on the counter were the same white glazed clay the army and prisons used in their mess halls. Ben had carried in his two chairs from the living room for Blackie and me. I sat opposite him and laid my cigarettes on the table. I waited to see whether he'd object. When he continued reading, I lit up. He finished a chapter, reached for a whittled cedar letter opener, and closed his place in the book over it.

"Written back in 1948 by a historian named Toynbee who claims Appalachian people are goners. Says history has passed us by or washed around us and we'll be phased out because we can't meet the challenges of modern life."

"Sounds like crap to me," I said.

"I hate to think that for those of us that have lived up here in the mountains all these years it don't mean anything," he said. The irises of his pale blue eyes contrasted startlingly with the darkness of the pupils. A prophet he could've been, living on locusts and wild honey in the wilderness.

"Most things don't mean anything," I said.

"I don't happen to believe that. Every man was put on this earth for some reason good or bad. And we here in Shawnee County keep going on going on no matter how bad conditions. Our big problem is the coal ran out. If that's a problem. Might not be long term."

"Right," I said and thought, Yeah, keep going on all the way to the boneyard.

We sat for a time without talking. The coals in his old Kalamazoo stove shifted slightly, and sparks dropped into the ash box. The clock ticked.

"You and Blackie plan to stay out in Montana?" he asked.

"No plans to change things if we close on a purchase of our leased ranch."

"She looks good. More at ease with life. You intend to marry her?"

"We don't talk about it."

"A man ought to marry."

"You haven't."

"But wish I had. Not having a wife's been like part of me's missing."

"You heard or know anything about Aunt Jessie Arbuckle dying?" I asked.

"Went to her funeral. Mighty fine woman. Not many of her kind left."

"What kind's that?"

"If she'd been a man, you'd say she was the sort you could trust to light the fuse in your powder charge."

"And Esmeralda?"

"From what I hear she's still out there somewheres."

"The police were at Aunt Jessie's."

"Don't know nothing about that."

I drank my coffee, finished my cigarette, thanked him, and removed the stove lid to drop the butt into the firebox. He was again reading.

"You ought to marry Blackie," he said but didn't look up.

FIVE

I carried a second mug of coffee to the front porch and watched the mist settle over the pasture and wet the grass. During the night I had reached for Blackie. Over past months in Montana when the wind played a howling tune off our chimney and sleet beat the roof and windows of our cabin, I'd grown to like the feeling of Blackie next to me—a hundred-and-eighty-degree break in the life I had lived alone.

I showered, pulled on khakis, and walked into the kitchen, where Ben stood at the stove. His skillet clanged. He had scrambled eggs, fried bacon, and boiled hominy. He drew a sheet of hot biscuits from the oven.

"You ever catch sight of Esmeralda?" I asked.

"Nope," he answered as he heavily peppered his eggs. His shakers were shaped like miniature kegs and looked as if made from cherry. My guess was he'd carved them too.

Blackie arrived in her quilted white bathrobe and barefooted, the lime-colored patch over her eye. Her hair hung long and loose down her back. Despite being a shorty, she ate man-sized meals. She reached for biscuits, dabbed on butter, and dripped molasses over them.

"I need to go down to town," Ben said. "You all want anything?"

"We doing all right here," Blackie said, and poured herself a glass of milk. At daylight I'd heard Ben's Guernsey lowing.

Blackie had a kind of shine on her from being back in Shawnee County. She was lit up from the inside. She thought Montana's plains too flat and peaks too high and threatening, maybe fine for tourists to gape at, yet not made for the likes of normal people to settle on or among. West Virginia hills, she believed, didn't want to buck you off like a wild-ass bronc but beckoned and were protective. During our second of Chinook's lashing winters, she had drawn a pencil sketch of Seneca County's Big Bear Mountain, a cabin on its slope, the sun shining, the dogwood and Judas trees blooming. It was pure homesickness.

After Ben left, Blackie and I washed the dishes before we walked out and watched the mist like a sheer curtain drifting across the land. Water gurgled among rocks in the creek, and ravens croaked from the ridges. Ben's cow, named Matilda, grazed at the far end of the fenced pasture. Somewhere dogs barked. Blackie raised her face, her expression worshipful. She breathed deep to fill herself with the goodness this country held for her.

"We ought to pick us some ramps," she said, ramps being what the locals called wild leeks. "Make a casserole and clean out the system."

She'd never been on horses till I taught her how to ride, but now mounted, became a part of them, like a female centaur. Best yet, she had a feeling for animals, what they wanted or needed. She spoke a silent language with them, a sort of communing. The one time I'd seen her bucked off by a hardmouth paint named Buster, he had returned and nosed her as if to let her know he was sorry.

"I don't like the police being after Esmeralda," I said.

"I don't either but don't mean we can do anything about it."

"We could set out food. She might find it hard making it without Aunt Jessie."

"How come you so all fired up about Esmeralda all of a sudden?"

"She's getting old. We ought to leave some money with Ben so he can take care of her."

"Talk to him," she said and started toward the house. "Me, I'm washing my hair."

Yeah, if it could be worked out, Ben was the one to keep looking after Esmeralda. I felt he and I belonged to the fraternity of those who had been to war and survived combat. That set you apart from others, an unbridgeable divide. Veterans might return and walk the streets like ordinary citizens, marry, buy insurance, and have children, but they carried around the rest of their lives a node at the back of their brains that contained the knowledge and certainty of death. Once you had that node, it flavored everything else and never let you forget that the very next step, the sudden turn around a corner, could take you and all else away.

Before I was born, Esmeralda had been spotted, a young girl who fled anyone who tried to approach or speak with her. She wore filthy clothes, hid in burrows or caves of the high-wall cliffs along the Wilderness River. People believed she'd arrived abandoned from some isolated mountain hollow, her parents killed in a rock slide or flash flood slashing down the mountains.

Esmeralda had scrounged around the fringes of the High Moor coal camp to find scraps of food. Welfare and Social Services workers from Charleston attempted to bring her in, but she was a fleeting vapor they could never close their hands on. Capturing Esmeralda turned into a game of her against authorities, and the people of Shawnee County, believing her lucky, became her allies. When questioned, they lied, played dumb, and were able to protect her.

Patient and gentle Lupi Fazio, the superintendent at the LeBlancs' High Moor colliery, won her trust over time. He had named her Esmeralda after Victor Hugo's *Hunchback of Notre Dame* heroine. It was to Lupi's doorstep Esmeralda brought a newborn baby wrapped in a sweater he had given her. He had heard Esmeralda keening up on the mountain. Only Lupi knew who the father was, not a hobo along the tracks or a rogue miner, and Lupi, while drinking Aunt Jessie's persimmon wine, had let out the truth to her. When I was on the run and needed that truth, Aunt Jessie had revealed it to me.

Taking insurance money I'd collected and my share of dollars escrowed by brother Edward from Bellerive's sale due me, I'd set up a trust that would pay out money to Ben to use for Esmeralda's care. He might have a problem establishing contact and winning her over, but if anybody could, Ben was the man.

When he drove up the lane, I walked out to his 1988 Chevy pickup to help carry in groceries. He had a dog tied in the truck's bed, a mixture of what appeared to be collie and German shepherd. I recognized Rattler, the animal Aunt Jessie had owned.

"They didn't know what to do with him in Cliffside, so I brought him along," Ben said and loosened Rattler. "He's old, but so am I. They might've put him to sleep. I'll keep him penned up a few days till he grows used to being around here. Fix him a place in the shed."

He lifted Rattler down, petted, sweet-talked him, and arranged burlap sacks on the shed's floor for bedding. He poured dry dog food into a bowl and filled a galvanized bucket with drinking water. He again patted the dog before closing and latching the door.

"And I got some news about Esmeralda for you," he said. "The word in Cliffside is the State Police using a bloodhound tracked her down. Early this morning captured and took her away. Lots of talk about it going 'round."

"Where'd they take her?"

"Word I got at the store is they rode her to the Appalachian General Hospital in Beckley."

"I'm gone," I said and walked to the house. Inside, Blackie, fresh from her shower, stood drying herself with a towel. Her hair hung wet and slinky. She cocked her head at me and tightened the towel around her breasts, though she wasn't shy about showing herself to me, and in our Montana cabin had become used to my seeing her walk past buck naked.

"Going to Beckley," I said and told her about Esmeralda.

"Not without me you're not."

I waited on the porch until she came out, her hair only partly dried. She'd changed into a yellow shirt, fresh and newly pressed Levi's, and leather sandals. She carried her ivory-handled brush, one of the few possessions she'd kept from Shawnee County days. It'd belonged to her mother.

"You're driving too fast," she said.

"I don't like the idea of the police carrying her off. She won't understand and be scared."

"They not likely to hurt her."

Because of high rich seams of low-sulfur bituminous coal that steel mills needed to coke their ovens, Beckley in Raleigh County had become a prosperous and modern city, providing malls, shops, and glassy office buildings in a backwoods setting. Ladies on the street wore stylish, brightly colored spring dresses, and the suited men hurried along the sidewalks carrying briefcases. "We no hicks or hillbillies here" they might be hoping to prove or demonstrate. The hicks and hillbillies had to be out there somewhere, but not on Main Street.

I stopped at an Amoco station for directions to the Appalachian General, which turned out to be a complex of white stucco buildings near the center of town. It took two circlings to find a parking space. When Blackie and I climbed steps to the front entrance, the broad glass door opened automatically before us. We stopped at the reception desk.

"We here to see a patient," I told the matronly woman whose rings clinked on her fingers. The lapel of her blue linen jacket had a jeweled dove pinned to it. I took her to be a volunteer doing the job because she felt it a duty of her upscale social position, a sort of chic self-sacrifice.

"Name of the patient," she said, and gave me a pleasant smile.

"First name's Esmeralda. Don't know the last."

"Oh," she said, and did not turn to the computer.

"What?" I asked.

"No visitors allowed."

"It's important we see her."

"Are you related?"

"I am," I said, and Blackie glanced at me.

"She's to have no visitors."

"Just give me her room number. She'll want to see us."

"I can't do that, sir. I'm sorry."

"Okay, thanks," I said, backed off, and moved Blackie along the corridor as if to leave. I turned not at the exit but toward the bank of elevators, where I paused to read the directory posted under glass on the wall. I picked what seemed the best choice—MEDICAL SECTION, THIRD FLOOR.

"You taking to lying?" Blackie asked as we rode the elevator.

"Just wait," I said.

"I never liked lying or waiting," she said.

As we left the elevator and walked the shiny antiseptic corridor of the third floor, I looked into rooms that had their doors open. Blackie's leather sandals squeaked and slapped along the way. The alcoholic disinfectant smells made me remember another place, another time—the infernal perfume of the near dead in a field hospital.

"You can't inspect them all," Blackie said. "You don't even know what she looks like."

"I'll know," I said. Aunt Jessie had shown me Lupi Fazio's crayon sketch of Esmeralda. It was the great swallowing dark eyes in a narrow childish face I most remembered.

When we reached the end of the hallway, I started to turn back toward the elevator and try another floor but saw the state policeman sitting on a straight chair outside a room. His trooper hat lay on his lap, and he held a folded newspaper. The door behind him was closed. He watched us approach.

"Esmeralda?" I asked, again tightening up in the presence of the law.

"You can't go in," he said.

"We're family," I said, and this time Blackie didn't react.

"No visitors of any kind," he said and put on his cap. He also looked at my Stetson and cowboy boots.

"Can we just peek in the door at her?" Blackie asked.

"Not without permission from Captain Jamerson."

"How do I reach him, honey?" Blackie asked and hipped out to assume her sexy pose. She awarded him a smile from the good side of her face.

"I'll give you a number, darling," he said, a pug-nosed officer who shaved his sideburns high.

I had no pencil. Blackie drew her pen from a gap between buttons on her shirt. She didn't carry pocketbooks but stuck her wallet in her jeans' hip pocket like a wrangler. She pulled out a dollar bill and wrote the number on its top edge.

"You know that's illegal," the trooper said.

"So put me in jail," she answered.

We walked back to the elevator, rode to the first floor, and found a battery of public pay phones in the waiting room. I fingered out coins. The number turned out to be State Police District Headquarters. Captain Jamerson wasn't at his office. I talked the dispatcher into paging him by radio and gave the hospital number. We sat fidgeting on molded plastic chairs until the captain called, using his cruiser's phone from somewhere out in the boonies.

"No can do," he said. "Doctor's orders."

"Who's the doctor?" I asked.

"Sir, I can't give out that information," he said and hung up without signing off.

I headed back toward the reception desk.

"We going to keep lying?" Blackie asked.

"You ask for the doctor's name."

At the desk she did. The matronly woman hesitated before clicking keys and scrolling the computer.

"Dr. Baldwin. Dr. Alexander Baldwin."

"How do we get in touch?"

"Dr. Baldwin's not on duty."

"Give me his telephone number," Blackie said.

"The doctors don't like to be called at home," the woman said. Not only rings on her fingers but a gold bracelet and choker around her neck. One-generation rich probably but maybe strong as iron under that polite smile.

"This a family emergency," Blackie said, assuming a desperate expression from the scarred side of her face.

"I can't break the rules," the lady said. She appeared regretful but determined.

"Like you never broke one in your life," Blackie said as I touched her arm to urge her back to the waiting room. I used the chain-bound phone book to find Dr. Alexander Baldwin's listed number. I punched in the number and after four rings listened to a recorded message announcing the doctor "is not available" but that I could leave a message after the frigging tone.

"Pick up," I said. "This an emergency."

Blackie took the phone from me. She listened and hung up.

"Let's go there," she said. She looked for the address, and her index finger traced it to 280 Beechwood Lane. We asked directions from an orderly pushing a cart piled with clean rattling bedpans.

"Just drive on out till you see where the money is," he said, pointed, and told us how to get there. "So many doctors, people call it Pill Hill."

At the parking lot sunlight reflecting from cars intensified heat rising off the gummy asphalt. We drove away and found the area named Beechwood two miles south of the city limits. It was rich all right, fronted by a gatehouse, though no sentry stood guard this time of day. Gaslights lined the streets, all lawns had been freshly mowed, and flowers bloomed in landscaped gardens. A blind man could've sensed the dollars.

I drove slow till we spotted Dr. Baldwin's residence at the end of a brick-paved cul-de-sac. The Tudor house sat on a bluff surrounded by a white hunt-country fence. A sign at the entrance read BEAU REPOSE, and evenly spaced beech trees dropped a cooling shade. The driveway paved with white pebbles curved to the front door. When we left the Caddy and I rang the doorbell, chimes sounded faintly inside.

"Keep your mouth shut and let me do the talking," Blackie said, pushing ahead of me.

A colored maid wearing a white uniform opened the door only partway. Blackie, who generally didn't do a lot of smiling, managed another one and gentled her voice, which had a tendency to become gravellike when she tensed up. The maid's eyes took in the scar.

"Dr. Baldwin's not home," she said. "This his day for golf."

"Where's he play?" Blackie asked.

"I don't know he'd want me to tell you that," the maid said, ready to close the door.

"Can't you page him?"

"He don't carry his pager when he's playing golf," she said and shut the door.

I started to use the knocker to bang on it, but Blackie blocked my hand and pulled me away. We walked to the car.

"Don't get her feathers up or she might call security," Blackie said. "We can find another way."

We left Beechwood, and at the bottom of the hill stopped at a Qwik Stop convenience store where a man unloaded beer from a Budweiser van. Blackie leaned out the car window.

"Where they play golf around here?" she asked.

"Do I look like a golfer?" the shirtless youth answered as he stacked six-packs on a dolly. He used his cap to wipe sweat off his face and rolled the dolly toward the store.

"Another shithead," Blackie said. "I'll go in and find out."

"No," I said. "Zeke."

"Zeke what?" she said.

Zeke Webb had been platoon radioman in Nam—short, heavyset, capable of carrying loads long distances. We'd kidded him about his hillbilly accent. He'd played a mean, whining harmonica, and the last I'd seen of him during the war he was being air-evac'd with mortar iron in his legs. He'd showed the wounds around and shouted, "I've seen the fucking light."

He'd also helped me while I was on the run by loaning me money he believed he'd never see again and letting me buy his old army-surplus Jeep. Respectable he had become now, solid middle-class, a CPA with a ranch-style brick house, a wife, child, and the node of memory he carried from hell.

At the Qwik Stop pay phone I looked up his number. I gave my name to his secretary, who put me through.

"Sure you're not a ghost?" he asked.

"Look, Zeke, I don't have time for chatting. You know any doctors at Appalachian General Hospital."

"I do some of their taxes. You in trouble again?"

"No trouble. Listen, how about Dr. Alexander Baldwin?"

"Sure, Alex."

"Where do doctors and lawyers and the like play golf around here?"

"Why?"

"Just tell me."

"The Rain Tree Country Club," he said.

"How do I get there?"

"I don't know I ought to tell you."

"Come on, Zeke. I won't cost you business."

"But you got to promise to come see me and my bride," he said, and gave me directions to the club. I remembered his wife's name was Alice Faye, and his daughter they called Suzy Q.

Blackie and I backtracked past Beechwood half a mile. The Rain Tree turned out to be about what I expected—a plantation-style clubhouse, an Olympic-size turquoise pool, all-weather tennis courts, and an eighteen-hole course laid out over the hilly terrain. What the tree rained was money. Coming upon the bloom of wealth in mining country always caused me a jolt—like an unsullied white lily springing up from beneath earth blackened by an overburden of mine waste called gob.

We left the car at the lot and found a sign painted in English script that pointed the way to the air-conditioned pro shop and caddy shack. Blackie asked the polo-shirted scheduler behind the counter not if but where Dr. Baldwin could be reached. Aging, wrinkled as dried-out rawhide, and likely a pro himself on his last lap, he looked her over before lifting a walkie-talkie to check with a course monitor.

"Dr. Baldwin's on fourteen, but you can't go out there," he said. His long-billed cap carried the Topflite logo, and his black sunglasses masked eyes that had probably looked across a wasteland of clubhouse alcohol and broken dreams.

"This a medical emergency," Blackie said.

"Dr. Baldwin won't want to be interrupted. It's his regular Wednesday foursome."

"A woman's life's in danger," Blackie said.

"Guess I can have one of the caddies carry you out to the fifteenth tee. Don't speak to Dr. Baldwin until they putt out."

The caddie, a gangly black in white coveralls, drove us in the battery-powered cart along the sandy path that circled a pond on which yellow barnyard ducks quacked and splashed. He stopped short of the green in the shade of a flowering crab apple at the edge of the rough.

The foursome approached in two carts. They stopped to make short-iron shots to the green. These men were no mere Sunday golfers but could play the game. Their swings had the grace of professional lessons only dollars could buy. As they drew close, the four glanced at us. I started toward them, but Blackie held me back until they holed out. Then she stepped forward.

"Dr. Baldwin," she called.

He was young, slim, and nattily turned out in a white knit shirt, peach slacks, and black-and-white shoes adorned with kilties. The bill of his immaculate white cap shadowed his face.

"Do I know you?" he asked Blackie.

"This about your patient named Esmeralda," Blackie said. "We need your permission to see her."

"How'd you find me?"

"Can't keep the dollars quiet," I said.

"We're family," Blackie said and again shot me a hard look.

"My information is Esmeralda Doe doesn't have family," Dr. Baldwin said.

"We're close friends and know she'd want to see us," Blackie said.

"Friends and kin," I said.

"That may be, but she's medicated and wouldn't know you. You'll have to wait another day."

"That the best you can do for us?" Blackie asked.

"Sorry, yes," he said. He still held his putter and started to move off toward the men, who watched and were anxious to get on with their game. A foursome waited on the fairway behind them.

"How do we arrange it?" Blackie called after him.

"Just phone my office. Has she ever spoken?"

"Yes," I said, though I wasn't certain she had used the English language.

"Been difficult getting through to her," Dr. Baldwin said. "Call my office."

He joined the others. I looked after them, all affluent, secure, certain of the insulated world they lived in. At best S#2s.

"We'll wait till tomorrow," Blackie said.

"Like you I don't care for waiting."

"Don't you think we're carrying this 'kin' business too far?"

"Just using what's at hand."

"Look, Charley, something's going on here you're not telling me."

"I don't want you to ask me about that right now."

"Why not?"

"There's stuff I don't ask you. Some things should stay buried."

"Trouble is, the bad stuff don't always does," she said and walked away from me to the golf cart.

SIX

On the drive back to Ben's, the occasional houses among the hooded mountains appeared lonely and brave, lights from their windows sending out feeble notice of their existence against the consuming night. "We are alive here" was the signal. "We count."

Ben had left his lights on for us. From the shed Rattler barked twice. We slipped into the house quietly, touched hands, and separated to our rooms. I had seen Blackie's, furnished not with a cot but a four-poster double bed. Maybe Ben had also constructed that. I undressed and stretched out on my cot, at the same time aching for a drink of liquor, wanting it to ease down to my belly and relax my muscles, joints, and bones.

I lay thinking of Brother Edward and our past at Bellerive, the family home of my father and the LeBlancs for more than twelve generations. My father hadn't wanted me. His wife, the woman I'd believed my mother, had shamed him into rearing me and had paid for it by his abuse. Though I didn't understand why at the time, I'd sensed his rancor all the days of my youth, until at age sixteen on a steamy afternoon I ran off from Bellerive. He had hit and knocked me to the lawn in front of the house's portico.

I slept little on the cot, the bad shapes again slipping into my mind.

I left Ben's house quietly and walked to the county road and back. Moonlight silvered the pasture, and a lonely owl sent out lingering sorrowful hoots for a mate. Before returning to the bed, I opened the Caddy's trunk and had a swig of Old Crow I chased down with palms of gritty cold water drawn from Ben's purling Laurel Creek.

At daybreak I drank Ben's strong coffee and purposely didn't wait for breakfast or Blackie but instead drove to Peck's Store, an unpainted frame building with a rusting tin roof set at the edge of the dusty road. Mr. Henry Peck, the owner, peered at me from around his cash register. He was thin, stooped, his scalp pink. A wattle of skin dangled from his throat.

According to Ben, Mr. Henry Peck lived alone upstairs in the store, which was from another time, a period of kerosene lamps, mule harness, and black powder used for shooting coal. Now many of its shelves offered goods nobody wanted any longer—rolls of faded calico, out-of-fashion clothing, shoes with the leather dry and cracked, flypaper, corroded cans of vegetables, and king-sized rat traps. Bins and flour barrels waited empty, the wooden scoops lying upside down inside them. Dust coated miners' picks and shovels. The moth-eaten head of a mounted buck deer had cobwebs strung between its antlers, and a few moldy country hams hung from nails in the oak rafters, the salt-and-smoke-cured meat faintly scenting the place.

"Use your phone?" I asked Mr. Henry Peck, who sat on a stool behind the gilded antique cash register that had a windup handle. His store served as the local post office, and behind him rose a bank of pigeonholes. No envelopes, newspapers, or mail of any sort stuck from them.

"Your money," he said, his voice weak and seeming to come from a distance.

"I need change."

"No charge for change," he said and cranked the cash register. The drawer sprang forward and sounded a gong. When he counted out eight quarters in exchange for my two dollars, his palsied, parchment-like fingers were reluctant to release the money.

I dialed Operator, gave her Dr. Baldwin's office number, and at her direction dropped in a dollar and dime. I was too early and got no answer. I waited.

"You a LeBlanc, ain't you?" Mr. Henry Peck asked, working his pink gums. He'd been watching me.

I nodded.

"Seen it in your chin," he said. "I remember Boss John. You one of his git?"

I said I was. Boss John was what the miners had called my father.

"Thought so," he said and nothing more.

I kept calling but didn't reach Dr. Baldwin's receptionist until eight-thirty. She told me he hadn't come in yet. I asked when I could expect to talk to him. She said he had surgery and wouldn't be available until ten or later at the hospital.

I decided to drive to Beckley. Logging trucks jammed the road too narrow for passing until I reached Interstate 77. At the hospital I skirted Reception and rode the elevator to the third floor. When I reached Esmeralda's room, the state trooper had gone, and an orderly worked making up the bed.

"Where is she?" I asked.

"Where who?" he asked, a young black whose hospital whites were nicely creased. He had a limp.

"The lady who was in this room."

"She gone before I came up," he said and stripped off sheets.

I rode the elevator down to Reception to face another matronly lady. Her cheeks were rouged, and she could have been dressed for a bridge luncheon. She had just hung up the telephone in a way to protect her long rose-colored fingernails. When I asked about Esmeralda Doe, she turned to the computer. Her arms were fair and downy.

"I find no Esmeralda Doe," she said after scrolling the monitor. "She must have been discharged."

"Wouldn't you have a list of the people discharged?"

Again she faced the monitor, carefully fingered buttons, shook her head.

"You're certain you're in the right hospital? There's been no Esmeralda Doe admitted."

"Yesterday she was in Room 3-D of the Medical Section."

"I have no way of knowing about that," she said, her expression wary.

"No way to find out?"

"I'll try the nurses' station," she said, lifted, and spoke into the phone. She listened and held it to her ample breasts. "Apparently she has been discharged, but her papers have yet to be processed through the office."

"Is that the usual procedure?"

"Well, no, actually it isn't. Possibly a clerical error."

"How do I find Dr. Baldwin?"

"I'll page him and see whether he's out of surgery," she said. She looked up his number. A red light on her console flashed. She lifted the phone, spoke, listened, and hung up.

"He's in the cafeteria eating breakfast," she said and gave me directions.

I took the stairs down rather than wait for the elevator and found Dr. Baldwin sitting in another of those molded plastic chairs before a plastic table. He chewed on a honey bun as he read the sports section of a newspaper. His operating greens hung loosely on him. When he looked up and saw me, his jaw stilled. He reached for a drink of orange juice before speaking.

"They've taken her," he said.

"Who has?"

"The State Police. They had an ambulance and court order."

"Taken her where?"

"I believe to Cliffside. The Shawnee County sheriff was with the police. They asked whether she could travel. I informed them she appeared physically able to do so."

I walked off and left the hospital. I drove back to Cliffside, where I parked by the courthouse and used the basement entrance to the jail. I found Sheriff Basil Lester alone at his desk. He leveled his white Panama as he looked up from a printed form he'd been filling out. He'd tied his expansive red tie in a Windsor knot.

"Where's Esmeralda?" I asked.

"Not here, Mr. LeBlanc."

"Where'd you take her?"

"I never took her anywhere. Esmeralda Doe's been transported to the Huntington State Hospital, where she'll be looked after."

"That the nuthouse?"

"Some people call it that. I don't. It's the state institution for the mentally impaired. I guarantee you she's in good hands. Nobody 'round here has it in for Esmeralda. She couldn't know what she done. We just want her taken care of before she hurts somebody else or herself."

"By 'what she done' you mean you believe she killed Aunt Jessie?"

"At this point I don't believe anything. The action was authorized by the court through Social Services. They been wanting Esmeralda a long time."

"She's under arrest?"

"She's being investigated. Everything's being investigated, including the vagrants. We been having trouble lately with them passing through the county. They go south during the winter, north in the spring. Come along the roads or railroad tracks, do some stealing. I went with the troopers to Appalachian General because District Attorney Sligh ordered me to. He speaks, I jump."

"You didn't notify anybody about Esmeralda?"

"Who's to notify? She's got no family or connections. We don't even have a legal name for her. Esmeralda was put on her way back by an Italian named Lupi Fazio out at the High Moor diggings. Now, they equipped in Huntington to care for people in her condition. Esmeralda's way out of it. She'll need confinement the rest of her life."

"I want to see her."

"Not my jurisdiction. You'll have to talk to the folks at Huntington State."

"I need a phone number."

"That I can furnish," he said and pressed a meaty thumb on an address book that had a spring cover that flipped open. He shuffled among the alphabetic tabs, lifted a pencil, and wrote the number on a page torn from a pad that advertised Purina Chow. He handed it to me. The ruby Masonic ring clunked against the desk when he dropped his hand.

"Use your phone?" I asked.

"Not for long distance, Mr. LeBlanc, unless you reverse the charges, which I doubt Huntington State will accept. You'll find a pay phone upstairs in the courthouse."

I walked out and climbed to the first floor of the building. The booth was at the far end of the corridor. At the treasurer's office I asked the clerk behind the counter to trade me change for a five-dollar bill. The clerk, a suited pinched-faced man, maybe the treasurer himself, counted out coins he lifted from a drawer set into his side of the counter.

"We not required to make change for people," he said.

"I'll vote for you next election," I told him and left his office for the phone booth. I closed its door before dialing Huntington State. A woman's voice at the other end instructed me to wait and then told me she had no record of a patient named Esmeralda Doe. I walked back down to the sheriff's office.

"That's where they took her," he said. He was cleaning his finger-nails with a pocketknife. "They keeping her under wraps, so to speak."

"Why?"

"Mr. LeBlanc, I don't know for certain, but my guess is they want to protect her from the press. Esmeralda's a story reporters would like to get hold of. They might mob her. Now, exactly what's your interest anyhow?"

"It's personal."

"Well, what's personal with me is I'm running behind on work I aim to do this day. You got any other questions, I recommend you ask them of Mr. Grover Sligh upstairs."

He stood and left. While I waited for him to return, I looked at the poster of him in his red, white, and blue wrestler shorts. I realized the sonofabitch wasn't coming back. All right, I'd go see District Attorney Sligh.

The marble steps to the second floor had dips in them from the past treads of a multitude of feet. The door's frosted glass displayed the black-lettered name GROVER A. SLIGH. Inside, a long-faced secretary with her gray hair pinned in a bun sat typing at a computer that appeared out of place in a room illuminated by brass light fixtures that had to have been converted from gas to electricity. When I told her I wanted to see Mr. Sligh, she looked at me without taking her hands off the keys. Her nameplate read MINERVA LEMON

"Nature of your business?" she asked.

"A private matter," I answered.

"He's in conference. Mr. Sligh's a very busy man. You'll have to make an appointment."

"I need to see him now."

"Then you'll have to wait," she said. "What's your name?"

I told her.

"You not a resident of or a voter in Shawnee County?"

"No."

"I thought not," she said and gave me a look that consigned me to the category of people not worthy of her time.

Three straight black chairs had been set back against the drab white plaster wall that could've used fresh paint. I sat and looked out an uncurtained window at Cliffside's Main Street. No cars or trucks drove by, no pedestrians strolled along the broken and sunken sidewalk, and the American flag hung undisturbed by any random movement of air. Pigeons had convened a session along the barrel of the World War I French 75 artillery piece.

I didn't like being here. I'd had too many dealings with the law ever to feel secure in its presence. I understood how being tagged by the police branded a man. In this computer age you became a folder that could be drawn from the file anytime the law took a notion. They could lay you out naked and open you up.

I heard talking from an inner office. The door opened, and two men walked out—one a uniformed captain of State Police, the other who had to be District Attorney Sligh, a miniature character at the most five feet tall, compact, sharp features, a trimmed brown mustache. His dark blue suit appeared tailored, his small black shoes had been polished. His eyes too were brown and took me in with a swift glance as he talked softly to the captain. A rodent's eyes, I thought.

"Grover, you'll hear from me," the captain said.

"And I'll keep in touch," the district attorney answered. His voice wasn't dwarfish but deep and resounding, as if from a much larger person.

The captain set on his trooper hat and strode out with the certainty of one carrying a full tank of power. The district attorney turned to me. "Be of help to you, sir?"

"Claims he needs to talk," Miss Minerva Lemon said as if she believed I'd lied to her. I definitely did not care for Miss Minerva.

"Your name?" Sligh asked.

"He's the LeBlanc," she said. "Charles LeBlanc."

"Indeed, a name well known around these parts, though none has been in residence for many a year," Sligh said and held out his hand. His shake was quick and elusive. "Sheriff Lester informed me you were in town."

He talked over teeth as small and moistly pearly as kernels of freshly picked corn. A white handkerchief folded to four points stuck from the breast pocket of his jacket. A dandy he was, and the sheriff would've told him I was the LeBlanc pursued and once believed guilty of my brother John's, his wife's, and their son's deaths at Bellerive. The sheriff would also have added I'd been dishonorably discharged from the army and served time at Leavenworth.

"You have need to talk to me, come on in, Mr. LeBlanc," he said.

His broad and deep office had three large globed light fixtures hanging by tarnished gilded chains from the high ceiling. An arched window gave out to the white oak tree whose leaves blocked sunlight. The office seemed much too large for him. Two diplomas from the University of Kentucky hung on the wall at the side of his desk, an oversized oaken Victorian piece that made him appear even smaller. The expanse of desk was bare except for a banker's lamp with a green shade, a pen-and-pencil set, a telephone, and an intercom. Two straight chairs had been placed symmetrically before the desk. His own was a swivel, leather high-back job that as he sat both elevated and further diminished his size. He was a farcical little Caesar, yet also bore the power of the state.

"Now, what is it you want from me, Mr. LeBlanc, assuming it is something you do want?" he asked and templed his small hands under his chin. A finger of his left hand held a gold wedding band. Despite the window, his lamp, and the chandelier, the light in the office seemed to bleed off into the buff-colored walls.

"Esmeralda," I said.

"Such a poor and unfortunate woman," he said and leaned back. "What's your interest in her?"

"My interest is I want to see her."

"Esmeralda is hospitalized and not able to have visitors at this time," he said, his voice dropping into an even lower register. He could have sung bass in a male choir.

"She hurt?"

"How much do you know of her history?"

"Right much."

"Then you have to be aware of her condition."

"I am and still want to see her."

"She knows you?" he asked and sat forward.

"I believe she might," I said and wondered how a man in this hillbilly county could be such a priggish prick.

"You believe. I'll rephrase my question. Have you ever been in her presence, spoken to her, or she to you?"

"I been in her presence," I said and had not only at my birth but also back at High Moor when on the run I saw her gliding like a spirit among the abandoned houses of the coal camp.

"That sounds like a further parsing of my question."

"It sounds like you're dodging me."

He laughed unexpectedly, the sound a titter over those tiny teeth. He flexed the fingers of his dainty hands.

"All right, Mr. LeBlanc, Esmeralda Doe was taken into custody and transported to Huntington by an action that originated in this office. She's being retained until she can be questioned."

"Charged with what?"

"As yet, no charges have been brought or sought."

"You're considering one?"

"Sir, you ask a heavy load of questions."

"Any reason you won't answer them?"

"Well, the fact is, you're not an attorney, and I'm not required to."

"It's the bundle she was seen carrying away from the cabin that makes you suspect her, right? That could've just been food. Aunt Jessie often fed her."

"I will tell you only that when she was captured by the State Police, the officers found among her possessions an object taken from Aunt Jessie's cabin."

"Can't be more specific?"

"Can but won't at this time."

"What would she want from Aunt Jessie that Aunt Jessie wouldn't give her?"

"I have no idea."

"So for the bundle you're jailing her in a mental hospital."

"She's not being jailed but treated. When and if the doctors report Esmeralda Doe can be questioned, she will be. From what we know of her condition, it's doubtful those questions will be answered."

"Does she have a lawyer?"

"At this point she has no need of an attorney. At the proper time, she will be apprised of her rights."

"What if there's no proper time?"

"Decisions will be made as called for."

"And habeas corpus?"

"Premature at this stage of affairs."

"I'd still like your permission to see her."

"I continue to wonder at your interest."

"I'd want to help if I can."

"You're not alone. People in the country have been looking after her for years. However, there may be a further complication."

"That being?"

"I can't reveal it at this moment as it might or might not be evidential. And I can't give you permission. That's out of my hands."

"Whose hands is it in?"

"At the moment Huntington State's, and the hospital's first concern is the condition of Esmeralda Doe's health."

No use in trying to push him farther. He'd only take me in circles. He gave me a chickenshit smile that seemed to say, "I can fuck you anytime I want and you can't do anything about it." With a little finger of his right hand, he stroked both sides of his mustache before he stood to walk me to the door.

"You staying long with Ben Henshaw?" he asked.

"How'd you know I was staying with Ben?"

"Mr. LeBlanc, I earn my pay by knowing," he said.

SEVEN

Twenty-seven miles from Cliffside, Interstate 77's bright bonds of concrete would carry me northward among the shadowed brooding mountains first to Charleston and then on westward to Huntington. The posted speed limit was seventy, and I stayed under it. Trucks and other cars washed around me like a stone in a creek. My regard for the law was knowledge of just how far it could screw you under any charge no matter how minor.

I'd bought gas and two and a half hours later crossed into the city limits, where I asked for directions to Huntington State from a postman wearing shorts and a pith helmet as he delivered mail along a shaded residential street. He explained I was already close and pointed.

"On a hill above Huntington, seven blocks to the light and turn left. Go another block and you'll see the entrance on your right."

The entrance had a stone archway with glistening ivy growing over it. Beyond lay a complex of multistoried red-brick buildings trimmed in white. An attempt had been made to relieve their uniformity by flower beds planted with pansies, iris, and daffodils. The place had the air of a college campus. Several patients wearing white pajamas, cloth slippers, and striped bathrobes sunned themselves on green benches arranged along the lawn. A hefty uniformed orderly, his thumbs hooked over his hip pockets, strolled among them.

A sign pointed to the parking area. When I left the Caddy, one of the patients, a smiling woman with stringy brown hair, crossed the grass toward me, her makeup applied so heavily she resembled a circus clown, though a sad and lost one.

"Hello, Freddy, I been missing you," she said.

She laid her hands on my shoulders to kiss me. I smelled soap and orange blossom perfume. She tasted of lipstick and mentholated cough drops. The orderly hurried to us to draw her away. I didn't wipe my mouth.

"Come on, Alice," he said. "Almost time for your sweet roll and glass of milk."

"But I haven't seen Freddy since the cotillion," the woman answered. She pouted.

"You need to be ready for the dance," the orderly said and gently prompted her toward a bench.

"I must have a new gown," she said. "You've been promising me a new gown."

When I was out of their sight I used my handkerchief on my mouth before following signs to the administration building. I climbed to a portico supported by Corinthian columns and entered the lobby. A pert young woman stood behind a counter holding a pencil and making notations on a pad. When she looked up at me, the pencil clicked impatiently against the countertop. I intended to bypass the bureaucracy.

"Let me speak to the medical director," I said.

"Your name?"

I told her.

"The nature of your business with the director?"

"I have confidential information to give him about a patient."

"Are you related to the patient?"

"I am."

"The patient's name?"

"Esmeralda Doe."

She gazed at me an instant before turning away to the switchboard, where she kept her back to me as she spoke softly into a headset held in her hand. She used the pencil to scratch at her hair. She again faced me.

"Dr. Fredrick will see you," she said. "You'll need a pass, which I am now preparing. You'll also want an orderly to show you the way. Pin this on."

She handed me the pass with my name, *Visitor*, and the date on it. While I pinned it to my shirt, she watched critically.

"Always wear it on the grounds," she said and spoke the name Bobby into the headset.

Bobby didn't arrive immediately. If I subtracted from my life the time I'd stood waiting, I'd be a boy again. Not that I wanted that. Hell no. I looked at the lobby and its scuffed hardwood floor. Portraits hung on walls, men I assumed to be either politicians or doctors. Someone had picked flowers and brought them inside to set around in vases. They appeared more startling than festive. Outside, a worker sprayed water from a hose on windows and used a squeegee with a long handle to wipe the panes clean.

Bobby arrived wearing whites. He spoke with the woman and motioned me to come along. His Nikes squeaked as he walked beside me along the corridor.

"You got somebody here?" he asked. He waddled and wheezed with every step.

I told him I did.

"Well, it ain't so bad. Once they get used to the place, lots of patients like it better than outside. Some that get released beg to come back."

At the far end of the corridor Bobby stopped at a door that had Dr. Joseph P. Fredrick's nameplate hung on it. Bobby opened it for me onto a windowless waiting room. Two bathrobed female patients sat on chairs opposite each other. A nurse appeared at a glassed-in booth that had a speaking hole. She crooked her finger at me, looked at my pass, and bent to the hole.

"Mr. LeBlanc, you're to go right in," she said and disappeared. A door beside the booth unlocked and opened. The nurse stood aside for me, closed the door after I walked past, and relocked it. As she led me along the hallway, a voice from the waiting room called out, "That's not fair. We was here first."

The nurse tapped on an unmarked door and opened it. Elderly Dr. Fredrick sat at his desk and looked at me over glasses that had slid low over his nose. He'd brushed his whitening hair straight back, but strands rose like hackles. His white unbuttoned medical jacket was rumpled, the knot of his black tie off center. When he stood to shake my hand across the desk, I expected him to creak. His fingers felt all bones, and he appeared very tired.

"Please seat yourself, Mr. LeBlanc. I'm anxious to hear anything you can tell me about the woman we presently have registered as Esmeralda Doe. You are related?"

He lowered himself delicately to his chair. On his desk he or the nurse had stacked manila folders holding patients' records alongside a laboratory flask filled with multicolored jelly beans. A silver frame held a color photograph of a well-dressed aged woman walking a Pekingese restrained by a leash beside a pagoda in what looked like a Chinese garden.

"I think so."

"You just think so?" He looked disappointed.

"I believe I am, yes, sir."

"What's the nature of your relationship?" he asked, his voice not much more than a whisper.

"I can't tell you exactly how we connect up. All I know is my mother once told me we're cousins."

I'd seen his question coming and had the lie ready.

"Does Esmeralda Doe have other family?"

"Not I know of, and I want to help any way I can."

"Tell me what you know about her."

"Not a lot. I was just a boy when Mother told me. Mom always felt sorry for her."

"Do you have a last name for Esmeralda?"

"I think I remember hearing the name Jenkins or Jordan, but it was usually just Esmeralda."

He sighed.

"I am disappointed, Mr. LeBlanc. We have so little information concerning Esmeralda Doe. From you I'd hoped for more. You're not by any chance connected to the press or media, are you?"

"No, sir, I'm not."

"I must be certain of that."

"I'm here to put up money for her care."

"Her care is presently being paid for by the state. How long have you known Esmeralda Doe?"

"We were never close. Just saw her once a couple of years ago."

"You spoke to her?"

"She wasn't doing any speaking."

"That's all you can tell me?"

"Dr. Fredrick, it's the best I can do, but I still am here to help."

"You're aware that she was brought to us by the police?"

"I know she hasn't done anything criminal."

"How can you be certain?"

"She runs from people, not hurts them."

"Perhaps she felt threatened."

"Never by a lady like Aunt Jessie Arbuckle."

Dr. Fredrick opened a manila folder and adjusted his glasses to read papers that lay inside. He fingered through them.

"I've been informed by the authorities that Miss Jessie Arbuckle is a homicide victim who previous to her demise was often in the company of Esmeralda Doe. You say you've seen her just the once?"

"That's it, though I feel sure she's seen me more than that."

"Please explain."

"I believe years ago when I was in Shawnee County she was watching me."

"Why would she do that?"

"She watched everybody."

"But you feel she did you in particular?"

"Yes, sir."

"If I allow you to see her, do you think she might show any sign of recognition or communicate with you in some manner?"

"I think there's a chance of it," I said, not a lie. She might remember my face or maybe the genes cry out. There were many ways of knowing.

"You'll possibly be surprised by her condition," Dr. Fredrick said as he gathered himself to stand. "She was badly disoriented when she arrived here. Thus far she's remained mute even while struggling. She is able to talk?"

"My guess is she has her own language."

"Which is?"

"The woods, the wind, the cries of birds and animals. Maybe she also learned words from Aunt Jessie, who somehow talked to her."

"All right, then," he said and again had difficulty rising to his feet, "we'll go this way."

We left his office not by the door I'd come through but another that gave onto a fire exit to the outside. Dr. Fredrick's footsteps were short and rapid along a gravel path that divided a circular flower garden on the way to a four-story building. No portico or Corinthian columns this time. A large white number 7 on a black oval background identified the building. The entrance doorway was locked. Dr. Fredrick tapped his knuckles lightly against the glass. An orderly looked out at us and used a key attached by a chain to his belt to open the door. His head had been shaved.

"Thomas," Dr. Fredrick greeted him as the orderly relocked the door after us. We walked past a nurses' station to an elevator. Thomas had a key to open and operate it. The three of us rode to the fourth floor. When the door slid open, we couldn't walk off because a screen of steel mesh blocked the exit. A nurse appeared, she too with keys, to swing the screen aside. She and the doctor spoke, and he introduced Miss Adams to me. She was buxom, her arms flesh heavy, her face rosy.

"You'll need to sign in," the doctor said.

Nurse Adams led me to her desk, where I wrote my name on a lined tablet. She looked at her wristwatch before adding the time and date. We followed her along a corridor to a grated door, the bars painted white. She unlocked and relocked it after us. The clang of the bolt was a knell of pain I well remembered.

We passed a recreation room where robed female patients sat playing cards at tables, turning pages of magazines, and drawing using crayons. A woman stacked checkers until they toppled. Others dozed or stared out the window at the top of a swaying willow tree. A female orderly paced among them. A young patient saw us and covered her eyes. Another pointed, grinned, and giggled as she beckoned by repeatedly drawing her palms toward her face.

Nurse Adams opened the entrance into a corridor along both sides of which were numbered doors all closed. Each room could be looked into by an observation window and held only a hospital bed and table. The bare walls had been painted white. She stopped before the third window.

Inside, Esmeralda lay strapped to side rails of her bed. I recognized her from Lupi Fazio's drawings Aunt Jessie had shown me, though Esmeralda was much changed from that time. Bones ridged her long lean face, her graying hair lay strung over her pillow, and lacerations scabbed her cheeks and forehead. Her eyes were not only closed but also clenched. She'd been washed as well as clothed in a hospital gown.

"She's still not spoken?" Dr. Fredrick asked Nurse Adams.

"Not a sound. We keep the intercom switched on and check her every thirty minutes. Her vital signs are near normal, though she refuses food."

"You had to strap her down?" I asked.

"She won't remain in the bed," Nurse Adams said. "She balls herself in a corner and hides her face. We had to tranquilize her before she'd release her arms from around her knees. She's never opened her eyes. We're attempting to keep her from hurting herself, nothing more."

I studied Esmeralda. I felt great concern and hurt for her but not love. Love wasn't automatic or triggered by genes. It needed to be earned. The two of us never had that chance.

Nurse Adams unlocked the door, and we moved inside. The window we'd been looking through provided one-way vision. We gathered at the side of the bed. Esmeralda kept her eyes shut. I saw no breathing.

"Esmeralda, we have your cousin here," Dr. Fredrick said. "He's come to see and visit you."

Esmeralda didn't respond. Nurse Adams took her pulse.

"You might try speaking to her," Dr. Fredrick whispered to me.

I spoke her name and my own three times. Still nothing from Esmeralda. The doctor shook his head and turned toward the door.

I cupped my hands over my mouth and surprised them by giving the mourning dove's call I'd learned as a boy when their plaints around Bellerive's cornfields announced the sunrise. At the five notes Esmeralda's eyes blinked open. They were black and much too large for her narrow face. She stared wildly about her, then again clenched them shut.

"Well," Dr. Fredrick said and looked at Nurse Adams and me. "Finally. Mr. LeBlanc, please attempt that once again."

I did the dove call, the crow's, blue jay's, and song sparrow's. Esmeralda's eyes stayed closed. I touched the back of her left hand. She tried to jerk away, but the straps held her wrist.

"I was hoping for more, but perhaps we have a start," Dr. Fredrick said.

"I'll want her moved to a private facility," I said.

"You'll need to get written authorization from the authorities for that. I assure you she's in good and competent hands here."

As we left the room, I looked back. Her thin body stretched taut, and her face had turned to the wall.

"I intend to keep in touch," I said.

EIGHT

On the return from Huntington, when I turned off Interstate 77 and crossed over the Shawnee County line, I saw ahead a black Mercedes SL500 convertible, its immaculate white top lowered, that had pulled to the weed-tangled shoulder of the road. The car's chrome trim shone bright as new money. The door opened, and a woman's bare legs swung out as she stood. She raised a hand to wave after me.

I slowed, stopped, and backed up. She strode toward the Caddy, a tall woman, at least six feet, yet shapely, her hair whitish blond. Her face, arms, and legs sported a golden tan. I took in her white leather moccasins, white shorts, white sleeveless shirt, and red billed cap.

"I can't get the goddamn thing started," she said as she bent forward to look in the Caddy's window at me. "You know anything about cars?"

"I know they're trouble," I said. "If I had my way I'd never own another one."

"We don't own them, they own us."

I parked on the shoulder, switched off my engine, and crossed to the convertible. She'd left the door open. A leather bag of golf clubs lay propped against the passenger seat. I sat to twist the ignition key. The engine turned over but wouldn't fire. The gas gauge registered half-full. I looked at the odometer. The Mercedes had less than seven thousand miles on it.

"I'm brainy enough to have checked the gas," she said. "I heard this thump, and the engine died. What you think?"

"What kind of thump?"

"How do you describe thumps? It was a noise under the hood."

I pulled the latch, stepped out, and crossed around to raise the hood. The engine shone as if it had been spit-polished. I spotted nothing wrong. Newer cars had such hidden complex electrical and mechanical systems it was impossible like in the old days to find something obvious like a cracked distributor cap or dirt-choked fuel line. Her wheels would need to be hauled to a garage and put on a diagnostic machine like an ailing human carried to the hospital.

"Best I can do is give you a ride or make a call for you," I said.

"I don't like leaving the car here. By the way, my name's Jeannie Bruce St. George, and I'm surprised to see a Montana license plate in Shawnee County."

I didn't hold out my hand to her. My grandfather Gaston LeBlanc, a courtly man of the old school, had taught me you should never shake a woman's hand unless she offered hers first.

"I'm kind of surprised to see a golfing lady driving a Mercedes in Shawnee County," I said.

"The trouble is I'm not driving it. My husband and I've been living here just a year or so. We're doing over the old MacGlauglin property that's been in his family almost a century. I'd make the call myself except my cell phone won't work among these damn mountains."

I wondered why anyone with her class and looks would want to settle in this wild, ragged country.

"I'll find you a repair garage," I said. "Or if you want I'll stay here with your wheels and you can use mine."

"That's sweet of you," she said and smiled. She had a full painted mouth, the lips tending toward a smirk, and she was definitely trim and fit. At her height her green eyes met mine leveled. I expected she worked out, likely ran, maybe lifted weights, and she carried evidence in the Mercedes of being a golfer.

I opened the Caddy's door for her. She pulled in those long, well-shaved legs and caught my glance at them. When she started the engine, she shifted into D while holding her foot on the brake. She pulled off her cap to shake out her hair. It curled upward and inward around her neck.

"Don't worry, I won't wreck your beast," she said but then drove off so fast the tires squealed before they took hold on the pavement.

I walked to the Mercedes and opened the glove compartment. Along with instruction and service booklets I found a registration card that named Jeannie Bruce St. George owner of the car, not her husband or a leasing company. Her address listed Wild Thorn, MacGlauglin's Knob, WV.

I opened the armrest compartment and found not only stacks of coins in the various slots of a toll-change holder but also thirty-seven dollars of paper money carelessly strewn about as well as a cell phone and a pearl-handled, nickel-plated Smith & Wesson .25-cal. automatic. The car smelled of leather, perfume, and a faint remnant of tobacco. I checked the ashtray. The Marlboro butts had lipstick stains.

I sat with my legs outside the car and watched turkey buzzards sail the thermals above the mountain's greening ridge. The buzzards wobbled slightly as if acknowledging my sighting them. The riddle was how such a bird could be so damn ugly and repulsive on the ground and yet so languidly graceful and beautifully suited to flight.

A brown pickup truck rattled along the road. Three yellow lights attached to the cab's roof flashed under a sign that read U.S. MAIL. The driver stopped, pushed up the bill of his CAT cap, and leaned to the window—a spare, elderly man who needed a shave.

"Do something to hep you?" he asked.

"Got help coming," I told him.

"I recognize that car. Belongs to Mrs. St. George, don't it?"

"You right."

"Where you hail from?"

"Montana."

"Whatcha doing in Shawnee County?"

"Passing through."

"You'd had to drive right far out of your way to pass through this place."

"You know Wild Thorn at MacGlauglin's Knob?"

"I carry the mail up to the Knob," he said and worked a wad of tobacco in his jaw. "You belong to them?"

"Them who?"

"The St. Georges."

"I belong to nobody," I said and thought, Except Blackie.

"They up at Wild Thorn. Just named it that not long ago. Get their mail addressed that way. In the lower end of the county. Big old mansion and more acres of land than most men able to count to. She and Mr. Duncan St. George has come back and be living in the house. Can't hire a carpenter or electrician no more in Shawnee County. They all working out at that place. You sure you don't need no hep?"

"You're wondering if I stole the car," I said. "I didn't. Engine trouble, and Mrs. St. George's coming back for it."

"Oh yeah, well, all the way from Montana, that's sure something," he said. "Far as I ever got is Kentucky. I always wanted to ride down to Texas and see the Alamo."

He geared up and drove off, sitting in the tilted manner that rural mail carriers develop because they steered on the left and needed to lean right to stick mail in the roadside boxes.

Again I sat in the Mercedes and called up what more I could remember my father had said about the MacGlauglins, particularly James MacGlauglin, a Scotsman and the first man to mine the Shawnee seams of coal. Old James MacGlauglin had taken on the unions during the mine wars of the 1920s, resulting in President Warren Harding sending in two thousand U.S. troops to stop the fighting. The MacGlauglins had owned some ten thousand acres of Shawnee County back then and held leases to coal rights on lots more.

It was late afternoon before Jeannie Bruce St. George returned in my car followed by a tow truck from Cliffside. She and I stood and watched the driver hitch and raise the front end to haul it away.

"They'll take it to Beckley," she said. "There's no garage around here that has the test equipment."

"You going with them?"

"I'm hoping you'll offer me a ride home," she said and again gave me the smile that verged on a smirk. She knew damn well I'd looked at the V neck of her shirt and seen top fringes of her athletic brassiere.

"Sure," I said.

She lifted her golf clubs from the Mercedes, and I set them in the rear of the Caddy. We watched the tow truck pull off. I again opened the door for her, though I'd long ago given up opening doors. Except for Blackie, I had given up women too, though I was very much aware of this one and she knew it. With her startling looks she undoubtedly expected it. Those long shaved legs stayed in my mind even when I made myself stop sneaking looks at them.

"You've not told me your name," she said.

"Charley LeBlanc."

She crossed her legs and turned her body toward me as she eyed my face.

"Of the LeBlanc LeBlancs and High Moor?"

"My father was John Maupin LeBlanc."

"Who took the last of the good coal out of Shawnee County. I don't suppose your father knew any of the MacGlauglins."

"They were gone from Shawnee County, but he talked about them. The MacGlauglins in their day were the big dogs around here."

"Actually I've never known any except my husband, Duncan, the great-grandson of James MacGlauglin. Duncan lived only a few years as a baby in Shawnee County. He inherited the property from his mother and considered selling it until we drove down from Baltimore

and took one look at the house and its breathtaking view. We decided
we wanted it ourselves. It's unique and truly beautiful. This morning I
had the bedroom window open and heard a rain crow as the sun
shone through the morning mist. The air was so moistly fresh and fragrant I kept breathing it to fill my lungs. Have you been to Wild
Thorn?"

I told her I hadn't.

"I'll give you directions."

Directions led to a badly paved county road so narrow south of
Cliffside that when we met another car each driver had to pull to the
shoulder to pass. Not many dwellings along the unmarked route and
those humble, most swaybacked, broken, or forsaken, and nearly all
swallowed up by forested land that rose on both sides of the valley and
covered slopes to the ridges. I assumed we had crossed a line onto the
MacGlauglin property when I saw posted signs nailed to hemlocks. A
fortune in timber grew here, and we crossed half a dozen streams that
fed under the road through galvanized drainage pipes. Shafts of sunlight like rapier blades penetrated the gloom.

"We face disadvantages living out here," Jeannie Bruce said. "No
grocery stores or Wal-Marts. On the other hand, in some ways those
same inconveniences are beneficial. We have a man who drives to
Beckley for our food supplies. If we need something more fashionable
or exotic, it's only ninety minutes or so to the Greenbrier, where we're
members of the Old White Club."

They had a man. Like they owned him and maybe they did.

"For a time it's been like camping out at the house," she said and
recrossed those legs. She jiggled her foot. "The water system needed
repairs, and the furnace to be replaced. Windows were broken. The
dining room had grackles nesting in a chandelier. Still, the house is
solid as a fortress, and most of the furniture is usable, though moths
had eaten up all the drapes and carpets. A caretaker did the best he
could but would've needed a staff to keep up the place. When he died,
Duncan and I came out to see what remained. Once here, we hardly

needed to discuss whether to stay or not. We turned to each other and knew without words."

"How much land?" I asked.

"At the moment fifty-seven hundred acres more or less."

More or less, I thought. When you had that much, who needed to be exact?

"We're having it surveyed to reestablish the boundaries, and Duncan hopes to acquire additional property."

"Fifty-seven hundred's not enough?" I asked and glanced at her. Her brows had been plucked, and she wore tiny diamond earrings— just right for golfing at the Greenbrier.

"Duncan wants to restore the original holdings of his great-grandfather."

"I heard that was about ten thousand," I said.

"Around ten thousand, who counted exactly?" she said and laughed. "It was a wilderness in the days old James MacGlauglin made his way here on a railroad work car along the river, discovered the coal, set up his mining operation, and built his town. For a while he turned his end of the county into a thriving community and owned every inch of it. Your father did the same at High Moor years later. Cliffside had a bank, movie theater, and Ford dealership. Now the economy is falling apart and the land reverting to the wilds. Call it Nature's revenge."

She was right. The camps and land around MacGlauglin and High Moor had once been kingdoms, or at least duchies.

"There," she said and pointed. "You can see the house."

The mansion sat like a fortification on the crest of a hill. Built not of brick but granite, it looked not only massive but also appeared a spooky white contradiction in coal country. The mullioned windows reflecting the afternoon sun flashed like molten silver, and the roof appeared to be a weird shade of pale green. A stone wall surrounded the house.

As the road dipped into the valley, we slowed at what was left of the town. Most buildings had been razed. A few still stood—a wind-scoured country church the belfry of which had been partially torn away, a windowless stone structure with an iron door that had probably been the powder house, and the two-story frame company store, its front porch collapsing. The shallow stream that ran through the center of the camp carried a tinge of pissy color.

"Hundreds dwelt here," Jeannie said. "James MacGlauglin expected his miners to fear the Lord and live upright lives. It was all his, even the church. He issued his own money called scrip. The coins were made of wood. In those days no one arrived at MacGlauglin except by rail. Once here, you were landlocked. He called the miners 'his people.'"

"My father admired him," I said.

"Duncan does too. James was a poor young boy when he came to this country. Life had made him hard. He'd never been to college, yet was able to lay out the town and engineer the headhouse and tipple as well as all the machinery. He talked the railroad into building a spur line. He became a benevolent despot, and for a while owned a private railroad car, the seats all plush, the walls decorated with murals, a dining salon as well as bedrooms. Duncan tried to find and restore it, but it's gone, possibly wrecked or junked. A shame."

"Sure, a crying shame," I said. "Every man should have one."

"It was a gaudy tasteless era," she said. "He had it all until 'his people' rebelled and wanted a union. Then it began to fall apart."

She raised her hand to indicate I was to take a twisting road that climbed toward the mansion. It had been paved but needed repair. The wall blocked my view of the house. We passed between stone gateposts that had wrought-iron lamps on top. Then the roof took shape, and at least a dozen paired chimneys rose from it.

"Solid copper," Jeannie Bruce said. "Only copper roof in this part of the country. It'll last forever. It's the way Duncan's great-grandfather liked doing things. He built them to last. At least he believed they would. Small, envious men attacked like a pack of dogs and brought him down."

Yeah, small men who bowed into the mountains each day to work in the wet blackness and hack out the bituminous James MacGlauglin transformed into dollars. They started work so early in the morning and stayed at it so late they forgot the look of sunshine and became pale as fish bellies. They heard the mountains talk—groan, strain, and crack above them. They died mangled by roof falls or became fried by firedamp, all for a few bucks a day. Then they had the nerve to want a fucking union.

Construction machinery lined the way, and men driving pickups left work. Once inside the wall a mowed lawn spread under ancient scabby oaks that dropped rich shadows on the grass. A few had their thick limbs chained to the trunks for support and made me think of Bellerive. I took in the three-tiered fountain, the iron benches painted white, and the croquet court. I glimpsed a swimming pool and tennis court being installed at the side of the house. Ivy covered a sundial.

"Isn't it so incongruous it's beautiful?" Jeannie Bruce asked. "James MacGlauglin considered unions socialistic evils. With his money he paid for his own private army to fight the miners, who marched all the way from Charleston, and he kept an arsenal of guns in the house's basement. What a man. They no longer make them that way."

Yeah, they do, I thought. They just slicker.

"I see you carry a pistol in the armrest," I said.

"Snooping on me, huh? Well, I did the same on you. Found you had liquor in the trunk and that the Cadillac was registered to a Mildred Spurlock. You a kept man?"

"More like a joint partner."

"Joint and joined at the hip and thigh, huh?" she asked, and this time gave me the smile along with a lifted right eyebrow.

I didn't answer. What was between Blackie and me was none of her feline business. The circular drive curved to cobblestones of a court-yard at the front of the mansion. I stopped before the entrance, where workers on ladders pulled down ivy and used mortar to point up the granite courses, which had been steam-cleaned. From an opened casement a white curtain fluttered out. Outsized brass knockers shaped like lions' heads hung from the massive wooden double doors.

"Appreciate your help, Charles. And you may call me Jeannie Bruce."

"Thanks for permission."

"Whoa now, don't turn nasty on me."

"I'm assuming you have other transportation," I said.

"Oh, we do. Duncan owns a Jag and our son Angus a Land Rover. There are also several trucks and a Jeep. Like to come in?"

"Not today. Got things on my mind."

"Who doesn't?" she asked and opened the door to leg out.

I might've helped with her golf clubs, but before I could lift the bag from the back a Latino servant hurried from the house to take it. Jeannie Bruce extended her hand to me, and I shook it. As her green eyes locked on mine, her hand gave mine a slight squeeze and was slow to release.

"Ta," she said when she stepped away and then slammed the door.

Driving off, I glanced in the rearview mirror and saw her enter the house, the Latino standing aside for her. The slant of sunlight reflecting off the mansion's windows made them appear silver no longer but as if flames burned behind them. Maybe it was Jeannie Bruce's presence. She was one hot bitch.

NINE

When I reached Ben's I found him sitting with Blackie on the porch steps peeling potatoes. Both were barefooted. Blackie looked good in her denim shorts and shirt, but nothing spit-licked and classy like Jeannie Bruce St. George. I felt disloyalty for thinking that. Blackie didn't have that tall statuesque body but was built neat and compact, no wasted curves. Her hair gave off a gloss from her washing it. Both of them looked me over as if taking measurement.

"Well, where you been holding yourself all the livelong day?" Blackie asked.

I told them about my trip to Huntington and that I'd finally seen Esmeralda.

"You should've invited me along," Blackie said.

"I had to move fast," I said, not completely a lie, but verging on it.

"I don't hold any world records, but I'm not exactly slow," Blackie said. "And they got her strapped down in the bed?"

"They have, and I mean to get her out of that place into a private facility."

"How'd she look?" Ben asked. Potato peelings curved off the sharpness of his knife's blade as if of their own free will and dropped into a five-gallon emptied salt can set between his feet.

"She scared and stretched out on the bed with her eyes kept closed. I hated seeing it."

"She hurt bad?" Blackie asked.

"The doc didn't seem to think so, yet she was skin and bones and scratched up. She opened her eyes a second, and they make you forget all about the rest of her—like she's reached out with them and touched you."

"Well, what you gonna do next?" Blackie asked.

"Talk to the district attorney to see if I can have her moved."

"You got to eat first," Blackie said.

I washed up for dinner, and she served Ben and me slices of country ham, boiled potatoes coated with country butter from Ben's churn, hot biscuits, and fresh-squeezed applesauce. I told them about stopping to help Jeannie Bruce St. George.

"You think her kind will last around Shawnee County?" I asked Ben.

"What you mean 'her kind'?" Blackie asked.

"She don't look cut out for backwoods West Virginia."

"They buying up land fast as people'll let go of it and doing a mountain of building," Ben said. "Paying top dollar too for any parcels that connects with their own holdings. Could have more money than sense. Word I hear is they talking of putting in a golf course, riding trails, and ski slopes to make the place a resort. Been all sorts of surveyors driving stakes and flagging property lines."

"Who'd come to a resort in this county?" Blackie asked. "Just as well toss the money off a bridge into the branch."

"Might be nothing to all I heard," Ben said. "People talking. Got nothing much else around here to do for entertainment. What I do know is the St. Georges provide jobs, and I hope they stick around as long as their money holds out."

Soon as I ate and we finished dishes, Blackie and I got in the car to drive to Peck's Store so I could use the phone to call District Attorney

Sligh. His name and office number were listed in the thin local directory that had an advertisement for the Duiguid Funeral Home on the front and the slogan WE CARE FOR YOU.

I didn't expect Sligh to be at his office, but that was the only number in the book. I listened to eleven rings before I hung up and then asked Mr. Henry Peck how to reach the house.

"Lives in Cliffside," Mr. Peck said. He sat on his stool, his body curved forward, his shaky hands stacking coins he'd drawn from the antique gilt-scrolled cash register. His skin appeared as pale and thin as rice paper. "Grover'd love to run for state attorney general and spends most of his time greasing them up that can do him some good at it. That means money or connections."

"Wait till morning?" Blackie asked me. "The world's not going to go to hellfire overnight."

"All my life I been chewed up with waiting," I said.

We drove into Cliffside. Sligh's white cottage was set back from the dark, lonesome street. No car in his drive or lights behind the house's windows. I parked in front and walked to the door. When I rang the bell, a dog barked inside, yet nobody answered. I crossed around to the rear. A rope swing hung from the limb of a maple tree, and two canvas beach chairs had been unfolded on the grass. I knocked on the back door. The dog continued to bark, and that was it.

We drove to Ben's and found him reading at the kitchen table. I touched Blackie's shoulder before turning in. She laid her hand on my waist and let her fingers trail around it. Except in bed, we weren't kissers.

Lying on the cot, I kept seeing Esmeralda's dark eyes and the way they'd taken me in. I again wondered whether she could have sensed something through the genes about me. I needed to be careful not to turn hope into being.

Jeannie Bruce St. George also appeared in my mind. Those green eyes and long shaved legs. Nah, man, none of that. I wiped her out like arcing a chalk eraser across a blackboard, but I needed to repeat it a couple of times.

I woke early, ate ham and eggs with Blackie, and waited till eight-thirty before driving to Cliffside. This time I asked Blackie whether she wanted to come along. She hesitated and said no, that she and Ben had made a date to pick cresses, which grew along the moist ferny banks of Laurel Creek. They carried buckets, and each held a knife to cut the stalks close to the ground.

At Cliffside a prisoner wearing bib overalls mowed grass in front of the courthouse. The district attorney's secretary, Miss Minerva Lemon, pursed her lips and looked sour as ever as she told me Mr. Sligh hadn't come in yet and I'd need to wait. She had coffee brewing but didn't offer me a mug. I sat in the chair and looked out the window. An aproned man swept the sidewalk in front of the Shawnee Grocery, a few people moved along Main Street, none seeming about much of anything, and an eighteen-wheeler Freightliner loaded with sawed red oak logs rumbled past and caused the courthouse to quiver.

"He usually this late?" I asked Miss Minerva at nine-fifteen by the electric clock on the wall above her desk.

"Nine-fifteen is not late for a man in Mr. Sligh's position," she said. "Many offices don't open until ten."

"In a place like Cliffside?"

She lifted her nose slightly, gave me a haughty look, and turned to her computer. I felt sorry I'd talked to her like that. Poor hassled little lady making her way in a dying town.

Mr. Sligh arrived at nine-forty. He appeared freshly shaved and energetic. You could've sawed wood using the sharp creases in the britches of his charcoal suit. His royal-blue bow tie was too large for his small face and spread beneath his chin like a butterfly. He poured coffee Miss Minerva had waiting not into one of the mugs but his set-aside private teacup and saucer before leading me into his office.

"Well, Mr. LeBlanc, here you visit us once again," he said and crossed to the Victorian desk to set the saucer on it. The silver spoon he used to stir with appeared dainty and delicate. The cup could've been Limoges. "Care for an eye-opener?"

When I shook my head, he closed the door and before sitting pulled upward on those creases of his pants. My grandfather Gaston LeBlanc had told me that no gentleman and only people in trade and men who knew no better did that.

"I have a bad feeling this is going to be one torturous day," Sligh said. "And I do hope you're not here to bring me problems. Fact is I can't see the day ending before late into this night."

"Life's a bitch, ain't it?"

"Indeed, though things in this office have been going fairly well until lately," he said and smoothed his tiny mustache before he allowed himself a sip of the coffee. "Nobody's done any knifing or shooting. A mountain man did drop his woman down his well, and another citizen kicked his neighbor's dog. Just the routine conduct of ordinary life around Shawnee County."

"Esmeralda," I said.

"And that too, of course."

"I saw her yesterday and tried to reach you last night."

"Last night I played bridge in Bluefield. That's how far I travel to find a decent game. You drove all the way to Huntington?"

"I don't count Huntington as being all the way."

"No, in Montana that must not seem much of a distance. But they allowed you to see her?"

"I didn't climb in a window."

"I expect you would have trouble doing that in Huntington. As I remember, the windows are secured."

"They are," I said and thought his twitching mustache was like a mouse that might scurry into his prissy mouth.

"They shouldn't have let you in without checking with this office. I just might give Huntington State a call."

"How do I go about a court order that would permit Esmeralda to be moved into a private-care facility?"

"Mr. LeBlanc, there's no way that can be done at this juncture. She is, as I told you, under investigation. Were she normal she would most

likely be in a cell this very moment with little chance of bail. Indictment is most likely only a question of her mental competence."

"You still hung up on whatever it was she carried in the bundle
from Aunt Jessie's?"

"I'm not hung up on anything. I do not become hung up."

"And maybe that further complication you mentioned last time I
was here."

"Mr. LeBlanc, as much as I'd like to help you, it's often the maybes
we have to deal with in the law. A whole world of maybes. We collect
and sift them through our legal fingers. The process requires time and
thought. Believe me, we are proceeding conscientiously." He leaned
forward to look at a notepad. "Now, I have miles to travel this day
before I sleep."

He finished his coffee and wiped his lips, not with the four-point
linen handkerchief displayed from his jacket pocket but an ordinary
everyday one drawn off his hip. The spread of handkerchief looked
much too profuse for his small mouth and face. He precisely refolded it.

"No way a person in Esmeralda's condition can be kept locked up
just for a maybe," I said.

"Actually Social Services is holding her and does have that right
because Esmeralda Doe is unable to care for herself. Mr. Leblanc, a life
has been lost. Evidence must be gathered and run through the judicial
system. The system is slow and cumbersome, a labor like hauling a
heavy load uphill, but eventually reaches its objective. Now please be
so good as to let me do my work."

"Esmeralda visited Aunt Jessie every day and might've become
scared at what she saw in the cabin and just run off."

"Might've is like a maybe. Look, I feel no obligation to tell you this,
but I will. When brought into custody, Esmeralda not only had in her
possession an item we know was taken from Aunt Jessie's but was also
found to have bloodstains on her dress. The State Police carried the
dress to forensics in Charleston. The report confirms that the blood
matches Aunt Jessie's DNA."

"Esmeralda could've gone to the cabin, found Aunt Jessie hurt, and bloodied her dress trying to help."

"Now we've gone from mights to coulds. This office, the sheriff, and the State Police are assuming nothing but carefully proceeding with an investigation. Esmeralda Doe will need to remain in custody until the legal process runs its course. It does appear the outcome might well be that Esmeralda Doe will be judged non compos mentis, require institutionalizing, and become a ward of the state for the remainder of her life."

"Not if I have anything to do with it."

"The question is, Mr. LeBlanc, just exactly what do you have to do with it?"

"I want her to receive the best of care in a first-class nursing facility."

"Huntington State Hospital has a very fine institutional reputation and is well prepared to take excellent care of her until this matter is adjudicated."

Sligh, hoping to be rid of me, looked at his wristwatch.

"Who found Aunt Jessie dead?" I asked.

"Mr. LeBlanc, please desist."

"Surely you can tell me that."

"A local citizen."

"That must have a name."

"He does."

"I'd like it."

"I'm not required to tell you."

"Why not tell me?"

"I worry that it might encourage you to attempt unauthorized and amateurish sleuthing."

"I can find out," I said and already knew it was Leroy Spears as the sheriff had told Blackie and me. "Somebody around here'll know."

"I have no doubt."

"What did Aunt Jessie die from?"

"Appeared to be heart failure until Bernard Duiguid, our local undertaker, discovered a puncture in her head."

"Caused by what?"

"We believed she had fallen."

"Believed, not believe now?"

"I misspoke. We're still looking into it."

"Who saw Esmeralda running away carrying the bundle from Aunt Jessie's?"

"Another citizen of the county."

"You won't tell me that name either?"

"No."

"Mr. Sligh, I'd sure like to have it."

"Mr. LeBlanc, the wheels of the law are turning slowly but will grind exceedingly fine. We don't want and in fact will oppose any intrusion from an unauthorized party into the death of Jessie Arbuckle. Allow us to do our work. Now, that's final."

I stood to leave. His chickenshit smile appeared.

"I want her moved," I said.

TEN

As I walked down the steps and started to leave the courthouse, I thought of again stopping and talking to Sheriff Basil Lester. No, the sheriff and district attorney would be acting in concert and give me nothing more.

When I reached the Caddy, I found I'd been ticketed. Dozens of empty spaces ranged along the street, and I'd figured the rusted parking meters had long ago stopped being checked. I carried the ticket back into the courthouse and the treasurer's office. A stout blowsy woman sat at a desk eating a Snickers bar. The nameplate on her desk read DARLENE.

"Parking space around here a problem?" I asked as I laid the ticket on the counter.

"It is for them that gets caught," Darlene said. Chocolate had coated a corner of her mouth. She examined the ticket. "That'll be fifteen dollars."

"Real bargain," I said.

"We aim to please," Darlene said and laughed.

All bureaucracies are the same, I thought as she counted out the change from my twenty and stamped the ticket PAID. Fleece the sheep.

"Hear Esmeralda's been taken into custody," I said on the chance I might learn something from courthouse chatter. There was bound to be talk.

"You know she has, Mr. LeBlanc."

"Why would I?"

"'Cause you been upstairs talking to Mr. Sligh."

"How'd you get my name?"

"Mr. LeBlanc, when strangers walk down Cliffside's Main Street the news about them gets found out as fast as greased pigs on ice."

I should've figured the courthouse of a hick town would be a leaking bucket of insider information. She lifted the Snickers bar and chewed it with a leisurely sideways movement of her jaws. A cow and its cud. I walked out.

I stood by my car wondering what next. A question took shape. The sheriff had said the local undertaker had discovered a puncture on Aunt Jessie's head. Wouldn't that have been a coroner's job? I remembered the sheriff had said the coroner, Doc Bailey, was old and had eyes gone bad. I'd seen the advertisement for the Duiguid Funeral Home in the phone book. I could take a look.

I crossed to the Shawnee Grocery, bought a pack of Camels, and asked a pale youth behind the cash register the location of the funeral home. He had three fingers missing from his right hand and used a thumb to punch the keys.

"Upper end of Jackson Street," he said. "You can't miss it even if you dead."

Jackson Street ran uphill, and the Duiguid sign painted in block black letters against a pukey yellow background had been planted on the front lawn. A cardinal decorated the left lower corner of the sign, its beak lifted as if singing a happy song. The frame Victorian house was a sprawling structure of porches, gables, and balconies, all painted the same yellow. Stained-glass windows gave off flashes of reds, blues, and oranges. Arrow-shaped lightning rods stuck up from the crown of the steeply pitched roof. An iron buck deer with its antlered head raised stood in shadows of a gnarled and sickly elm.

Stone urns that held petunias flanked the steps to the porch, and a film of pollen lay over the railings, the gray floorboards, and a line of wooden rocking chairs you might've seen at a resort hotel of old. I tapped on the screen door and looked into the shadowed interior. The ticking of a clock sounded slowly persistent. I glimpsed the pendulum swinging a golden glint. A black woman holding a broom appeared. She had tied a red bandanna around her head.

"Mr. Duiguid, he in back," she said and pointed using the handle of the broom. "Just go 'round the house there."

I passed flower beds growing blooming hydrangeas and hollyhocks. Trumpet vine snaked up a latticework. I let myself through a latched gate into the backyard, where a man standing on the lawn held a fishing rod to cast a wooden practice plug at a galvanized washtub of water at least seventy-five feet distant. He was good. As I watched, the plug splashed into the water three times without a miss.

He appeared flushed and pudgy, his red hair newly clipped around the rear of his neck. He'd rolled up the sleeves of his white shirt and loosened his tie. He reeled in the plug by dragging it across the grass, then lifted it for another cast. This time the plug clinked the lip of the washtub.

"Well, hell," he said. "Keep your eye on the doggone ball."

"Sir?" I called.

I'd startled him, and he took a step sideways. When he finished reeling in, he laid his rod across a lawn chair, rolled down his sleeves, and tightened his black tie. His face became mournfully sympathetic.

"Bernard Duiguid, brother," he said and held out his hand. His fingers felt softly moist. He'd pronounced *Bernard* with the accent on the second syllable. "You here in the service of a loved one?"

"Not yet," I said. I wanted to get to Esmeralda but not ask questions so directly they'd spook him. "I'm interested in your house."

"In buying it?" he asked and became more alert. He glanced at my Stetson and cowboy boots.

"No, the architecture. It's a beauty."

"Sure was a glory in her day. Lots of people used to stop to ask about it. Built and lived in originally by a gentleman who owned the bank here. Sprague his name. The Miners and Merchants Bank. Failed during the Great Depression. People around here called it the Great Compression. My daddy who ran this business before me bought the house at public auction in 1931. No other bidders."

"What happened to the banker?" I asked.

"Shot himself in the mouth. Used an English twelve-gauge. Dressed up even to wearing spats and a derby hat to do it. His big toe was too large to fit in the trigger guard, so he used a little one. My daddy buried him. It was tight times for many around here. People hungry and knocking on doors. Beggars riding the rails. My mama and daddy always fed them. The mines shutting down. A terrible, terrible time for one and all."

Except for undertakers, I thought. Times would've been good for them. Plenty of bodies around.

"My mama and daddy operated the business before me, and lately I been thinking of retiring," Bernard said. "Still got their furniture inside. My wife left me. Said she could no longer stand the odor of lilies and formaldehyde. My children live in Atlanta, where they making money hand over fist. You have no interest in the house other than curiosity? I'd be willing to let her go at a good and fair price."

"Just impressed by the way you've kept things up."

"My daddy always told me if you take care of your business, your business will take care of you."

"You have a nice action with that fishing rod."

"I compete in tournaments and won several prizes—a second-place at Smith Mountain Lake down in Virginia just last week. I'd like to go on the road full-time. Travel all over the country catching fish. Kind of a dream of mine." He scratched his reddened nose. It bespoke liquor drinking. "I don't believe I caught your name."

"LeBlanc. Charles LeBlanc."

"Oh yes, I've heard that name and been told you was in town."

"Who told you?"

"Down at the Shawnee Grocery people talking. John Maupin LeBlanc the Third your father, right?"

I admitted he had been. Bernard started to ask another question but recaptured it in his loose-hanging mouth. I answered it.

"I'm the LeBlanc the police were after a couple of years ago."

"Surely, well, I remember your father from when I was a little tyke, a fine cultured gentleman he was who for a time brought jobs and hope back to Shawnee County. Business was good during those days. Cliffside boomed and the lights never went out at night. How things changed. Oh my, yes they have, they have indeed."

My father John Maupin LeBlanc III had come to despise me and I'd learned to hate him. Rich and supposedly a gentleman, on one of his wild and violent drunks he'd raped Esmeralda and fathered me.

"You remember Lupi Fazio?" I asked.

"Oh surely. Everybody remembers Lupi. Ugly little man who made the High Moor diggings work and pay. Sat out there in that stone office and froze to death after the coal played out. He didn't have much else in his life except the mines. My daddy buried him too. Lupi was the last resident of the High Moor camp."

"Except for Esmeralda," I said.

"Yes, her, of course. She often bedded down at High Moor after it was deserted, and she keened for Lupi. People on the mountain heard her wail. That poor frightened woman surely's not responsible for anything she's done. Oh yes, so much has changed in my time. Is there any way I can serve you, Mr. Leblanc?"

"Tell me about Aunt Jessie," I said. "I came back to the county to see her. Hadn't heard she'd died."

"Oh my, our Aunt Jessie, such a great and fine lady. Indeed gone to glory."

"What I hear is she might've died from a fall when she fell and hit her head against her hearthstone."

"Well, now, that's somewhat questionable. They carried her body down from the cabin to me here after old Doc Bailey the coroner from over in Seneca County examined her. He'd missed the head puncture. Not his fault. Doc's almost blind and near worked to death. I discovered the wound while I was preparing her for burial. The police had missed it too. Went on and buried her anyhow and now they just dug her up again."

"She gone from the grave? Whyn't you all wait for an autopsy to start with?"

"Everything was set for the service. Church service, flowers, and all. Autopsy hadn't yet been decided on. I was rushing around. People had come in for the funeral. Lots of confusion. The sheriff told me to just go on and bury her."

"The sheriff?"

"Yeah, Basil. We disinterred her last evening and sent her to Charleston."

Sligh hadn't told me about that. God, I hated to think of Aunt Jessie lying on a cold morgue drainage slab and the rubber-gloved pathologists and their assistants taking knives and saws to her body.

"Hardly no external bleeding. I located the puncture under clotted hair and probed it. She had nice thick hair, a vigorous woman for her age. What stopped and clogged the bleeding was a small piece of steel about the size and shape of a twenty-two-caliber bullet."

"I didn't know they made steel twenty-two-caliber ammo."

"Well, they not certain what it is exactly, or if they are they keeping it to themselves."

"But you think it was a bullet?"

He gazed at me and rubbed his nose. I was moving in too fast and about to silence him.

"Mr. LeBlanc, why you asking me all these questions?"

"Aunt Jessie meant a lot to me."

"I don't think it'd be smart for me to be telling you anything further."

"But there's a chance she fell after being shot in the head with a twenty-two and that the bullet, not the fall, killed her?"

"I'm not telling you that. It's up to the state medical examiner. Not my business to bring in findings."

"Where on her head is the puncture?"

"The posterior region."

"Meaning the rear."

"The rear above the hairline."

"Indicating she might not've seen it coming."

"I've reached no conclusion, nor is it my business to do so. Her body was brought here, I prepared her for burial, and informed the State Police that I found the puncture and had probed out the twenty-two-caliber bullet or whatever it is."

"What happened to the bullet?"

"A trooper stuck it in a glassine envelope and carried it off to Charleston."

"It must've been a custom load to be made of steel."

"I don't know about that. Guns not my thing."

"Who found her?"

"A rural mail carrier by the name of Leroy Spears."

Okay, the second time I'd gotten that name.

"Was he the man who saw Esmeralda running away from the cabin carrying a bundle?"

"I believe that was Angus St. George."

"Who's Angus St. George?"

"He Mr. Duncan St. George's son."

"They question him?"

"I expect so."

"What was a St. George doing out at her place?"

"Chances are riding his horse. Angus is a horseman. Likes to gallop over the countryside and jump fences. Maybe you know the St. Georges are restoring things out at Wild Thorn."

"I heard," I said and thought of Jeannie Bruce.

"Spending dollars like they own a bank. Fact is there's talk they plan to open one in Cliffside. Mostly to hold their own money, I expect. They a real blessing to Shawnee County. People finding work. Bread on the table."

"Angus just happened to be riding by, huh?"

"Well, you'd have to ask him, and I'm not answering any more questions. I already talked more than I intended to."

"Well then, Mr. Duiguid, guess I'll be going."

"You didn't really stop by my place here to find out about the house, did you?"

"I was drawn to it," I said. "Appreciate you taking the time to chat with me."

"Sure, and what I learned in my business is death always draws an audience."

As I walked away, he lifted the rod from the chair, flexed it, and made a cast. The plug hit the exact center of the tub and splashed out water.

ELEVEN

At Cousin Ben's, Blackie walked around the far side of his house. She'd used shears to cut a few of his roses and wore his cuffed oversized work gloves to protect her hands from thorns. She arranged the roses in a mason jar she set on the kitchen table. She had her own garden out in Chinook, where I'd often watched her kneeling. The sight made me remember Bellerive and the woman I'd believed to be my mother wearing the broad straw hat that shaded her face as she gathered daffodils she placed in a silver vase on the breakfast table. Flowers gentled women, transformed them, a nurturing, spiritual thing few men fully understood. And such women gentled men.

"That lawyer of yours over in Jessup's Wharf called for you," she said as she washed her hands at the kitchen sink. "He talked the sheriff into tracking you. The sheriff sent Deputy Lester out here with the message and left a telephone number."

"They dug up Aunt Jessie's body," I said.

"Why?" she asked and handed me a slip of paper with the number and the name Walter B. Frampton on it. Walt had been my attorney when I was accused of setting off the explosion under the portico at

Bellerive. I hadn't thought much of him at first, considered him a snot-ass college boy, but he'd stuck by me during the bad time, and I'd grown not only to trust and respect him but also to like him. He possessed staying power. Walter had the possibility of making an NS#3. He just had to come to believe he had the stuff within himself.

"I don't know but mean to find out," I said and drove to Peck's Store. Mr. Henry sat on his stool and used a magnifying glass to read the newspaper. He traced words with a trembling, crooked index finger. I asked him to change five dollars into quarters. He focused his pale rheumy eyes on me.

"I don't like running short of change," he said. "Make me need to drive to the bank in Fayetteville. Don't like driving either. Go once a week at most. And it burns gas."

"You heard anything about Aunt Jessie's body being taken to Charleston?"

"News to me," he said and groaned working down off his stool. He sank to a knee before a black iron safe that must've been a hundred years old. He set his glasses, spun the dial, and pulled the heavy door open. He stood with a shoebox that held neatly stacked coins. With serious concentration he counted out twenty for me. Then he counted them a second time. He took my five-dollar bill and snapped it between his fingers to test its authenticity and rang up a No Sale key on the cash register before placing the bill in a bin.

I dialed Walt's number, looked at a shelf that held rat poison marked with skull and crossbones on the carton, and heard the voice of his secretary. When I'd first met him, he hadn't been able to afford help. She switched me over to his phone.

"How'd you find me?" I asked.

"Called your Chinook bank. Explained who I was and asked them to help locate you. They sent a teller out to talk to the man named Albert who's feeding your horses. He said you'd gone to West Virginia. I figured you had to be in Shawnee County and called the sheriff in Cliffside. Charles, it's good to hear your voice."

"Same here, Walt," I said. He always called me Charles, not Charley. "We got problems?"

"I don't know. Your brother Edward wants to talk to you. He acts as if it's a serious matter. I tried to find precisely what's bothering him, but he's being tight-mouthed. That sounds like money to me."

"Give me his number and I'll call."

"He wants to see you in person. He's emphatic about that."

"The road between Richmond and Cliffside runs the same distance in both directions."

"He'd like you to come to Richmond. In fact he insists upon it."

"What right's he got to insist?"

"Charles, I'm in the middle here, but I think you ought to do it."

"That all he told you?"

"He made reference to a complication in the sale of Bellerive, nothing more."

"Why can't he speak to me over the phone?"

"I have no answer to that."

"He hasn't paid us out any money yet. You think he's weaseling?"

"Just come on, Charles. You can stay with Mary Ellen and me."

"Mary Ellen?"

"My secretary."

"You living with your secretary?"

"My wife now, Charles."

"You could've sent an invite to the wedding, though weddings always make me cry for the wrong reason. People not knowing what a mess they getting into."

"We had a private wedding. She wanted it that way, and you wouldn't have attended anyhow. What you doing in Shawnee County?"

"I'll tell you when I see you."

"I'd like to set up an appointment with Brother Edward."

"Tomorrow at ten," I said. "I'll head straight for Richmond."

I used my fifteen remaining quarters as part payment for two packs of Camels bought to keep Mr. Henry happy and drove back to Ben's.

My business with Esmeralda would have to be put off a day as I turned to what promised to be a problem with Brother Edward, Bellerive, and the dollars I had coming.

"Why not use your smarts, drive to Richmond tonight, and stay at a motel?" Blackie asked. "Then you'd be fresh in the morning."

"The last time I stayed in a motel I felt the room was closing in on me. The place smelled of too many people's scents, and the window was fixed so I couldn't open it and get at fresh air."

"Looks like your brother could've invited you to stay with him."

"He probably thinks I'd carry in germs. He's very big on germs."

Edward and I were never close. During our boyhoods, though he was two years older, I'd caught him behind Bellerive's stable, beat him up for ratting on me to our father, and sent him crying to the house. I'd inherited nothing from my father or older brother John. Edward had it all. Over the years he'd been glad to be shut of me. He'd surprised me after I was cleared of the murder charge by offering me half the proceeds from the sale of Bellerive, which he figured would amount before taxes to a million dollars a year over seven years. I'd retained Walt to handle the business end of the transaction. Walt was both my lawyer and moneyman. Dollars of the first payment remained escrowed.

That night, alone on the bed, I found myself again remembering the kind and gentle woman I'd believed to be my mother and how she had tried to protect me from my father. Montana and Blackie had not erased those days but at least helped push them into a back corner of my mind. I didn't like seeing into that corner even for jerky instant flashes of vision.

I allowed myself seven hours to reach Richmond. I swung out of bed at two in the morning to shower and shave. Blackie had orange juice, buttermilk pancakes, and hot-peppered sausage ready in the kitchen.

"Sure you don't want to come along?" I asked.

"Richmond's got nothing I need," she said and tightened the belt of her bathrobe as she sat across from me. "All them bluebloods sticking up their noses. But don't you go getting into trouble. You walk wide around it."

"My style these days."

"Shouldn't you wear a tie to the city?"

"I don't own a tie."

"Ben's got one."

"I don't wear ties."

"You'd make a mule look willing," she said and reached her hand across the table to touch mine. A touch could say a lot about what we had come to feel for each other. It needed no theatrics.

As I drove into the foggy morning darkness, I looked back to see Blackie's shape in the lighted doorway of Ben's house. Lucky I had been with her. I passed a deer standing at the edge of the road, its eyes like a demon's reflecting the Caddy's headlights. A few windows shone at the courthouse and the Shawnee Grocery. The Confederate statue on the lawn appeared spectral, marching from the pit of night.

I knew the way to Richmond. I drove over to Lewisburg and got on I-64. It was a straight run down to Staunton, Charlottesville, and what some called the Holy City. I set the cruise control at the sixty-five-mph speed limit. Like on the way to Huntington State, cars washed past me. I stopped for gas and coffee at Midlothian before reaching the outskirts of the capital.

The sun rose red above the city and spread itself over the high-rise temples of finance, commerce, and law. They became thinly silhouetted against the fireball's rise. Their blue-tinted windows reminded me of snake doctors' eyes. All fall down, I thought. An artillery round here, a mortar shell there, and you're rubble. The only permanent residence was a hole in the ground.

One of those buildings held Brother Edward's office at Boone & Massey. In fact Edward owned Boone & Massey plus the building. As a boy he had become interested in bugology and impaled butterflies, beetles, and moths on pins, his collections framed along walls of his book-stuffed bedroom. He'd sit hours under a hooded lamp at his desk and arrange before him what he'd captured with his net and chloroformed. My parents and brother John had been certain Edward would find an academic college career in a laboratory or become a medical doctor.

Instead of attending the University of Virginia, Edward had chosen Wharton, studied business, and brought to the gathering of money the same fierce concentration that he'd once awarded to bugs. He impaled each dollar, placed it where it could re-create itself most bountifully, and built edifices of finance with them. To him the neatness of numbers had the same beauty as a monarch butterfly or tiger moth skewered under glass.

Though the dollars multiplied and begat themselves, rarely did his name appear in the news. He dodged publicity and any show of what he considered vulgar wealth, while among Richmond's moneymen his cunning spread through boardrooms of the great. When he walked quietly into the best clubs, members sensed his presence as if a draft had wafted through from the doorway, causing heads to turn.

I arrived downtown an hour early, found an underground parking garage, and walked the streets. The day was still cloudy but warm, the air scented by flower stalls and exhaust fumes. I passed Mr. Jefferson's capitol, where girls in bright summer dresses and pigeons strolled the lawn among green benches and blooming dogwoods. Then east along Main Street to the intimidating banks, the iron storefronts with their stylish offerings, and down to the glistening new towers built above the James River. People had faces and paces set to the tempo of money. They lacked the absolute knowledge that all this magnificence could be smashed and blood run in gutters—the node at the back of my brain.

On Fifth Street I stopped at a narrow, crowded café named Benny's for coffee. So many city people in such a freaking rush. One rule I'd made for myself when I reached Montana was I would never again hurry unless my ass was on fire. I aimed to keep the beat of my blood calm and constant throughout the day and pretty well stuck to that except moments when I was in the bed with Blackie or breaking horses—two exceptions, but good ones.

When I left Benny's I stopped not before one of the imperial high-risers but stepped through an unpretentious doorway into an aging brick structure that looked begrimed and out of place among its brethren. The building had an address, yet no name. The terrazzo floor of the bare lobby had become abraded and needed sweeping. The single elevator wasn't paneled or supplied with brass rails and soothing music but moved slowly upward and rattled as if links of a chain were being dragged across the roof.

I took off my Stetson. The elevator did have a circular mirror in which I caught reflections of my khaki shirt open at the neck and dark brown hair in need of a comb. In Montana I'd let it grow like an Indian's. When it needed cutting real bad, Blackie brought out her scissors and clippers she used on the horses.

I received looks from two men, executive types, not directly at me but sneaky sidled glances. Maybe they believed I should've used the service elevator. They got off in a hurry.

At the eighth and top floor, the elevator door slid open onto the front office of Boone & Massey, which hadn't been laid out to impress but appeared starkly functional. The off-white walls remained undecorated, the desks and furniture might've come from the 1970s, and the floors had no carpets. By a window that could've used washing, a large clay urn held an artificial plant that was supposed to represent elephant ears. The pale green fronds drooped and had become ragged. My brother Edward didn't believe in opulence except within the confines of his own house. Beauty to him lay not in paintings or art but in the mounting balances of his bank accounts. His bedrock belief was that numbers did not lie. You were what you could count.

Yet a surprisingly young and alluring brunette sat at the reception desk. Her lavender-framed glasses peaked at the corners like a lynx's eyes. She was too stylishly cute to be working for Brother Edward.

Maybe he had her on the payroll so he could dick her. Get two for one. No, Brother Edward would never put himself in sexual jeopardy. For a dollar maybe, but not a body. Probably she was a temp.

As I approached the desk, her expression became uncertain. The nameplate read VICKY BEAUFORT. Her mouth opened and closed as if sucking a soda through a straw. She stared at my boots.

"You from maintenance?" she asked.

"Well, yes and no," I said. "I maintain my own maintenance."

"Sir, what do you want? We're busy here."

"I'm busy here too."

"Sir—"

"Just kidding around, Miss Vicky," I said. "Please tell Edward I'm waiting."

"You're—?" she asked, and I watched the thought take shape in her mind.

"I'm Brother Charley. I believe I have an appointment at ten."

"Oh," she said and touched her brow to wipe away a lock of hair. "Yes, of course." Never taking her eyes off me, she leaned to her intercom and spoke the words "He's here."

I waited by the window. The view was to the side of another building. A shirtsleeved man sitting at a desk punched numbers into a calculator. All at once he pounded the desk, bumped his head against it, and shouted silently. Poor trapped bastard.

"Boone and Massey having a good and bountiful year?" I asked, turning back to Miss Vicky.

"I believe we are, yes, sir." She breasted and then adjusted her skirt.

"That's the kind of belief to have," I said.

She remained uncertain, tried to compose herself, and asked, "Did you have a nice drive to Richmond?" Pleasant-conversation time.

"Actually, Miss Vicky, I'd like us to go back to horses. It would not only save gasoline and screw the A-rabs but also slow everything down. That's what we need in this country, something to slow everything down, don't you think?"

She glanced behind her to the corridor, and to her relief there came Edward. He ran a hand over limp, faintly blondish hair and removed his scholarly glasses. No matter what he paid for his suits, they bunched at the stoop of his shoulders. His skin had always been wan and sunburned easily. At least my brother John had been bold and shown guts. John had once tried to drown me in the Axapomimi River. Edward was the essence of an S#1.

He adjusted his striped red-and-black regimental tie, glanced at Miss Vicky, who still appeared flustered, and held out his hand to me. It felt a fugitive thing. On his index finger glinted the gold signet ring that carried the LeBlanc coat of arms. For generations, heads of the family had worn it. When pressed into hot sealing wax, the coat of arms reproduced itself and you could read the Latin word *virtute*. Grandfather Gaston LeBlanc had taught me *virtute* was an ablative of means denoting the sum of a man's character, composed of his strength, courage, manliness, mental aptness, virtue, and excellence among other things. What a laugh.

"Charles, you are good to come," Edward said and turned back toward his office. He allowed me to precede him. "No interruptions," he called to Vicky, who stood gazing after us.

As we walked, I spotted employees working at mechanical-drawing tables. Blueprints had been taped to walls. A woman stood at a machine cranking out photocopies. A beefy man in gray coveralls and holding a wastebasket waited at the end of the corridor. He eyed me.

Edward's office was no larger than others I'd passed. The chairs weren't genuine but imitation leather. Green file cabinets lined walls and architectural sketches lay across a card table. The floor had no rug. Still he'd set on his gray metal desk an antique from Bellerive I recognized—an ornate French eighteenth-century silver inkwell with a feathered quill that my grandfather Gaston had liked to use when writing friends or composing invitations. The object seemed way too out of character for the desk and Edward.

The dreary atmosphere of his lair could not undermine his slice of view to the tree-flanked James River and the rapids that formed the fall line. Boulders in its course broke the flow, sluicing white, and laughing gulls spiraled above it, their wings finding thermals to hold them suspended in delicate flight. The gull a lovely bird that if you fell dead at sea would pick out your eyes and eat them as a delicacy.

"You're looking well, Charles," Edward said. "Montana must be treating you royally. I'd like to travel out to that country one day."

"I don't think it's your type of show, Edward."

"What do you mean?"

"Well, the room service out my way's lacking."

"Ah, Charles, let's try to be family again," he said, and leveled his glasses. He'd aged. Lines spread fanlike from corners of his eyes.

"That's going to be tough. You and I were never much family."

"Can't we put those bad times behind us. I'm willing. Where are you staying?"

"I'm not staying anywhere, and notice you didn't invite me to bed down at your place."

"I apologize. Patricia's having our house remodeled. I can hardly find my shoes and socks. I wish you could meet my daughter Janice, who today's having her riding lesson. Shall we sit?" he asked and indicated the straight chair in front of his desk.

"We shall," I said and we did.

"You have family these days?" he asked.

"I live with a woman. She's my family."

"I'm happy you've become domesticated."

"That's not what I've become," I said. Edward had no sense of humor. In my whole life I'd never heard him guffaw. When tempted to laughter, he swallowed and choked upon it.

"Well, I know Ms. Beaufort and Mr. Frampton had difficulty locating you. I was surprised to learn you were in Shawnee County. Whatever could have drawn you there?"

"Just took a notion." He'd never taken a notion in his life either.

"You wouldn't have happened to run into any of the St. Georges?"

"I didn't run into any of them, but I met one named Jeannie Bruce."

"Oh, yes, a beautiful and talented woman. Are you aware she's able to trace her lineage back to Robert the Bruce of Scotland."

"Somehow that knowledge has escaped me."

"I know her husband Duncan. A brilliant man with an unerring instinct for making money. Absolutely fearless in his investment style."

"How'd you know him?"

"We collaborated in a real-estate venture. I've had word he's up to a new project in Shawnee County, a resort of sorts. I wonder whether he might not be overstepping, but I never underrate him. He's been right too often in the past. Really a financial genius. Claims he has a secret formula for investing in the stock market. Told me it had never failed. Of course he wouldn't reveal it to me or anyone else. Too many of us using it might dilute the system's effectiveness. If you run into him, give him my best."

I looked out the window as a helicopter flew past his slice of view. The rumbling beat of its blades caused a shudder to pass through the building. I no longer experienced the sick fear I'd known in Nam, but even now I sensed a giving way of my body as it sought the ground for cover.

"What's on your mind, Edward? The message I got from Walt Frampton was it's something about Bellerive."

"We went to some pains finding you, I can tell you that. You apparently have an unlisted number in Montana."

"I don't have a number. I don't own a telephone, air conditioner, TV, or a clock. Blackie and I live by the sun. When it's up, we work. When it's down, we're in the sack. Means hard labor during the summers, plenty of warm bedtime during the winter. We think that's the way it was meant to be."

"It obviously suits you. Who's Blackie?"

"The woman."

"What are you really doing out there in Shawnee County?"

"Visiting a friend."

"Have you been by Father's old High Moor mines?"

"No, nothing left there but shacks and rats."

"We owe a lot to that coal. It kept the roof over our heads."

"Some roof," I said.

"Charles, Charles."

"Edward, Edward."

He sat looking at me, his hands resting lightly on the edge of the desk.

"I'll try again," he said. "I want us to be friends."

"Edward, why'd you really ask me to come here?"

He shifted, removed his hands from the desk, sat straighter. He had my father's gray eyes and the LeBlanc chin, which was broad and blunt like my own.

"It's a delicate matter," he said. "Look, would you mind if I tape our conversation here?"

"I might. I don't know."

"Just so we have some sort of record."

"Why do we need a record if we're family?"

"I find this troublesome. Very much so, in fact, and don't know quite how I should proceed."

"Try speaking things straight out."

"All right, you're of course aware of our agreement on the sale of Bellerive. You and I were to share the proceeds to be paid out over a term of seven years. It would come to a half-million dollars a year or so for each of us."

"I don't think I like hearing the words *were* and *would*. What happened to payout time?"

"The first year's proceeds remain escrowed, a routine procedure to allow the buyers and us to make certain that all pledges made are kept and secure. The second payment will, I'm happy to say, be made shortly. The developers have achieved significant progress at Bellerive. You must take a look."

"What about the family graveyard?"

"The plot is still owned by us, fenced, and protected by means of a documented covenant." He touched his brow. It wasn't sweat. I'd never seen him sweat. "Charles, this is extremely hard for me. Actually, I've been losing sleep wondering how to approach our problem here. I want to be fair and intend to be so."

"Ed, I don't know what you're talking about."

"I thought we ought to have a written understanding as to the payment of revenues from the sale of Bellerive in the event something happens to either or both of us. Our estates need that. Several weeks ago I asked my attorney to draw up papers, and he called to inquire about the date and place of your birth. I knew the year of course, but I couldn't remember whether it was May sixteenth or twenty-sixth."

"The sixteenth."

"Yes, well, I was able to find that by our baby books. You remember our mother had a book for each of us. After John died, I discovered them in her cedar chest. Both John's and mine had a copy of our birth certificates pasted inside the covers. Yours did not, though there were photographs of Mother holding you. The usual kind of pictures—you blowing out candles on your birthday cake, opening Christmas presents, sitting on a pony. So next I had my attorney contact the King County clerk's office, but he came up empty. I then remembered you were born in Shawnee County, and he tried the courthouse there. Again he could find no record. I thought perhaps you had been born in Fayette or Raleigh County, and he sought information from those clerks to no avail."

I watched and waited.

"You of course remember Juno," he said.

I remembered her, the black cook who had treated me so kindly when I was a boy at Bellerive. After the explosion that killed my brother John and his family as well as Gaius, an old retainer, Juno had gone to live and work for Edward in Richmond. As a youth I'd come in wet and cold from duck hunting on the Axapomimi, and Juno had stood me beside the kitchen's wood cookstove to warm myself and offered me buttered cinnamon tarts hot from her oven.

"She still works for us," Edward said. "She's eighty-four now, healthy and willing, though her mind has given back somewhat. I asked her did she remember anything about your birth. Each time I questioned her she failed to respond and found reasons to turn away. Why do you suppose that is?"

I saw what was coming.

"It's a question I put to myself," Edward said. "Why would your birth record be so hard to locate? I sensed Juno knew something. I pressed her a bit. I didn't like doing it, but it was necessary. She began weeping, twisted her hands, and covered her face, but finally confessed. I believe you know what."

"You tell me."

"All right. My mother never bore you, Charles. It was another woman at High Moor. There is also no record of adoption. We are brothers, true enough, but only by half."

"How'd you wring it from Juno—by threatening to turn her out?"

"That's immaterial. I was shocked and disheartened to learn the truth. How could it be? My mother loved and treasured you. If anything, she favored you. I thought back to the ways she protected you when you and our father were at odds."

"We were more than at odds. We hated each other."

"I well remember, and your birth explains much of that unhappiness. I'm sorry about it. You are my father's son but not my mother's. That's not your fault or mine, yet it does change things."

"Let's get to how."

"The agreement to share the sales price of Bellerive between us was based on my belief you were my full brother. Now that I know you're not, I believe it's only right and proper that we make an adjustment."

"Ed, you're getting ready to welsh on me."

"You knew the truth. All this time you've known it."

"Not so long. Just a few years."

"You think you've been honest with me?"

"I think I paid plenty of dues to my fascist of a father."

"I contend that an adjustment in the agreement is called for. My thought is we reduce your share from Bellerive to a quarter. That would provide you with approximately two hundred fifty thousand a year for the seven years before payment of various taxes and fees."

"You prick, you just couldn't stand to let go of the money, could you?"

"I played fair. You didn't. You could and should have told me who was your real mother."

"Your mother was mine in ways beyond just getting born."

"My mother loved everyone, and that doesn't give you an entitlement to more than a quarter share."

I stood slowly and moved toward his desk. He became alarmed. His right hand moved under the edge of the desk. An electrical button. Sure, he would have a button to press for security. I lifted the inkwell from its filigreed rack as I edged around the desk. He shoved away on the chair until it struck the wall. I raised the inkwell and emptied it over him. Ink streamed down his hair, across his face, and dripped on his tie and white shirt.

"Oh, oh, oh," he said and brushed at himself. He smeared and spread ink from his fingers over his jacket and pants. I dropped the inkwell onto his lap.

The door opened. The beefy man in gray coveralls I'd seen earlier along the corridor entered. Edward must've alerted him to wait in the wings. Arms spread, he lunged at me. I ducked under them and hooked my shoulder into his belly. It drove him back until he slammed hard against a file cabinet. As he slumped and gulped for air, I grabbed my Stetson from the floor and made it fast out of the office to the elevator. Miss Vicky stood frightened at her desk. The elevator door had just opened to let off a lawyer type who held an attaché case. I stepped on, punched the down button, and at the lobby walked fast to the street. I double-timed it to the parking garage. I meant to be out of the city before sirens sounded for me.

TWELVE

I headed for Jessup's Wharf in King County, a small Tidewater town that lay alongside Virginia's Axapomimi River. The lazy tidal stream had once thrived on commercial traffic, the shallow-draft paddle-wheel boats carrying finished goods from Baltimore upstream and hauling cotton, tobacco, and timber down to the Chesapeake Bay and north again to the Maryland city.

I knew the town well. As a boy I'd walked its rounded brick sidewalks and passed the Dew Drop Inn, the Jessup's Mercantile, and the King County Bank at which my father had been a director and kept only part of his money pile. His major account had rested with a blueblood Richmond bank where old dollars resided and seasoned like tobacco hung on racks in curing barns. A few of those barns still survived, though collapsing along dusty roads partially shaded by ragged pines.

Bellerive, the plantation where I'd lived as a boy, lay upstream. Owned by the LeBlanc family since 1740 when my Huguenot ancestors had sailed from La Rochelle to escape religious harassment during the reign of Louis XV. Money from its sale and transformation into an exclusive residential community was what Edward and I supposedly had agreed to split half and half.

I parked in the customer lot behind the King County Bank to walk along River Street. The old LeBlanc warehouse, empty and moldering, still stood by the river, its bricks bleeding down its sides. I'd used my Daisy air rifle to shoot sleek rats that nested among its dark underpiling. The rats toppled thrashing and squealing into the river's meandering flow.

I paused at the Planters Drugstore. The town ladies had sipped their lemonade and cherry Cokes here as they sat on wire-back chairs around marble-topped tables. Multicolored apothecary bottles still lined the window. I remembered the taste of cod-liver oil spooned to me by the woman I'd believed to be my mother. Her patient urgings had made the gluey stuff swallowable.

Farther along the street pigeons that fed on grain spilled from the Southern States loading dock grew obese and acted, like those around the Cliffside courthouse, as if the territory belonged to them. They flew from the dock to the eighteenth-century St. Luke's Church, where they rested and digested their meals beneath its hallowed eaves.

I walked up Hill Street to find Walter B. Frampton's office. The *B* stood for Beauregard. Walt was a throwback to another time. He should've lived his life during antebellum days, when ladies wore bell-shaped silk gowns and cavaliers swept feathered hats before them. Yet he'd come to believe in me, and that belief had saved me from a seat on a needle-injected journey to a far dark place.

I climbed to his second-floor office above an antique store, the display windows of which offered dusty porcelain dishes, tarnished silver, and an oil painting of a foxhunting scene, its canvas cracked. The red fox looked to be smiling as riders were thrown ass over head at rail fences. When I tried Walt's door, it was locked. I looked through a dirty pane of glass. The place lay deserted.

I walked back down the steps and entered the antique store. It smelled of cats and mothballs. A humpbacked old lady sat at the rear crocheting among a collection of pewter tankards, her arthritic fingers shaky on the curved flexible needle they grasped.

"Mr. Frampton's on River Street now," she said. "Got a new office. Come a little closer so I can see you good."

I obeyed. A calico cat sitting among balls of varicolored yarn eyed me.

"You a LeBlanc, ain't you? You got the chin. I bet you Charley."

"Sorry, I don't recognize you."

"Not much left to recognize. The name's Laura May Ellis. I used to sew for your mama. You was always in trouble. So you back to town for a visit?"

"Not for long," I said, thanked her, and left.

Always in trouble, particularly with my father and my older brother John. He could whip me, but I at least stung him back. He knew that if he took me on, he'd come out of the fight hurting.

I walked the other side of River Street. The shoe repair shop had closed, but the Little Ritz Beauty Parlor still served the ladies under its two hooded dryers. A uniformed town cop watched me. I passed him by and felt his eyes on my back. At the Jessup's Mercantile shoppers lifted apples, Irish potatoes, and butter beans from sidewalk bins and placed them in paper sacks before weighing them on a scale swinging from a thin chain. Old men used a bench set in front of the King County Bank to loaf and sun themselves. The bank had a classical stone facade styled, my grandfather had told me, after Florence's Medici Chapel.

Walter B. Frampton II's office had been the old bakery. His name painted in gold leaf arched across the window where I'd once stood to look at doughnuts and sweet rolls fresh from the ovens. Now potted plants lined the sill beneath a three-quarters-closed venetian blind.

When I opened the door, I faced a woman at a desk. She'd tied her neat brown hair back with a length of red yarn. Beside her on a chair sat a young boy who watched from guarded eyes. The softly feminine woman raised her face. A slim glass vase held a single freshly picked yellow iris. Walt had said he'd married his secretary, so this had to be her.

"Mr. Frampton in?" I asked.

"He's at court," she said. "I expect him within the hour."

Everywhere in the office potted plants and greenery had been set around. Undoubtedly her doings. The boy held a book on his lap. The way he looked at me caused me to think of Esmeralda. The dark eyes in his thin face weren't nearly as large but almost as devouring.

"What you reading?" I asked.

"*Robinson Crusoe*," she answered for him.

"Used to be my favorite," I said. "I guess I read it ten times."

"So's my son Jason," she said, indicating the boy. "Would you like to leave your name?"

"LeBlanc. Charley LeBlanc."

"Ah," she said, pushed away from the desk, and stood. "Walter's been expecting you."

"I'll come back," I said.

"I'm Mary Ellen. It's so good to have you here. Walter frequently talks of you."

Walt hadn't told me anything about the boy. I'd wait to find out. I thanked her, continued on down River Street, and crossed over to the courthouse—one-story Colonial built of outsized bricks the birds had pecked on and pocked. Four square white columns supported a small porch. Green louvered blinds at the windows.

I slipped into the rear of the courtroom. Balding Judge Pechinny still sat on the bench, and Ben Falkoner, the commonwealth's attorney, slumped heavy-lidded at the prosecutor's table, legal papers spread before him. Some two years ago he'd attempted to have me indicted and arraigned on a capital murder charge.

Walt stood addressing the jury made up mostly of farmers and watermen, but all wore Sunday suits and ties except for a black woman who had on a blue dress and white pillbox hat. Walt laid a hand over the rail of the jury box. He didn't have to act sincere. He was built of sincerity.

"Aren't there times when we must feel that anger is momentarily justified?" he asked. His seersucker suit was fresh and crisp. "Not to excuse anger but to understand it? No man should raise his hand against another, but when a neighbor in the dark of the night repeat-

edly changes the fence line in an attempt to enlarge his property
boundary, surely you can understand that there is a limit to patience.
Put yourself in my client's place. He forgave his neighbor twice for
twice removing that stob."

I left and stopped by the Dew Drop Inn for a beer. I held my alcohol
intake pretty much under control. More than once I'd stood at the
abyss and almost toppled over in surrender to Mr. John Barleycorn.
Blackie never asked me to stop drinking but had a way of looking at
me that sapped the pleasure I took from liquor. I'd slacked off the bottle to dim her smoldering eyes.

The Dew Drop operated under new management. I'd left my Stetson
on, and men sitting at the counter looked me over. I didn't know any of
them, though they might've recognized me from my fucking LeBlanc
chin. Through the window I spotted Walt carrying a briefcase walking
back to his office. He appeared seriously professional. I'd never seen
him with his hair messed or his tie off center. I paid for my beer, used
the john, and crossed the street. When I opened the door, his wife smiled.

"He's waiting," she said.

Walt walked out to greet me. He was tall, gangly, his waist too high.
His glasses, like Mr. Henry Peck's, slid low on his nose, and he often
seemed to be looking over rather than through them. He'd aged since
I'd last seen him. He took off the glasses with his left hand to shake my
hand with his right. Yeah, life had put lines of character on that once
boyish face, which meant somewhere since I'd last seen him he had
come to know pain and maybe grief, the universal marksmen.

"You win?" I asked as we shook. "I caught your act over at court."

"My client got off with a warning and fine," he said. "I'm satisfied
and so is he."

"Big case," I said.

"Like fishing, you have to catch the small ones to land the big one."
He turned to the woman. "You met Mary Ellen?"

"Not officially, but I'd say you did pretty well, though I don't know
about her," I said and didn't offer to shake her hand. Instead of extend-

ing hers, she stood, lifted the hem of her dress slightly, and curtsied.

"Thank you, kind sir. The things I've heard about you."

She was pretty in the settled way of a happily domesticated woman. I thought of Blackie, who stayed edgy and seemed unable to sit for long in any one place. Quieting her was like trying to tame a hawk.

"You're lucky it's just the good stuff," Walt said. "And I had to dig for that."

"How about you eating and staying with us tonight?" she asked. "I have a rib roast and chess pie."

"Thanks, I need to be getting back."

"Well, dern it then," she said, and my sense was that Walt had picked a winner or the winner him. Likely a convergence.

"And this is our son, Jason," Walt said.

"Hey," I said. The boy didn't speak but looked down at the book as he turned a page.

"Let's go in my office," Walt said and stood aside for me at the door. There on the wall he'd hung his large framed photograph of Robert E. Lee, who looked more like someone's elderly uncle than the general who had led the Army of Virginia into the Valley of Death. I wondered whether Walt had any black clients and what they'd think of the picture. From what I knew about Walt, he'd never take it down even if it cost him money.

"You look like you doing all right," I said. The office too had Mary Ellen's touch, particularly its orderliness and the daffodils along the window. Her perfumed presence scented the air. I looked out across the street to the King County Bank and the steeple of St. Luke's Church behind it. Many LeBlancs had worshiped there. I had myself. My first prayer had been for a shotgun to shoot ducks along the Axapomimi.

"You too, Charles," Walt said. Even if I'd asked him to call me Charley, he wouldn't. The code of manners he lived by was as out-of-date as a Packard touring sedan. "How are things in Chinook?"

"Bread on the table, a roof that don't leak, and a woman."

"You married too?"

"Not been around to that yet. I see you got a son in your deal."

"A good boy. I'm teaching him to fish. His father was a soldier, a helicopter pilot killed in peacetime Germany. Jason and I are in the process of reaching out to each other. You still smoke?"

We lit up his Winstons. All the pencils in his W&L mug had been sharpened and his paper clips arranged in a row of small glass bins according to their size. That had to be more of Mary Ellen's touch.

"So you met with your brother?" Walt asked, already bearing the look of a settled family man, though little more than thirty. He was meant for marriage, would fit it like ham did eggs. But I again saw he'd suffered, and whatever that suffering, it had laid lines on him that augmented the dignity of his bearing.

"Wondered when you'd ask that question," I said and stretched my legs. "No use dodging the issue. Brother Edward's trying to screw us. Intends to cut my share of money from half to a quarter."

"He can't do that," Walt said and shoved his hands forward on the desk. His KA fraternity ring enclosed a finger.

"Yeah he can, Walt."

"What reason did he give?"

I hesitated. I'd never tell him about Esmeralda being my mother unless I had no way out.

"He changed his mind how much I'm worth."

"Charles, it has to be more than that."

"We got nothing in writing. Means he can do anything he wants."

"What about the money in escrow?"

"My guess is he indirectly controls the escrow and its distribution."

"But everything was set. Edward's even showed a genial side. Something happened between you."

"I can't tell you."

"You'd better. We may have grounds for legal action. Maybe nothing on paper, but you had his word and so did I. He and I talked about the disposition of the money. You two fight?"

"Ed doesn't fight. He dodges."

"What's his explanation?"

"It's a private matter."

"You're refusing to tell me?"

"Looks that way."

"You'll just walk away from all that money?"

"That money's walking away from me," I said and felt sorry now not for what I'd done to Brother Edward but to Esmeralda. I'd put in jeopardy dollars needed to pay for the care I wanted her to have. I had in effect screwed myself.

"Charles, stay the night with Mary Ellen and me. We'll talk it out and plan a response."

"Can't do it, Walt," I said and stood. "At the moment got other business to tend to."

"You're not in trouble out there, are you? If so, I know a sheriff in Seneca County, which adjoins Shawnee. A good man who helped me with a hunting accident case I had. His name's Bruce Sawyers. I'll write it down for you. Look him up if you need help."

"Generally I try not to run to sheriffs," I said as I took the slip of paper.

"Won't hurt to stick that in your pocket."

I spoke my good-byes to Jason and Mary Ellen. Walt walked with me across the street to the King County Bank parking lot.

"I want you to authorize me to meet and talk further with Edward," he said.

"I know my brother. It'll be a waste of your time."

"Nevertheless, I'd like to do what I can to patch things up."

"You're one of the few people I know who use the word *nevertheless* in ordinary conversation," I said. "Been good seeing you again, Walt."

"Charles, I'm your attorney, and you're holding out on me."

"You don't need to know everything," I said.

He opened the Caddy's door for me. Walt had made it to an NS#3, no doubt about it. Still, I couldn't tell him about Esmeralda.

"Let me hear from you," he called as I drove away.

I left him standing spick-and-span at the curb shaking his head.

THIRTEEN

I drove away from Jessup's Wharf and reached Shawnee County just as the mountains blocked the reddish setting sun, dropped deep flowing shadows over Cliffside, and filled the valleys with a hazy dusk. To check on Esmeralda, I stopped at Peck's Store, and this time had quarters. When I dialed Huntington State, I asked the switchboard to transfer the call to Building 7 and identified myself to Nurse Adams.

"I'd like to help, Mr. LeBlanc," she said, "but we're not permitted to give out information on Esmeralda Doe."

"I was there with Dr. Fredrick."

"I remember. Thing is, Dr. Fredrick's not available right now."

"Just tell me her condition."

"Why don't you try Dr. Fredrick in the morning."

It was more of a statement than a question. All right, she had her orders. I drove on to Ben's, where Rattler lay on the lawn before loping to the Caddy. I allowed him to take my scent before I patted him. His tail wagged, yet not with a fullness of swing that denoted total acceptance. I rubbed his head. Maybe Blackie and I could take him to Montana, the place for man and dog.

Ben and Blackie had eaten. She fixed a plate for me she'd stuck in the oven to keep warm—fried apples, a bowl of collards, and lamb stew served over split hot buttered biscuits. Ben left to do his milking. I'd watched Blackie's hands set out my dinner and thought how nice she was to come home to.

"Well, when you going to tell me what happened in the big city?" she asked.

"Crap chin high. We might have to make do with less money than I been figuring on. Mightn't be any money at all."

"Just what you gone and done now?" she asked and sat across from me.

"The question is what have I been done to," I said as I chewed. She'd spiced the stew up the way I liked it.

"Meaning I'm going to have on my hands not only a jailbird but a broke one?"

"With your talents you can always work. You shoe a horse better than I do."

"I don't mean to use up the rest of my life shoeing nags. What you fixing to do about your brother?"

"Run it through my mind a spell."

"What mind?"

"You could slip in and lie beside me tonight?"

"Why would I want to do a fool thing like that when you come here telling me we about out of money?"

Yet she entered my room after Ben closed his door and started snoring. Blackie walked softly in darkness, and I listened to the rustle of her nightgown as she lifted it over her head and dropped it on the chair. Her skin caught a gleam of moonlight passing through the window. When you looked at Blackie, you might think she was cold, but her blood ran so hot her skin gave off radiator heat. I felt her gasp and the release of her fingers as they dropped away.

"Anything else I can do for you?" she whispered after a time.

"Pray," I whispered back.

"Done done that for a loser," she said. She left the bed, lifted her nightgown, and allowed it to settle over her. She peeped through the door before stepping out and closing it softly behind her.

I put Brother Edward out of my mind. Let Walt handle that end of things, at least temporarily. I'd also not allow myself to think of what the pathologist was doing to Aunt Jessie's body. First thing on my platter had to be figuring out just what had happened between Aunt Jessie and Esmeralda. The next how to spring Esmeralda from Huntington State and settle her into a private facility. I'd worry later about the money to pay for it.

After breakfast I rode to Peck's Store and again called the hospital. When I asked for Dr. Fredrick, the switchboard rang his office, and his nurse said he hadn't yet come in. I drank a Pepsi, smoked, and waited fifteen minutes before I dialed a second time. I believed I'd been cut off until Dr. Fredrick spoke. His scratchy voice again sounded as if it came from a faraway country.

"No change," he told me. "No response from her since she opened her eyes briefly while you were present."

"Dr. Fredrick, let me give you a number and ask you or your nurse to contact me if anything does change."

He agreed. I read out the Peck's Store phone number and thanked him, though not convinced he'd call or even remember he'd agreed to. Mr. Henry Peck with his lidless eyes had watched and listened to my side of the conversation.

"Got anything to add?" I asked him.

"You spending lots of quarters," he said. "And you was talking about Esmeralda."

"I'd appreciate it if you didn't spread that word."

"I don't spread words, just manure," he said. "I did hear about them digging up Aunt Jessie. Talk's moving the news around."

"Always talk," I said and next phoned District Attorney Sligh at his office. To my surprise Miss Minerva Lemon passed me through to him without question. I started to turn my back on Mr. Henry Peck but didn't bother because he'd still be able to hear unless I spoke into my hand cupped over the phone.

"Have you decided yet whether the county intends to bring a charge against Esmeralda?" I asked Sligh.

"Mr. LeBlanc, no change since the day before yesterday. As I indicated then, in her present state she's in no condition to withstand arraignment even if a Shawnee County grand jury moves for a true bill of indictment. Meanwhile the police will continue to investigate and her doctor consulted."

"Any chance you changed your mind about telling what was in the bundle Esmeralda carried away from Aunt Jessie's?"

"None."

And no use for me to hound him further. Still, I wanted to keep the line open for future inquiries and thanked him before hanging up. I walked out to sit in the car, where I closed my eyes and attempted to get my thoughts in order. Fuck Brother Edward and keeping Esmeralda first in mind was still the order of the day. I wanted to try talking to the man who'd discovered Aunt Jessie dead. And what about the St. George son Angus, who had seen Esmeralda fleeing the cabin with the bundle?

I decided I'd again drive out to Aunt Jessie's cabin without telling Blackie. She'd be all right. I'd heard her talking to Ben about going fishing. I stopped first at Mt. Olivet Church to check Aunt Jessie's grave. It lay ugly and empty, the flowers tossed aside, some covered or flattened under tire marks and chunks of moist red clay.

I continued south to Persimmon Creek. What did I expect to find? Aunt Jessie would have nothing much worth stealing unless it was the silver candlestick I'd noticed the first time I'd been in her cabin. I wanted to look around and get a feel for the place. I turned up beside the full flow of the creek. It wasn't the yellow tape fluttering in the breeze but the trooper's car parked beside the cabin that caused my foot to hit the brake. Okay, I'd come another time.

I backed off slowly, but when I turned onto the hard surface and started toward Cliffside, I heard the siren and saw the flashing blue lights on top the trooper's souped-up Crown Victoria. They filled my rearview mirror. He had come fast down off the mountain. I pulled to the road's shoulder. He swerved his car in front of the Caddy.

A large, lumbering officer moved toward me with a hand resting on his Heckler-Koch .40-cal. automatic. I stepped from the Caddy because I wanted to meet on his level any man who accosted me, a lesson I'd learned at Leavenworth. As in warfare, high ground was advantage.

"Something wrong, Officer?" I asked. He wore the trooper hat at a forward tilt as they all did and had a meaty, porous face.

"Your operator's license," he said.

I slid it from my wallet and handed it to him. He studied it before checking my face with the picture. Dark hairs grew from the back of his fingers. Before he returned the license, he walked to the Crown Victoria, drew out a clipboard, and copied down the operator's license number as well as the Caddy's. He spoke into a radio mike, waited until he heard the word "Negative," and returned to me.

"Don't get many cars from Montana," he said. "What you doing here?"

"Visiting friends," I said and felt like telling him it was none of his frigging business but wasn't about to give him a reason to get pissed and haul me in.

"What friends?"

"Ben Henshaw's who I'm staying with."

"I know Ben. How come you drove up to the cabin?"

"I knew Aunt Jessie way back and thought I'd stop by."

"Aunt Jessie's dead, and her place is part of an ongoing investigation. You keep away. All right, get on out of here and remember I know you in the county."

"I'll do that, Officer," I said as I slid back into the Caddy. When I drove off, he looked after me. I wiped my palms on my pants.

I decided I'd travel to Wild Thorn and try to talk to Angus St. George. Worst that could happen was he'd refuse to speak to me. Traffic increased as I crossed over onto St. George property. I passed a crew cutting timber up the side of the mountain. A skidder dragged down logs that left behind spirals of dust and disturbed earth.

At the mansion's walled entrance an electrician worked rewiring an iron lamp on a gatepost. Laborers had parked their cars, vans, and trucks along the drive. Plumbers stood at the rear of a pickup threading pipes clamped in vises. A man cleaning out the tiered fountain laid down his brush to finger his nose and blow snot. I parked behind a lowboy that held ladders and ten-gallon cans of paint.

One of the mansion's great oak doors stood ajar, but I used a lion's-head knocker, and the rap sounded through the house like a bass drum. I heard something else, maybe an oboe, the tune low and haunting, and it made me remember the Frankenstein movie I'd seen back at a Jessup's Wharf tent show as a boy—the horn the hunchback played while standing on a misty rampart to call the monster to the castle.

A maid wearing a black uniform with a white collar appeared from the interior shadows of the mansion. A Latina. I told her I wanted to speak to Angus St. George.

"He gone today," she said. She was built heavy, her ankles thick.

"Anyone else here?" I asked. I'd left my Stetson in the car. Because of my clothes, she might believe I was one of the workers.

"Mr. Duncan, but he don't like be interrupted at his music time."

"How about Mrs. St. George?"

"What your name?"

When I told her, she pushed the door to. A cement truck rumbling by caused the ground to tremble. As I waited, I counted the number of men I could see on the job. Twenty-seven. When I turned back to the door, Jeannie Bruce St. George stood watching me. Her long red T-shirt hung loose around shorts that had been cut from Levi's, and a hank of her whitish-blond hair hung over her left eye. She wiped the hank away. She held a putty knife and smelled of turpentine.

"My gallant rescuer," she said.

She was a beauty even dressed this way. I tried to keep my eyes off her breasts and expanse of legs. She stood on a step higher than mine, so I had to look up into her aggressive green eyes. I was breast-high to her. Her smirk mocked me.

"Didn't mean to bother anybody," I said. "Just hoping to have a word with your son."

"You haven't bothered me. Come in this house." When she stepped away, she led me into a reception hall two stories high, its vaulted ceiling hung with a massive Teutonic-like chandelier. The stone walls had been wainscoted with dark mahogany, and a grand staircase rose to a landing lighted by a stained-glass window that dropped a spectrum of colors over carpeted steps.

The window depicted coal-camp scenes—among them a helmeted miner leading a mule from a black portal in the mountain, the chute of a tipple pouring coal into a railroad car, and women wearing hats and holding the hands of children leaving a steepled white church.

Walls supported electric candles held in pewter sconces. A square ebony table, its legs carved like griffons, held an outsized Chinese vase and a silver tray that had probably been of use during days when people left calling cards. There were portraits, the heads of the same bewigged types that had hung at Bellerive when I was a boy. My grandfather Gaston had made me remember and recite their full names. He'd also insisted I study Latin. Each evening I'd stood before his armchair and read my assignment from Virgil's *Aeneid*.

A brass lamp lighted a small circular oil painting under glass of a bearded warrior in armor and holding a mace. The canvas had cracked, the colors faded. His tawny beard flowed to his chest, and his green eyes were not so much warlike and threatening as saddened by whatever he sighted in the distance.

"Robert the First de Bruce, King of Scotland," she said. "Not a St. George kinsman but mine. I had the lineage traced to Sir Robert and authenticated at Edinburgh Castle. The portrait's been in the possession of successive members of the Bruce family for some six hundred years. I tracked it to a maiden great-aunt living at Inverness and paid a king's ransom for it."

As if I gave a damn. I'd been made to climb enough genealogical trees while growing up at Bellerive. What really held me was her. She made the frazzled denims appear stylish and would have been a knockout in a burlap sack—or out of one.

Again the mournful music, which came from somewhere on an upper floor.

"My husband Duncan," she said. "He plays the oboe d'amore, a cherished instrument from olden times. Would you like to see more of the house?"

She led me first into a formal room, its stone fireplace large enough to park a small car. Sycamore logs had been precisely sawed and laid across massive andirons, the wood, I assumed, chosen not for fuel value but the decorative effect of its brown-and-green patch coloration. Above it hung another portrait, this one large and of a short, elderly white-haired man wearing a tuxedo who had dark blue eyes and a set jaw. He stood next to a marble bust on a pedestal of a man I didn't recognize. Each had an expression stern and righteous.

"James MacGlauglin," Jeannie Bruce said. "Founder of the present family and its wealth."

There was something about her voice, an underlying tone of sarcasm, yet not Yankee or southern. *Neutral* was the best word for it.

"A lowland Scot," she said, and maybe the Bruces, as Highlanders, looked down on the MacGlauglins as commoners no matter how rich, powerful, or titled. Did she chide her husband?

"Who's the bust?" I asked.

"A sixteenth-century Scot and Calvinist preacher named John Knox. What an incongruity—divine election of the saints, predestination, and evening dress."

Solid ponderous pieces furnished the room, in no way stylish but made to last generations for people of weight and substance. The winged lid of the grand piano had been closed, the keys covered. Tiered chandelier's bulbs were flame-shaped, and several lamps standing about had leaded-glass shades. Even with the sunshine through the mullioned windows, the room had a somber quality, as if it resisted the intrusion of ordinary daylight.

The view from the windows looked down over the wall at the west to a grassy valley and the remnants of the camp where miners had lived. A yellow bulldozer worked razing all that had remained of a dozen roofless Jenny Linds. The dozer pushed the debris to a mound of burning wreckage, and black smoke curved upward to drift over the forested green mountainside and white tombstones of a cemetery at the center of which rose a stone obelisk—my guess the grave of James MacGlauglin himself.

She led me to the dining room with its long polished table that had ten high-back seats along both sides as well as a thronelike one at each end. Set the length of the table were six silver candelabra. Blackened wicks of long slender white candles indicated they'd been burned. Did this woman, her husband, and their son, a party of three, use the room for meals? They'd need to communicate by waving or shouting.

Jeannie Bruce's portrait hung over this fireplace. Her pearl-gray dress bared her arms and shoulders. The artist had caught the golden glow of her skin. A jeweled tiara held her hair in place, and a diamond brooch bound the silken V between her breasts. At her waist she held a bouquet of white roses. She appeared genuinely regal.

She showed me the library, the walls covered by shelves so high that a ladder on a rail and rollers waited handily so that a person could climb all the way to the ceiling to find volumes. Floor lamps had been placed behind leather armchairs and beside a desk inlaid with different kinds of wood. Oriental rugs felt soft underfoot. This room too had a fireplace, but instead of a portrait the space above had been hung with the St. George coat of arms—a knight's profiled head surmounting a triangular shield and the Latin word *fidelis.* Faithful to what? I wondered.

"Anyone read these books?" I asked.

"Actually my husband does. He's made that one of his projects. He always has projects. The books have been cataloged. Some are rare and valuable."

Next was the game room, which held a billiard table as well as rifles, shotguns, and pistols kept in cabinets fronted by locked glass doors. Between the cabinets framed prints displayed sporting scenes—bird hunts, dogs on point, horses jumping fences, bucks fleeing hounds that bayed after them during the chase.

"Duncan's great-grandfather always had guns around," she explained. "There's part of a machine gun in the basement. During the mine wars it became an armory. Over a hundred Belgian rifles and wooden crates of ammunition. Riotous times when men were shot daily, tipples blown up, trains derailed. Like the Wild, Wild West. Would you care for a drink?"

"I hoped to speak to your son," I said as we walked back to the library.

"Angus? What about?"

"He reported seeing Esmeralda run off from Aunt Jessie's cabin the day she died. I'd like the details."

"Whatever for?" she asked and raised the plucked eyebrow. "Aren't the police conducting an investigation?"

"They are, but not letting out much information."

"They might not like your butting in. And why do you need information?"

Back at the library, she leaned against the ladder and lifted a foot in a tennis shoe to the first rung. Her posture pulled the denim tight around a thigh. God, I thought, the power in female thighs among even the most feminine, cultivated ladies.

"A personal interest I have in Esmeralda."

"That doesn't explain much. Well, Angus did see her running from Aunt Jessie's. He was riding a chestnut gelding he's schooling. I'll ask him to call you."

"Don't have a phone. Be better if I call him."

"I'll give you the number."

She walked us to the entrance hall. I heard the oboe d'amore playing. At the ebony table she opened a drawer to lift out a notepad and a pen. She rapidly scratched out Angus's name, number, and Wild Thorn's address, her handwriting looped and full of curlicues. She tore off the page for me.

"Anything I can offer you?" she asked. Her smile seemed a tease.

"I appreciate the tour."

"My husband will be sorry he missed you. Please come back. I'm interested in the LeBlancs. I'm certain you could tell us stories about them."

She extended her hand. The large emerald ring on her finger closely matched the color of her eyes. Maybe it was a piece of jewelry she had chosen to wear with cutoff denim shorts, her putty knife, and red T-shirt.

"And you must come dine with us," she said. "You staying awhile in Shawnee County?"

"Looks that way."

"You'll hear from Wild Thorn," she said.

FOURTEEN

As I left and crossed toward the Caddy, a man walked after me from the mansion's doorway and called, "Mr. LeBlanc." Tall and pale, he appeared fragile and careful of his step. He held a hand to me. His graying hair lay shallow over his scalp, the tips partially white. His smile was like that of a person gritting his teeth.

"Mr. LeBlanc, forgive me for being so inhospitable as not to have come down to greet you. I'm Duncan St. George."

His grip was merely a touch of our fingers, and his face in profile had all its features in line as if vertically sliced—the forehead, brows, nose, and downswept chin.

"Please come in," he went on. "It happens I know your brother Edward. The fact is, I've talked to him a bit about the projects that engage us here at Wild Thorn. I'd like to show you what we have in mind if you'd care to take a minute."

"I care," I said and thought this poor piece of man flesh was not her father but her husband. He must've either possessed a hot tongue or she be frigid. His white summer jacket and trousers hung loosely about him. Around his neck he'd tied a blue scarf. His polished black loafers enclosed long slender feet. Yet Edward had called him a bold financial genius.

"I believe Jeannie Bruce has already given you a bit of a tour."

He escorted me back inside. I looked for Jeannie Bruce, but she had gone. We walked to and climbed the grand staircase past the landing's stained-glass window, which laid the spectrum's glow on his face and would be doing the same to mine. We continued to the second floor and then to the third, where the steps narrowed and steepened.

"I find my exercise this way," Duncan said. "Good for the legs and lungs. We have an elevator, yet I seldom use it to ascend."

His breath became short as he climbed and talked. Definitely no athlete or swordsman under the covers. We walked along the hallway past closed doors I assumed were bedrooms to the end of the passage, where a large office held desks, tables, a Xerox, and a computer. Colored pins fastened geological surveys, topographical maps, and aerial photographs to corked surfaces of wallboards.

"Perhaps you've heard we're in the process of developing and opening a resort here at Wild Thorn?"

"The talk of Shawnee County," I said. The windows on this side of the house gave onto a view across green fields to an outcropping of boulders that overhung the mountain at the south end of the camp.

"Well, that doesn't take much. These days our county doesn't offer a great deal to talk about. The curse of coal is here today, gone tomorrow. There was a time it supplied the power that kept the machines of this nation humming. Coal's days are numbered, perhaps another thirty or forty years, and what we owe it will be forgotten and the fuel termed by historians as a hazardous and barbaric polluter."

Centered on his desk he'd set a picture of Jeannie Bruce. She sat astride a bay horse and wore hunt attire—top hat, a lady's shadbelly, and black boots with spurs. She appeared as stately as royalty on parade. Beside her another photograph of a young man dressed for tennis and holding a racket. He had the tanned smooth muscles of an athlete, straw-blond hair, and grinned over teeth almost too pretty to be real.

"Angus, my son," he said.

At least in his twenties, Angus sure God couldn't have been Jeannie Bruce's son. Or could he? Who these days could tell the mileage a woman had on her? A whole industry of doctors and pharmaceutical companies strove to keep them ageless and beautiful.

"You and Jeannie Bruce have other children?"

"No, I'm sad to confess. And Angus is not Jeannie Bruce's." His laugh was timid, like an apology. "She might be offended if you thought so. No, my first wife Phyllis died of uremic poison twelve years ago—a lovely woman trained in opera. She performed *Traviata* with the Baltimore Symphony."

"I heard you playing the oboe."

"Yes, the oboe d'amore, an instrument almost forgotten. I've always loved the old things of this world."

Except for Jeannie Bruce, I thought. She definitely lacked that qualification. My sense was that Duncan, a rich, introverted man who'd lost a wife, had bought himself a younger one to keep life around him at the boil. And somewhere under his quiet presence lay the financial genius.

"Let me show you what we plan here at Wild Thorn," he said and crossed to a wallboard. He'd lifted an adjustable steel pointer from a desk and tapped it against a map. "This is a recent aerial view of our acres shot from a plane. Look at the long winding drops from the ridges to the valleys. These mountains cry out for ski slopes. We are within a day's drive to many centers of population, particularly in the south. We intend to lay out our runs to make the best use of the land, with the major slope challenging enough to draw expert skiers and provide competitive events."

"You ski?" I asked. I couldn't believe he did.

"No, but it isn't necessary that I do. I admire the sport. The concept of a resort here is Jeannie Bruce's as well as her dream, though I'm enthusiastically joining in not only for her but also for Shawnee County. It could revive the economy."

He again tapped the pointer lightly against the map.

"This is Bull Mountain, our highest peak, nearly four thousand feet. We might have as many as half a dozen shorter runs, but Bull will be our premier attraction. We'll soon be installing pylons for the lift. Of course it might take three or more years before we carry our first dime of profit to the bank."

"Lots of work," I said as I studied the map.

"Jeannie Bruce and I are committed to it. She's the skier and does everything well."

Like laying you, I thought.

"We won't restrict activities at Wild Thorn to skiing. Our lake during the winter will freeze over and provide ice-skating. Possibly there will also be an indoor rink. We plan toboggan runs, cross-country trails, and sleigh rides."

I stood orientating myself to the map and the lay of his land.

"Our house here will serve as the center of activities. There are twenty-five bedrooms. We will, if necessary, also build cottages for guests. It's possible in time we will add a conference hall, though I'm not certain Jeannie Bruce and I'd want that sort of trade. She's been very much involved in the planning, her ideas daring and original."

"This a boundary of your property?" I asked and with my finger traced a broad expanse of land shaped like a double-headed ax blade.

"It is. During the summers we'll offer eighteen holes of golf as well as swimming, tennis, and fishing. The climate will be cool in these mountains, an escape from the heat of cities. This is beautiful country, could be a little Switzerland, and as I've indicated, it's accessible from many cities along the southeastern seaboard. When we're ready to accept guests, we'll mount an extensive advertising campaign in select publications."

"The kind the rich read," I said.

"Exactly. Wild Thorn will be expensive, yet worth it. We'll have to gate the resort, but think of what it'll mean to Shawnee County—the jobs, income, the pride that could be restored to a people who've nearly given up."

"No problem hiring labor with all the unemployed around here."

"Indeed. Of course they'll need to be trained, but they are good people, many of fine stock. And they have endured."

Fine stock. Like they were cattle. Big money did that to the rich. Dollars had protected Duncan from the relentless grind of most people's daily existence, though the blood appeared to have run thin by the time it reached his generation. Still, with thin blood often came gentility and grace, and I felt myself drawn to him.

"When you expect to operate?"

"It's our hope and desire to be ready for summer guests a year from now, perhaps a Memorial Day opening. So far we're on schedule. Everyone's been very cooperative. Jeannie Bruce has made her dream mine. She's thrown herself into the work and is in charge of the various decorating motifs. I need and am happy for her okay on the critical decisions."

I couldn't help thinking of them in bed. She struck me as a woman who would take vigorous loving. Well, there could be lots of answers there. Duncan might've learned elaborate techniques that evolved along with genteel decay. Or maybe all the dollars set her off better than a hard dick.

"Your brother Edward's been a great help to me," Duncan said. "He explained how they've been developing the private community at Bellerive and offered to invest money in Wild Thorn Corporation, but while I'm grateful, I told him I wanted to keep the business in the family. Jeannie Bruce and I are the sole stockholders."

I had picked out Persimmon Creek on the map and what had to be Aunt Jessie's place. A red line crossed a portion of her land, and an *X* had been penciled in northwest of her cabin.

"What's that about?" I asked.

"It's a section of the most desired route for our major run," Duncan said.

"Not Aunt Jessie Arbuckle's property?"

"It is. We were in negotiation with that fine lady before she died. A shocking event. Jeannie Bruce and I had grown very fond of her."

"You were asking her to sell out?"

"Not her entire property. We wanted that strip of land that lies across her holdings. Or a long-term easement and right to use the strip. We made her an offer that she was seriously considering. We had planned further talks."

"You believe she would've let you have it?"

"I do," he said and laid the pointer back on the table. "She was a kindly woman and had every wish to help us here at Wild Thorn."

When we left the office, he stopped at a door along the hallway and opened it.

"Excuse me a moment," he said, and walked into a room that held a collapsible music stand, a chair, piano, and in a corner the bust of John Knox I'd seen in James MacGlauglin's portrait. On the chair lay his oboe d'amore. He lifted a sheet of music from the stand, drew a pencil from his jacket to make a notation, and set the music back in place. He then crossed to me and shut the door after us.

"I've learned that if I don't write things down soon as they cross my mind I often forget them," he said. "Are you fond of music, Mr. LeBlanc?"

"Call me Charley. I used to be. Now I hear a different kind of music."

"What kind is that?"

"What the wind or water or the nights compose. I like listening to the land."

"And the music of people?"

"I don't hear much music from people."

Instead of using the staircase to go down, we took an elevator, which I first thought was just a closet door. Well oiled, the elevator ran almost silently. When we reached the first floor, I again glanced around for Jeannie Bruce, but she didn't appear. Duncan walked me to the front door. He glanced at my cowboy boots.

"Do you have equestrian interests, Charley? You being from Montana I thought you might."

"How'd you know I was from Montana?"

"Jeannie Bruce told me. We keep horses here that need exercising. I don't participate myself."

"I ride western, not English."

"I'm certain Jeannie Bruce and Angus see to it our stable's equipped with a variety of tack."

"Am I allowed to bring a friend?"

"Surely. Feel free to come. No appointment necessary."

As I drove away, I judged Duncan to be all right. At the same time I reminded myself to stay wary. Trusting was like hope—either could hurt you real bad.

FIFTEEN

When I reached Ben's, I found Blackie and him in the kitchen. She again moved about barefooted, her shirttail out. They were fixing six mountain trout they'd caught at upper reaches of Laurel Creek.

"Where you been?" she asked as her eyes swept over me.

I told her.

"They make you go to the back door?"

"No, and didn't seem all that bad."

"Look who's taking up for the bluebloods, the original loner himself. Never called on a neighbor or went into town if he could help it. Carried around with him his own hole to hide in."

"You aching for a fight?"

"I'm a woman around a man. That's a situation always near the ignition point and fire in the hole. I like to know where you are and what you doing."

"I'm taking a shower."

"Yellow belly won't fight," she said as I walked out.

After the shower and a change of clothes, I walked back to the kitchen, where Ben had the trout about ready. I watched him salt and pepper the fish, dice over them wild mushrooms he'd picked in his pasture, squeeze on fresh lemon juice, shake cayenne pepper, and wrap the three fish in wild grape leaves. Using country butter, he sautéed the trout until they were brown and dry. He unfolded the grape leaves to serve us. The fish were so hot and savory they could almost make a man believe in the goodness of this world.

"Trout like these is living proof of a benevolent God," Ben said.

Afterwards Blackie and I sat the porch swing to drink mint iced tea. I kept thinking of Aunt Jessie's body up in Charleston and wondered what would happen to her cabin and land. When Ben came out, I asked him.

"What I hear is Aunt Jessie meant to leave her belongings to Mt. Olivet Church," he said. "She was the heart of the congregation, the little that's left. And you got another call down at Peck's Store."

"Your lawyer," Blackie said. "We didn't want to tell you till you'd eaten the trout. They got to be fresh in and out of the pan while less important things like lawyers can wait."

I stood and finished my tea.

"Can't you wait till morning?" Blackie asked.

"I better go see. Come on if you'd like."

"I don't like doing anything but sitting right here and swinging after that feed. You go ahead."

I drove to the store. Mr. Henry Peck had written down Walt's number in his shaky handwriting. On the third ring I got through to Mary Ellen.

"He's on the other line," she said. "I'll have him phone you right back."

While I waited I chatted with Mr. Henry. He had an unlit stogie in his mouth and chewed on its butt end. I asked about the Mac-Glauglins.

"I was just a tad," he said. "Old man James MacGlauglin ruled that roost like a king. When he passed on the road, you even felt a little fear. Men took their hats off to him. Lots of important people came visiting—the governor, a Rockefeller, and the opera singer Lotte Lehman stopped by while passing through headed south. James MacGlauglin was increasing his holdings ever' year. If he'd lived long enough, he'd owned the whole of Shawnee County. Had his heart attack when the president sent in the troops and they came to arrest him. Lived a while afterwards but couldn't fight the U.S. Government. He's buried in the cemetery up at Wild Thorn. For a while it went to thistle and briars. What I hear is Mr. St. George has seen it's been cleaned up. Supposed to have scrubbed off the tombstones."

The phone rang. Mr. Henry Peck allowed me answer it.

"I talked with your brother," Walt said. "Charles, why in the world did you have to act that way? Poured ink on him. My God, man."

"Brother Edward lives on ink."

"But you should've just walked out and come to me. I'm attempting damage control here. I drove over to Richmond, where Edward and I ate lunch. He was almost affable but won't be moved. He contends he's under no legal obligation to share any money from Bellerive with you. I asked him about keeping his word. He said he hadn't known all the facts when he promised you half the proceeds from the sale. I asked him what facts. He wouldn't elaborate. You want to fill me in on what he's talking about?"

"Nothing to fill you in with. He just don't want to turn loose the money."

"So you poured the ink on him."

"Ink's his bread of life. Cut him, and it'd leak out his veins."

"You're not giving me anything to work with."

"Best I can do at the moment, Walt."

"You expect me to take legal action? I don't think there's a chance as things stand now we could prevail in court. Moreover he's so furious with you he practically quivered every time your name came up."

"He's a prick. It's time somebody let him know."

"What do you want me to do?"

"I'll think about it," I said, thanked him, and hung up.

Mr. Henry Peck as usual had been watching and listening. He shifted his cigar by pushing at it with his tongue.

"You know or ever heard anything about the St. Georges trying to buy Aunt Jessie's property?" I asked.

"Word that's come to me is the St. Georges was dickering with Aunt Jessie for a portion of it."

"You think she seriously considered selling?"

"I don't know nothing about that."

While at the store I called the Huntington State Hospital. I got through to Building 7 and again talked to Nurse Adams. She recognized my voice. This time I pleaded and pulled a little more out of her.

"There's been no change. Esmeralda's not opened her eyes or communicated with the staff or Dr. Fredrick in any manner. We continue to feed her through a tube."

I drove back to Ben's feeling tired, opened the Caddy's trunk, and helped myself to a swig of Old Crow before walking in the house. Ben and Blackie sat at the kitchen table reading. I told them I was ready to turn in.

"Nobody's stopping you," Blackie said.

I slept awhile, woke a couple of times, reached for my Camels, and thought of Duncan St. George and Jeannie Bruce. Especially Jeannie Bruce. I was glad to see the sunrise color the clouds pink. After breakfast Blackie hung washing on the line, where a breeze caused the sheets to billow. Dogs barked and ravens called from up toward the ridge of Big Bear Mountain.

"How'd you like to go riding?" I asked.

She turned, clothespins held in her mouth.

"Car riding?"

"Nags."

"You got us horses?"

"Just a thought," I said and walked away without explaining. I weighed in my mind Duncan St. George's disclosure that he wanted to buy or secure an easement across Aunt Jessie's property against what

Ben had heard about Aunt Jessie meaning to leave all her land to the Mt. Olivet Church.

"Who's the preacher out at Mt. Olivet?" I asked Ben in his shed, where he sharpened his hay mower's blade. I liked watching his knowing fingers on the file and teeth of the blade. Good mechanics had an innate feel for tools and machinery. To such men engines were alive and, like women, needed a delicate touch.

"Bartholomew Asberry," Ben answered, looking over his shoulder at me. "You thinking of churching?"

"Just might."

"Preaching out at Mt. Olivet's not a full-time any longer. The church can't afford a pastor these days, though years ago they had plenty of members. If the wind blew right, you could hear them singing all the way to Cliffside. Sad it is what's left there today."

"How does Bartholomew earn his bread?"

"Coal leavings mostly. Got himself a little two-man punch mine. He and his brother Tolliver. The good seams long played out, but there are scraps left. Not enough for the big operators to bring in million-dollar dozers and draglines. Bartholomew makes a little money alongside his preaching. Probably his diggings disregard safety regulations. Once the unions would've driven him out of business, but now nobody much cares. He keeps it all in the family."

"How do I find him?"

"Weekdays he'd be working. His hole is hard to find. I can fix you directions that'll put you close."

Back at the house, he opened the lined writing tablet. Again I noted his exact engineer's handwriting. He didn't tear off the page, but cut away the part he'd penciled by using his pocketknife. Nothing wasted by Ben. I asked Blackie whether she'd like to go.

"I'm thinking of giving myself to the sun today," she said. She had changed into her yellow shorts and halter as well as a matching eye patch. She sure didn't need a tan, as her skin was dusky by nature.

I drove west eleven miles to a desolate section of Shawnee County and a place named Rich Find, now a broken-down and abandoned frame store in the clutches of kudzu and poison ivy, the vines as thick and hairy as a brawny man's arm. I looked at foundations where once other buildings stood. A blacksnake slithered among pokeweeds that had grown up so lushly they tipped over from being top-heavy. The berries were turning purple.

I checked Ben's directions. The bent, rusted Rich Find sign marked the end of the pavement. I followed tracks along a dirt road that wound among the narrow valley. Second-growth poplars and striped maples grew up the mountainsides. I forded a creek that riffled from shade of the trees. As the tires splashed water up under the Caddy, I worried it'd hit a rock and bust the oil pan. Blackie'd have my scalp if she could see how rough I treated her car.

I lucked into the turnoff for Bartholomew's diggings, a steep climb over crushed rocks that had been dumped along the road to give tires traction. When I felt lost and searched for a place to turn back, I reached a bench of land where a two-and-a-half-ton truck waited parked under a loading ramp. Beyond it the black mine entry had been cut into the side of the mountain. The portal wasn't high enough for a grown man to walk upright. Two narrow railroad tracks tapered away into the blackness. An aged front-end loader had most of its yellow paint flaked away, the tin-roof shed housed a gasoline generator, and tires and broken pieces of equipment lay about.

I left the Caddy, crossed to the mine entry, and thought of men back under the full weight of the mountain. I'd heard about low coal, seams so thin the miners needed to lie down to work them and load their buggies. The men hammered the crooks out of their shovel handles so that they became straight and could be used more easily in the cramped space. I'd also heard my father claim some miners grew to prefer low coal. "Gets in their blood," he'd said.

I knelt waiting until I heard a growing rumble in the mountain. As I stood aside, the battery-powered motor drew two coal buggies into the sunlight. The motorman sat up. He'd been lying flat on his back at the controls. The tracks circled toward the elevated ramp, which was supported by sawed locust trunks that still had bark clinging to them. The motorman braked his load, stepped out, and hauled at a lever to dump the buggies' loads into the truck's bed. Coal crashed down and made the old Dodge squat as blackened dust spun around it.

The motorman beat dust off his coveralls. A power cord attached to a battery holster at his side led to a lamp plugged into his blackened white helmet. As he pushed up his goggles, the revealed whites around his eyes made him appear like an actor from a minstrel show. When he climbed down a ladder, he pulled off gloves and took notice of me.

"You here to buy I can sell you this load," he said. "Eighteen dollars a ton delivered up to twenty mile. Twenty-five cents a mile add-on after that."

"Cheap," I said.

"Everything goes up 'cept coal," he said, his voice a growl-like rasp likely caused by dust lodged in his throat. His lungs had to be a dirty mess. His broad, chunky body moved heavily. Using a dipper, he drank water from a galvanized bucket set beside the trunk of a papaw tree. A green, broken porch glider had been placed in the shade.

"If I needed coal, I'd buy it here," I said. "You Bartholomew?"

"That's the name laid on me. Who you?"

"Go by Charley."

"What you want, Charley?"

"Talk to you a minute."

"I don't get paid nothing for talking."

"I'll pay you for your time or buy you a beer."

"I don't drink liquor or beer. 'Wine is a mocker; strong drink is raging, and he who is deceived thereby is not wise.' Proverbs."

"Got to be true," I said. "I heard you're the preaching man at Mt. Olivet."

"You not buying and want to talk to me, you wait till me and Tolliver eat lunch," he said.

"Tolliver being your brother."

"Was when I got out of the bed this morning and reckon will keep on being till dark."

"I'll wait," I said.

He climbed up to the loading dock, settled into the motor, and reversed it along the tracks to the mine. He lay back flat just as the motor entered the dark portal.

I drove to Rich Find, turned at an intersection, and found a settlement called Ordinary that had a one-pump gas station at a flat-roofed cinderblock store with bars across its windows. I bought Moon Pies, potato chips, and six cold Big Oranges. I opened the Caddy's trunk to set the bottles in my cooler before ripping open a bag of cracked ice to pour over them. Back at the mine, I sat not on the dirty swaybacked glider but, after using my handkerchief to wipe it, the seat of the backhoe. I stared at the sky. Fat cumulus clouds drifted over the sun and created shadows that fled along the length of the valley. Doves called from deep in the woods.

When the motor again rattled from the black entry into the light, this time it carried Bartholomew and Tolliver. They emptied the load into the truck. It groaned under the weight like a hurt animal. They climbed down the ladder, took off their helmets, and crossed to another bucket set on the hood of a mud-scabbed Ford tractor to dip and soap their hands. They flung them about to dry them. Tolliver emptied the dirty water on the ground as he hiked to the branch, where he hunkered to rinse out and refill the bucket.

"Well, see you still here," Bartholomew said and spat to the side. His spit too had been blackened by coal dust.

"Right enough," I said. I had the Playmate in hand and opened it. "Thought you might be thirsty."

Bartholomew looked at the iced Big Oranges and drew out a bottle. He used his teeth to twist off the cap. Tolliver returned with the bucket. His tangled towhead hair hung long, and his nose looked as if it'd been broken. I held out a dripping Big Orange.

"He's a Charley," Bartholomew said to him.

Tolliver accepted the drink without speaking.

"Tolliver don't talk much," Bartholomew said. "He mostly give that up after his wife run out on him. He come home and she'd taken everything from the house and run off with a diesel mechanic from Oak Hill. He ain't seen much need for words since."

"He's welcome to chips and a Moon Pie," I said.

"Let's get to the shade," Bartholomew said and walked toward the glider with the steady step of a man not to be hurried and who would never tire. The glider's cushions had become torn, the stuffing poked out. One of its feet was missing, causing it to lurch and tilt when Bartholomew gave his weight to it.

"Nice of you to bring the drinks," he said, lifted out a lunch box from under the glider, and clicked it open. He handed Tolliver a sandwich wrapped in newspaper. They bowed their heads.

"We thank You, Lord, for the food we eat and the ground You give us to stand on, amen," Bartholomew said and unwrapped his sandwiches. Hunks of meat lay between thick slices of white bread. No lettuce or tomatoes. Both men took full grips with their hands and used their teeth to tear off chunks. Though they'd washed their hands, their fingers still soiled the bread.

"Now, just what is it you want from me, Charley?" Bartholomew asked, his jaw working mightily. "If you selling, I ain't buying."

"It's about Aunt Jessie Arbuckle," I said.

Both he and Tolliver lowered their sandwiches.

"Just what in particular about Aunt Jessie?"

"You were her minister at Mt. Olivet."

"Been called that. When our regular preacher left, the people come to me to fill in. I ain't never been to no Bible college, but I fear God. Bud, fear of God's the beginning of wisdom, in case you done forgot. You go in the mountain and hear the roof talking like a bunch of bones breaking, you learn about fear all right. You in that tomb of dark and the mountain's talking, you go to your knees fast and God's right alongside you."

"I heard Aunt Jessie was active in your church?"

"Not my church but the Lord's. She might near was the church, right, brother?"

Tolliver nodded. One nod.

"When I was a boy the pews filled up," Bartholomew said. "We'd have services that lasted all day Sundays and meet two or three times a week between. People brought picnic baskets and stayed sunup to sundown. We had mighty men of the cloth. Circuit riders traveled over from Virginia and Kentucky. Powerful preaching that brought sinners to weeping."

This time I nodded.

"But it was coal that held us together. Men need work. Without work men ain't nothing. They like walnuts you crack open and don't have no meat inside. Some go on welfare, but that's no life. Most upped and left. They drained the blood from Mt. Olivet."

He took another twisting bite from the sandwich, reached for his Big Orange, and drank, causing his Adam's apple to bob. The meat had to be hog or mutton.

"But Aunt Jessie never give up," Bartholomew said. "She held us together. She'd show up at your door if you missed church. She said it would all come back if we waited on the Lord. Told us waiting was the same as worshiping. 'Just hold on, and the Lord will handle it' was her words."

"Yep," Tolliver said, his first utterance.

"I do the ministering now," Bartholomew said. "I told Aunt Jessie she should be the one to stand in the pulpit. She claimed it wont women's work. They's only eleven of us left. Most old farts with no children. The children all gone. But those of us left still meet three times a week. We faithful to meet, and I do some sorry preaching. I give them one sermon I keep repeating in ten different ways. 'Come to me all ye that are heavy laden, and I will grant you rest.' Yes, sir, ever'thing I tell them comes off that verse of Scripture."

"I heard Aunt Jessie might've left Mt. Olivet her property."

"Words that has come to my ears too."

"From where?"

"Her mouth."

"She had a will?"

"She did. Writ in her own hand. I seen and witnessed it. Kept it folded in her Bible."

"Where's it now?"

"Reckon the law has it. They took the Bible with some other belongings. Least that's what I been told by Mr. Sligh. He said they was being held till the police investigation finished. You know them lawyers. They get paid for making easy things hard. It's a moneymaking circle of thieves you can't break into unless you one of them."

"Un-huh," Tolliver said and drew a second Big Orange from the Playmate.

"Her land ought to be worth considerable money," I said and laid out the Moon Pies and chips on top of the cooler. "How many acres?"

"My understanding it'll come to more than three hundred," he said.

"The St. Georges were interested in purchasing part of it."

"Them St. Georges trying to buy ever'thing. She wouldn't turn her land loosen."

"I've been told she was negotiating with them."

"You been hearing lots, ain't you? Maybe you call it negotiating. They was offering her money, and she was turning it down. They wanted that high land where some of her people died."

"Died how?"

"Way back when they was still Injuns in this part of the country. Some of her kin had just come over the ocean, and while clearing a homestead and working the fields, the Injuns hit them. The settlers fought and drove them off, but men, women, and children got scalped, killed, or dragged away. Them that was left came on down to settle in the glens. They buried the dead up there. Rocks mark the graves. Aunt Jessie liked to hike up and carry flowers."

"That land the St. Georges wanted to buy?"

"Part of it anyway. She wasn't about to sell. She expected the church to own and use it for picnics and gatherings. We might need to sell most of what she left us, but that section she meant us to keep up the way she'd kept it."

"I seen bears up 'er," Tolliver said. "Bunch of 'em."

He ate potato chips, chewing with his mouth open. When he drank from the Big Orange, a spill ran down his chin and dripped into his beard. He brushed at it as if not worth the effort. His fingers left a clean swipe across the chin.

"You ever catch sight of Esmeralda?" I asked.

"Couple of times. She'd took to visiting Aunt Jessie. Once when I stopped by to have a prayer, I seen Esmeralda skirting off to the woods. Aunt Jessie told me that when she died the church was to keep looking after Esmeralda, putting out food, clothes, and them lemon drops."

"Angus St. George told the police he saw Esmeralda running off carrying a bundle. You got any idea what that would be?"

"Nope. Bread's my guess. Aunt Jessie baked her own loaves. Best bread I ever wrapped my tongue around."

"Un-huh," Tollliver said. He tore open a second Moon Pie.

"Anything else in the cabin Esmeralda might've wanted?"

"You mean did Esmeralda steal from Aunt Jessie? Hold it right there. I won't never believe it. It just don't add up do it, brother?"

"Nope," Tolliver said. He'd chewed off half of the Moon Pie with one bite. He also reached for more chips.

"Nothing Esmeralda could've been attracted to?" I asked.

"Aunt Jessie didn't have much. She made do. You set her out in the middle of the woods anywheres and she could make it. She lived outside more than in. Days other people wouldn't leave the front door, she'd be chopping wood, feeding or milking her cow, collecting eggs from her chickens."

"I remember when I was in her cabin a couple of years ago she had a trunk at the foot of her bed."

"Yeah, that trunk. Come over from the old country. She kept quilts and stuff in there. A wool shawl that'd belonged to her mother and an old picture album she liked to lay across her lap and look at."

"But nothing anybody would want to steal?" I asked and again thought of the silver English candlestick set on her mantel.

"Nah, nothing nobody would've taken to get money for."

"Who'd hurt a woman like Aunt Jessie?"

"Don't know. The county's been having trouble with vagrants. Could've been one of them. Now, I don't mean to show bad manners, but me and Brother has to go back into that mountain."

"Yep," Tolliver said and ran his hand across his mouth to wipe away crumbs from the chips and Moon Pie. He finished his Big Orange.

I thanked them and set the rest of the sodas, chips, and Moon Pies in the shade beside the glider.

"I believe I got you figured," Bartholomew said. "You a LeBlanc, ain't you, the one that was in prison? I heard talk in Cliffside."

"You heard right," I said.

"It's a hard path we all walk in this life. Put your trust in the Lord, and He'll see you through."

"Yep," Tolliver said.

SIXTEEN

I still wanted to talk to Duncan St. George's son Angus, and I had the invite from Duncan to come ride Wild Thorn's mounts.

"We'll drive over and saddle up," I explained to Blackie, though I didn't give her my real reason for doing it. "I feel the need of a horse under me." A small lie.

"You sure we can without letting them know we coming?"

She had pulled on her Levi's and was sticking her small arched feet into her western boots. Hers, like mine, were scuffed and worn. We set on our Stetsons. Blackie knotted a bandanna around her neck.

"The man told me to feel free to bring a friend. You my friend, aren't you?"

"Sometimes I wonder about that," she said, "and I not sure I like any of this."

Mostly from her reading Blackie had learned to use near parlor English if she chose to but remained most comfortable when she dropped back into her Shawnee County lingo. Talking like that also announced her loyalty to ways of her past and the people she'd loved. Most of all she hated pretense.

"When did you start having to like things in this screwed-up life?"

"When I first laid this eye of mine on a poor thing like you," she said.

As we drove toward Wild Thorn, I told her what I knew about the MacGlauglins and St. Georges.

"The first St. Georges came to Shawnee County around 1830. They owned land passed down through the family from an English gentleman named Charles Gordon St. George, who had a coat of arms and Oxford education. When he immigrated to this country a few years before the Revolutionary War, he received through his service to the new government patents to land in the western wilds of what was then still Virginia, yet never rode out to inspect the thousands of acres recorded in his name."

"So?" Blackie asked. She'd lit up one of my Camels. She liked to leave a cigarette dangling in her lips and smoke around it like a gun moll.

"The first St. Georges to cross the mountains didn't stick here long. Living was way too rough. Then just before the Civil War one of the descendants inherited the land and decided he could make a go of it being a planter and growing tobacco. It was a dumb idea. The mountains weren't suited for that kind of farming, but he kept trying and spent all the family money doing it. His offsprings would've gone under except for James MacGlauglin, the smart and tough Scotsman who toward the end of the century discovered coal on the property. By then the St. Georges were surviving hand to mouth by selling off their land to MacGlauglin. He already owned or had leases on the best seams."

"Probably crooked them out of it."

"Maybe. The St. George blood had pretty well run thin. James was a powerful man, strong and hungry for money. He built his mining camp and brought in workers, blacks from the south, immigrants from all over the world. He also hated the unions, particularly the United Mine Workers."

"The union had ever' right to organize," Blackie said. "The operators treated men like mules. My daddy used to say, 'Kill a mule, buy another one. Kill a man, hire another one.'"

"James MacGlauglin was a throwback. He had a daughter named Sarah who married a William St. George. Maybe she reinvigorated the blood when she bore a son named Jamie, who as best I can figure it is the father of Duncan, the supposed financial genius, which is hard to believe when you look at him."

"I heard tell my granddaddy worked MacGlauglin coal, but it was in a LeBlanc mine he died," she said.

"Don't blame me, I wasn't around."

"They probably going to be shocked when they see me," Blackie said. She had put on a clean white eye patch.

"You a knockout."

"That's what I'm afraid of. I seen the look on too many faces when they first eyeball mine."

The Caddy's engine automatically downshifted as we climbed toward Wild Thorn. The forest of great oaks, spruce, and hemlock must've been like what the pioneers or original settlers faced when they first hiked the Allegheny Mountains and pushed westward into this country. They had crossed the ocean and found a sea of trees that seemed to lie ahead without boundary.

"Whoa now," Blackie said as we drove from the forest's green gloom into sunlight and she saw the mansion on the hill. She looked at me as if to ask what are we doing here. She'd been poor, worked hard, and as best she could tell had the Spanish and just maybe a drop of Polish blood flowing in her veins. She blamed the Spanish for the olive cast of her skin. She'd never been to or in a place like Wild Thorn. The sun shone on the copper roof and steam-cleaned granite stones of the mansion so out of character with the rest of Shawnee County none of it seemed real.

"I don't want to go up there," she said.

"Too late to back out."

"Funny talk from a man who's been backing out most of his life."

We drove between the gateposts. Construction crews worked. Men measured lumber, mixed mortar, climbed scaffolds. Two stood inside the fountain's scalloped bowl, one lifting the dolphin while the other drew out a corroded pipe he hacksawed before tossing aside. The hoary elms laid shadows on the lawn, white lounging chairs, and croquet court.

"This not a house but a hotel," Blackie said.

"Surprised you never been out here before."

"They didn't let us come out here. They kept the roads blocked with chains and had a caretaker who walked around carrying a twelve-gauge shotgun. If he caught you hunting, he hauled you before the county judge."

I parked behind a furniture van. As we left the Caddy, we heard shooting in the distance. A shotgun, not a rifle. Blackie looked to me.

"They having another war here?" she asked as we moved on toward the front door. Before we reached it, the slick-haired Latino stepped out to meet us. He had tied on a blue apron. We heard more firing.

"He gonna send us to the servants' entrance," Blackie whispered.

"What they shooting at?" I asked him. He might have done that except he recognized me.

"Busting traps," he said and pointed toward the rear of the mansion. "By the lake."

He could've asked us to walk through the house but didn't. Blackie and I circled it and crossed over the mowed lawn to clipped evergreen hedges that enclosed a flower garden where long-stemmed tiger lilies bloomed yellow and swayed in a random breeze. The black industrial water tank that rose on girdered legs above the red oak trees jarred with all else around it. At the wall a latched iron gate blocked our way. I thought of the fighting that had taken place when Wild Thorn lay under siege. Iron and granite had been needed.

Yet the gate opened easily. Someone had oiled its hinges. Slate steps descended the terraced hillside to the lake, around which willow trees grew and dipped dangling branches into breeze-ruffled water. A moored powerboat bobbed at a landing. At the far end swans had huddled. Upset by the firing, they climbed to shore and looked back.

The gunners had gathered on a raised deck at the edge of lapping water. Beneath the deck a trap flung a clay pigeon out over the lake. Jeannie Bruce stood at the railing, a shotgun in hand. She dusted a pigeon. Duncan sat in a wicker chair before a round metal table. A young man, also holding a gun, moved into firing position when Jeannie Bruce stepped away.

Blackie and I quietly walked up behind them. Duncan operated the electrical control box that released the pigeons. Also acting as score-keeper, he held a silver pencil that reflected sunlight. In his soft canvas hat, white jacket, and red bow tie, he appeared very much an anti-quated squire of the manor.

I recognized the young man as Angus from the photograph I'd seen in Duncan's office. He spread his feet to take his shooting stance. "Pull," he called, and at a press of Duncan's finger a clay pigeon spun from beneath the deck. With a casual grace Angus shattered it. Pieces splashed into water.

They hadn't noticed us yet. Jeannie Bruce again took her place at the firing line. She looked sporty in a long-billed red cap, sunglasses, a white shirt, a black leather belt, stylish gray slacks, and black high heels. The heels accentuated her height, making her even taller and beautifully aloof. Instead of calling "pull," she nodded to Duncan, who pressed the release. She winged the pigeon, causing it to flop crippled into the lake. Duncan made a mark on his scorecard.

"We can still beat it out of here," Blackie whispered, hanging back.

"No retreat," I said and pressed my hand to the rear of her waist.

As Jeannie Bruce turned, she gazed at us as if searching for recognition, but then waved a greeting. Duncan stood, raised his hat, and crossed the platform to greet us.

"Your invitation for a ride still open?" I asked and remembered my manners. "This is Mildred Spurlock." She wouldn't want me to call her Blackie among these people.

"We're delighted you're here," Duncan said and knew not to shake Blackie's hand unless she offered it. "Do you shoot?"

"Mostly other people," Blackie said. "Or varmints, if there's any difference."

Duncan coughed up his feeble laugh, his lips tight over gritted teeth.

"Come, join us," he said and acted genuinely pleased. The young man waited to be introduced. He looked older than in the photograph, maybe twenty-five or so, his straw-colored hair blow-dried and wavy. His arms had not the lumpy muscles that resulted from lifting and labor but were smoothed out, most likely from the gentlemanly pursuits of tennis, swimming, and golf. He gave off the easy confidence of the born rich. Blackie attempted to keep her scarred profile faced away from him.

Jeannie Bruce strode across the platform, haughty, her heels tapping. What style, wearing stilettos to shoot trap.

"My Sir Lancelot of the Cadillac," she said to me. "Hey, Mildred."

Blackie lifted a hand and dropped it.

"So happy you've come," Duncan said. "You must shoot."

They did their best not to notice Blackie's scar or eye patch and were much too well-bred ever to ask about it.

"Use mine," Angus said and offered Blackie the twenty-gauge Parker side-by-side he held. I recognized the Trojan field-grade model, for when we were boys my brother John had owned one. It was Edward's now. He'd taken all from Bellerive when he sold the property, including the firearms. He hadn't used the Parker or cared to hunt but would never let go anything of value. You didn't stay rich by letting go.

"I don't know," Blackie said and again looked to me.

"Sure," I said.

"You can handle a gun?" Angus asked.

She took it from him without answering, tested its heft, and drew the stock to her shoulder. Blackie could shoot a rifle. She had killed Montana mule deer and dressed them out to put meat on our table.

She didn't have much experience with shotguns. As she assumed the ready position by the rail, she balanced her weight, brought the stock to her cheek, and lifted her chin. Duncan pressed the release. The pigeon swept out low but rising. She fired twice behind the target.

"Don't stop your swing but let it ride on through," Angus advised. "Now let's try another one." He leaned over the railing. "Wayne, level it a couple of clicks."

I'd believed the trap had an automatic loader. Instead, a boy, his face smudged, stuck his head up from beneath the deck. He ducked back under. When Blackie's chin lifted, the pigeon flew straight away. Her first shot missed, but the second clipped the pigeon, which wobbled to the water. They congratulated her as if she'd done something terrific. She knew it was phony praise and didn't like it. They should've seen what she could do with her Winchester.

"You've got the eye," Angus said, his gleaming teeth bared for her. "Just a matter of practice." He then realized what he'd said and for an instant became embarrassed. He quickly turned to me.

"Like a go at it, Mr. LeBlanc?"

"Call me Charley," I said.

"I'll do that thing," he said.

I took the Parker from Blackie and loaded up from a box of shells set on the railing. "Send out a double," I called down to Wayne.

The gun felt good in my fingers, like an old friend come home. I sighted along the plane of barrels and thought of the mallards and black ducks I'd dropped and bagged during frigid early mornings along the Axapomimi. I narrowed my eyes to focus them.

"Pull," I said, and at the release I busted the first pigeons with a snap shot so fast that the pieces hardly made it beyond the lake's edge. The second load struck cleanly, and pieces scattered across the water.

"Whoa, I think we got a pro on board," Angus said. Duncan stood to tip his hat to me. Jeannie Bruce raised that plucked right eyebrow and clapped her hands just once and that silently.

"Well done, sir," Duncan said.

"You ever shoot competition?" Angus asked.

"Bird-hunted mostly," I said. "Partridges and pheasants."

Jeannie Bruce's turn. She tapped across the deck to the rail. The heels sculpted her ass. She had an insolent manner of moving, a woman sure of her body and its power. I liked seeing the confident way she handled the Parker.

"Pull," she said, not calling but forming the word with her lips. As if unconcerned, she powdered two pigeons. Their dust sprinkled the water. She shrugged as if it were nothing.

"I'd like to try again," Blackie said.

"Of course," Jeannie Bruce said and gave over the Parker. Blackie stepped into position. She wasn't about to allow Jeannie Bruce to show her up without a scrap. She adjusted her Stetson, hunched forward, and drew in her body as if about to spring forward. She pulverized the first pigeon, yet hesitated before firing at the second. Too far and away, I thought, but as it dipped, a pellet caught and brought it down in three twirling shards.

Applause from Angus, who grinned his pearlies. Duncan again tipped his hat. Jeannie Bruce's lips lifted in her smirk of a smile. I felt proud of Blackie. She and Jeannie Bruce locked eyes an instant. Something womanly passed between them, maybe Blackie sending the message "Don't fuck with me."

"Let's have a drink," Duncan said and reached down beside the table to open a cooler from which he lifted a bottle of Rhine wine. Ice slid down sides of its long emerald neck. He set on the table what appeared to be a small leather suitcase that opened onto glasses and bartending paraphernalia. His delicate veined hands trembled as he attempted to use the corkscrew. He glanced to Angus, who took it and the bottle, easily removed the cork, and poured wine.

"Here's further evidence," Duncan said and touched his glass to Blackie's and my own.

From the house came sounds of pounding and the shrill of saws, yet here we were partying in sight of real people sweating out a day's work.

Only the rich, I thought, could be so uncaring. Let the peasants eat cake.

As I wondered how to draw Angus aside and ask him about Esmeralda, Duncan opened a wicker hamper and brought out sandwiches wrapped in wax paper. He offered the first to Blackie.

"You have aplenty?" she asked, uncertain.

"We could feed an army," Duncan said.

She accepted the sandwich, and he pulled back a chair at the table for her. Angus held a chair for Jeannie Bruce. The bacon, lettuce, and tomato sandwiches were laid out on thin slices of rye bread, the crusts removed. Duncan produced pickles, mustard, and horseradish from the hamper. The wine went down cool and easy. I could've drunk a whole bottle.

"Mildred, you live in Seneca County?" Jeannie Bruce asked Blackie. She'd eyed and awarded her half smile to our Stetsons. I had uncovered my head, but Blackie wasn't about to.

"Once upon a time," Blackie said. That's all.

"I thought I detected a mite of the local tongue," Jeannie Bruce said, a bitch remark.

"You mean hillbilly," Blackie said, and I saw the fight in her. She'd take no crap from Jeannie Bruce.

"I use the word *mountaineer,* not hillbilly," Jeannie Bruce said. "And I love the colorful, quaint dialect."

"An honest idiom that gets the job done," Duncan said. He'd picked up on a confrontation and intended to block it. "No frills, and its foundation a mix of Celtic and Anglo-Saxon."

"Really nothing to be sensitive about," Angus said. He had sat by Blackie.

"I don't get sensitive," Blackie said, but she was smoldering.

"Music to my ears," Duncan said. "I'm weary to the point of death at TV babble all cut from the same cloth, most of it mere noise and devoid of content."

In trying to appease Blackie, they went too far. She wouldn't be talked down to.

"We always been colorful and quaint at my house," she said. "But we got standards and never let the hogs upstairs except on Saturday nights for their weekly baths."

For an instant they stared, and then Duncan and Angus laughed. Jeannie Bruce smiled and sipped at her wine. Blackie gave me a hard look. She wanted to get the hell out of there. I avoided her eye.

Sunlight glimmered off water reflecting the blue sky and startlingly white feathers of the swans gliding from the far end of the lake. The southern breeze carried the scents of spruce and damp forest mast. I heard a single croak from a raven perched on some distant ridge. Ravens loved the high misty country. They believed it theirs.

When we finished eating, Jeannie Bruce stood to arrange things back in the hamper and bar case. Her sign to us it was time to leave. I still meant to talk to Angus.

"Blackie and I just walk down to the stable?" I asked Duncan.

"I'll come and get you started," Angus offered. He leaned over the railing to drop Wayne a five-dollar bill. The ragged, barefoot boy scampered off up the slope.

"Please enjoy your ride and do come again," Duncan said. If he didn't mean it, he played the part of a gentleman well. A fourth time he doffed his hat.

"Wish I could come along," Jeannie Bruce said. "I've an appointment with a decorator from Richmond."

I doubted the truth of it. Her green eyes ran over me, and she offered me her hand. When we shook, I was again surprised at the warm lingering pressure. Her smile now seemed a taunt.

"I'll send Pepe to clean up," Duncan said.

He and Jeannie Bruce walked up toward the mansion while Angus led Blackie and me along a graveled path outside the wall to the stable—an elongated two-story structure, its white plank siding freshly painted, the doors and windows trimmed in midnight green. A weather vane topped the louvered steeple and the loft held fragrant baled hay. The far end opened onto a paddock connected to a fenced ring set with a pattern of show jumps.

"You done much riding?" Angus asked. His curly chest hair stuck out above the collar of his short-sleeved pink shirt.

"We been knowing which end of the horse you supposed to sit facing," Blackie said.

Angus again laughed. He liked Blackie, and she had softened her voice for him.

"Mind if I join you?" he asked.

"Yeah, we going to take and use your horses and mind if you come along," she said. "Think we that dumb?"

"Definitely not, Miss Annie Oakley," he said.

She granted him a wary smile. She wasn't about to pay herself out fully to a person she hadn't known and learned to trust. That was truly hillbilly.

The stable had twelve stalls, six on each side of the throughway. Eight held horses, and one nickered to Angus.

"Western not English, right?" he asked. "I'll get the darky to saddle up." He hollered, "Toby."

Toby stuck his head from the tack room. He was aged, not black but more like coffee with cream. He held a stirrup strap he'd been soaping. Angus didn't bother introducing him. I looked into the tack room, where a dozen saddles waited arranged over conformed horizontal racks bolted to walls. Bridles dangled from hooks fastened to ceiling beams. A wooden cabinet held veterinary ointments and supplies. A foxhunting whip lay coiled on the cleaning bench.

Toby led out the haltered horses—a bay, a chestnut, a gray—and fastened them in the throughway using cross ties. He left to bring grooming equipment he carried in a long-handled wooden toolbox. Blackie selected a brush and I a mane comb.

"Toby can do them," Angus said. He stood watching as Toby used the hoof pick.

"I can handle it," Blackie said and began grooming the bay. Swipes of her brush laid a gloss on the horse's coat.

"I got this feeling you can handle about anything," Angus said.

"Try me," she answered.

The chestnut was his, a Thoroughbred at least sixteen hands. Toby set an English saddle on it and tightened the girth. Angus checked it. Blackie chose to ride the bay mare, leaving me the gelding. Blackie and I helped saddle them western. The chestnut stomped as it walled its eyes. Angus changed his Docksiders for boots kept in the tack room. He zipped up leather chaps around his legs and set on a hunt helmet, which had a strap he fastened under his chin. He had brought along the whip.

"Wild dogs," he said when I glanced at it. "We having trouble with them chasing our swans. I thought you two might like a ride to the river overlook. I've had trails cut."

My gray was a rocking-chair nag. I loosened the reins, and he lazed along the path. Blackie's bay also moved easily to the fine hands she had for horses. Angus's chestnut wanted to surge ahead and stayed on the bit. Angus held him in check. The horse arched its neck, shook its head, and snorted.

We moved across pasture and through a gate into the valley where a clean stream coursed among rocks. The trail wound among a forest of spruce and hemlocks, their lower limbs pruned. Trunks bled a milky sap. A ruffed grouse's flush startled the horses. Angus's chestnut swerved, but Angus sat tight in the saddle. The bird banked through shadows, and my eyes tracked it as if I held a gun.

"Wild Thorn will offer guests equestrian options when we're set up," Angus said. "We might add a polo field."

"A polo field in Shawnee County?" Blackie asked. "That'd sure be a first."

"And could be a draw," Angus said. "Laying one out doesn't take that much of an effort. Plenty of land available."

"Oh sure, available," Blackie said.

The stream ran purling beside us and broadened out. Spray had beaded ferns growing along the bank. The drops sparkled in shafts of sunlight that found ways through a latticework of tree limbs.

"We'll have fishing," Angus said. "The upland creeks are cold enough for trout, and I caught a mess of smallmouth bass last week in the river. Noah fried them up for breakfast."

"Noah?" Blackie asked.

"Our cook."

"Your cook's a man?"

"That strikes you as odd?"

"In these hills women do most the cooking," she said.

"Noah's been with the family for years. We inherited him."

"I didn't know you could inherit people any longer," Blackie said.

"Just a term. Noah's an old family retainer. Care to trot a bit?"

"A bit," Blackie said.

We set off, my horse, name of Windlord, moving reluctantly. Blackie sat secure in the saddle, using one hand on the reins, her heels urging the bay to maintain pace with Angus as he posted. When Gallant, the chestnut, became long striding, Blackie's Ginger broke into a canter to keep up. Windlord followed at the same gait. Angus glanced over his shoulder before he let out Gallant to send the horses flying along the trail at a gallop, each of us bent forward, hooves pounding and throwing up soil. The path narrowed, limbs hung low, and swished past our faces. We bowed under them.

Angus pulled farther ahead. He waved us on and drew out of sight. Blackie and I gave chase till the horses heaved for breath and broke sweats. We caught up with him waiting on an outcropping of rock that overlooked the Wilderness River. He had turned his chestnut back toward us. Blackie and I pulled up hard. The shod hooves slid and cracked against the ledge. Another ten yards or so and we might've gone over into the gorge like the stream sluicing away and falling apart in air.

"Invigorating?" Angus asked and laughed, the sonofabitch. That had been dangerous stuff, and though I could take danger, I never went looking for it. Blackie's lips moved silently. I read them. She was cussing him too.

"And beautiful," Angus said of the river some thousands of feet below. It ran full and furious among bone-colored boulders tamed over time by the relentless battering of the water. Rapids thrashed white and twisted heaving between the boulders. Even this high we heard the flow, which sounded like the ocean's distant roar.

"That was a dumb-ass thing to do," Blackie said to Angus. "A horse could've slipped and killed itself and the rider."

"A bit scary, but these horses are old hands at it and in the know. Speeds up the blood, right? We're thinking of offering raft trips on the river. That'll quicken the guests' heartbeats."

"River be hard to reach from up here," I said.

"We'll use all-terrain vehicles to carry them down and bring them back from the mighty water."

"How far are we from Aunt Jessie Arbuckle's?" I asked.

He brought the chestnut around to face me. It pranced, snorted, and stomped.

"That's right, you knew Aunt Jessie. Wonderful old lady. I rode over to visit when she made her cider. She mixed cinnamon in it. The best cider ever put on this earth. I'd sit on her bench under that persimmon tree and listen to her stories about the old days in Shawnee County."

"I heard you all were trying to buy her place for a ski run."

"Not her cabin. Just a down-mountain slab of her land. Jeannie Bruce proposed to leave her a couple of hundred acres and of course the cabin, which is picturesque and a plus for guests in search of local color. Aunt Jessie wore bonnets and clothes that looked as if they came from another century. Sightseers would've eaten up her and her ways. Of course we at Wild Thorn were willing to take all her land had she wanted to sell."

"Doubt she'd much taken to being sight-seen," Blackie said.

"She refused to sell?" I asked.

"Mom and Aunt Jessie were talking terms," Angus said. "Jeannie Bruce believed the old lady would come around in time."

"Jeannie Bruce your mother?" Blackie asked.

"No," he said and laughed as he pulled at the chestnut. "Sort of an inside family joke. Jeannie Bruce has more or less taken charge. It was her idea to develop Wild Thorn, not Dad's. She likes to keep busy."

"I don't think so," Blackie said.

"You don't think what?" Angus asked. Each time his chestnut tried to move out he made it circle.

"Aunt Jessie's family's owned that land for over two hundred years, and money never meant anything to her. Way she was set up, she could live without it except for paying taxes. And she liked her privacy. Plus there was the pioneer graveyard she cared for."

"We offered to relocate the cemetery, and it was Mom's impression Aunt Jessie was beginning to see the advantages of our offer. The old lady wanted money not for herself but to rebuild her church. Unfortunately that's all moot now she's gone."

"You'd still like to buy her land?" I asked.

"Sure. It's a logical action in our case. I hope we get things operating here before long. To be frank, at present there isn't much to do around Shawnee County. We need to liven things up."

"Yeah, becomes boring, particularly working in the mines when the mountain's talking," Blackie said.

"Talking?" Angus asked, puzzled and frowning.

"You ever see Esmeralda?" I asked.

"Let's move it on back," he said and started along the path. "Yes, I saw her once."

"That when she ran away from the cabin the day Aunt Jessie died?"

He pulled in the chestnut and brought him around to me.

"You've been speaking with somebody?"

"Sheriff Lester and District Attorney Sligh."

"Now why would you do that?"

"I heard she was carrying a bundle."

"That's true."

"What'd it look like?"

"An object wrapped in cloth or clothing. I couldn't be certain. Had only a glimpse of her. Then she was gone into the woods."

He reined away, and we rode toward Wild Thorn along another trail. A hemlock that'd been struck by lightning had fallen across it. Angus allowed Gallant to canter, and the chestnut jumped the trunk effortlessly. They galloped ahead. Blackie and I held our horses to a walk and maneuvered around the trunk.

"A classy rider," I said to Blackie. "How does he strike you?"

"I didn't like him calling Toby a darky," she said.

"Anything else?" I asked. I hadn't either, and though Angus rode well and boldly, at this point I'd not grant him more than an S#2.

"But he's a beauty," she said. "I could eat him up."

SEVENTEEN

On the way to Ben's we stopped at Peck's Store, and as Blackie picked up sugar and coffee I again phoned Huntington State to ask about Esmeralda. Nurse Adams reported that while Esmeralda still needed continued tube feeding, they'd removed the wrist restraints and observed her withdrawing a hand from the water carafe on her bedside table. Dr. Fredrick believed Esmeralda would have had to open her eyes to locate the water, though no one had observed her doing so.

"Another message for you here," Mr. Henry Peck said. On the back of a grocery sack he'd written Walter Frampton's number.

I dialed and spoke to Mary Ellen. Walt got right to it.

"I've been attempting to pacify Edward, who believes you're fortunate he hasn't charged you with assault and battery."

"He wasn't assaulted or battered. He was inked."

"Charles, get serious."

"It was serious ink."

"You don't want to lose any part of that money. Attempt to make it up to him. Tell him you want a rapprochement."

"Fancy word *rapprochement*."

"A reconciliation. You could try."

"No I couldn't, Walt."

"Why not?"

"The way I'm built."

"If you won't help me make amends, I might as well hang up and let go."

"He'll need mending if he crosses me again."

"Entirely the wrong attitude."

"Okay, Walt, what's the right attitude?"

"Let me tell him you're anxious to patch things up."

"Fine. Just as long as I don't have to do it."

"Edward's full of himself. He's been nominated for an award given out by the Chamber of Commerce. Richmond's Entrepreneur of the Year. Quite an honor."

"Glad he's making it in this tough old world, but I want to talk about something else. What happens to a person's real property if he dies without a will and no heirs?"

"The court appoints an administrator who will put the property up for sale. The money from the sale remains in escrow for an extended time, and if no claims are made on it, the proceeds remand to the state."

"Sold at auction?"

"Could be sold on the courthouse steps by the sheriff, but not necessarily, though if not, it would have to be advertised and put out for bids. Need I remark you don't have much money in the bank to be buying property?"

"Thanks, Walt. I'll keep that in mind."

I hung up. So without a will Aunt Jessie's property would come up for sale and who in Shawnee County would be able to bid against St. George money to buy? Come on, Charley, I thought, you can't connect Angus to Aunt Jessie's death because he claims he saw Esmeralda fleeing with a bundle or Wild Thorn's needing the old lady's land to install a first-class ski run. Too much of a stretch, at least with what you know now.

When Blackie and I reached Ben's, he stood on a ladder pruning dead branches from a Yellow Delicious apple tree. Blackie put away her purchases while I sat thinking and smoking on the porch. She brought me a tall glass of tea with plenty of ice and a sprig of mint freshly picked just outside the kitchen door.

"How long we gonna stick around here?" she asked. She sat beside me, and her bare feet pushed the swing. Her toes touched the floor each time we swung back.

"You suffering?"

"I'm liking it here, but you better call Albert and check on the horses."

"I'll do that thing," I said. Maybe no Jeannie Bruce, but Blackie did look good. She'd given up cosmetics in Montana, no face powder, lipstick, or eye shadow. Her beauty was as natural as grass of the plains. She had also stopped wearing earrings.

Ben came down from his ladder and crossed the lawn dragging the dead branches to a pit behind his shed where he burned cuttings. I helped pile them, and when he lit the fire, we watched it burn. Smoke twirled away and leveled out over sycamores along the creek.

"Where'd the law finally catch up with Esmeralda?" I asked.

"Word around town is it was up above Aunt Jessie's property in a mountainside burrow hidden by laurel."

"Think we could find it?"

"We?" he asked and turned to eye me.

"Thought you and I might find it and have a look."

"I don't reckon the sheriff would be much help, but you might try him first while I ask around."

"One more thing," I said. "How do I get in touch with Leroy Spears, the mail carrier?"

"You getting curiouser and curiouser about Aunt Jessie, ain't you?"

"I'd appreciate the directions."

"You'll see the sign," he said and gave me the directions.

"What sign?"

"Boats."

"He sells boats?"

"You'll see."

That evening after eating and cleaning up, I left Ben and Blackie reading at the kitchen table. From a West Virginia Mobile Library bus he'd picked out *Jane Eyre* for her. The dictionary and the pad for writing down unknown words lay positioned between them. Ben believed if you didn't write the words down and try to use them three times in conversation, you'd forget.

I drove four miles to what had once been a mining settlement named Boomville. A few houses still perched on the side of the mountain, small dwellings but well kept, most with garden plots, and some had chickens running around. A railroad track curved along the narrow valley. The rails had rusted, and the cindered bed between the rotted ties grown up thick with weeds and briars. No coal, no trains.

The sign BOATS had been nailed to a post in the yard. The brown frame dwelling appeared freshly painted, and a TV antenna stuck from the roof. Potted geraniums grew along the porch railing. A heavyset woman in a loose-hanging faded purple dress looked out the screen door at me.

"You wanting to see about a boat?" she asked. She opened the door partway. Inside, the TV played what sounded like a quiz program. "How far north is the North Pole?" the moderator asked.

"No'm," I said, still wondering what kind of boats would be sold in this place so far from big water. Maybe something fit for rafting the Wilderness River. "Just like a word with Mr. Spears."

"He in his workshop," she said and pointed behind the house. She let the door draw to. "He might near lives with them boats."

I walked to the rear of the house. The workshop, a square plank building, had no porch and only a single door. When I tapped on it, I heard shuffling around inside. Leroy opened it and blinked at me. I recognized him—a bent, skinny man, his hair little more than gray threads atop a bony face. He held a small paintbrush. He'd splotched his denim work apron with dried and crusted colors. I thought of Jeannie Bruce's cutoff Levi's and her holding a putty knife at Wild Thorn. Leroy's glasses had wire rims, the kind the army issued soldiers.

"Why, you Mr. LeBlanc, the man in that Mercedes, ain't you? You come to see my boats?"

He stepped away from the door to allow me to enter. I thought the boats couldn't be much to have been built in such a small workshop. Then I saw them on shelves, benches, hanging from the ceiling, all model vessels from the age of sail—barks, cutters, schooners, and ships of the line, their rigging, spars, ratlines, windlasses, anchors, and sailors all created in miniature. They were not high art, yet they were damn good craftsmanship here on the side of a West Virginia mountain. He'd been using the brush to paint the cannons black on a Spanish galleon.

"You in the navy?" I asked.

"No, sir, never seen the ocean. Fact is, I hardly been out of Shawnee County. Biggest body of water I ever laid my eyes on is the Bluestone River at Hinton."

"You must've dreamed about the sea."

"Yes, sir, I have done that."

"How'd you get into this business?" He'd painted tiny mustaches, sideburns, and beards on many of his sailors.

"Not much of a business. Each year I carry a load of my ships to Greenbrier County for the State Fair. Make myself a little money. Enough to keep buying supplies. Never seen a ship. Can't swim. Don't particularly care for water even to drink. But I love the sight of boats."

"If you never been to the ocean, how do you catch sight of them?"

"The *National Geographic* got me started. They had copies at the Shawnee County High School. Then I found other magazines and pictures. I'm in mail and see lots of magazines. People save them for me. What's in the newspapers too. They know I'm on the watch. You come to look or buy."

"Sorry, neither one."

"Nothing to be sorry about. I hate to let them go anyhow. I sometimes sit here amongst my ships just to be with them. Like they was the children me and Lucy Ann never had."

"I came to ask you a few questions about Aunt Jessie Arbuckle. Understand you two were close."

"We was. I stopped by whenever I could make time. She'd never let me leave without feeding me her baked bread or in season a dish of persimmon pudding."

"You the one who found her after she died."

"I am and did. Went up 'er, knocked on her door, got no answer. Pushed it open, and she was laid out on the floor. Lying on her back, her head resting on the hearth. Had blood on her. I feared moving her, but it wouldn't have been no use. She had left this world. I know dead when I see it. I drove hell-bent back to Cliffside to tell the sheriff. He sent for old Doc Bailey and an ambulance. Did no good. She lay stone dead."

"Where was she bleeding from?"

"Mostly her nose and a cut on her mouth. It was the terriblest day ever. I don't even like to remember it."

"You believe it was an accident?"

"I did until they dug her up. Hard to find out what's what. The sheriff and Mr. Sligh keeping things under a tight lid."

He laid aside the brush to draw out the stool from his workbench. He indicated I was to sit in a stuffed easy chair set by a coal stove flued to the ceiling. Maybe it was his dreaming seat, the place he settled in to watch great ships parade along a sea that filled his mind.

"You often at Aunt Jessie's cabin?" I asked.

"Sure, lots of times. We friends."

"Ever get a look at Esmeralda?"

"Not up close."

"The sheriff claims she was seen running from the cabin the day Aunt Jessie died and carried a bundle. Have any idea what that would be?"

"Beats me. Aunt Jessie never owned much, just her bed, table, some old-timey things like an ox yoke, her cooking stuff, her dog Rattler. She had a few dollars, but money would've never meant nothing to Esmeralda. Esmeralda never went anywheres to buy stuff. Nobody ever seen her in a store."

"I remember a silver candlestick," I said.

"What would Esmeralda do with a silver candlestick? Sell or trade it? That don't make no sense."

"I remember a trunk at the foot of Aunt Jessie's bed."

"I seen that trunk. Some quilts, an old doll that had come over from Scotland that Aunt Jessie sewed up clothes for and replaced the dried-out hair with fresh locks cut off from a child's head down at Mt. Olivet during a barbering. She used to cut lots of hair around. Wouldn't charge nothing. Old album in the trunk too. She showed me her snapshot taken just before she was thinking of getting married. She was a pretty woman—long brown hair, a fair round face, strong in the body. She stood by the run, and the wind was blowing her skirt up against her legs. She never reached the altar 'cause her man got killed in the war. Lots of other old pictures in the album—her mama and daddy, cousins and kin. She owned an old gun, a single-shot Henry rifle. She used it once to scare off bears. She never killed nothing except to put meat on her table."

"Was Esmeralda ever at the cabin? When I was last in the county she kept her distance from everybody."

"After Lupi Fazio died, Emeralda grew to trusting Aunt Jessie, who in time coaxed her inside the cabin, give her food, clothes, and lots of plain old loving-kindness. Treated her like a child."

"You ever seen vagrants around Shawnee County."

"Now and again during harvesttime they pass through on their way to somewheres else."

"They cause trouble?"

"Nothing real big I heard of, and if it'd happened I would. They'd do a little stealing if you don't keep a sharp eye. Slip into yards and taken people's clothes off the line or raid their gardens."

"Want to thank you," I said and stood. "And I'd like to buy a boat. How much for the three-masted clipper ship?"

I touched the ship that in her day had been called the greyhound of the seas. She had shear lines and sported raked masts. He'd painted her sleek hull black, and her white sails billowed as if feeling wind. She looked fast just sitting on Leroy's shelf. He'd named her the *Lady Mary*.

"I'm asking seventy-five dollars."

"It's worth more. You take my check?"

"I will but can't let you have the *Lady Mary* till the check clears at the Mt. Hope Bank."

"I'll come back for the boat," I said and wrote the check on his workbench.

"You might want to be careful where you poke your nose," he said as he pushed up stiffly to walk me to the door.

"Meaning?"

"Meaning poked noses sometimes get hard bumped."

"You're telling me what?"

"I'm telling you what's a fact of life," he said. "And I'd look to keep from stepping on anything wearing a badge. I'll hold your boat for you."

EIGHTEEN

I assumed the badge I'd better be careful of stepping on belonged to Sheriff Basil Lester. During the night I listened to the rain gather and work its way over the trees and pasture. The lightning stayed distant, the thunder rolled like artillery fire. The rain rapped the roof, water gurgled along the gutters, and splashed from downspouts.

Blackie and I drove into Cliffside after breakfast because she wanted a bottle of shampoo and Peck's Store didn't carry any. She remained particular about her hair. The day was fresh and clean. Everything—the road, the trees, the grass—gave off shines and shimmers.

Despite the warning, I meant to see the sheriff. While Blackie walked to the Shawnee Grocery, I crossed the street to the basement of the courthouse. Basil sat alone at his desk, a newspaper spread over it. He'd pushed back his Panama hat and loosened the large Windsor knot of his blue tie that was speckled with white fleurs-de-lis.

"You still around I see," he said, raising his eyes from beneath his overhanging brows. He tipped back his chair.

"You got some objection?"

"Not objection. Last time I checked this was still a free country."

"What then?"

"Heard you been out to Wild Thorn asking questions."

"Why would you hear that?"

"Hearing's what I do best."

"There's got to be a voice before you can hear it."

"I seen Miss Jeannie Bruce at the store. She told me you and your lady friend had paid them a visit. She wanted to know more about you. I told her all I could come up with."

"That being?"

"Same as I told you, that you the LeBlanc family black sheep, have served time, and gotten a bad discharge from the United States Army."

"I appreciate it."

"People ask, I answer," he said and rubbed his ring over his sleeve to shine the ruby. He laid those meaty hands over his stomach. "Mr. LeBlanc, you going to be around here much longer?"

"You thinking of running me out of town?"

"I'm thinking I don't know exactly what it is you're messing with and up to."

"What I'm up to is wanting to see the burrow where you all caught and captured Esmeralda."

"It's off-limits to you."

"You still gathering evidence there?"

"Just wait a damn minute," he said and sat forward. "You got no right to be in here questioning me like you doing."

"I hoped you'd be obliging."

"There's a time to be and a time there ain't. Me, the State Police, and the district attorney want it taped off, and I'm advising you to keep away from that place."

"When do they release Aunt Jessie's body?"

"When they damn well feel like it."

"Thanks for your help," I said and started to leave.

"Mr. LeBlanc, you should've learned by now you don't get anywhere by kicking the ass of the law."

He stared at me from under those thick brows, and the threat was not only in his voice but also the hardness of his face and steadiness of his eyes.

"I always been slow picking up on things," I said and left.

I felt queasy as always when in the presence of the law. I wasn't aching for trouble, but I'd risk it if it opened a window on what or who had killed Aunt Jessie. The one thing I did know it wasn't Esmeralda. Blackie waited for me in the Caddy. She had found her shampoo and had bought gum.

"What you been doing?" she asked as she chewed a stick. Even in Montana she had to have her Juicy Fruit.

"Went to see the man about Esmeralda."

"That do you any good?"

"That man's got no good for me."

"Then stay wide of him."

We drove back to Ben's. Crows fussed in the woods. I narrowed my eyes. The crows had spotted a great horned owl perched on the top limb of a sycamore tree along Laurel Creek. They flailed their wings around him. The owl acted unconcerned. Screw them, the owl's body language seemed to indicate. He was snubbing them.

We found Ben in his garden gathering English peas. Blackie and I carried empty gallon cans from his shed to join him. As we picked, I split pods, thumbed out the peas, and chewed them. They tasted sweetly cool and just as fine raw as cooked.

"What I get from talk going 'round is the place they captured Esmeralda was not far off from Aunt Jessie's cabin," Ben said. "Esmeralda kept moving in closer to Aunt Jessie these last few years. You still have it in your bonnet to take a look?"

I told him I had. We washed the peas under his well pump and left them in the kitchen sink.

"I don't know you ought to be doing this, but I mean to come along," Blackie said.

Ben brought his flashlight, and we rolled in his Chevy pickup through Cliffside and down toward Persimmon Creek. We wouldn't attempt to drive head on up to Aunt Jessie's cabin but to park farther down the road half a mile and to hike back along the mountain's slope.

We left the Chevy locked in a cut of fire trail through the woods and climbed among ash and sweet-gum trees to the sod, where we worked our way keeping to the edge until we came out above Jessie's pasture. We stopped to figure out how best to go about searching. We were so high that buzzards circled lazily on thermals below us. We heard the sluggish flaps of their wings.

"If they got the burrow taped, we ought to be able to find it," Ben said.

We walked under the deep shade dropped by the great oaks Aunt Jessie had never allowed anyone to hack even a notch in. Again I thought of how the timber companies would love to feed these royal trees to their sawmills. We crossed the patch of cleared land where flowers grew among field stones heaped in pyramid fashion to serve as markers for the ancient graves in what had to be the pioneers' cemetery. Laurel grew thick around it, some blooming lavender. This was big laurel, not the catalpa variety from North Carolina, but head high. We skirted it as best we could. You'd wear yourself out trying to beat a path through.

"The police bound to have left tracks," Ben said.

We found footprints but lost them among the sea of laurel. We figured we'd gone wrong until Blackie stopped to retie her Bean boot and spotted a flash of yellow tape while she knelt. We moved sideways, pushed and breasted quietly through laurel in the direction of the tape. Water from a mossy spring had softened the leafy ground we crossed. It squeezed up about our boots. We stopped to wait and listen before shoving closer in case a deputy had been posted to watch the place. By the time we reached the tape, we were wiping sweat and sucking hard for air.

The police had torn away laurel from the entrance to the cave at the side of the mountain. Ben clicked on the flashlight, peered in, and ducked under the entrance. Blackie and I followed on our hands and knees. My back scraped rock of the roof. Once through, the cave opened enough so that we could stand. I held out my hand for Blackie. She brushed soil from her jeans.

The beam of Ben's flashlight swept side to side. It stopped on blackened stones that formed a round open fireplace full of ashes. An iron skillet and dented aluminum pan lay nearby. The beam drifted across a drinking glass with yellow daisies painted on its sides, blankets, and a pallet made from feed sacks and stuffed with leaves. Piles of clothing lay about, the cast-off stuff Aunt Jessie and other people around the countryside had left out for Esmeralda over the years. A wooden box had been smashed to use as kindling. Firewood Esmeralda had stacked against a wall. Rows of bottles and jars she must've picked up from the town dump lined the floor.

"Guess she got her drinking water out there from the spring," Ben said. "The laurel shielded this place from the wind, and being underground it'd retain some of the earth's warmth. Temperature'd not vary greatly. Dry in here, and enough circulation to draw off smoke from her fire. Plenty of clothes, hats, and that old overcoat to wrap herself tight." He lifted the coat and dropped it. "She could survive the winters and make out okay. Proof of that is she has."

A crate had been set upright and on top held a bar of soap, a wash pan, and a comb. Lots of trash, but all seemed neatly arranged. She had folded the clothes. We found candle stubs, a galvanized bucket, a hammer, a crosscut saw, an ax.

The piles of old magazines had also likely come from the dump. She'd torn pages from them and fastened the tops to a ledge by weighting them down with chunks of rock. The pictures she'd chosen were cereal and soap advertisements, all of babies—babies in baths, in beds, on lawns, babies with their arms raised, smiling, white, healthy, shiny, and happy.

"What's this about?" Blackie asked. She'd taken the flashlight from Ben to look at each picture.

"Must've loved children," Ben said.

"Maybe longed for one," I said, thinking the one longed for would surely have been me.

"She's been spotted spying on them," Ben said. "They've caught sight of her in bushes on the hillside above Cliffside Elementary."

"The poor thing," Blackie said and handed the flashlight back to Ben.

"We better get on out of here," he said.

"The poor lonely woman," Blackie said and touched a torn page as if bestowing comfort through her fingers to the pictured baby just learning to stand.

"Come on," I said.

"But the poor, poor thing," Blackie said, her one eye teary.

NINETEEN

In Ben's kitchen, as we ate fried eggs, venison sausage, and buttered grits for breakfast, we heard a vehicle stop out on the road in front of the house and a horn honk. Ben stood from the kitchen table to go see about it.

"For you," he said to me when he came back.

I walked to the porch and down the steps. A Jeep had parked at the fence gate. The Latino from out at the St. Georges' stood waiting with a hand on the gate. He held a pale blue envelope with my name on it in a certain large, loopy handwriting full of curlicues that I recognized. The rear flap of the envelope had been embossed with the words *Wild Thorn.* Inside, the name Jeannie Bruce St. George, also embossed, headed the folded sheet of paper, which read, "Please, you and Mildred come dine with Duncan, Angus, and me tomorrow at seven. Just give Pepe your answer."

"Will do," I told him.

He drove off, and I carried the note back into the house to show to Blackie. After she read it, she tossed it on the kitchen table.

"You accepted this thing? I'm telling you here and now I'm not going."

"Sure you are."

Ben picked up the note and studied it.

"What'm I supposed to wear—jeans?" Blackie asked.

"We'll head for town and buy you a dress."

"Oh, right, they got all kinds of fancy ladies' stores in Cliffside. Movie stars come there to do their shopping."

"Beckley," I said. "Stores in Beckley."

"What'll you wear? You don't even own a jacket."

"I'll borrow Ben's along with his tie," I said.

"Courtesy of Monkey Wards," Ben said, and laid the note back on the table.

"You who was supposed to give up ties and jackets forever," she said to me and lifted the invitation to read it a second time. She held it as if it might contaminate her small, efficient fingers.

"I could buy a tie," I said. "Use it for a wipe-down rag when we get back to Montana and the horses."

"I know we never waited till seven to eat dinner."

"That's before drinks," I said. "The food'll come later."

"I not going. I mean to be sick with the twenty-four-hour virus."

"You going, Blackie."

"Tell me just why in the hell why?"

"'Cause I'm asking you to. Now please do it and quit acting like a woman."

"Which is what I am in case you ain't forgot."

But she gave in. We stopped by Peck's Store so that I could call Zeke Webb in Beckley to tell him we were on our way. He invited us to have lunch at his house and afterwards his wife, Alice Faye, would take Blackie shopping. They waited for us in their brick rancher with its white shutters and a three-bay garage. We ate around a table shaded by a fringed yellow umbrella on their flagstone patio. At the center of the patio a circular fishpond grew water lilies, and goldfish lazily nudged among them. I thought of Zeke, the platoon's radioman, who'd been a bitching, foulmouthed, stinking grunt. Now he owned this house, had himself a pretty blond wife, and had fathered a cute, bright little blond girl who peeked around doors at us and giggled. Zeke, who'd been damn near a wild man in Nam and still carried shrapnel in his legs, now wore his hair fashionably barbered and used his fork and knife like a gentleman.

He'd taken time off from his CPA office to be with us. Alice Faye served a vegetable quiche and white wine. I remembered the binding, revolting C and K rations that had lumped up in our stomachs and caused them to rumble. At the same time I watched Blackie relax. She and Alice Faye hit it off speaking woman talk.

"I know the stores," Alice Faye said.

"Believe me, she do," Zeke said.

"And if you know what's good for you, you'll stay out of this conversation, buster," Alice Faye said.

Zeke grinned and pretended to shrink back from her.

Blackie took the checkbook, and away they drove. Zeke told me he was awarding himself the rest of the day. We sat on the patio, where we kicked off his shoes and my boots to drink beer, yet the scene didn't feel real or substantial for either of us. What did were nodes at the rear of our brains that revived memories of body counts, terror, and the reek of shit and putrid flesh. We were both stuck with the absolute knowledge that at any instant everything in the world that had any value to us could be seized and taken away.

"You still play the harmonica?" I asked. He'd been able to make one cry, whine, whimper, and howl.

"I got it in the house somewhere," he said. "Charley, can you believe we sitting here like this?"

"We're not," I said. "This a dream. We under fire in a flooded rice paddy that smells like piss."

"Was piss," he said. "These nights I lie listening to Alice Faye breathing easy beside me in a soft clean bed. I slip out to Suzy Q's room and look at my daughter sleeping so sweet and peaceful. I get scared for them. I never get over being scared for them."

By the time Alice Faye and Blackie came back, Zeke and I'd drunk up all his beer and gotten into bourbon. We were bombed, our condition disgusting the gals. Blackie had to do the driving returning to Ben's. I took a cold shower, lay down for an hour, and ate a lonely chicken leg for my supper.

Blackie, still sulking at me, modeled her purchases for Ben in his living room—first the dove-gray dress with black piping on the collar and around the hem. It fit her well, showing off her trim body, especially her small waist. She'd also bought a pair of matching gray heels and panty hose. The shoes muscled her calves. I'd never seen her so dolled up. From her collection, she put on a gray satin eye patch she had sewed during the past Montana winter. She looked damned good.

"Any way I can get a date with you?" I asked.

"Don't talk to me till tomorrow," she said and walked out.

"You ought to be in pictures," I called after her.

"I been in pictures and so have you," she said. She meant our police and prison photographs.

By morning she had cooled. After breakfast she wanted to go out and snip wildflowers to put in the mason jar. I asked whether I had her permission to come along.

"Sometimes I like being out by myself," she said.

I let her go and drove to Peck's Store. I'd been thinking about Aunt Jessie and the conversation I'd had with mail carrier Leroy Spears. He'd told me when he discovered her in her cabin, the blood had come from her nose and mouth, meaning he hadn't known about the puncture of the steel .22-caliber bullet or whatever it was found in her head. Neither had anybody until undertaker Bernard Duiguid discovered it while preparing Aunt Jessie's body for burial and notified the State Police. I wanted more information but would surely get none from the sheriff or district attorney even if they had answers. They had closed their doors on me. In the sheriff's case, maybe more than just closed the door. Yeah, he definitely appeared on the offense against me.

I needed more answers, yet didn't know who or where to ask for them next until at Peck's I opened my wallet. I saw lying alongside a dollar bill the slip of paper Walt Frampton had given me with the name and number of lawman Bruce Sawyers over in Seneca County. I exchanged money for quarters from Mr. Henry Peck, dialed, but Sawyer's office line was busy.

"You wearing out my phone," Mr. Henry Peck said. He spat into the five-gallon lard can half filled with soil he used as his spittoon.

"You need a new one anyhow," I said. "The kind with push buttons."

"New ain't always good," he said.

"When is new ever good?" I asked.

A couple of timberhicks came in the store, bearded men who'd left their International diesel rig parked, the engine running, in front of the store. Red oak logs straddled by iron retaining posts lay across the flatbed. The men bought a dozen bananas and two tins of Honest snuff.

"You can't find no plumber," one said to the other. "They all out at MacGlauglin's Knob."

"What all ain't out 'ere? Whole county's being sucked away like water spinning down the drain."

As they left, I got through to the Seneca County Sheriff's Office, where a kindly sounding woman answered and clicked me through to Sawyers. I explained Walt had put me on to him.

"I'd take it as a favor if you'd allow me to drive over and talk to you," I said.

"Why?" he asked.

"Pick your brain about a couple of things."

"Picking brains's not like picking beans," he said. "I got court today. Come on in the morning about ten."

"I'll be there."

I always tried to figure out from voices I heard only on the phone what the people were like on the other end. Sawyers's had been expressionless, a touch of hillbilly, a clipped monotone maybe of a man who had seen so much lying, cheating, hurting, and killing that it had eroded away all capacity for emotion. On the other hand, he probably had two voices—one for the law, another for the times he escaped from it, if ever.

"So you was talking to Sheriff Sawyers over in High Gap," Mr. Peck said.

"Always glad you enjoy my conversations," I said.

"My phone," he said. "Sawyers a good man. Heard he was running for the legislature. He'll win. Yep, he's well liked in Seneca. Heard something else too. Sheriff Basil Lester might not again be throwing his hat in the ring come the next election."

"What'll he do with himself?"

"Heard he might be thinking of taking a job out at Wild Thorn."

"What kind of job?"

"Head of maintenance, in charge of security. He asked for a raise in his sheriff's pay, but the county didn't grant it. They don't have the money to grant a hound a ham bone. He might could better himself out there. Supposed to have offered him the job. But only what I heard. Don't try putting it in the bank."

Okay, I thought, there's nothing wrong with a man wanting to better himself, but what if there was more to it, like a payoff for doing the St. Georges favors? What kind of favors? The sheriff might have inside information of use to the St. Georges concerning the part of Aunt Jessie's land they wanted and needed for the ski slope. Wasn't it the sheriff on the courthouse steps who auctioned off property that became tax delinquent and no heirs stepped forward to claim?

Yeah, it was.

TWENTY

Blackie stayed spooked about dinner at Wild Thorn and again washed her hair. After drying it, she sat in her new nylon slip to brush the hair a hundred strokes and coax out a sheen. She had come back from Beckley not only with new clothes but also makeup. She painted her face and primped before the mirror in ways I hadn't seen since we left Shawnee County together for Montana.

"I thought you'd given up that stuff for good," I said as she worked her mouth to spread the crimson lipstick.

"You could've washed the car and need a haircut," she said.

"Not running for office," I said but did hose the Caddy. I didn't have time to do anything about the haircut and wouldn't have anyhow. I pulled on the khaki pants she'd washed and pressed, a white shirt she'd bought me, and Ben's black tie and lightweight brown jacket he used for churchgoing during summer. It had been well taken care of but was nearly threadbare, the sleeves frayed, the lining patched, and still carried the Montgomery Ward label inside. Blackie was against us setting on our Stetsons. She didn't like me wearing my boots either, but luckily I had no choice.

"We going to be late," Blackie said as we drove out to Wild Thorn.

She had fastened on earrings too—small ceramic bluebirds, not the gypsy jangling stuff she'd worn when she owned The Pit.

"These people like late," I said.

When we reached the mansion gateway, the sun sinking to the mountain's ridge reddened the clouds. Workers had left their construction equipment lying about the grounds. The repaired fountain had been switched on, and dripping descending tiers also captured a reddish tint from the light. The black water tank cast a long shadow over the sundial, the white seats of the lawn, the croquet balls lying on the grass, and the chained oaks.

Pepe, dressed to serve in a white jacket and black bow tie, opened the door. His hair had again been combed straight back from his forehead. You could've planted corn in the deep furrows. We followed him through the hollow-sounding entrance hall and past the portraits, including the one under glass of Robert the Bruce. Blackie paused to look at it.

"Ever had portraits in your family?" she asked.

"Once," I said and thought of the more than a dozen that had been displayed at Bellerive. Edward would own them now and have hung them in his Richmond house.

"Don't think anyone in my family ever got himself painted except when he fell from a ladder and spilled the bucket," Blackie said.

Jeannie Bruce, Duncan, Angus, and a girl were gathered not inside but on the screened stone porch reached through French doors off what in the old days people might've called a drawing room. They sat having drinks while sitting in white wicker chairs, each chair with a broad right arm and pocket to hold a glass.

Duncan and Angus stood. They'd decked themselves out in dinner jackets and fucking Scottish kilts. Jeannie Bruce and the girl wore evening gowns, Jeannie Bruce's a silky black that bared her shoulders, the girl's a pale lemony shade. Blackie glanced at me. She felt even more out of place.

"So happy you could make it," Duncan said. "You do us honor."

Angus and Duncan shook my hand. Jeannie Bruce stood to greet

Blackie. They eyed each other. Jeannie Bruce looked sleek in the gown. It dipped low between her breasts. Angus introduced us to the brunette named Liz—she younger than Angus, who drew out chairs for us. I caught a snotty fleeting smile on Jeannie Bruce's face as her green eyes took in Blackie's dress, which in this company appeared unstylish and off- the-rack.

"What'll you drink?" Angus asked. His shirt had a winged collar, and his bow tie matched his kilt. No doubt about it, he was one good-looking prick. He and Duncan repositioned chairs. Angus held Blackie's for her. Her face had become set so rigidly the jawbones outlined themselves along her cheeks. Liz had been surprised by the sight of Blackie's scar and pretended not to see. Pepe took our drink orders. Blackie, whom I'd never known to touch a martini, ordered one. Maybe she believed that was what all the rich drank. I asked for bourbon on the rocks. Music, Mozart, played from speakers set in the porch ceiling. Our view looked down over the terrace to the lake, where swans gathered around the dock.

"Liz comes to us from Newport, Rhode Island," Jeannie Bruce said. Her whitish-blond eyelashes curled upward. Those bare shoulders gave off a subdued gleam in the lowering twilight. Blackie's breasts were small and tight. Jeannie's had weight against her dress. She again caught me looking,

"Where I spend summers and met Angus," Liz explained.

"Didn't know I was supposed to get all the way dressed up," Blackie said. Her chin had pushed out as if challenged.

"I apologize," Duncan said. His old legs looked comical and rickety in knee-length argyle socks. "We've been reviving the tradition of dressing for dinner at Wild Thorn. I'm sorry that wasn't made clear to you but is of no account. We're truly delighted you're here with us."

Yeah, I thought, Jeannie Bruce could've and should've made it clear about dressing but hadn't.

"Certain things ought be held on to no matter how out-of-date, don't you think?" Angus asked.

"I do, and believe it's wonderful," Liz said. She had a round, energetic face and a voice that had to be the product of money, good schools, and country clubs. "I've never been to West Virginia before," she went on, "and had no idea a place like Wild Thorn existed. It's terribly interesting. And Cliffside's like entering a bygone age." She turned to Blackie. "Don't you think, Mildred?"

"When I can't get out of it," Blackie answered.

"I beg your pardon. Get out of what?"

"Thinking," Blackie said.

Uncertain glances exchanged. Jeannie Bruce appeared amused.

"Mildred comes from Seneca County," she said.

"Oh, please, I don't mean to make fun of it," Liz said. "It's all beautiful—the mountains, the streams, yes, just beautiful. I expected to see so much coal and haven't laid my eyes on the first lump."

"Most coal's gone," Angus said. "Nature's taking the land back and restoring it to what it was once."

"Were your people in mining like so many in the area?" Liz asked Blackie.

"Yep, we was in coal, and I wore it," Blackie said. She was laying on the hillbilly now and not about to allow anybody to patronize her.

"Wore it?" Liz asked, puzzled.

"Coal paid for the food I ate and the clothes I put on. Men of my family worked it all their lives. A passel of them left their bodies under the mountains. Mountains became their tombstones."

"Oh," Liz said and gave a look that begged for help from Angus.

"Liz and I did some sailing together," he said. His crested ring shone, as did his watch with its gold band.

"The only thing I ever sailed was rocks on a pond," Blackie said. She had finished her martini quickly and held up her glass for another. Pepe appeared to take it without anyone signaling him.

"She can ride like the wind," Angus said and smiled his million-dollar teeth at Blackie. "I'll vouch for that."

"Next time you visit us, maybe you can fly in," Jeannie Bruce said to

Liz, and took charge of the conversation. "The surveyors have laid off land for the airport. Not in the valley but on a hilltop. And we're having more wells dug so there'll be plenty of good water."

She acted as if it were her right to do the speaking for the family. Duncan and Angus appeared willing to allow her to dominate.

"At our opening we'll have celebrities, an orchestra, fireworks, all of course preceded by targeted advertising."

"Targeted?" Blackie asked. She was halfway through her second martini. "You mean like shooting at something?"

"I do," Jeannie Bruce said. She pulled at her skirt and crossed her leg. It was a deliberate movement, and you couldn't miss the whisper of the fabric as it lapped over her nylon-clad ankles. "At the right people."

"What about the left people?" Blackie asked. She was becoming tight and more combative. She licked at her lips.

"Left?" Angus asked.

"Left behind," Blackie said.

That brought silence and another swift exchange of eyes.

"Notice the reflected light on the water," Duncan said to change direction. He sure God appeared too old and frail to be a financial genius. "I often sit here at the end of the day and have my drinks."

We all looked at the lake. The swans, their feathers appearing unnaturally white, crossed the water in stately procession as if directed to perform. Their reflections rode under them as they trailed wakes and gathered alongside bowed branches of willows growing from the bank.

Angus pointed. A dappled faun had slipped from the woods and crossed the pasture to drink. It looked about before it lowered its head and then stood staring up at the house, its ears too large for the thin, delicate body. The faun turned suddenly and bounded back into cover of the trees.

"So enchanting," Liz said. "I know Wild Thorn will be a success."

Pepe appeared and leaned to Duncan to whisper in his ear. Duncan nodded.

"Anyone wish to sweeten his drink before we're called to dinner?" he asked.

"Here," I said and raised my glass.

"Me too," Blackie said. Hers had been emptied.

"Indians actually lived in this part of the country during the earliest days?" Liz asked. She tilted her head to the side when she talked and nibbled at her words.

"Yes, Indians and even mound builders at first, but then the Scots replaced them, followed by a flood tide of immigrants and blacks needed to work coal," Angus said.

"My family came in with the wops, the Pollocks, and pickaninnies," Blackie said.

Liz stared. Duncan and Angus's expressions didn't change, as if we were all still politely conversing. Jeannie Bruce again smiled.

"The Scots didn't quietly replace them," I said. "They either drove out or killed all the Indians. Nobody around here in those days could kill more efficiently than those boys, particularly the Highlanders."

"Well," Angus said. "I think maybe he's talking about our forebears."

"James MacGlauglin was a lowland Scot," I said, trying to draw them off Blackie. "So maybe you're excused."

"You a history lover?" Jeannie Bruce asked. She'd picked up on Highlanders and dwelt an instant on the word *lover*, extending the last syllable.

"My grandfather was," I said. "I don't much believe in history. It's all on the outside of people. Historians can try but really never know the inside."

"Very cynical," Jeannie Bruce said. She gave me the smirk.

"But I agree," Duncan said. "Who can really know what happens in the minds or hearts of men? Often they don't know themselves."

Something was going on among the swans. They had begun an excited hissing and swam toward the middle of the lake. Dogs ran along the bank, a pack of five. They splashed into the water and tried to grab a cygnet whose feathers weren't as white as the more mature birds. It thrashed free.

"The wild dogs," Angus explained, standing, "I'll get my rifle."

"Tomorrow will do for that," Duncan said.

The dogs ran toward the lower end of the lake and crossed pasture to the woods. I hoped they wouldn't scent and track the faun.

"Let's eat," Jeannie Bruce said. She had seen Pepe standing in the doorway.

We stood and walked through the house to the dining room. The long cherry table had been set with the three lit silver candelabra. Duncan held a chair for Jeannie Bruce, Angus for Liz, I for Blackie. Duncan walked around to the other end opposite Jeannie Bruce. Blackie was on his right, I on Jeannie Bruce's, Liz next to me, Angus beside Blackie. Duncan bowed his head for a blessing.

"Our most gracious heavenly Father, we here give thanks for the undeserved redemption that You out of Your love and grace have bestowed upon mankind through the crucifixion, death, and resurrection of Thy Son Jesus, our Savior in this world and the next."

Duncan sounded sincere enough, his voice quaking slightly. Pepe served honeydew melons in cut-glass bowls of cracked ice. We waited until Jeannie Bruce lifted a spoon before the rest of us began to eat. The heavy silverware had been engraved with a coat of arms. I watched Blackie. She'd picked not a spoon but a fork from the setting spread beside her plate. Before using it, she wiped it with her linen napkin. Liz cut her eyes to Angus, and Jeannie Bruce covered her mouth as if she needed to cough. Duncan pretended not to notice.

"The St. George or Robert the Bruce crest?" I asked Duncan.

"Well, neither actually," Duncan said. "My great-grandfather James MacGlauglin bought his silver on a trip to England. Sold to him by a noble house in need of money. Many of the robber barons used the opportunity to make purchases."

"You call your grandfather a robber baron?" Liz asked. She sipped at white wine Pepe poured into one of the three glasses at each setting. Blackie had put her fork down to drink hers.

"No, I wouldn't, but the newspapers did. He was a very determined man. He arrived in this country at a rough and rowdy time, and through hard work and daring made his fortune against incredible odds."

"He wrote his mother in Scotland to send him a good Christian woman for a wife," Jeannie Bruce said. "They had never met until he fetched her at the train station. They crossed the street to a Presbyterian church and were married by the preacher. On the first night they lived together, he hung his pants on the hotel bedpost and in the morning ordered his wife to put them on. She refused. 'All right,' he told her, 'just remember I wear the pants in this family.'"

You, I thought, seem to wear the pants in this one if you wear any pants at all.

Pepe appeared to take our plates. He brought in avocados set on iceberg lettuce and sprinkled with grated cheese. Instead of using a fork, Blackie lifted her avocado, peeled off a piece with a thumb and forefinger, and chewed.

"Don't have much taste," she said and wiped her hands on her napkin.

"Great-Grandfather MacGlauglin was in his way a pioneer," Duncan said. "It was a treacherous life. A lot of men died in the mines. He gave his own son to the mountain. An explosion and fire, and the only way the fire could be extinguished was by sealing the entry to cut off oxygen."

"He allowed his son to die?" Liz asked.

"The son was almost surely dead, and my great-grandfather could see no other way to save the mine."

"Almost surely?" Liz asked.

"Firedamp," Blackie said.

"What?" Liz asked.

"Sounds like firedamp caused the explosion."

"I didn't know fire could be damp," Liz said.

"Probably a lot you don't know," Blackie said. "Methane."

"They were tougher in those days," Duncan said, again intervening. "Men as well as their women had to be."

And the blood has run thin, I thought, financial genius though you might be. These charming cultured people wouldn't have lasted a week through the howling mountain winters or in the wet black muck of the mines.

"My daddy had a saying," Blackie said. 'Kill a mule, buy another one. Kill a man, hire another one.'"

Liz's mouth opened and closed, but no words came out.

"A different era certainly," Duncan said. "Only the strongest survived."

"And lots of them didn't either," Blackie said.

Pepe had taken the salad plates and carried in a silver salver that held a roast of beef. He also set a carving knife and fork in front of Duncan and a stack of gold-rimmed white china plates. Duncan stood, expertly sharpened the knife by drawing each side of the blade quickly along the cone-shaped whetstone that had a bone handle, and started carving. The roast was cooked blood rare, and he cut the slices so thin the shadow of the blade shone through. He laid two slices on a plate that he passed to Blackie. She stared down at it.

"This thing's bleeding," she said and reached for her wine, drank, and swallowed. "It ain't half cooked."

Silence as everyone gazed at her. Damn if she wont something.

"Perhaps you'd rather have chicken," Duncan said. "I'm certain Pepe can find a piece in the kitchen."

"Yeah, go find a piece in the kitchen, Pepe," Blackie said.

A Latina maid wearing a black uniform and white apron served the asparagus and buttered potatoes. Pepe filled glasses with red wine. Blackie used a fork on her vegetables but picked up the breast of cold fried chicken in her fingers.

"What happened to your great-grandfather," Liz asked Duncan. She pretended not to watch Blackie.

"He never recovered from the strike violence around this house, the federal troops, and a congressional investigation," Duncan said. "It was the end of an empire."

"This was considered an empire?" Liz asked.

"He owned it all around here," Angus said. "The school, the store, the churches, three of them, one for whites, one for blacks, one for foreigners who were mostly Catholic, some Russian Orthodox. Interestingly, a fine distinction was made between the native and foreign-born miners, a class system within the camps."

"Isn't it fascinating?" Liz asked.

"That's the way we always thought of it in the camps, fascinating," Blackie said. She was soused from the wine on top the gin.

Jeannie Bruce laughed first. The others took it up. Blackie hadn't intended to be funny and glared about suspiciously.

"They were great men, those Scots," Jeannie Bruce said. "Not only strong but smart. They made things happen."

"Jeannie, please don't start on Robert the Bruce," Angus said.

"Who?" Blackie asked.

"A King of Scotland," Angus explained as he leaned to her. "Freed his people of English domination, at least for a while."

"It's good to hold strong men in the mind," Jeannie Bruce said. "American males are becoming both effete and effeminate."

"So this is what she really thinks of us," Duncan said, his teeth gritted in his style of smiling.

The candle flames wavered from a breeze, their glows enhanced by glitterings reflected from silver, china, and crystal. For dessert, Pepe brought in strawberries and whipped cream as well as chocolate mints shaped like whelks. As Angus lifted a spoon, he suddenly exhaled so powerfully his breath blew the whipped cream off his spoon to the tablecloth. We looked at him, except Blackie, who continued to eat.

"What is it?" Jeannie Bruce asked.

"A cramp in my leg," he said. "Excuse me, I need to walk it off."

He stood and, holding his napkin against a thigh, listed from the room. Pepe cleaned up the whipped cream. More shifty glances until Duncan asked Liz what she planned to major in at Dartmouth.

"Art history," she said.

"You'll have to go to Paris," Duncan said.

"I plan to."

"I been there," Blackie said.

"You have?" Liz asked. They were all surprised.

"Sure, Paris, West Virginia."

"Of course," Liz said. "Dumb me."

"Yeah, there's a London too," Blackie said.

When Angus came back, he seemed all right, though he sat very carefully beside Blackie and gave her an attentive look.

"Anyone for brandy and a cigar?" Duncan asked as we finished.

"Count me in," Blackie said. "Nothing like a good cigar, 'less it's two good cigars."

They were again amused, except for Angus, who seemed out of it for the moment.

"When do I get to see the jail?" Liz asked. She turned to me. "Did you know they have one right here in this house?"

"Installed during the bad times," Duncan explained. "More of a holding pen. When men broke the law, there were days when snow, flooding, or other mishaps prevented taking them into custody at Cliffside. Prisoners were kept here until authorities could arrive to pick them up."

"A pen," Blackie said. "Like for animals."

"I apologize," Duncan said. "I should've called it a cell."

"I want to see it," Liz said.

"All right," Duncan said. "Then we'll have the cigars and brandy. If you'll allow me to lead the way."

"Sure," Blackie said. "Lead on."

We followed him through the house to a back hallway. A wooden door gave onto a black iron one. An outsized jailer's key hung from its copper knob, and Angus used it to unlock the door. It swung open heavily. He switched on lights. The spiral steel staircase wound down into the basement, where we passed vegetable bins, lawn equipment, and a laundry room at the center of which a gas-fired mangle had been bolted to the concrete floor. At the far end of the passageway we reached the cell, its size maybe eight by ten feet and furnished with a sink, a toilet, and three canvas cots folded to the wall, each supported by chains at two corners when let down. The bars reached from floor to ceiling.

"It was rarely occupied," Duncan explained. He pointed to another iron door, this one providing an outside exit from the mansion. "Meant to be used for apprehending or escorting out those arrested so they needn't be paraded through the house."

"Escorting, like they had dates for a dance, huh?" Blackie asked. "And that would be some kind of parade, wouldn't it? Don't everybody love a parade? Never seen one in a house."

She got no answer. Instead Duncan showed us what he called the "armory," a room where the Belgian rifles had been stored. Empty vertical racks lined the walls, and below them on the floor lay long wooden crates that had held ammunition. The tripod of a Browning .30-caliber water-cooled machine gun sat in the center of the room under a naked lightbulb.

"I don't believe it was ever fired, at least not against the miners," Duncan said. "I hate to think so."

"They might've hated it too," Blackie said.

We climbed back up the steps and trailed Duncan to the drawing room. Pepe had coffee, brandy, and cigars waiting. When he carried the box past her, Blackie pulled him back by the tail of his jacket and selected an Uppman. Jeannie Bruce, smiling, Duncan, and I chose the same. Liz and Angus didn't smoke. He sat by her on pink velvety cushions of a Victorian love seat. Gingerly he touched his thigh as he adjusted his kilt along the leg that'd been cramped.

Blackie laid her cigar on a glass ashtray fitted into a stand set beside her chair. Her eyelids drooped.

"How's your brother Edward?" Duncan asked me.

"Last I heard he'd been nominated for Richmond's Entrepreneur of the Year."

"I'm certain he deserves that honor. It was always a pleasure doing business with him."

"He called you a financial genius. Said you had a secret formula for making money in the stock market."

"He's too gracious. I've just been lucky."

"He does have a formula, and it works," Jeannie Bruce said. She held her cigar as a man would. Her painted lips settled around its tip. She had crossed her legs. Her slippered foot dangled and bobbed.

I drank a brandy. Liz and Angus walked out the French doors to look at the moonlight glaze on the lake. Jeannie Bruce talked about plans for Wild Thorn. She thought they might provide horse-drawn carriages to bring people down from the airport. The swimming pool would be enlarged. Blackie had nearly nodded off. I needed to use the john and asked about the facilities.

"Down the hall to your left," Duncan said and offered to show me. I told him I'd find it.

Paneling darkened the hall. I passed the library, where more lamps with leaded tinted-glass shades burned on the ornate table and beside leather easy chairs, yet the library seemed under assault by shadows. I found a bathroom large enough to hold a dance in. Golden spigots, marble washbowls, and full-length mirrors located so that you could see yourself from three angles at the same time. Clean fluffy hand towels had been laid out on a shelf.

As I walked back, Jeannie Bruce stepped from the library doorway. She reached to the crook of my right arm, drew me to her, and pressed herself against me.

"You've been looking at my legs and breasts all night," she said, then kissed and tongued me. I tasted the cigar she'd been smoking. "Why don't you give me a call, and we'll go riding together?" she asked.

She released me and walked away, her hips swinging against the clinging fabric of her gown, toward the drawing room. I gave her a minute to be ahead of me. When I joined the group, Blackie's head hung. Liz and Angus had come back from the terrace. Jeannie stood with a hand on Duncan's shoulder.

"Duncan's agreed to play the oboe d'amore for us," she said.

"The what?" Blackie asked, coming awake.

"It's an old and beautiful instrument," Jeannie Bruce said. She squeezed Duncan's shoulder affectionately.

"If you insist," he said but appeared more pleased than reluctant. He laid his cigar aside as he stood. I helped Blackie up, and we trooped to the music room, where shelves held scores and recordings as well as bronze busts of Beethoven, Schubert, and Wagner. A section had been set aside for a phonograph console and recording equipment. The strings of a golden harp beside the grand piano glimmered. A music stand had been set up and cushioned seats placed in a semicircle before the piano. So Duncan had intended to play all the while. On a straight chair lay the gleaming wooden instrument that resembled a clarinet except for a crooked soda-straw-like mouthpiece and a pear-shaped bell.

"Perhaps they'd really rather not," Duncan said.

"They'd rather," Jeannie Bruce said, her words a command.

Poor fellow, I thought, completely under her control. She seated us and strode, heels clicking, to the piano. She pulled at her skirt as she sat on the bench, then leaned forward to reach to the music.

"Scarlatti, a sonata," she announced.

She looked to Duncan as he settled himself and lifted the instrument. Jeannie Bruce struck an A. Duncan returned the note from his oboe. He played a scale before nodding to her, positioning the oboe in his small mouth, and raising his brows to Jeannie Bruce to send them off together.

It was the same piece I'd heard the first time I came to the mansion, the tempo slow, and the tone even more mournful and weird. Again I called up the hunchback standing on the wall of the castle playing his horn to call Dr. Frankenstein's monster back through the mist.

Duncan became intense. His small foxy face twisted in effort, and his veiny cheeks puffed. No natural musician, he fought the music and was losing. He looked as if he might break a sweat. His fingers trembled, his mouth puckered. I felt sorry for him.

My gaze slipped away from him to Jeannie. She was the better musician, though not professionally accomplished. Her playing held Duncan up and on course. She had long lovely arms, and she raised the left one to turn pages of the music. Each time she bent to the score, her breasts spilled against her gown, which had drawn tight around her hips. Her muscled calf moved her slippered foot forward to strike the piano pedals.

When Duncan finished, we applauded. He stood, bowed, and laid the instrument on the chair. He used his handkerchief to dab at his brow. He acted modest but pleased. He gave us the gritted smile as well as kissed Jeannie Bruce on her cheek. In the kilt and with his spindly legs, he looked more like a vaudeville comedian who should've been cracking jokes than a musician. I hoped he'd put the oboe d'amore away, but no.

"This time Brahms," Jeannie Bruce announced.

This, I thought, is how we have to pay for our dinner. I again watched her. I had this feeling that she was not accompanying and supporting Duncan as much as displaying herself. For an instant her green eyes turned and caught mine before swerving back to the music. Had she kissed me for sport and amusement or did she need a good lay? Amber from the chandelier gathered on her shoulder and along her arms. She was goddamn sexy and at the same time remote.

The performance finally ended. Blackie's head had hinged forward, her eyes had closed, and she breathed through her mouth. Our applause roused her. She blinked around as if wondering what'd happened.

I wanted to get her out of there. I thanked Duncan and told him we needed to leave. He protested in gentlemanly fashion. I said good-bye to Liz and shook Angus's hand. I supported Blackie as they walked us to the door. Jeannie Bruce stepped up beside me and presented her cheek for a kiss. At the same time her fingers squeezed my wrist.

"Please come back," she said.

Pepe had turned on the spotlights at the front of the mansion. The Caddy waited, its engine running. From the entrance, Duncan, Jeannie Bruce, Liz, and Angus waved us off.

Blackie slumped against me, her arms limp at her sides.

"That bitch could've warned me how to dress," she said. "She didn't want no competition. Vibes bad in that house. Something going on there. Things not what they seem. They using us somehow."

"Angus had eyes for you," I said.

"I fixed the good-looking hunk."

"Fixed him how?"

"Under the table he put his hand on my knee. I pushed it off. He did it again higher, trying to feel me up. I shoved it away hard and was ready for his third try. I lifted his skirt and got him." She laughed and let her head fall back against the seat. "With my salad fork. Boy did he ever spew that whipped cream. Left the table for some kind of patching job. But he's a beautiful hunk. I'll say that for him."

She got the hiccups and giggled through them off and on all the way to Ben's.

TWENTY-ONE

I lay in the bed thinking of Jeannie Bruce, those jiggling breasts, her rounded hips, her bare shoulders and arms. I didn't want to be doing that, but she kept slipping into my half sleep and taking up residence. That kiss at the library had meant nothing. She was the standard prick teaser who got it off by exciting men. Well, maybe not so standard.

A rain shower blew in. When the wind rattled my window, I pushed from the bed to close it. I had more important things on my mind than Jeannie Bruce. First Ben's well-worn dictionary, which he'd left on the kitchen table. I looked up the dates on Robert the Bruce. Next what to do about Esmeralda. Wasn't much I could at the time except keep calling and checking. When and if she improved and the law turned her loose, I'd need more money to see she received the care she ought to have.

Before I drove over to Seneca County to talk to Sheriff Bruce Sawyers, I meant to call Walt Frampton. I'd been doing considerable thinking about how to handle Brother Edward. I explained to Blackie where I was going but didn't mention Edward.

"What you expect to find in Seneca County?" she asked. All the liquor and wine she'd drunk at Wild Thorn hadn't affected her. She'd been up early, showered, and helped Ben cook breakfast.

"Maybe nothing," I said.

"Your gasoline," she said.

"Have fun last night?"

"Don't start on me. Just get out of here."

"Sure, boss," I answered.

Not wanting Mr. Henry listening to what I had to say, I didn't stop at Peck's Store. Instead I continued on past to the phone booth in front of the Cliffside post office, swung the door shut, dialed Walt's office, and dropped in the money. Walt answered, his voice polite and accommodating but at the same time restrained.

"Hear anything from Brother Edward?" I asked.

"He's not making himself available to me."

"I thought maybe he'd cooled off and could've had second thoughts about the money."

"My impression is he doesn't have second thoughts about money. He sees it as a one-way street leading to his door."

"Suppose we got something to use on him."

"I'm listening."

"Here's what you do. Either call or find a way to see him. Congratulate him on being nominated for Richmond's Entrepreneur of the Year. Make a big deal of it. Then suggest that if he won't keep to the original agreement about Bellerive, I'll come to Richmond, go to the *Times-Dispatch*, and tell the paper what kind of man my father really was— how he bullied his wife, beat me up, fooled with other women, raped a young girl, and fathered a bastard child. Let Edward know if that gets out, he won't be receiving any awards anyhow, anytime, anywhere."

"What's this about rape and a bastard child?"

"Ace in the hole."

"You're not telling me?"

"Not if I can help it."

"Charles, I don't like it. You're treading on extortion or blackmail. I won't be any part of it."

"Righteous extortion and blackmail."

"I can't, Charles. You shouldn't ask me."

"All right, Walt. Something else I will ask. I want to know if during the life and reign of Robert the Bruce any portraits were painted of him. Like in oil and color. Do that for me?"

I'd been thinking about Robert the Bruce and his likeness under glass at Wild Thorn. What I'd found when I looked up the dates in Ben's dictionary was that the king of the Scots had lived during the thirteenth and fourteenth centuries. The way I figured it artistic representations of any kind from that era would have not only been primitive but also damn near impossible to preserve through the wear and tear of those violent times, yet Jeannie Bruce'd claimed her family had been able to hold on to their Robert some six or seven hundred years. Hard to accept even if an expert restorer had worked some fancy magic on the original portrait.

"How am I supposed to do that?" Walt asked.

"Used to be an art museum in Richmond."

"There is still a very fine art museum in the city."

"Somebody there ought to know. You could ask around for me."

"That I can do," he said.

I hung up. It was time to take on Edward. I dialed information for Boone & Massey's number. When Miss Vicky answered, I gave my name and listened to pauses and clicks from the telephone as well as what sounded like scuffling somewhere in the office.

"He's unavailable at this time," she said.

"Miss Vicky, you tell him he better come on and talk to me or he'll suffer boils, frogs, and worse."

As I waited, I looked at people entering and leaving the one-story post office with its faded and frayed American flag above the doorway. The place could've used paint. All of Shawnee County could have except for Wild Thorn.

I saw District Attorney Sligh walk over from the courthouse, step inside to check his mail, and come out holding letters he fanned through. He spotted me as he passed the booth, raised a small hand, but crossed back to his office. Next was Sheriff Lester. He had the upright big-bellied stride of a man who possessed the authority to frighten, humble, and hurt others. Likely he packed a pistol under his jacket. He gave me the eye but moved on with no sign of recognition.

"What do you want?" Edward asked. "I don't know why I'm even talking to you."

"I'll tell you, brother of mine. I'm thinking of visiting Richmond and stopping by the newspaper to tell them what a great man we had for a father. I'll let it be known how he was often liquored up, mistreated his wife and children, and turned his back on the people in Shawnee County who believed they were his friends, particularly Lupi Fazio, who saved the beans when Dad reopened the mines. For a clincher I'll throw in rape and bastardy."

"What are you talking about rape and bastardy?"

"Caught your attention, huh?"

"I don't believe any of this."

"I can prove it. I got a living witness, and, Brother Edward, when all is revealed there won't be any Richmond Entrepreneur of the Year award for you. You'll need to hide your face walking down the street."

Edward didn't speak.

"You got a pretty, growing daughter. You'll be sending her to a fine private school, allowing her to travel in Europe, and want her to come out in time as a ravishing offering at Richmond's Debutante Ball. It'll be tough on her and your bride when they learn the true history of the illustrious LeBlancs."

"I'll go to the police and sue you for defamation," Edward said.

"They don't arrest people for telling the truth, and I'll take my chances in civil court. Think of the publicity, all the talk in the board-rooms and clubs. No matter what happens, you lose."

"This conversation's finished," Edward said, and hung up.

I left the booth and walked to the car. I figured it would take about an hour to reach High Gap, the seat of government for Seneca County. I drove the winding road through the narrow valley. The sun had only partially risen over a mountain bald from timbering. I felt the warm touch of light that flooded away shadows lying deep. The western slope glistened from the night's shower.

At the outskirts of High Gap I passed dwellings, mostly one story, a few sided with tarpaper patterned like bricks. Firewood had been stacked on porches. I stopped at a Marathon gas station to ask about the sheriff's office. The one-armed attendant pointed the way along the street. I passed a stone courthouse that appeared much too large and grand for the small shops and businesses that lay across from and alongside it.

I located the sheriff's office at the rear in a flat-roofed cinderblock addition to the courthouse. His sign hung above the doorway. I parked on the gravel lot, crossed to the entrance, and pushed open the door. Overhead fluorescent tubes brightened the white walls and green linoleum floor.

I stopped at the window of an office where a uniformed matronly lady sat at a desk that held a control panel dotted with red-and-green lights. Behind her were a computer, a monitor, and a buzzing police radio. She wore a plastic nameplate that read MAUDE and nibbled on a doughnut. A mug of coffee steamed at her elbow. I gave my name.

"Yes, sir, Mr. LeBlanc, you just go on down the hall to the office at the very end." She lifted a phone. "I'll tell Bruce you on the way."

The door at the end was closed, and I knocked before turning the knob and walking in. The sheriff sat at a plain oak desk that looked like something sold by army surplus. He wasn't what I expected, no florid, potbellied lifer, but young, at the most his mid-forties, his red hair cropped, his skin lightly freckled, eyes the color of slate. His sharply pressed brown uniform fit him smartly, and the knot of his black tie snugged to the collar.

"Sawyers," he said, stood, and shook my hand with a quick hard grip that was maybe testing me. Two metal folding chairs had been set before his desk. A rack of rifles and shotguns were locked in place by a chain through their trigger guards. He'd tacked up a calendar from the

Appalachian Bank and a yellow handbill listing the game schedule of the West Virginia Mountaineers football team. His holstered .45-caliber automatic in an oxblood holster hung from its belt looped over deer antlers screwed to the wall.

"Sit if you care to," he said.

I looked at the framed picture on the iron safe behind him—a glossy photograph of a bare-chested grunt wearing camouflaged battle fatigue pants and holding an M-16. The soldier appeared more boy than man.

"You?" I asked.

"Me."

"You must've lied about your age."

"You have identification?"

I nodded, took out my driver's license, and handed it over.

"And you claim to know Walter Frampton?" he asked, studying the license.

"I do."

"This your Social Security number on here?"

"It is."

He flipped open the top of his telephone pad, fingered a listing, and dialed. He leaned back and watched me while he waited.

"Speak to Mr. Frampton, please," he said. "Sheriff Bruce Sawyers of Seneca County."

His eyes settled on me. In the face of the law I had trouble holding my own steady but did.

"Mr. Frampton, fellow here by the name of Charles M. LeBlanc. Said he's a friend of yours. Yeah, tall, lean, dark brown hair that needs cutting, wears a Stetson and cowboy boots. You vouching for him?"

He listened, but the slate eyes never left me.

"All right, sir. We fine here. Hope to come down and fish with you one day before the summer's over. My thanks."

He hung up.

"So you in the service too," he said.

"Walt tell you that?"

"You call him Walt?"

Before I answered, his phone rang. He lifted it, listened, and said, "Serve the warrant." He set the phone back.

"I like to know who and what I'm dealing with," he said. "Let's hear your story."

"No story. Just like your help."

"Why should I help a man dishonorably discharged from the service, is a felon, and has been a fugitive?"

"Walt wouldn't have told you all that."

"No, I'd already heard about you, Mr. LeBlanc. What Mr. Frampton told me was that you're his friend and he'd be grateful if I could be of any assistance to you. I have an enduring respect for Mr. Frampton."

"So do I," I said. Sawyers spoke with the nasal hillbilly monotone. I'd already awarded him an S#2, but no NS#3, not yet. It was my belief that to find what most men were made of you had best see them at war or in situations like flood or fire that paralleled it. Few who hadn't been in combat knew their essence. Civilian life rarely demanded that knowledge, and the majority of men went to their graves deceived and never knowing who they really were at the center of themselves.

"Okay, what particular help you want, Mr. LeBlanc?"

"I'm assuming you heard about the death of the woman named Jessie Arbuckle in Shawnee County?"

"Mr. LeBlanc, this is mountain country. Gossip is just as much a staple as food. They hear about us over in Shawnee County, we hear about them. So you don't have to assume."

"Then you know about the woman the law calls Esmeralda Doe."

He nodded. My sense was he'd seen a lot both here in Seneca County and Nam. Likely the dead ran in his mind, and because of the node, he too fully understood how easily everything could come tumbling down.

"I'm after information," I said. "It looks like District Attorney Sligh, Sheriff Lester, and the State Police are bent on making a case against the woman named Esmeralda who at the time of Jessie Arbuckle's death was seen running away from her cabin carrying a bundle. The State Police have that bundle, and I want to know what's inside."

"You ask either Sheriff Lester or Mr. Sligh?"

"I did and got no answer."

"Why should they answer? You have no legal authority. It's an ongoing investigation and police matter. They won't show their cards until they have a case or close it."

"I'd still like to know about the bundle."

"You'd like. Mr. LeBlanc, I'm a law officer. I work and cooperate with other law enforcement personnel. We one of a kind."

"You one of a kind with a man like Sheriff Lester?"

He didn't like that, and his lips thinned.

"You think I'm going to answer a poisoned question like that?" he asked as he abruptly sat forward.

"My grandfather taught me you don't answer a question with a question," I said.

"I'm not your grandfather."

"Shouldn't people around these parts have been given some account in the newspapers of what happened to Aunt Jessie and Esmeralda?"

"First of all, Shawnee County no longer has a paper. There were accounts in other news media around the state, including our local Seneca County rag, *The Mountain Bugle*. The public will eventually get all the details. Second, you're not one of the people around these parts but an outsider. The LeBlancs have always been outsiders, even when they ran High Moor and mined its coal."

"I'm on my way," I said and stood.

"Sit down," he said. "Walter Frampton thinks highly of you. I think highly of him. He was never in the service, but two years ago he showed bravery under fire right here on a mountain of this county. I'd like to accommodate him if I can. I'll speak to Sheriff Lester, ask for that information and his permission to pass it on to an interested party. I doubt he'll go along. He won't want any but authorized personnel involved in his investigation. Give me your phone number."

I gave him the number of Peck's Store, and he wrote it on his pad. Again I stood.

"Anything else?" he asked.

"Aunt Jessie had been hit in the head with a bullet or pointed object about the size of a .22-caliber long rifle, not lead, but steel. You ever hear of any such ammo?"

"How'd you find that out?"

"Bernard Duiguid, the undertaker over in Cliffside, let it slip."

"I know Bernard."

"You haven't answered me about the ammo?"

"You talk to me like that, I don't take it kindly or feel like answering. But I will. No, I never heard of a .22 cartridge that used a steel slug."

"I'd appreciate if you find about that for me too."

"You'd appreciate. That's something."

"Could be Sheriff Lester won't mind passing that bit of information along to you. Word I get is he won't be running for office again when his term ends."

"The word you get," Sawyers said. "The man's getting words."

I waited for more, but when it didn't come, I thanked him and started out.

"I'll do what I can for you, Mr. LeBlanc, but won't cross the line," he said.

"What line's that?" I asked.

"The one I set for myself."

"I know about those," I said and left the jail, started the Caddy, and drove back toward Shawnee County. As for Sheriff Sawyers, I liked the cut of him. Yeah, almost certainly another rare NS#3.

TWENTY-TWO

Istopped at Peck's Store and learned from Mr. Henry I'd had a phone call from Dr. Fredrick at Huntington State. When I dialed the number, his nurse said the doctor wanted to see me. I drove on to Ben's first and told Blackie. I didn't mean for her to come along, but couldn't tell her no.

"I never seen her and would like to this once," she said.

She carried a book along in the car. She had finished *Jane Eyre* and held Dickens's *Great Expectations,* which Ben had signed out for her from the mobile library.

"I don't believe any of this stuff but still like it," she said.

"That's reason enough for doing most things," I said.

"When's the last time you read a book?"

"At the place. *Robinson Crusoe.* I'd taken to it as a boy and tried it again. It's still a great work."

"Yeah, out on an island alone with cannibals. That suits you just fine."

Dr. Fredrick's nurse had made an appointment for me, yet Blackie and I had to sit on chairs in the waiting room outside his office thirty minutes before he could see us. An orderly wheeled an agitated elderly patient past us.

"They coming," the hysterical man said and pointed a wobbling finger at us. "They're out there watching. And they coming to get us."

Dr. Fredrick looked more worn and weary. The way his medical smock, shirt, and trousers drooped on his body bespoke fatigue. Papers and folders littered his desk. He stood to meet Blackie and waited till she offered her hand before he held out his spindly fingers. He too had learned old-world manners.

"I am hopeful," he said. "We've cut Esmerelda's medication, taken her off forced feeding, and she's begun to eat a few bites, yet only when she believes herself alone and unobserved. She reaches to bread or fruit we leave on the bedside table and snatches them up to gnaw on and swallow. Certainly a step forward."

"What's next?" I asked.

"We'll leave her off the tube and set more food in her room to see whether or not she'll continue to feed herself. I believe you told me you're certain she has a voice, that she's been heard keening by people in the vicinity of High Moor. Is there a chance she has ever spoken directly to anyone?"

"Not I know about unless it was a dead man named Lupi Fazio and Aunt Jessie Arbuckle, now also supposed to be in the grave," I said.

"Supposed to be?"

"The police dug her up for an autopsy. Aunt Jessie was the one person in this world Esmeralda trusted after Lupi Fazio died."

"Who is Lupi Fazio?"

I explained about Lupi, the mechanical genius who had taken it on himself to look after Esmeralda at High Moor. I didn't tell the doctor it was also Lupi who'd found me as a newborn baby at his door and had set the dynamite charge under the portico at Bellerive that killed my brother John, his wife, and their infant son.

"That's a disappointment," Dr. Fredrick said. "We'd hoped there might be an individual still living who could coax a spoken response from her. Do you know of anyone anywhere, no matter how slight the possibility, who might break through to her?"

"Not a spoken response. You remember she did open her eyes the last time I was here."

"Only for an instant," Dr. Fredrick said. "We need something further, yet don't want to frighten her into an even more defensive mode."

Blackie and I followed him out the door at the rear of his office and over to Building 7. The doctor's lips moved as if he were carrying on a conversation with himself. About what—the long line of desperate people who needed his help and the little time he had to give each of them?

The orderly named Thomas unlocked the door for us. When we rode up to the third floor on the elevator, Nurse Adams slid aside the grid that guarded the exit and led us past the ward's recreation room where ambulatory patients in colored bathrobes played their card games and stared from the windows, maybe trying to catch sight of lives and dreams once whole, now broken or lost.

Blackie stopped and stood before the one-way window to stare at Esmeralda, who lay stiff on the bed, her arms at her sides, her eyes shut. The food tray beside the bed held a peeled orange and a glass of water. Esmeralda's graying hair, which looked as if it had been brushed, lay across her pillow.

"The nurses and orderlies tend her faithfully," Dr. Fredrick said. "They've taken a more than usual interest."

"God, she's so thin but must've been beautiful once," Blackie said.

"Indeed, now, Mr. LeBlanc, why don't you go in and speak softly to her. Nurse Adams, Miss Spurlock, and I shall wait here."

"Can't I go in too?" Blackie asked.

"I think it best he try this alone," Dr. Fredrick said.

Nurse Adams held the door for me. I crossed to the bed and stood beside it. Esmeralda didn't respond. Again I couldn't see her breathing, yet her color was better, the scratches on her face healing, and her hands lay unclenched, palms upward, at her sides. I spoke her name. She didn't stir. I leaned forward and touched my fingers to her right palm. Her great dark eyes blinked open. She looked at me, and her hand didn't pull away. I spoke her name a second time as I took the hand gently in my own. I felt a slight pressure from her fingers before the hand relaxed, let go, and she closed her eyes.

When I left the room, Nurse Adams again shut the door on Esmeralda.

"Well, something's going on here, but I was hoping for more," Dr. Fredrick said.

"There was more. I felt it through her fingers."

"You felt what?" he asked and reset his glasses to focus on me.

"She squeezed my hand."

"You're certain?"

"I believe I am."

"Either you are or aren't. It could've been an involuntary muscular contraction."

"Wait," Nurse Adams said as he drew away.

We turned back to the window. Esmeralda had again opened her eyes. She slowly raised her arms until they stretched straight above her and lowered them slowly, curved and rounded, to her breasts as if to embrace herself. The arms faltered, released, and slipped to her sides. Her eyelids fluttered closed.

"Well," Dr. Fredrick said, "what do you suppose that was about? Mr. LeBlanc, will you be good enough to go back into the room, speak to her a second time, and touch her as you did previously."

I did as he asked, yet this time received no response. Her eyes remained shut, though I repeated her name and touched not only her hand but also her cheek and forehead. Maybe I hadn't felt anything the first time but been deceived by the hope I had for her. Reluctantly I left the room. We stood watching and waiting for something else. Esmeralda remained motionless.

"If you actually felt pressure from her hand, it might be of some useful significance," Dr. Fredrick said. "You did tell me you'd never in your life known her?"

"Never," I said and felt Blackie watching.

"Let's call it another step," Dr. Fredrick said, "though I don't know as yet where it's taking us."

When we left Building 7, Blackie and I thanked and said our good-byes to the doctor, who again agreed to notify me of any new developments. Blackie and I walked to the Caddy. We left the city and drove toward Shawnee County. Blackie closed her book. She looked at me as if waiting for me to speak.

"What was going on back there?" she asked finally.

"Beats me," I answered, and it did.

"I thought a felon and jailbird like you would've learned how to lie better," she said.

She again opened her book, and that was the last word she spoke to me on the way to Shawnee County.

At Peck's Store, I stopped and Blackie waited in the car while I checked on the chance of a call from Brother Edward who might've had time to reconsider his options. Mr. Peck did have a number for me I didn't recognize. When I dialed, Pepe picked up and identified Wild Thorn. I told him my name.

"Sure, I recognize," he said. "Hold a minute, please."

I waited. The next voice I heard belonged to Jeannie Bruce.

"Been wondering about you," she said.

"Wondering what?"

"Why I've not heard from you."

"Why would you hear from me?"

"Let's not play footsy and pretend. You know why. The way you looked at me at the dinner."

"Don't you think it's kind of risky to be phoning me?" I asked, my face turned away from Mr. Henry Peck and my hand cupped over the phone's mouthpiece.

"Not from my end," she said and laughed.

"It is from mine."

"Your little one-eyed gal got claws?"

"Most women do."

"Meow," she said. "You'll be sorry."

She hung up, and I wondered how much Mr. Henry Peck had heard. He couldn't know who'd been on the other end. Out at the Caddy Blackie looked up from her book.

"Something?" she asked.

"Just talking to Mr. Henry Peck," I said, and, Jesus, that was another lie to her.

"When you going to tell me?"

"Tell you what?" I asked and my stomach tightened. How could she have found out anything about Jeannie Bruce kissing me?

"Why you so set on this Esmeralda business?"

"With Aunt Jessie gone, somebody had to take charge."

"She's in good hands at Huntington. They doing okay by her."

"Once they lose interest, she'll just be warehoused."

"She'll have food, clothes, a roof, a doctor's care. That's a lot more than before."

"It's slow death," I said.

"What isn't?" Blackie asked.

TWENTY-THREE

When we reached Ben's, he had picked his first Big Boy tomatoes of the season from the staked vines of the garden. His sharp kitchen knife sliced effortlessly through them, and he made us sandwiches doused with thick, creamy homemade mayonnaise. Lord, the goodness of a tomato at full fresh ripeness. I thought of Bellerive and its extensive vegetable rows. Gaius, my father's black servant, had tended it for us. In those days I'd like to twist the Rutgers and Marglobes right off the vine and bite deep into their flesh while they still held the sunshine's warmth.

As I ate, I again tried to figure what it was Esmeralda might've taken from Aunt Jessie's place. I pictured the yellow-taped cabin out on the mountainside above Persimmon Creek. The police couldn't have it under surveillance twenty-four hours a day. I still wanted a look.

Blackie had her mind set on reading *Great Expectations*. She'd spread a blanket on the grass of the front yard, stretched out on her stomach, loosened her halter, and opened the book. She held her breasts as she raised her head to speak to me.

"I might just drive around awhile," I told her, another lie. "Or find a good place for a hike in the woods."

"There's not plenty of woods right here?"

"And do some thinking."

"The man can't think around this joint, huh?" she asked and one-handing her halter to keep from losing it turned back down to the book.

She was a get-in-the-last-word expert, the champ at it. I walked to the house and changed into a pair of patched khakis before lacing up my Bean boots. I found Ben, hoe in hand, working his garden. Rattler lay watching him. The dog followed him everywhere now and had made a transfer of at least a split loyalty from Aunt Jessie to Ben.

"You own any field glasses?" I asked.

"An old pair I took off a dead panzer corporal near Aachen," he said.

We walked to the house, and he lifted the binoculars from beneath shirts in his dresser drawer. They were military, gray Zeiss 8X30s with a neck strap. I sighted them through the window at Blackie. The clean lens focused tight. I saw her toes wiggle and the pink polish on their nails.

"You a bird-watcher?" Ben asked.

"Lots of different birds," I answered.

As I drove back through Cliffside and toward Persimmon Creek, I passed a man hiking along the side of the road. He was bearded, dark-skinned, and used a walking stick. Across his back he'd strapped a pack. A vagrant or somebody just enjoying a ramble among the mountains? He glared at me when I stopped to look back at him. Not exactly friendly. I moved on.

At the dirt road up to Aunt Jessie's place I slowed and saw no sign of a police car, deputies, or troopers. I didn't pull in but continued on to the fire trail, where I parked far enough off the pavement to keep any-body from spotting and becoming curious about the Caddy.

I climbed through the woods until I was high above her property, sat on an outcropping of limestone, and used the field glasses to watch the cabin. Sun heated the pasture, causing air to shimmy upward. Crows scavenged among sprouting weeds of Aunt Jessie's abandoned garden. A strand of the tape had torn loose from the persimmon tree, and a breeze worried it. I repeatedly focused on the windows. Nothing moved inside. Unless they were sitting or lazing around, no trooper or other lawman on duty.

I waited what I figured to be a good hour before I worked my way down the slope, crossed the pasture behind the cabin, climbed the split-rail fence, and sprinted to the back door. I stood holding my breath while I listened. Nothing. I laid my right ear against the weathered wood. No sound. I tried the knob. The door gave a little but wouldn't open. I circled to the front and saw that the police had secured its door with a padlock closed through a hasp.

At the side of the house, I tried the window and found it held shut by a wooden dowel inserted into holes where the frame met the sill. I took out my Old Pal and worked it between the space to lever the blade until it popped the dowel.

I waited and again listened before I raised the window, legged up, and stepped inside Aunt Jessie's bedroom. I eyed the roughly hewn oak bed covered by a patch quilt and her walnut bureau that dealers in Early American antiques would've loved to put on sale. I flinched at my own reflection in the circular mirror. She had no closet, and her clothes dangled from rows of whittled pegs mortised into the logs. At the foot of the bed was the trunk that had supposedly come over from Scotland with the earliest of Aunt Jessie's Highland kin. Propped in a corner stood her rifle, the old .40-caliber Henry she'd kept oiled and ready.

I crossed from the bedroom into her kitchen. The stone fireplace she'd used for cooking had also warmed her during the winters. Dried vegetables, fruits, and sun-cured leaf tobacco hung from nails. Her wooden plates and mugs lined a shelf. I turned to the mantel and found the tarnished silver candlestick that carried an English benchmark. So neither Esmeralda nor vagrants had taken that. I checked the hearthstone. The brown spots on it had to be Aunt Jessie's dried blood.

I walked back to the trunk and raised the lid. The paper shopping bag with twine handles lay on top. I opened it to look at the crayon portrait Lupi Fazio had drawn of the thin, black-haired young girl with the enormous dark eyes who became my mother. I laid it aside on the bed.

Next I uncovered beneath a folded wool blanket a limp, dog-eared photograph album. A few pictures had names written under them in a spidery script. Some were dated as early as 1915. None had been taken with a modern camera, and they'd become yellowed, the edges curled—snapshots of men in derby hats standing before a shay engine at a sawmill, women wearing long dresses and bonnets setting food on an outdoor picnic table beside a church, a group of three children sitting astride a mule, and one photo of Aunt Jessie herself when young. It was marked ME. She held herself erect, her light brown hair pulled to a bun, her hands at her waist holding what looked to be a bouquet of mountain daisies.

On the last filled page she'd pasted the single picture of a girl maybe ten or twelve. At first I thought it might be Esmeralda, but neither her eyes nor hair looked black. The girl wore a white dress with a large bow tied at the waist and stood at the doorway of what I recognized as Mt. Olivet Church. Her name had been written beneath it. *Violette Slaughter.* Violette's hair hung in braided pigtails across her shoulders, and she appeared resentful or sullen.

I laid the album back under the blanket, Lupi's drawings on top, and closed the trunk. I ran my hand over the smooth grain of the kitchen table that looked as if made from the butt end of a felled oak. The wood had never been shellacked or stained and had taken on an ivory tint from age and wipings of Aunt Jessie's lye soap. A quart jar held a dried crackly spray of wildflowers. Withered blooms had dropped to the table.

Leroy Spears told me he'd found Aunt Jessie with her head on the hearth, blood over her face and dress. According to undertaker Bernard Duiguid, the police had first believed she might have tripped or suffered heart failure and fallen. Then Bernard Duiguid had discovered the puncture in her head and what he believed to be the steel .22-caliber bullet that had caused her death.

I stood thinking about Aunt Jessie's large family Bible handed down
to her by her forebears. I'd seen it at the center of the kitchen table my
first time in the cabin. Bartholomew Asberry said the police had taken
the Bible. What about the will he claimed she'd written and stuck
between the pages?

I heard crows sounding off. Something had disturbed them, and
they cawed in woods west of the house. I stepped to the window. The
crows spiraled above the trees and circled squawking. Another owl, I
thought, but as I started to turn away, a shape emerged from shadows.
A deer, I believed, slipping among the trees in search of graze.

It faded away, but the crows kept up their fussing. I used the field
glasses and scanned the woods. What materialized from shade wasn't
a deer but a horse and rider. They halted and remained motionless
before skirting the edge of the pasture. They ambled down along the
rear of Aunt Jessie's garden and turned toward the cabin. I lost sight of
them a moment but then heard hooves outside. I moved fast to the bedroom, quietly closed the window I'd climbed through, and stepped
back from it. When the rider circled the tape, I saw it was Jeannie
Bruce decked out in fawn jodhpurs, a denim shirt, and a riding helmet. She carried a hunt whip. She sat forward in the saddle as she
walked the bay twice around the cabin.

She dismounted, tied the bay to the persimmon tree, and ducked
under tape to approach the front door. She rattled the padlock. Her
footsteps moved away. I glimpsed her at a side window. She bent
down and shaded her eyes to peer in. I stood very still against the wall.
She straightened and passed on toward the rear.

I hurried to the back door. It was held shut not by a lock but a two-
by-eight-inch wooden plank laid across and set into carved U-shaped
wood blocks bolted to the wall. I lifted the plank and set it aside. When
Jeannie Bruce tried the knob, I jerked open the door and faced her.
She stumbled in frightened.

"You scared the shit out of me," she said, and righted herself. "What
the hell you doing here?"

"Same question to you."

"I don't have to explain."

"Me neither."

"Let me tell you that they damn well know at Wild Thorn where I am. If I'm not back right away, they'll come looking for me."

"By that time I'll have finished raping you and be long gone."

Those green eyes steadied on me. She still held the whip. She slapped it across a thigh.

"I assume if I were to have the great good fortune to be raped by you, it would be happening by now," she said.

"Good thinking."

"You're a cool one, Charley. So why are you here?"

"I wanted to see for myself how Aunt Jessie left this life."

"I believe Esmeralda Doe has the answer to that question for you."

"Esmeralda never answers anything."

"But you think otherwise."

"Why would she harm her best friend in this world?"

"Esmeralda Doe's not responsible for her actions."

"Yet not crazy."

"I don't use the word *crazy*. I'd call her unfortunate."

"Did they question your son Angus?"

"Stop calling him my son. He's my stepson. And why should they question him?"

"He saw Esmeralda running off from here. Means he was in the area when Aunt Jessie died."

"In the area, nothing more. Angus is no killer. He's so tender-hearted he won't clean and eat the wild game I shoot. He hates dirtying his hands with any mess. Why would he attack Aunt Jessie? She had nothing he wanted. The police questioned him and are satisfied with his explanation."

She unfastened the helmet's chin strap and let it dangle.

"You and your husband been trying to buy land off Aunt Jessie and she wouldn't sell," I said.

"Perhaps not sell, but we believed in time she would've come around to a fair and generous leasing arrangement."

"What I heard is she meant to leave all her property to Mt. Olivet Church."

"She would've still been able to leave it to Mt. Olivet if the lease were not renewed as well as pass on to the church a good bit of money."

"When and if her land comes up for sale, will Wild Thorn make a bid?"

"We have every right to. Now I think I've done enough explaining. Are you going to let me pass? The police aren't looking after this place as they should, and there are vagrants around. Aunt Jessie didn't have much, but what things are here should be cared for."

"Aunt Jessie had a whole lot. More than most people."

"In character, I agree, but not goods of this world, though a few old pieces have value and ought to be preserved. I intend to ask Sheriff Lester if he'll allow us to carry her things to Wild Thorn, where we can inventory and store them until the court orders distribution."

"Couldn't you've asked the sheriff first instead of trying to sneak in the cabin?"

"Charles LeBlanc, I'm beginning to believe you're a real mean and sorry sonofabitch. Now get the hell out of my way, I'm coming by."

She brushed past me, stripped off her thin leather riding gloves, and stuck them in her hip pocket. She ran fingers over Aunt Jessie's clothes hanging from pegs.

"Might as well give them away," she said as she moved on to the kitchen. "Who would want them? Maybe a museum. But these wooden plates and cups are of interest as well as the pewter bowl."

She removed her helmet and laid it and the whip on the table before crossing to the mantel. "This silver candlestick ought to be polished and tended to." She pointed up the loft ladder to the ox yoke. "That would bring money."

Jeannie Bruce looked so damn good in the jodhpurs that set off her hips, thighs, and long legs. When she pulled down at her shirt, the action tightened the denim over her breasts. She trailed a faint perfume. Black-on-white representations of ancient Greek horses ornamented her round earrings. Her style was that of disdainful arrogance.

She set the candlestick on the mantel and strolled back to Aunt Jessie's bedroom, where she opened the trunk and lifted out Lupi Fazo's crayon drawings. She selected the one of Esmeralda, which she held to the light from the window.

"What a tragic face," she said. "But that still doesn't explain your extraordinary interest in her."

"I stop on the road to help hurt animals," I said.

"Yes, though I'd never have spotted you for a philanthropic type, Charles. It doesn't quite seem to fit your sort of person."

"What you know about my sort?"

"Lots of talk. Apparently you're a maverick and rogue, but I must confess an attractive one."

She set the drawing aside and dug around in the trunk until from under the blanket she brought up the photo album. The pages flopped loosely bound, and she needed both hands to collect them. She laid the album on the bed to look at pictures.

"Like inhabitants from another time and world," she said. "In their era they really believed they had it all. I suppose one day people will feel the same when they look at photos of us."

She paused at the picture of the sullen girl standing on the Mt. Olivet Church steps before leafing on.

"You must wonder about me as I have about you, Charles. I mean, my husband's twenty-eight years older than I. You do wonder, don't you?"

"I heard he's a financial genius," I said and watched her set the photo album back in the trunk but not under the blanket. She laid Lupi's drawings on top before closing the lid.

"Oh, definitely he is. He waves his hand magically and creates rivers of money. He hires dozens of other men just to keep up with it. He's been good to me and has a wonderfully kind and loving nature."

I felt tempted to ask did he know she went around tonguing guests at Wild Thorn but didn't as she lifted the quilt from Aunt Jessie's bed and fingered it like a buyer testing the fabric's quality at a bazaar.

"I expect you wonder about our love life," she said and looked at me as she spoke. Her lips shaped themselves to the smirk of a smile.

"Yeah, who wouldn't?"

"What's your best guess?"

"You're not getting enough."

She laughed and sat on the bed. She leaned over to unstrap one jodhpur boot and then the other. She toed the boots from her feet and peeled down her white socks. Her toenails were a glossy scarlet.

"You hit it on the head, Charley boy. There are times at Wild Thorn I long for love. At times I burn for it, and so little is available hereabouts."

She stood, lowered the jodhpurs over her hips and down each tanned shaved leg. She sat again to pull them off. She had on white silk panties. She stood, and this time unbuttoned the denim shirt, let it slip back over her arms to the bed. Her brassiere was of the same shiny white silk. She unscrewed her earrings and set them in a boot.

"How'm I doing so far?" she asked and cocked her head before crossing to me. She raised her arms around my neck and pushed her pelvis against mine. The green eyes mocked. When she kissed me, I smelled her perfume and felt her woman heat.

"I think you like to take big chances," I said.

She was so goddamn appealing, and in all my life I'd never laid a really classy woman.

"Some consider danger the spice of life," she said, and this time when she kissed me I was ready for her tongue, which with my own I pushed back into her mouth. Her body gave way, became submissive and lingering.

"And you're dangerous," she said. "I knew it the second I saw you."

Oh Christ, I thought, kissed her, bent her backwards as she

unhooked her brassiere and tossed it aside. I got my mouth on her nipples, let her down on the bed, and yanked off her panties. As I shucked my clothes to the floor, she lay propped on an elbow smiling.

It was crazy stuff. I believed I'd long ago finished with gut-wrenching lust. At times I felt passion for Blackie, but nothing like this since the day I got out of prison and had all my money stolen during the Kansas City knee-walking drunk. I went at this woman as if I meant to pound under and smash her—to destroy us both by fucking. She was as wild. She surged, bit, and raked my back. She wanted and liked it rough, and I snarled as I rammed it to her. This wasn't loving but battle. Die, bitch, I thought, die.

When I came, I lay pumping into and sprawled across her as if I'd been poleaxed. She sighed into my ear. I flopped away to my back. She turned on her side, and her eyes glittered.

"One big wow," she said, sat up, held her hands over her breasts, exhaled, and laughed.

I thought of Blackie and betrayal. Jesus, did a man with a woman ever really have control of himself? Nature's aeons of creative force conspiring and powering him into screwing no matter what the consequences. Yet I knew Jeannie Bruce had used me, not the other way around. She pushed her fingers through her hair to collect and lift it. She rolled on top of me and allowed the hair to string over my face.

"You're quite the bedroom athlete," she said.

"What I am is a dumb shit."

"And human, as are we all."

"What if your husband finds out?"

"He understands desire and looks aside as long as I remain discreet." She again laughed. "You might say he's not always up to it. Now I'm beginning to get the impression you're not about to avail yourself of second helpings."

I squirmed from beneath her. She shrugged, swung her legs from the bed, and reached for her brassiere. She leaned forward to dip her breasts into its cups before fastening it behind her, drew on her panties, and unhurriedly buttoned her shirt. I set my feet on the floor and rubbed my face. I bad wanted a drink of water. I pulled on my pants to walk to the kitchen and Aunt Jessie's pitcher pump. I cranked the handle to splash my face and slurp up water from my palms.

"Hard day at the office, eh?" Jeannie Bruce called. She had finished dressing and, her back to me, was fastening on her earrings. She stood at the trunk, opened it, and again fingered through its contents. I had another drink from the pump. She straightened things before closing the trunk's lid. As she walked from the bedroom to the kitchen, she pushed at her hair, lifted her helmet, and gathered up the whip. She crossed to the bedroom and checked the terrain before opening the door wide enough to step through.

"Call me anytime," she said and drew on her gloves.

"No calling," I said. "No nothing."

"We'll see," she said and smiled back at me. She left and walked away around the cabin fastening the helmet's chin strap. Through the front window I watched her untie the bay, step into a stirrup, and swing the other leg over onto the saddle. When she cantered off, she raised an arm to circle the hunt whip above her head. She then jumped the bay over the pasture fence, and they galloped into dappled shadows of the woods.

I stepped back from the window. I took a departing look at the table and shelves before walking into the bedroom. What had she been doing in the trunk a second time? I opened it, found Lupi's crayon drawings, a pair of old-fashioned high-top button-on women's shoes, and the album. I gathered it up. Wait a second. A page had been torn from the cord binding and left shreds of its edge. I fanned through the album. The photo missing was the last one—the sullen young girl at the church, the name beneath it what? Violet. No. Violette. Violette Slaughter.

TWENTY-FOUR

I stood at Aunt Jessie's mirror to twist around and look at my back. Jeannie Bruce's painted nails had drawn streaks of blood. Wetting my undershirt under the pitcher pump, I cleaned at myself as best I could. She'd also bitten my shoulder and ear. Somehow I had to get past Blackie without her seeing and demanding answers. I balled up the undershirt and buttoned on the khaki. I hated lying to her again but would if cornered.

When I returned to Ben's, I slowed at the gate to see whether she still lay reading and sunning herself on the grass. No, I glimpsed her back of the house with Ben in his garden. I parked and got inside quick. I thought of hiding or throwing away the blooded shirts, but Blackie kept count of my clothes and would expect to know what'd happened to them. I locked the bathroom, ran water in the sink to soap up a lather, and scrubbed both shirts hard until all the blood-stains had seeped out down the drain.

Now what the hell was I going to do with them? I pushed off my boots, socks, pants, and undershorts to dunk them. To make my story work, everything had to be wet. A towel wrapped around my waist, I carried the clothes to the wood-burning water heater in Ben's utility room, where he also stored can goods so they'd not freeze during the winter. I hung the clothes from the line. Lastly I set the binoculars on his bureau.

I was able to dress just in time. Blackie and Ben walked into the kitchen carrying pails of snap beans. Blackie stopped short and stared at me.

"Bear get ahold of you?" she asked and set her pail in the sink.

"I had a fall," I said, truth of a kind. "Tumbled into a creek."

"You hurt your ear," she said, squinted, and reached to me to touch it. "Drop of dried blood on the lobe."

"Scratched it when I fell down the slope."

"What slope?"

"I decided to sneak a look at Aunt Jessie's."

"You ought've told me that's what you went to do."

"Didn't know what I was going to do until I did it."

I got a look from Ben. Maybe he was thinking about the binoculars and why I'd really needed them. He set his pail in the sink.

"You see anything at her place?" Blackie asked.

"Nothing that counts," I answered. Lies piling up. "Ben, your binoculars okay. I was able to keep them dry."

"Where's your other clothes?" she asked.

I told her, and she headed for the utility room.

"I'll wash them," she said.

"Just need to dry," I said, following her.

She ignored me, shook them out, and dumped them into the old Maytag Ben kept running by salvaging parts whenever it needed fixing. She shook on soap powder and flipped the switch, causing water to swish noisily into the tub. The machine began to wobble slightly.

"You come with me," she said, and I trailed her to the bathroom. She stood close to dab iodine on my ear. She was so soft with the applicator I hardly felt the sting. What I felt was more guilt.

"What'd you expect to find at Aunt Jessie's?" Blackie asked, eyeing me.

"I don't know. Thought I ought to try something instead of just waiting around. Scouted her place through the woods."

She studied me a moment before she turned away, set the iodine back on the shelf, and walked to the kitchen. Ben had gone out to his shed. Blackie carried both pails of beans to the front porch, where she sat on the swing to snap them. I sat beside her to help and began to feel safe.

"I keep thinking of Esmeralda," Blackie said.

"She gets to you."

"Those eyes of hers, all the fear and misery in them."

When we finished, she carried the snaps to the kitchen to wash and soak them in the sink. I walked around the house and found Ben feeding his chickens. He favored Rhode Island Reds but had a few Dominickers. He tossed out handfuls of scratch from a lard can, and the chickens came running and cackling for it. I'd been thinking about the page torn from Aunt Jessie's photo album.

"You ever hear the name Violette Slaughter?" I asked.

"Nope," he said, laid the lard can back in the bin where he kept his feed, and closed the lid. He'd tacked wire mesh around it to keep out rats. "Why?"

"A name I came across."

"Nobody 'round here I know of," he said and patted Rattler, who geared his tail into motion at full throttle.

"You ever wonder what it'd be like to be a chicken and know you got a date with the chopping block?" I asked.

"You think chickens know that?"

"Sure. They just hoping the ax happens to somebody else first."

"Well, at least they got odds," Ben said.

That night before bed I showered and checked my back in the bathroom mirror. The scratches had scabbed up. I might be in trouble if they became infected. The bitch Jeannie Bruce had meant to put her mark on me, not giving a damn what I had to contend with, yet I kept seeing and thinking about her. As I lay in the bed, her features took shape in the restless darkness behind my shut eyes.

First thing in the morning I drove to Peck's Store and called Huntington State for another report on Esmeralda. I was able to get through to Dr. Fredrick after a wait of only eight minutes by the ticking of Mr. Henry Peck's slowly swinging pendulum clock, the glass panel front of which advertised Black Draught tonic. I could just hear the doctor over the phone, and it wasn't the connection. He sounded like a man who had finished a long run.

"We're cutting her medication altogether because she's eating more and drinking her juice, though she does both quickly and turns to the wall hunched over, eyes closed. Still, I am allowing myself a further modicum of hope."

"Of what?"

"That at the very least we are on the road to a partial recovery. We're still working at eliciting a verbal response from her. I've ordered all who come in contact with her to make it a practice of speaking at every opportunity. We see indications she's listening. There's nothing wrong with her hearing that we can discern. We checked her ears, and she responds to noises that surprise her. When one day she might acknowledge us, we can then begin the task of diminishing the terror that lives in her eyes."

I thanked him. Mr. Henry Peck had been listening. I'd purposely not used Esmeralda's name in front of him. Might as well put it on the radio.

"Like to have the money you spend on phone calls," he said. "Be a rich man today."

"What would you do with the money?"

"Go to Hawaii. Always wanted to see some hula dancers. Now, that would be a sight, those hips a-swinging under them grass skirts. Like they got oiled ball bearings in their female joints."

I started out but turned back.

"Mr. Henry, you been around Shawnee County a long time."

"All the many years of my sorry life on this poor old earth."

"You ever hear the name Violette Slaughter?"

He shifted the unlit King Edward in his mouth, took time to run the question through his mind, and shook his head.

"Seems I have but can't connect it to no face. My mind's done rusted up on me. It'll happen to you one day if you last long enough."

I again wondered about Aunt Jessie's Bible, what the police were doing with it and the handwritten will supposedly kept inside. That thought brought to my mind Bartholomew Asberry, the jackleg miner and preacher at the Mt. Olivet Church. If that photo of Violette Slaughter had been snapped at Mt. Olivet, he ought to be able to remember something about her.

As I drove the eleven miles toward the desolation of Rich Find with its abandoned store in the clutches of poison ivy and kudzu, a car honked and whizzed curving past the Caddy. Jeannie Bruce sat behind the wheel of her black Mercedes convertible. She raised a hand, and I saw the flash of her teeth. A red band kept her hair from flying loose. Likely she was headed toward the Greenbrier for another day of high-class golfing and maybe something more.

I stopped at Ordinary's cinderblock grocery store to buy more Moon Pies and sodas before turning up toward Bartholomew's two-man coal diggings. After I splashed across the creek, bounced along the dirt road, and parked beside the front-end loader, neither Bartholomew nor Tolliver appeared to be anywhere around, but the old Dodge truck waited under the loading ramp. As I had last time here, I left the Caddy to walk over to the portal and to listen. I heard a faint hum along the rails, meaning the brothers were back somewhere under the mountain. I carried the cooler and Moon Pies over to set beside the beat-up glider, again waited on the seat of the backhoe, and smoked until I heard the motor and mine buggy clanking from the portal. Its jolting headlights emerged from darkness.

As if they had springs on their backs, both men sat up soon as sun-shine struck their faces. Bartholomew powered them up the ramp, where he braked to dump the load into the Dodge. When he saw me, he cut off the motor to climb down the ladder to the ground. Tolliver followed, and they pulled off their helmets. Each had soiled leather pads strapped around his knees.

"Well, I see you come back," Bartholomew said, lumbering toward me. He swiped at his face with a dirty bandanna. His heavy, square-built body had confirmed itself to hard labor. If he were a horse, it would be a Percheron.

"Help yourself to a cold one," I said, indicating the cooler.

"Tolliver, you figure a man being so nice to us might want something or maybe taken us to raise?" he asked.

Tolliver managed a grunt. His long tangled hair was black on the ends but lightened where his helmet had protected it. When I opened the cooler, they reached in for the Big Oranges. Each used his teeth to open the bottle and spat out the cap. Both stunk of sweat and coal. They could probably never rid themselves of coal's smell so much had been inhaled and ground into their bodies over the years, and maybe to their nostrils the odor became transformed to the sweet scent of money.

"So you planning to tell me what it is you want or is we wasting time talking about the weather, crops, and price of a load?" Bartholomew went on.

"I'm hoping you can help me by remembering a young girl that might've lived in Shawnee County some years ago. I saw her picture in Aunt Jessie's photo album. The girl was standing on the steps of what looked to me like Mt. Olivet Church."

"She got a name?"

"Violette Slaughter."

A beat of time while Bartholomew drank from and finished the Big Orange. He wiped his mouth with the back of his hand and turned to Tolliver, whose jaw had stilled.

"We able to tell him anything about a girl named Violette?"

Tolliver shook his head just once and reached for a Moon Pie. He tore off the wrapper and tossed it to the ground.

"Well, there you are," Bartholomew said as he turned away to the cooler.

"Funny you wouldn't know or heard about her, you being so close to Aunt Jessie and the church," I said.

"What's funny about it?" Bartholomew asked, again facing me.

"I figured you'd know about everybody that ever went to Mt. Olivet."

"Ever's a long time, and figuring don't always work out," he said and bent over for a Moon Pie.

This time Tolliver nodded before tipping his Big Orange bottle up for a deep gurgling swallow.

"Help yourself to another," I said to him.

"Reckon I was planning on it," he answered, and did.

"You been a member of that church all your life, haven't you?" I asked Bartholomew. "Seems you ought to recollect."

He stopped chewing and scowled at me.

"Mister, you accusing me of lying?"

His china-blue eyes appeared too clean and lustrous to be set in such a filthy face.

"No, sir, I'm not. I know you're a good man and don't think you'd ever lie, but you kind of slid around my question about Violette Slaughter."

"No law says I got to answer you anything."

"That's right, you don't."

His eyes broke contact, and he hocked up to spit on the ground. The hock had coal dust and Big Orange mixed in it.

"Why you need to know for?" he asked.

"To help Esmeralda. I don't believe she had anything to do with what happened to Aunt Jessie Arbuckle."

He studied me, took another swig of soda, and dragged a wrist across his mouth.

"I don't neither," he said. He hesitated. "What you think, Tolliver?"

Tolliver shrugged, using only one shoulder.

"You ever heard of Red Eye?" Bartholomew asked me.

"Don't get your meaning," I said. "You talking about liquor?"

"Gone now. Never was on the map or had a post office. Just what people around here called it. Up on the mountain, a big old frame house that used to be lived in by a horse doctor. When he died, his widow stayed 'ere a couple more years before she passed on. The house put up for sale but nobody bought it. Then it was empty a long spell before a woman named Juanita moved in and fixed it up some. She hadn't bought it neither. Just a squatter till she made her money. She had ladies with her, three of them, two white, one black. They prettied the house with paint, puttied glass in the broken window-panes, hung curtains. Set it up to do business. Lonesome men could go up 'ere, buy a drink, get more than liquor. The white girls had the upstairs bedrooms. The black girl the basement. They kept a red light burning on the porch even during daylight."

Bartholomew stopped talking. He looked toward the mountain, where billowing cumulus clouds sliding over seemed barely to escape collisions with the rocky ridge. He again spat, and the blob raised dust at his feet.

"Juanita had borned her a little girl," he said. "We wouldn't've known 'cept a truant officer seen her and brought the girl to school. She was ten or eleven best as I remember."

He again stopped talking. Tolliver let down to the glider and sat chewing, his body tilted to adjust for the slant.

"Some larger boys at the school got to know her," Bartholomew said.

I waited for more. It didn't come.

"Know her?" I asked.

"In the Bible meaning of that word," he said. "She'd go out in the woods behind the school or at the house. They had to give her something—a nickel, a bar of candy, a pretty marble, gum, a dime-store bracelet. She was selling herself. Just like her mama, she was selling that skinny little body."

"Lord God," Tolliver said.

"Terriblest thing for a child to do," Bartholomew said. "Don't even like to think of it for the pictures it calls to my mind. The school principal learned about it and went to the sheriff, and the sheriff drove out there with a woman from the Health Department. Back then Shawnee County and the mines was still going pretty good, and we had us a full-time nurse and the doctor at High Moor. The sheriff and the nurse took the child. Juanita Slaughter didn't even put up much of a fuss. She was glad to get shut of Violette."

"Violette Slaughter," I said.

"That was her name. We paid a full-time preacher at Mt. Olivet those days, his name Abraham Sharp. He had a voice that could raise fire and brimstone and spin the dead in their graves. People sat shaking in the pews, and children cried, but he was a good man and didn't want that pitiful little girl to go to the state orphanage. They arrested her mother, she paid the fine, and was turned loose to go the devil knows where. She didn't even ask about the child. Preacher Sharp thought Mt. Olivet should take Violette in, feed, clothe, and raise her. Save her for the Lord. We voted to share her amongst members of the congregation. Bring her up like she was one of us."

In the distance we heard shots. A light rifle, .22 caliber. Neither Bartholomew nor Tolliver showed interest. I shifted around to look in the direction of the shooting.

"Boys squirrel hunting," Bartholomew said. "Their mama'll make them a stew tonight."

"This hunting season?"

"Around here hunting season's whenever you got a gun in your hand and you can pull down its sight on your dinner."

"You ever hear of a twenty-two with a steel-tipped bullet?" I asked.

"No, sir, not in these parts."

"Then your congregation at Mt. Olivet took Violette to raise," I said.

"We did. Me and my wife kept Violette awhile. The girl didn't much take to us. Always sneaking looks at you like she was up to something.

Never asked about her natural mother. We couldn't trust her not to slip away to see the boys. They'd whistle or make bird noises to her from the woods. It looked like we was going to have to give her up to the state people, but Aunt Jessie'd have none of that. Claimed it was our duty to keep on trying."

"Aunt Jessie took her?"

"She did, and could handle her better than most. Taught Violette to plant a garden and sew. They read the Good Book together. Looked like the child might be going to be all right. She could sing the hymns pretty. She was smart and recited the catechism quicker than other children her age. Aunt Jessie taught her to respect her elders. Violette learned to cook and play the church piano. Then one night she slipped out a window to run off. Aunt Jessie didn't know nothing about it till morning. Violette had stole her egg money. Wasn't anything to do but tell the sheriff. The police found Violette hitchhiking alongside the road in Logan County. They took her to the orphanage. Aunt Jessie wanted her back, but the judge said no. The orphanage held Violette awhile and she run off again. They think she snuck out to some boy who gave her a ride in his pickup. That was the end of it as far as we ever knew. Nobody never found her."

Bartholomew shifted his body and stood, meaning he was ready to get back to work.

"Aunt Jessie good to her?" I asked.

"Aunt Jessie been good to ever'body," he said and turned to amble toward the ladder up the ramp. Tolliver fell in behind him.

I thanked and watched them climb, reset their helmets, and lie on their backs to sweep rumbling from the full warm sunlight into the portal's swallowing blackness.

TWENTY-FIVE

Riding away, I again thought about that supposedly steel .22-caliber bullet. The effort might be wasted, but I could again try to get something from Sheriff Bruce Sawyers over in Seneca County. I called not from Peck's Store, where I'd be overheard, but a third time used the phone booth in front of Cliffside's post office. A postal employee stood on a ladder to install a new American flag over the doorway. I watched him struggle with the handle's fitting until Sawyers himself answered the call.

"Mr. LeBlanc, I don't mean to sound inhospitable, but I been wishing I wouldn't hear from you again."

"I not been wanting to bother you either, Sheriff. Just hoped you could tell me something more about the bullet or whatever it was found by Bernard Duiguid in Aunt Jessie's skull."

"The State Police are still examining it at the crime lab in Charleston."

"I thought by now maybe you had some idea of what to make of such an offbeat kind of ammo."

"My answer is that what the lab makes of it is not public knowledge at this time."

"I understand that, but what I'm asking you for is to give me your unofficial opinion of what they likely to find."

"It's not in my purview to give unofficial opinions."

Purview, I thought, not a word you'd expect from a rural West Virginia sheriff. But then he'd been hanging around politicians and had ambition to become one himself. He was learning their lingo.

"Sheriff, how about taking a guess?"

"You bound and determined to put your foot in the middle of this cow pie, are you?"

"I don't see how you playing a hunch could hurt anybody. I promise anything I hear from you will be kept under an airtight lid."

"Hold on, I got another call," he said.

I stood waiting. People going to and from the post office glanced at me. I again had the sense that the citizens of Cliffside had survived from another period of time. Their clothes, habits, and manner of life seemed twenty or thirty years behind the rest of the country. That had to be good.

"All right, I'm back," Sawyers said.

"A steel bullet don't make sense," I said. "Unless it's tied to some kind of weird bunch of self-loaders, and why would they go to such trouble? They'd had to machine-tool it. And what kind of game would you use it on?"

"Mr. LeBlanc, if Walter Frampton hadn't called this office on your behalf, I'd not be talking to you but off the phone. Now I'm going to give you some information you've no right to know. Walter Frampton believes you can be trusted. I expect you to honor his confidence and mine by protecting your source."

"I guarantee it."

"The guarantees I've heard in this office. If they were dollars, I'd have myself a yacht. All right. First thing, it's not a bullet but hollow inside and might be a fitting of some sort. Bernard Duiguid believed it to be solid because it was filled with bone and brain matter, which gave it body and heft."

"What's the second thing?"

"It's not steel but silver. Last thing is, it's not a projectile of any sort and has definitely never been fired from a gun."

"What you telling me?"

"No barrel markings. Forensics first believed it was an industrial alloy until they cleaned and tested it. Silver. One theory is it was attached to the end of whatever weapon or device struck Aunt Jessie Arbuckle and that the blow could have caused the fitting to dislodge inside her skull."

"Weapon or device means what?"

"No conclusions yet. The lab men continue to test and search."

"You're telling me Aunt Jessie was killed by a silver fitting?"

"I didn't say that."

"What did you say?"

"Mr. LeBlanc, you're testing my patience."

"You can't leave me hanging after taking me this far."

"I can, but won't. The state pathologist doesn't believe the skull puncture killed Aunt Jessie. It didn't go deep enough to her brainpan. The thinking first was the blow caused her shock followed by heart arrest and a fall against her hearth."

"First was?"

"The pathologist has concluded she was strangled."

"Wait a minute now. How could they have missed that earlier?"

"She was an old lady, her skin wrinkled and rough as rawhide, particularly on her neck, where bruises at the first examination by the coroner were not apparent and overlooked. A lab incision revealed a crushed larynx."

"Esmeralda's supposed to have choked her?"

"Possibly hit her first and then killed her."

"And hit her with what?"

"I told you that's an unknown."

"Why would Esmeralda kill a woman who'd done nothing but help and treat her with kindness?"

"That's the missing piece that can't be known until it comes from Esmeralda's mouth alone, if ever."

"But what you make of it?" I asked. I heard indecipherable voices from his police radio and then a ten-four.

"I don't make anything of it. This not my investigation. It shouldn't be yours. Mr. LeBlanc, I've given you more than you have any right to know. Don't phone me again. I'm not answering further questions from you."

He hung up on me. I stood a moment before stepping from the booth. No use calling back. No way either that Esmeralda could have strangled Aunt Jessie. That was crazy thinking. Had to be another answer. Or did there? Who really knew what Esmeralda's mind was like after all these years of wandering and loneliness? Maybe something had happened in the cabin that'd pushed her over the edge. No, I couldn't accept that.

I left the phone booth. A scrim of clouds now overlay the sun, diluting its light and warmth. A voice called my name. Angus St. George had walked from the post office holding a package. His wavy blond hair bounced with each step, and in his tennis whites he appeared as out of place on Cliffside's drab street as a newly minted silver dollar among a handful of petty change.

"When you coming to Wild Thorn and ride again?" he asked. "I'm having the workers cut a new trail you and Mildred might enjoy. It'll wind us down to the river."

"Maybe one day," I said, thinking, Yeah, not doing it himself but having the workers do it. Doubtful he'd ever lifted an ax or chain saw.

"We heard you've been to Huntington trying to help Esmeralda. Glad somebody is."

"Where'd you hear it?"

"This morning from Jeannie Bruce. The police shouldn't charge Esmeralda. She's definitely non compos mentis and better off at a state facility. It's where she's belonged all these years, for her own good."

"Hard to tell what somebody else's own good is," I said as two young women walking to the post office eyed him. They whispered to each other.

"I believe it's obvious in Esmeralda's case," he said.

"How's your leg?" I asked.

"Leg?"

"A salad fork can be a dangerous weapon."

He turned abruptly and walked to a Land Rover parked at the curb. When he drove away, his lips were moving, and he shot me a nasty look. Tenderhearted, Jeannie Bruce had called him. Meaning not capable of hitting an old lady in the head and strangling her?

"I'd drop my drawers for him in a second," I heard one of the young women say leaving the post office. They giggled until they caught me watching, then became correctly ladylike as they walked on across the street toward the courthouse.

I stopped by Peck's Store. The old man was again counting his money and pressing his palm against the bills to flatten them before he bound them in packs with rubber bands. I'd been hoping to hear from Walt and asked about calls.

"Mr. Frampton, same number," Mr. Henry said.

By now I knew the number well. I had to wait to use the phone until a farmer finished. He'd called the market to find out the sell price for feeder calves.

"Mr. Walter B. Frampton's law office," a voice said. It sounded childish and had to be Walt's stepson Jason. My guess his mother Mary Ellen was either training or entertaining him. I told him I wanted to speak with Mr. Frampton. The kid asked me who was calling. I gave my name. Walt came to the phone.

"I've managed to schedule a meeting with Edward," he said. "So you had to go and attempt to intimidate him. I explained I had no part in that. That was a dumb thing to do, Charles."

"He wants that award and will cave on the money," I said.

"I don't like him thinking I advised or had any part in your threatening him."

"Okay, so?"

"I'll meet with him to see if some modicum of damage repair is possible, nothing more."

"You're my main man, Walt."

"Don't try to mollify me."

"I'm not the mollifying type, Walt."

"That's for damn sure. Now let's see here. I'm checking my notes. You asked about a portrait of Robert the Bruce. I talked to an expert at the Virginia Museum who told me no oil portraits of the Scottish king were painted during his own time, which is 1274 to 1329. There are various representations including lithographs as well as busts and other sculpture from the sixteenth, seventeenth, and eighteenth centuries, but I repeat, nothing in oil during his life. Does that answer your question?"

"It does."

"All right, Charles, try to stay out of trouble, will you?"

"I will if it stays out of me," I said.

I drove to Ben's thinking about Jeannie Bruce's portrait of the king turning out to be a fake. The question was did she know it or had she been tricked and cheated? Nah, she was too smart for that.

Blackie and Ben weren't at the house. I drank a glass of tea and swung on the porch swing. Thoughts of Esmeralda, the theft of Violette Slaughter's photograph, the faked portrait, and the silver fitting lodged in Aunt Jessie's brainpan filtered through my mind.

I heard Blackie and Ben in the kitchen. They'd been up on the mountain searching for ramps and returned with sacks full of the wild leeks they'd dug up.

"Make us a sausage casserole using them," Ben said. "Might stink up the place, but some stinks are good."

I laid my hand on Blackie's shoulder as she stood at the sink washing ramps under the faucet. I felt the need to hold her. She slid the shoulder out from beneath my fingers. I stood waiting.

"Something?" I asked.

"I'm busy," she said.

So there was something. I again touched her, this time her waist. She stepped away and looked at me, her face taut, her dark eye wide and angry, then turned back to the sink.

I waited for a chance to get her alone. When she walked to her bedroom, I followed and circled my arms around her.

"Just get on away from me," she said and twisted loose.

"What is it?"

"You think I wouldn't smell that bitch's perfume on you when you came back from Aunt Jessie's cabin yesterday?" she asked.

"Blackie, give me a chance to explain."

"You had your chance and plenty of time to do that. I been waiting. You didn't mean ever to open your damn mouth to me about your slutting. Now get out of here before I shoot you."

She shoved me from the room and slammed the door.

TWENTY-SIX

That evening I bad felt the need to go to my bottle of Old Crow in the Caddy's trunk but had enough sense left to know it was no time to take up with whiskey. I set the table, Blackie served the meal, and Ben glanced at the two of us as if wondering why nobody was much talking. While I cleaned the dishes, Blackie walked to her room and closed the door.

"Thought I felt a cold draft run through here," Ben said. He sat at the table and looked at me over the edge of the book he'd been reading. It was Eisenhower's *The Great Crusade*.

"Weather change coming," I said and left him alone. I undressed, settled on the bed, and would've kicked my own ass if possible. To have fuckedupped at this time with Blackie alongside everything else that had happened. I lay through the night hearing the throbbing insects gradually quiet to a rhythmic purr—the way I liked it, no sounds from man, no cars or trucks on the road, no planes, no train whistle or banging hopper cars. This, I thought, was how it'd been for the first men who pioneered the Alleghenies, the Daniel Boones who felt crowded at the sight of another man's chimney, and how it should've been for me except Blackie had become part of my life, not something I was able to abandon or lop off any more than I could take a knife and carve out my own heart.

I rolled from the bed before dawn, made the coffee, and carried a mug out to Laurel Creek to smoke a Camel. I listened to the sibilance caused by the flow of water over and around the course of rocks. A hawk cried on Bear Mountain, a shrill piercing screech that quieted the finches, jays, and doves that had been tuning up. The mist drifting over the glen left the pasture and apple trees of the orchard wet and dripping.

When I walked back to the kitchen, Ben had finished mixing a batch of buckwheat pancakes and offered me a stack. I shook my head. He looked toward Blackie's room.

"Troubles?" he asked.

"Appears so."

"Make it up," he said. "You got yourself a fine woman there."

He rinsed and left his plate in the sink before going out to see about his cow and to feed Rattler and the chickens. I sat and waited. When Blackie came in, she didn't look at me. I offered to fix and serve her pancakes along with bacon and eggs. She acted as if she didn't hear, poured herself a mug of coffee, and went out to talk to Ben. I didn't realize she was leaving till I heard the Caddy start up. She drove off under the mist hanging low above the road. No, I thought, and hurried to her room. She hadn't taken her suitcase or clothes bag. I felt shaky but could again breathe.

I found Ben in the garden, where he stooped cutting collards. I knelt facing him to help. Without rising, he moved sideways along the row and collected salad in a plastic sack that had Dollar General's name on it.

"So she's gone?" he said.

"Not for good or she would've packed her stuff."

"You better hope."

"I do, and she'd never leave for good without telling you good-bye."

When he stood to go to the house, I used his hoe to chop at the few weeds I could find. I kept looking toward the road. My thoughts jumbled up. I couldn't wait but had to go try and find her. I asked Ben to let me use his truck. I meant to drive to Cliffside, seek her out, and make her look at and listen to me apologize.

Without comment, Ben tossed me the keys to the 1988 Chevy that he'd kept so clean you could have licked soup off the floor. I left and first stopped by Peck's Store to see whether Blackie had been there.

"She ain't been in but you got a letter," Mr. Henry Peck said. He slipped from his stool to limp slowly from the cash register to the pigeonholes of his post office. He laid on the counter a pale blue stamped envelope that I recognized and had my name on it in her cursive feminine handwriting. I scented Jeannie Bruce's perfume before I opened it. Unfolded, the letter had only one word on it:

Scaredy-cat!

"Smells nice, don't it?" Mr. Henry Peck asked as he sat watching from his stool.

I nodded and walked out. I had to stop this thing with Jeannie Bruce and make her know it. In Cliffside, I drove up and down streets slow to look for Blackie and the Caddy but couldn't locate them. I rolled on south toward Wild Thorn. The sun found gaps through clouds white on the top, dark at the bottom, and its light scythed the forest and mountainside.

I passed trucks traveling to and from Wild Thorn. The gatepost lights hadn't been switched off. I parked in the courtyard among the construction crews' trucks and gear. When I used the brass lion's head to knock at the door, Pepe answered it. He held a silver bowl he'd been polishing. I asked for Mrs. St. George as I heard faint notes of Duncan's oboe d'amore sound from the mansion's upstairs.

"She at the stable," Pepe said and blew his breath on the bowl before wiping it with a white cotton cloth.

I walked around the house, through the flower garden, and out the wall's back gate. Swans gathered around the shore dipped their heads beneath the water, spreading ripples. A flight of pigeons swooped toward the stable and circled the louvered spire and vane. Toby, the groom, walked from the throughway to the open door of the two-and-a-half-ton Ford truck, its engine running.

"Miss Jeannie and Mr. Angus riding and ought to be back 'fore long," he said. "I got to get myself to town for a load of sweet feed and fifty bales of alfalfa hay."

I watched him drive away before looking into the stable. Both the chestnut and bay were missing from their stalls. The gray stopped munching hay to watch me. Ceiling fans spun to create a cooling downdraft. A golf cart had been parked beyond the tack room. The paddock was empty.

From the grain bin I scooped up oats and fed a handful each to the gray and four other horses. When I heard dogs barking, I crossed back through the stable entrance. Swans hissed and flapped their wings frantically as they retreated to the center of the lake. The dogs ran baying around the water's edge. One had caught a bird he dragged off. Its wings beat at him while the others tried to seize it. From the house came a rifle shot. The pack scattered into the woods, the leader still gripping the swan in his mouth, a wing now dragging the ground. Whoever used the gun had missed.

A single swan lifted hooting off the water. I watched it climb to the mountain's ridge and become a white speck that faded into a clearing blue sky. It couldn't have been pinioned like the others but must've been a wayward tundra drawn in by the majestic mutes to feed on grain the St. Georges left out for them.

I sat on the tack-room steps to wait. I wouldn't smoke in a stable. When the gray nickered and another horse answered from a distance, I shaded my eyes to look out along the trail that led beneath overhanging spruce pines. Jeannie Bruce and Angus approached holding their mounts with loose reins toward the stable. Each was helmeted and carried a hunt whip. Angus reached across from the chestnut to

Jeannie Bruce's hand. What the hell was that about? Her bay had a gimp in its near foreleg.

"Toby," Angus called.

They hadn't seen me in the shadowed throughway, and I backed off and climbed the three steps to the tack room. As the horses entered the stable, their shod hooves clanged on concrete. I watched Jeannie Bruce and Angus dismount, snap cross ties on their horses, and loosen their saddle girths. I edged into the feed storage recess and stood behind the door. They carried up their saddles, pads, bridles, and whips to the tack room. Angus switched on the ceiling light. When they left to attend the horses, I knelt to ventilation slats at the base of the exterior wall to see Jeannie Bruce stoop and squeeze the bay's ankle to lift the hoof.

"Maybe a stone bruise," she said. "We shouldn't put them away hot."

"Us either," Angus said and laughed.

"Let's hose and turn them into the paddock to cool," she said. "Toby can rub them down when he comes back. Where is he when you need him?"

Angus held the horses while Jeannie Bruce did the hosing. The horses lifted their mouths to drink from the nozzle. They closed their eyes and shook their heads as water splashed over their faces. Jeannie Bruce stroked their flanks with a sweat scrapper.

"Our tack ought to be soaped," she said.

"I'll see that trifling darky does it," Angus said.

He led the horses to the far end of the haulway and the paddock while Jeannie Bruce removed her helmet and shook out her hair. I thought I ought to step out and show myself, yet no way could I explain what I'd been doing in feed storage all this time. When Angus came back, Jeannie Bruce started off, but Angus reached for her wrist, drew her to him, and kissed her. She responded willingly, and they shoved it at each other.

"Not now, darling," she said and blew into his ear.

"I need the hose on me," he said. "Nothing like a morning ride to get the blood up."

"It'll keep till tonight," she said, laughed, and pushed away. They moved beyond range of my sight. I heard the whir of the golf cart starting. Jeannie Bruce sat behind the wheel. She stopped it for Angus to sit beside her. He cocked a booted foot to the dashboard, and they sped from the stable and up the hill toward the mansion.

I gave them time to be gone before I crossed into the tack room. So Jeannie Bruce was screwing her stepson and everything else that moved. They had left the ceiling light switched on. I looked over the English saddles they'd set on the cleaning stand. Their helmets and coiled whips hung from the wall—the heavy, thickly braided lash that Angus carried to scare off wild dogs, the more ladylike model that belonged to Jeannie Bruce.

I started away, stopped, crossed back to the whips. The staghorn handles had been made not only for gripping but also to hook over gates while mounted to hold them open or pull them closed. I leaned closer. Both whips had tarnished silver bands around their shanks. Angus's was also fitted with a silver cap at the grip's curved tip. I lifted the whip to finger the cap. It was bullet-shaped, though larger than a .22 caliber. I set the whip back and reached to Jeannie Bruce's smaller and lighter one. No cap. I held the grip close to my eyes under the ceiling bulb and made out a quarter-inch discoloration at the tip. Caused by what—a fitting that had once decorated it and become dislodged? Jesus, what was I thinking?

I rehung the whip and walked to the end of the stable to look up the slope. The golf cart had turned into the wall entrance. I tried to order my mind. It was crazy to believe Jeannie Bruce might've struck Aunt Jessie with a whip and strangled her. Why would she? Because Aunt Jessie wouldn't sell or lease land to Wild Thorn? No, that didn't wash and wasn't enough reason for murdering anybody. Could be there had never been a cap on Jeannie Bruce's whip, or if so, it'd been lost some other time or place. The grip's discoloration might be natural or caused by routine abrasions from the normal wear and tear of use. I had to be forcing proof.

The wall phone in the tack room had a vertical row of ivory punch buttons at its base. One had been designated House #2. I waited to allow Jeannie Bruce time to get settled inside the mansion before I pressed my thumb against the extension. After two rings, the Latina answered. When I asked for Mrs. St. George, I identified myself and waited.

"I got your note," I said when Jeannie Bruce answered.

"Where are you?"

"Not far. I'd like to stop by."

"Ummm," she said, her laugh throaty. "Whatever for?"

"We'll find something to talk about."

"Surely, but I've been riding and need a shower. I'll be looking for you."

As I continued to wait, I again examined Jeannie Bruce's whip. I held the shank as I would a hammer and rapped the grip against the tack room's wall. When I coiled the lash before setting the whip back, I heard the wild dogs barking in the woods beyond the stable. One had a wavering cry like a foxhound gone away. My guess was the pack had finished the swan and ran scouting for another meal— maybe the big-eared fawn seen by the lake the night Blackie and I ate dinner at the mansion.

I hiked up the slope to the house. At the front I met Angus leaving and crossing the courtyard toward his Land Rover. He carried a couple of tennis rackets. When he saw me, he hesitated, tossed a lank of blond hair off his tanned brow, and hurried on without speaking. He drove away fast. And he had a date that night with Jeannie Bruce.

Pepe let me in the house. I glanced at the illuminated portrait of Robert the Bruce in its climate-controlled glass repository. Why would Jeannie Bruce fake her aristocratic lineage unless she felt the need to prove its authenticity? Pepe showed me into the library. He switched on lamps and left me. I touched the ladder that moved on rails before the shelves of books. It gave easily to my fingers. The room had an amber ambience spread from the shelves' leather-backed tomes. They gave off the manly scent of their covers. Gold lettering embossed titles and authors' names.

Sunshine from a mullioned window shone on the polished brass knobs of the card-catalog cabinets. I opened the door to look into the adjoining room, which held the billiard table, hunting prints, and sporting guns. Books and guns, I thought, unusual neighbors. When I pushed the door to, I heard mournful tones of the oboe d'amore.

Jeannie Bruce slipped in from the hallway so quietly I didn't hear her footsteps. She'd tied the tails of her white sleeveless shirt in a knot at her navel rather than tuck them into her khaki skirt. Her belly skin had a satin gleam. Thongs of leather sandals separated her toes with their scarlet nails. She pushed the door closed, approached me sweet and freshened from her shower, and kissed my mouth. When she drew away and looked at me from those feline green eyes, even now I wanted her.

"It's okay," she said. "Angus is gone, and Duncan's got his blessed oboe to keep him company. So wrap your arms around me."

"I don't think that'd be such a good idea."

"You afraid of me?" she asked and touched my cheeks with long cool fingers of both hands. "I like that."

"Why?"

"It gives me a certain control over events."

"You need control?"

"It's one more spice to enliven a drab life here in the wilderness."

"What about the people you hurt?"

"What people—you?"

"Not me. And I'm not afraid of you but myself."

"Lover, what in the world are you talking about?"

She stepped back to gaze at me. I couldn't shake the thought of a missing silver cap from her whip. Maybe it would be forcing proof but worth finding out for sure by attempting a bluff spoken with certainty.

"Why'd you hit that fine old lady in her head?"

It startled her. She blinked her long upswept lashes, and her lips opened and closed without forming words. She joined her hands, and the fingers clenched.

"Charley, what has gotten into you?" she asked and laughed.

"I keep asking myself what Aunt Jessie could have done to make you that desperate?"

"Wait a minute. Let's get this straight. You're really accusing me of attacking Aunt Jessie?"

"Appears that way."

"And killing her?"

"Yeah, I guess I am."

"Just get out of this house," she said and backed off a step. "I mean this goddamn instant."

"I can go to the law with what I know." What the hell did I know? "I'm giving you a chance to explain."

"I don't have to explain anything to trash like you."

"Your call," I said and moved toward the hallway door.

"Wait, you sonofabitch," she said, crossed to me, and knocked my hand away from the brass knob. Her face had drawn tight over her cheekbones. "Why are you doing this to me?"

Christ, this fucking bait was working. I moved toward and stared hard and mean at her.

"What Aunt Jessie did must've been some kind of bad to make you hit her with your whip," I said.

"I don't know what you're talking about and you can never prove that I hit anybody," she said and managed to call up half a smirk. "Why did we ever let filth like you in this house?"

"I figure it's because you wanted a piece of my dick."

She walked to me and tried to smack my face. I'd already noted she was right-handed. I caught not her wrist but the hand and squeezed it hard. I felt the rings she wore and the collapse of her fingers. She dipped away in pain until I released her. She held to and rubbed the hand, those green eyes watching me with the intensity of a cat about to pounce.

"What rock did you climb out from under?" she asked as she stroked her long scarlet-tipped fingers.

"You did hit her. The whip proves that. The grip's silver fitting they found in Aunt Jessie's skull. They don't know yet what it is. I could tell them. Maybe I should've already, but I'm giving you a chance to tell me why."

"What did I ever see in a piece of shit like you?" she asked, not in the refined style of cultured people who believed profanity chic, but down and dirty, those full lips gathered and twisting as if about to spit.

"Okay," I said and again reached for the knob.

She moved fast to intercept me and pressed her back against the door.

"And what will you do if I tell you that?" she asked.

"I don't know yet."

"You won't go to the police?"

"I don't have any great love for the police."

"A convicted felon, who'd believe you anyway?"

"Maybe not me, but they'll believe the evidence when they see that silver cap fits your whip."

"There are thousands of whips with that fitting."

"Agreed."

"Or somebody else could've used mine that day."

"Who else? You the only lady around here that rides."

She bit at her lower lip, and I raised a hand, ready to duck, because I believed she meant to swing at me again.

"You have a wire on you?" she asked.

"So you familiar with wires?"

"Like I'd believe you," she said and stepped to me to pat me down along my chest, back, arms, and legs. She knew the procedure. I stood quietly and let her finish.

"You slimy bastard," she said, rising and pulling at her blouse so that it tightened over her tits.

"Let's get you started," I said. "You were trying to buy the land for the ski run and Aunt Jessie wouldn't sell or lease."

"She was country stubborn. Stuck out her jaw, shook her head, and refused to discuss it. I offered her more money than she'd ever seen in her life. She didn't listen. Just kept smiling, gumming her snuff, and going about baking bread. She acted as if she didn't hear me."

"That's enough reason to use the whip?"

"I saw our plan for an Olympic-class ski run ruined. This whole development of Wild Thorn was my idea, not Duncan's. He would've been content to sit in our Baltimore house and plot his financial coups the rest of his life. I'd been begging Aunt Jessie, pleading with her. For an instant I lost control. She was like a deaf-and-dumb wooden post. A dozen times I tried to make her see it was the best thing for her, Mt. Olivet, and Shawnee County. I didn't mean to strike her hard. Certainly not with the pointed tip of the grip. I was just so goddamned frustrated trying to get her attention. I hit her, yes, harder maybe than I intended, but not to hurt her. If she'd just listened. Even afterwards she seemed all right, sat down in her chair, kept smiling. There was no blood. She didn't appear hurt. I was deeply sorry and sincerely apologized. When I left the cabin she was still sitting in the chair smiling."

Wait a second, I thought. No blood? Leroy Spears had told it otherwise. And forensics in Charleston had found Aunt Jessie's blood on Esmeralda's dress.

"You hit her and nothing else?" I asked.

"Just once and what else? It was an involuntary reaction. I kept telling her I was sorry. I told her time and time again before I left. She said, 'It's all right, child. It's all right.'"

"Your story doesn't wash," I said. "There's got to be something more."

"Goddamn you, I'm telling the truth," she said, but the fight was ebbing from her. She again put her arms around my neck and pulled herself to me. I smelled the bittersweet perfume Blackie had picked up off my skin. "Believe that I never wanted to hurt her or anyone."

She worked her body against mine and tried to kiss me. It would've been easy to believe her. But if not her, who? A vagrant in the county? No, it was too distant from the railroad, though I'd seen the bearded man hiking along the road shoulder not too far from Persimmon Creek and Aunt Jessie's cabin. Angus? He might have a hell of a tennis game, but he didn't like to soil his hands, and I doubted he had the balls for the dirty job of killing.

Jeannie Bruce clung to me. I looked over her shoulder at books on the shelves. So many unsullied amber volumes and thousands of pages. They made me think first of Aunt Jessie's Bible, its whereabouts, and her ragged album with the yellowed photo of the sullen little girl standing on Mt. Olivet's church steps.

"Red Eye," I said, another chance shot.

"What?" she asked, and her arms loosened. She looked into my face.

"Violette Slaughter," I said.

She stopped breathing, and her hands slowly fell away. Then she squared her shoulders and inhaled as she collected herself to try to brave it out, but fear lived in her eyes. She swallowed.

"Who?" she asked.

"Violette Slaughter, the young girl who met boys in the woods and traded herself for their nickels and dimes. Violette Slaughter, reared by Mt. Olivet Church and Aunt Jessie. Violette Slaughter, who stole Aunt Jessie's money and ran away, was sent to the orphanage, and escaped again, not to be found."

"There's no Violette Slaughter," she said, the coarse tone back in her voice. "She was shucked off and by dint of brains and her hunger she became someone else."

"Meaning you," I said, thinking, Pay dirt.

"Look at me. You believe I have anything in common with that poor ignorant child? I've made my own way in this dirty world. I've had to fight for everything I got and am—and yes, I used men to do it. It is the thing I do best, my big talent. They used me, I used them. I discovered I was smart, had the brains, and fought my way up through the shit. God, the work I've done—stuffing pig guts to make sausage, a waitress, cook, hospital orderly, manicurist, beautician. But with every dollar I could hold to I took college courses, learned how to dress, speak the language, now even French, and can converse about Marcel Proust. Three husbands I married before Duncan, each a step up. I put it all together, and a turd like you comes along and threatens to take it away."

She was rallying, standing taller and squaring her shoulders. She raised her chin. She was beautiful.

"Oh sure, I've fucked," she said and nodded. She clasped her hands. "A woman uses what she has to. I gave as good as I got."

"Aunt Jessie remembered you," I said.

"I didn't believe anybody in Shawnee County or the world could remember or connect me to that hillbilly urchin. How can they see her in me? I'm not the same person. I'm educated, stylish, accomplished. One husband was a classical pianist who taught me to play his kind of music on the Steinway. He insisted I had a natural talent. I have curtsied before Queen Elizabeth. I bear no resemblance to that pitiful little girl standing on the Mt. Olivet Church steps."

"Why'd you come back to Shawnee County?"

"I never intended to until I found Duncan owned Wild Thorn. He brought me here on a visit to his list of properties. He was thinking of selling it all to a timber company. I saw what the place could become with his money. And maybe deep in me I wanted to have the satisfaction and pleasure of lording it over these sanctimonious peasants who treated me like white trash. I wanted them to make way for me when I walked down the street, to say 'yes, ma'am' to me, suck up, and kiss my ass for money."

"When you were a kid Aunt Jessie treated you bad?"

"All that Bible reading she made me do and the preaching and the praying. She never whipped me, but she believed in stupid, strict rules from another century. I had to obey them and learn endless verses. She made me stand before her and recite before I could eat my supper. If I refused, I went hungry. I was suffocating. I was dying and had to run off."

She moved away from me, her hands clasping and unclasping as she circled the ornate table so highly polished that it caught the ghost of her reflection. The leaded stained-glass lamp splayed a span of colors across her face.

"Yet Aunt Jessie recognized you," I said.

"She wasn't sure at first," Jeannie Bruce said as she walked back to me. "She was not so much suspicious as puzzled. Every time I'd go to see her, she'd watch me as if she sensed or suspected something, but I looked her straight in the eye and stared her down."

"How'd she figure it out?"

"That last day I was there and she was baking bread, I sat at her table. She slipped around behind me and lifted up my hair before I could stop her. 'Violette,' she said and hugged me. I'd fallen out of her apple tree when I was a child, hit my head on the stub of a limb, and it left a scar above my temple. "

She touched the temple but didn't finger away the hair.

"When Aunt Jessie let go and turned, I stood and hit her. I was holding the whip by its shank. Hitting her was a reflex that happened fast without thought. And she didn't fall, cry out, or anything. She just sat in her chair and smiled."

"But after she died you remembered the album she kept in her trunk and went back to the cabin for your picture. You were scared somebody might pick up on it and make a connection."

"Yes."

"And you screwed me to cover up what you were after."

"I had to have the picture but was strongly attracted to you and still am."

"Did you tell anybody what you'd done."

"Only Duncan."

"What did he do?"

"He drove the golf cart over there to check on her, came back, and told me she'd died."

"You didn't touch her again after you hit her?"

"Just her hand when I told her how sorry I felt."

"Something more happened to her."

"I didn't do anything else and couldn't believe I'd hit her hard enough to hurt her seriously. I've done lots of bad things in my life, but never killed. I hope you believe that."

Before I could answer, the door from the game room swung fully open, and Duncan stepped through. In his thin, veined hands he held one of his shotguns—the sixteen-gauge Parker Trojan we'd used shooting trap by the lake.

TWENTY-SEVEN

Duncan appeared the country squire out for gentleman sport in his buttoned green summer jacket, white silk throat scarf, and white linen cap. His narrow thumb rested on the Parker's safety, ready to slide it forward. The bony index finger of his right hand curled to the shotgun's trigger.

"Mr. LeBlanc, I'm no expert like Jeannie Bruce, Angus, and you, but I do know something about the use of firearms, which if you remember during Old West days were and still are deemed the great equalizers between men large and small. I'm fairly certain I can wing you if you try to attack me or flee."

"You heard us?" Jeannie Bruce asked and moved to his side.

"Heard enough, yes, my dear. I think it's best for you to pack a bag as quickly as possible and take a little trip."

"Where?" she asked as she glanced at me.

"The place you and I have loved so well we call Xanadu. Be sure to carry your checkbook and credit cards. And do hurry. You'll hear from me soon."

"Yes," she said, her body posture submissive now, a woman following orders. Without another look at me she turned to leave. As soon as she passed through the hallway door Duncan held for her, he shut it. He stood with a casual posture but kept the Parker steady.

"I'm unhappy it's come to this," he said as he adjusted his glasses.

"To what?" I asked. If I could get at him, he was so frail I'd take him easily.

"Well, let's seat you first, Mr. LeBlanc. Please, I insist."

With the shotgun's barrel he indicated a leather wing chair set on the Persian carpet at the center of the library. I sat while he positioned himself behind a second chair directly across from me. Smart. If I tried to rush him, I'd need to charge past or over the chair he'd use to protect himself and gain time. He rested the shotgun on the chair's back and sighed.

"The misfortune of our lives," he said. "Always dangers lurking at every turn. We never know what horrors life has prepared for us along the way."

"I could do without a philosophy lecture."

"Of course. I was, however, hopeful that none of this would come to pass."

"None of what?"

"How would it have been damaging to allow Aunt Jessie's death to play out the way it was before you interfered? It's my opinion your Esmeralda will never be prosecuted. Guilty or not, she'll remain a ward of the state, and everything could have continued as before."

"A fact of this life is you can't ever get back to before," I said and thought of Blackie.

"That's philosophy also. We shall see."

"You think your bride killed Aunt Jessie?"

"Don't you?"

"I know it wasn't Esmeralda and don't believe it was Angus or a vagrant who just happened to be in the vicinity."

"It could have been more than one vagrant. They often travel in packs."

"Makes a good story."

"The legal authorities might have bought that explanation even if Esmeralda were cleared until you happened along. If not vagrants, you're right, it certainly wasn't Angus. He lacks the killer instinct even on the tennis court."

"You make that sound like a weakness."

"In the world of finance it often is."

"You know your wife's been screwing him and probably somebody else over at the Greenbrier? Maybe the golf pro."

It didn't shake him as I'd hoped. He gave me his gritted-teeth smile.

"There are things I choose not to know."

"You're so civilized they don't bother you?"

"Bothered, yes, but I'm an aging man only occasionally able to make love to my wife—at that somewhat shakily, as I have a heart condition. Jeannie Bruce is a strong and vibrant woman with a zest for what each day brings. She requires love as much as air. I've never criticized her straying. We have an unspoken understanding. Whatever she does is to be circumspect. I am not happy that she and Angus found a need for each other, but then they are both so healthy and spirited their eventual attraction was inevitable. It's a passing thing, and you see, Mr. LeBlanc, I love Jeannie Bruce deeply, and as Mr. Shakespeare tells us, love 'bears it out to the edge of doom.' I can't endure the thought of living without her. She loves me as best she can. I accept that, and life goes on."

"Not for Aunt Jessie it won't," I said and still meant to take him down. I watched that index finger that remained on the trigger.

"No, not good for Aunt Jessie. Believe me, I am greatly distressed."

"What I'm thinking is there was one other person at her cabin the day she died."

"Oh?" He raised his graying eyebrows.

"You rode over there on a golf cart after Jeannie Bruce came back to this house. Could be you were the last person to see Aunt Jessie alive."

"No, when I last saw her she was dead. She had fallen from her chair and struck her face on the hearthstone."

"She lay face down?"

"Yes."

"She was face up when Leroy Spears found her."

"I have no explanation."

"How'd you know she was dead?"

"I felt for her pulse and heartbeat."

"You try resuscitation?"

"I'm not skilled in that department."

"You notice any wounds?"

"She had blood dripping from her nose, blood in her mouth, and blood on her dress," he said and shifted the shotgun slightly.

"Though she was lying face down, you saw all that?"

"I did. Her face rested on a cheek."

"You think the fall killed her?"

"At the time I thought so."

"She was strangled."

Again he showed no surprise or alarm.

"Maybe you know about that," I said.

"I didn't at the time. I've learned since. It appears that finding exonerates Jeannie Bruce and the matter of the whip."

"How'd you find out?"

"I have ways of doing so."

"Sure, Sheriff Lester's in your pocket. He'd keep the man about to hire him informed. To recap, I don't buy the vagrants or Angus, who was bored around here. Esmeralda had no need to kill Aunt Jessie, who'd befriended and was caring for her. And if it wasn't Jeannie Bruce, I come back to you. You say when you last saw Aunt Jessie she was dead. You mean when you first walked into the cabin or had left it?"

"Mr. LeBlanc, are you suggesting I had something to do with Aunt Jessie's death?" He lifted the shotgun.

I was taking a chance pressing him too hard, but if he became distracted or rattled, I'd lunge, knock the chair he stood behind into him, and bowl him over with it. I watched his finger resnug itself on the trigger.

"I'm asking myself why you went over to the cabin after Jeannie Bruce came back here."

"To help Aunt Jessie in any way I could," he answered and again lowered the barrel of the gun to the chair. "Consider, Mr. Blanc, how would I have done it? Choke a woman? Strangle her? Aunt Jessie was old but fit. Even had she fallen and hit her head on the hearthstone, I would've needed to turn her over and press my thumbs against her throat and windpipe. Think not only of how appalling such an act would be but also of the difficulty. Do you have any idea how arduous the physical act of killing is, how strongly even an unconscious body resists death?"

"Do you?"

"I've read about it."

"There are ways of strangling. Even a person of little strength might turn a body over and use twine twisted around the throat or maybe a broomstick or fireplace poker laid across it, then pressed down with a foot and body weight."

"But the killer would need to clean the blood off such instruments as well as his hands and clothes and be certain to wipe away all fingerprints. He'd have to leave the cabin and find a place of refuge where he could remove his bloodstained clothes and discard them as well as clean himself without anyone taking notice."

He again smiled, and I sensed he was playing with me and possibly even enjoying this moment. Puny he might be, yet he was considered a brilliant man who dealt with huge sums of money and had the respect of smart, hungry, and ambitious competitors in the jungle of the marketplace. Weak of body, he had to be strong and bold of character to have succeeded—maybe a feared manipulator who loved and became excited living on the dollar's edge. This delicate, languid man would possess the know-how and nerve to kill a woman who lay helpless. He would also have it to pull the trigger of the Parker aimed at me.

"Violette Slaughter," I said. "That name mean anything to you?"

"It means very much to me, and if you're asking did I know that about Jeannie Bruce, I did even before we married. I had her investigated, though it wasn't necessary. On her own she confessed her past to me."

"Then only the two of you knew until Aunt Jessie found out. Aunt Jessie not only wouldn't sell you land, but on her discovery of Violette being Jeannie Bruce she also became a danger."

"Such a revelation would obviously be devastating to Jeannie Bruce and her social position in this world."

"And to you?"

"Only in the sense it hurt Jeannie Bruce."

"So you went over to the cabin not mainly to see about Aunt Jessie but to protect your wife's past from becoming known."

"Unfortunate indeed that Aunt Jessie recognized Jeannie Bruce as Violette. You can understand why a woman like Jeannie, who has against all odds won for herself a life of elegance and distinction, became enraged and used the whip. Jeannie Bruce believed she had escaped Violette Slaughter for good and all."

He moved his weight from one foot to the other, but his eyes never shifted from me.

"Aunt Jessie would never have told anyone."

"Perhaps not willfully, but she carried the knowledge and remained a reminder to Jeannie Bruce of her past. Jeannie couldn't escape that reminder as long as she was at Wild Thorn, or perhaps anywhere else. Secrets have a way of making themselves known. They lie in wait for the opportunity to escape. Aunt Jessie might have become addled or demented, and a single careless word or action from her could open doors to what is best forgotten. There could be no absolutely secure place for Jeannie Bruce while Aunt Jessie lived."

Yeah, he killed Aunt Jessie all right. I felt certain now. What I wondered was did this little fucker mean to kill me too?

"Aunt Jessie was old, her days in this world nearly finished, while

Jeannie Bruce is still lovely, with years of life ahead of her," he said. "I remember the first time I saw her climbing the ladder out of the club swimming pool at Boca Raton. She was beautifully tanned, her blond hair strung along her back, the water beaded and dripping off the stretch of her dazzling legs. I knew I had to have her. If nothing else in this world, it had to be her."

"You bought her."

"I did, and mean to keep her. Have you ever truly loved a woman, Mr. LeBlanc? I mean to such an extent that everything else is subservient to a desire to please and hold her? I never believed I would until I met Jeannie Bruce. She set out to catch me. She'd already had three husbands. I knew all that but was still smitten. The investigation I'd ordered a private detective to pursue revealed she was an exploiter of men to further her ends. I wanted her so completely that before our marriage I made a financial settlement on her. She didn't understand I was the fisherman, she the fish. I love her as much today as at Boca Raton the evening I saw her wearing a great yellow hat and blue cocktail dress under the ivory glow of Japanese lanterns during the hotel's courtyard party."

"So what now?" I asked.

"I believe we've gone far enough with this, Mr. LeBlanc. Jeannie Bruce's dream of resurrecting Wild Thorn is over, at least for the while. I'll continue to hold the property. If she wants never to return, I'll put it up for sale. International Paper is clamoring to have the timber. I'll find something else for Jeannie Bruce, perhaps a sunny spot in Europe or the Caribbean."

"Where'd she get the oil portrait of Robert the Bruce?"

"She had it painted by an artist she lived with for a while in the SoHo district of New York City."

"You knew it was fake?"

"Certainly."

"You're quite a guy, Mr. St. George," I said, and it was then something else took shape in my mind. He hadn't told Jeannie Bruce what he'd done to Aunt Jessie. Jeannie Bruce still believed her hunt whip had caused the old lady's death. Suppose he'd strangled Aunt Jessie not only to protect Jeannie Bruce's name but also to hold over her what she believed was her guilt? She could've already been looking around for another man. She had her settlement and the means to do so. Duncan was a daring tactician. As long as she believed herself responsible for Aunt Jessie's death, he'd have power to control her. With Aunt Jessie he'd used what was at hand.

"Yes, it's been my advantage that people have often misread me," he said. "Now you may stand, but carefully. I'll need to detain you for a time."

"How much time?" I asked as I stood. I watched the shotgun.

"Three days ought to be sufficient."

"For what?"

"You don't need to know."

"Where's Xanadu?"

> "'In Xanadu did Kubla Kahn
> A stately pleasure-dome decree
> Where Alph, the sacred river, ran
> Through caverns measureless to man
> Down to a sunless sea.'

"I expect you're familiar with those lines."

"Yeah, I been to school," I said and thought of Miss Mabel Tascott, who had been my teacher back in Jessup's Wharf. She had whipped my legs with a ruler for looking up a girl's dress.

"I know what you've done Mr. LeBlanc. I've had you looked into and must tell you that it will be useless of you to go to the police after Jeannie Bruce and I are gone from Shawnee County. We can, if we wish, leave this country for another that has no extradition agreement, live well, and after a few years return to the United States. By then any evidence would be old and untrustworthy, and the one man who could testify against us is a felon who received a dishonorable discharge from the army—the only witness and unreliable. I have the best lawyers, attorneys very resourceful and clever who know how to stall and throw up intricate legal barricades. Years could pass, and even if charges against Jeannie Bruce or me are brought and we come to trial, there would be only the slightest chance of conviction."

"Money works miracles, don't it?"

"Mr. LeBlanc, it has always been thus. Now put your hands palms outward under your belt at the rear of your trousers. Stick them as far down as you can thrust them."

I obeyed. I still had my feet and could kick if he got in range, but he continued to stand off from me.

"Let's move you ahead into the hall, turn right, keep your hands as they are, and proceed slowly," he said as he opened the door.

I did as he told me, at the same time watching as we passed for something I could grab, whirl, and throw at him—the porcelain vase, the Tiffany lamp, the Greek amphora—yet there was no way I'd have time enough to free my hands before he could use the Parker.

"Mr. LeBlanc, don't even think of it. Now stop and keep your back to me three paces past the door on your right."

I remembered where the door on the right led. I listened to him unlock it and the second iron one that opened onto the basement.

"Very carefully descend the steps," he said.

The steps were the spiral metal staircase he'd taken Blackie, Angus, Angus's girlfriend Liz, and me down during the dinner party. At the bottom we passed the laundry room, with its sinks, kettles, ironing tables, and mangle. Duncan could have returned from Aunt Jessie's after killing her, entered unseen by the outside door, and cleaned himself as well as found scrubbed clothes hanging from the line or in the dryer. He might have prearranged to have them waiting. He'd stick all the bloody stuff in one of the electric washers. Evidence drained away.

Next along the passageway was the arsenal where his great-grandfather James MacGlauglin had kept the Belgian rifles, the

Browning machine gun, and the wooden crates of cartridges. Only a shaft of light from the hallway's ceiling bulb penetrated the room's darkness.

We reached the jail cell. The outsized key hung from its hook on the wall.

"Stop and continue to keep your back to me," he ordered.

I heard him lift down the key and unlock the cell door. I waited for him to prod me inside. If he did, I had a chance of whirling, knocking away the shotgun, and grabbing him.

"Mr. LeBlanc, don't be foolish now. Just enter the cell."

I walked in, and he quickly shut the door and relocked it before I could face him.

"Now remove all your clothes except for your underwear and hand them between the bars to me," he said and hung the key on the wall.

I took off my boots first. I thought of throwing them at him, but that would do me no good. At my thigh I felt for the Old Pal pocketknife that I'd carried and kept sharp many a year. If I could somehow hold on to it, I might be able to spring the door's lock. While I took off my pants, I tried to work my hand into the pocket and palm the knife.

"No, that won't do," Duncan said. "Leave everything inside your pants and give them to me."

I hoped to jerk him back against the bars as he took hold of the pants, but, no, he stood away, reached long, and his grip on them wasn't firm enough. I released them. Next was my khaki shirt that had a pack of Camels in the pocket. He laid my clothes on a wooden bench against the wall outside the cell. He set my boots under the bench.

"You leaving me here for three days without food or water?" I asked.

"I'll bring provisions and blankets. The help will be given time off for a vacation. I'll see that Pepe returns to release you. He won't know you're down here or where the key will be to gain entrance to the basement until he receives my instructions. It will be of no avail for you to shout or scream. The sounds won't penetrate these thick stone walls even if someone is upstairs. I suggest you relax and make the best of a quiet and enforced rest."

"Can I have my cigarettes?"

"They are no use to you without matches, which I can't allow you to have. Your lungs will rejoice at their freedom from nicotine."

He turned, walked through the basement, and I heard a chiming of his feet on the spiral staircase followed by the sound of his closing and locking the doors at its head. I turned to inspect the bunks, sink, and john. I found nothing I could use to break out. I rattled the cell door, pushed a hand between bars, and worked a finger into the keyhole. No chance I could move the heavy bolt.

I let down a bunk from the wall. It was made of steel and had a thin cotton pallet over it. A chain at each end allowed it to unfold flat. No springs or movable parts I might break loose and use to lever the bolt.

I heard Duncan coming back. He carried two white blankets on top of a cardboard box. He set them in front of the cell door.

"Stand back," he said. "You have water from the sink. Here is bread, cereal, pastries, cheese, and milk—food enough to last you until you're released. There is also a pie I found in the pantry. You'll need to use your hands to eat. I do have paper napkins here. I'd have brought soup, but you would need a can opener and possibly be able to fashion it to some use. You can reach through the bars and gather these items as you want them."

Using a foot, he pushed them closer.

"You think of everything," I said, and fastened up the bunk.

"I've always tried to look ahead and be thorough."

"But Jeannie Bruce threw you off stride."

"Indeed she did, and still does. Uxorious am I, a fatal malady. I'll be going now."

"Look, you could at least tell me your secret formula for making money," I said. I wanted to keep him here talking as long as possible. Maybe someone might see Ben's pickup outside and wonder. Pepe and the Latina could come looking for him and learn I was here.

"It's partly a myth I don't mind sharing with you," he said. "All very simple. I call it my Contrary Indicator. It's made up not primarily of numbers but seven men of varied professions and ways of life. One is a doctor, another a lawyer, a third an accountant, a fourth a Harvard sociologist, the fifth a former president of a major corporation he drove almost into bankruptcy, the sixth a stock analyst who puts out his own publication, and the seventh a congressman. They are all intelligent, good, and honorable men. None knows the other. What they have in common is that as a body they are almost always wrong about financial markets, interest rates, foreign currencies, and other monetary instruments. Have you done any investing?"

"Not money."

"Once a quarter I wine and dine these gentlemen individually at dinner, chat them up, and ask for their opinions because as a body they more often than not sell low and buy high. Maybe two or even three make the right calls at random moments, but as a majority they are wrong more than seventy percent of the time. Occasionally they are a hundred percent mistaken. My strategy is simply to move in contrary fashion to the general consensus. When they are all in agreement, I bet against the market whether it be to go long or sell short."

"Don't suppose you'd give me their names," I said, anything to delay his leaving.

"No, that would be a violation of confidence, but let me remind you of the Greek poet Archilochus' aphorism that is translated: 'The fox knows many things, but the hedgehog knows one big thing.' You might ask yourself who among such men is the hedgehog. Now I must be on my way. I'll leave the light on for you. So many people fear the dark."

The only light was attached to the ceiling outside the cell and way beyond reach. A wire cage protected it.

"You don't fear it?" I asked.

"Actually I do."

He started to walk away.

"Give Jeannie Bruce my big hello," I said.

He stopped to look back at me. His eyes narrowed as if he was calculating. I wondered whether he knew about Jeannie Bruce and me, what had happened between us in the cabin. Maybe that had escaped him, at least until now.

"I will," he said. "She'll be sorry. She was very much taken by you."

"And I was taken by her," I said.

He gave me the clinched-teeth grin.

TWENTY-EIGHT

I stood listening for life or activity of any sort in the mansion and heard water running through pipes. Duncan could be washing his hands or having himself a shower. Or maybe Jeannie hadn't already left and was using the bathroom. The water stopped. A distant motor hummed, my guess the mansion's air-conditioning system kicking in. No coolness needed down here in the depths of the basement.

I let down a bunk. Three days. Three days if Duncan had told the truth. The devious bastard could mean never to let me out. Or if for some reason he had an accident, heart attack, anything unforeseen, he might not be able to reach Pepe to order him to free me. I saw myself eventually growing weaker, starving, letting go of life. I pictured writhing from hunger pains followed by the putrefaction of flesh. The stench of that I remembered well.

That kind of thinking was panic. I had to block such stuff from my mind. Again I tried the cell door. I'd sworn never again to allow myself to be locked up. Feeling a chill, I stooped to reach through the bars to draw in a blanket. I wrapped it around my shoulders. Next I opened the cardboard box. The first thing my fingers brought up from inside it was Wheaties, of all fucking things. Next I lifted sticky buns dotted with raisins, all Glad-wrapped. The pie was so round I needed to angle it between the bars. Turned out to be pecan. Something else—Lux soap and a towel. I found those reassuring. If Duncan meant for me to die, he wouldn't have provided them. On the other hand maybe they could be the little joke of a warped and sadistic sense of humor.

I kept listening. When I arrived, a dozen or more men had been working outside on the grounds around the house, most operating machinery. They had to be making a racket, yet I heard nothing except the quiet whir of the air-conditioning or whatever it was. The thick walls built by old James MacGlauglin had been mortared and made to last. In the end they had become his fortress.

I drew in and arranged the second blanket on the bunk. Lots of bedtime ahead. To stay in shape I'd exercise as I had at Leavenworth. Enough room in this cell for push-ups and jumping jacks—called the side-straddle hop during my army days. Yet why the hell would I ever again want to repeat anything I'd done in the army or its prison? No choice. I lowered myself to the concrete floor for the push-ups, thirty of them. Once I'd done a hundred easy.

Sitting on the bunk with the blanket draped around my body and pulled in about my stomach, I felt temporary warmth. In this basement the temperature would likely remain constant the year around—like the coal mines, the same summer or winter, about forty degrees, maybe sixty in the basement. No real comparison. The mines stayed dark, wet, and befouled, while at least I was dry, clean, and had light.

I felt thirsty. Duncan had provided no glass or cup. Smart again. He'd allow me nothing I might use to break free. I held a hand under the faucet and found it provided both hot and cold water. I drank from my cupped palms. The water had a slight taste of copper. Old James MacGlauglin would've had nothing but the best plumbing, which in those days was copper like on his roof. I flushed the john. It drained briskly. A fine gray dust coated the white plastic seat.

All right, I'd rest. I lay back on the bunk. The blanket partially softened it. I'd known lots worse beds, some with no pallets, others made of sidewalk concrete. I couldn't get over all this being done to me by Duncan, the delicate, gentlemanly player of a weird and whiny oboe d'amore. Yet I had to hand it to him. Despite his age and fragile appearance, he had the makings of a first-class NS#3.

I wished I hadn't abandoned time tellers. I'd left my wristwatch unworn and unwound in Montana. How long had I been here? Thirty minutes, an hour? Go to sleep, I told myself. Close your eyes and empty everything else from your mind. Allow time to drift past like the easy flow of Laurel Creek. But I kept thinking of Blackie and wondered whether she might be thinking of me. She was white-hot angry, with reason. Goddamn you, Jeannie Bruce. Yet I thought of how driven and perversely brave her life had been. Maybe knight her a Dame of the Garter Belt. Such thinking was even further betrayal of Blackie. "I didn't want or mean any of this to happen," I said aloud. "I'd like you to know that."

By nightfall she and Ben should miss me and do what? Probably check at Peck's Store or call around. Blackie could believe I'd run out on her or was holed up with a bottle and Jeannie Bruce. After a couple of days Blackie and Ben might have to act even if they figured I'd gone for keeps—Ben to phone the State Police to put out a want on his pickup, Blackie maybe to leave Shawnee County, meaning never again to have any care for or thought about me.

Jeannie Bruce on her way to Xanadu. Duncan and probably Angus would join her, whether that was in Baltimore, this continent, or across the big water. Maybe Duncan owned a yacht, and they'd soon be gone from the territorial waters of the United States and beyond the reach of its laws.

Where would they land? How about Spain or Italy? Sure, a man as rich as Duncan could have a casa on a mountainside overlooking the Mediterranean. Or in Monaco a white villa with louvered green shutters, a swimming pool, all located near a golf course, stables, a casino, and whatever else Jeannie Bruce called for. Then there was Switzerland or France, a château, the Loire, those lazy rivers shaded by overhanging birch trees. Jeannie Bruce would find men. Wherever she traveled, she'd always find men, and Duncan would play the mournful oboe d'amore, but he had her now and maybe for good.

If Duncan were ever brought to trial and convicted, he wouldn't last more than a couple of weeks in prison. He'd be like a dry leaf floating down into fire and flames. Woof and gone. I could be wrong. At the place, his brains and cunning might bear him up so that he not only survived but also managed to tend to his portfolio of securities from the cellblock.

How many days or years could he keep from Jeannie Bruce the knowledge that she'd not killed Aunt Jessie with the whip? He had her boxed in as long as she didn't know what really happened, and he'd use his brain to prevent her from ever learning the truth. Unless she did him in. After the life she'd lived, she could have the daring to drop a little poison into his two-olive martini. He'd realize that and might tell her he'd left a sealed letter with his attorney or locked in a safety-deposit box that was to be opened at his death and reveal all. He could force Jeannie Bruce to care for him the rest of his life. Maybe even be faithful to him. He'd imprisoned her. I pictured Jeannie Bruce desperate and afraid. Yeah, Duncan never made a move without thinking it through. He was one slick sonofabitch.

I couldn't sleep or doze. I stood and paced off the cell. I had to swing up and fasten the bunk to do that. The cell's dimensions were eight by twelve feet. I felt the compression of being enclosed. I stood at the bars and again rattled them. I tried shouting. I looked at the ceiling and hollered, "Pepe, anyone anywhere, help."

That was stupid. That was chicken. Lie down, believe that Duncan hadn't lied about getting in touch with Pepe, close off your mind, and let time run. The way you'd done at Leavenworth? Well, you'd had books. You'd been able to study and earn your GED. Seven of us got diplomas on the same day at a ceremony before other prisoners in the mess hall. The warden had shaken our hands and seen to it the awards were entered on our records. I'd also used the kitchen's steam hose to kill another prisoner, the leader of a gang who jumped me in the laundry room. The roiling steam sent him into a screaming dance of death and allowed me to escape detection and punishment. The GED helped with my early release, earned chiefly by the good time I was believed to have served.

What had I done at nights in my cell when the lights switched off? I'd thought about the woman who I'd believed was my mother. I remembered her trying to stand between my father and me. He'd never written while I was locked up, and when she died and I was permitted under guard to go to her funeral, he had stood on the side of her grave opposite me. "You more than anything else put her in the ground," he'd said at the end of the service before the guards returned me in shackles and belly cuffs to the Norfolk Airport, a plane back to Kansas City, and the hole.

I thought of hunting, of squatting in reeds along the alluvial Axapomimi River, the cold mist shifting low, the water just a murmur, the reeds leaning and leaving slight furrows in the flow. I heard mallards' wings beating as the ducks circled and I honked them in, shifted the twenty-gauge L.C. Smith side-by-side, and sprang up from the blind I'd built. The pair of drakes canted from out of the mist, wings spread, landing gear lowered. I dropped both with quick, clean snap shots that left them limp. They splashed into the water. "Get 'em," I told Reb, my yellow Lab, and he leaped into the river and carried both back with one proud retrieve. His eyes alight, he shook his wet hair over me, and I kissed him.

I thought of other women I'd known, the earliest one not a woman at all but a teenager named Laurie in Jessup's Wharf who was the first girl to bare her young breasts to me. She had rose-tipped fingernails and smelled of mint-scented soap. I pictured the almond-eyed Oriental ladies of the night willing to trade their goods for American cigarettes or army rations. And Blackie. Of course, good and honest Blackie.

I pictured Esmeralda at the Huntington State Hospital, those dark eyes that had opened on me for a second as she lay strapped to the bed. I wanted her never again to know want, fear, and hurt. Yet here I sprawled helpless.

Relax and let go, I told myself. Let the tide take you out. I'd once been able to sleep. I had slept under shell fire and after a deadly game of hide-and-seek with little men in black pajamas who squatted amid elephant grass. Sleep had been my hideaway, like Esmeralda with her caves and burrows. I'd been a drunk on sleep. Yet by the time I left Leavenworth, I'd lost that refuge. Too much bad stuff year after year and different shapes in the night. Sleep had become a shallow alert even now when I stretched out beside Blackie. Or had with Blackie, if never again.

I turned and twisted on the bunk. My eyes burned. Imagine yourself in a bathtub of rising warm water, I told myself. You're feeling comfortable. You're letting go. As it was starting to work and my muscles loosened and relaxed, I heard a noise and sat up. No, the lack of noise. The air-conditioning had shut down. The question was, had it done so because the temperature outside cooled or somebody upstairs had flipped a switch?

I stood and flexed my fingers. I did some knee-bend military calisthenics. I sat. I stood a second time. My guess was that everybody had left the mansion by now and locked up. Then a compressor whined, and the air conditioner again kicked in. What did it mean? Nothing. Duncan, Jeannie Bruce, and the help could all have cleared out. The thermostat would've been left set on automatic.

I ate a pastry, chewed it methodically. I wanted to make my food last. I used the soap to wash my hands afterwards and drank water, a second time sucking it up from my palms. I lay down. I hoped Blackie was thinking about me. I wanted her to be worried. Worried meant she cared. I wanted her to be so anxious she'd forgive. We'd never used the word *love* between us, but it now formed in my mind and worked my lips.

I slept finally, just off the edge of consciousness. No way I could tell how much time had passed. Maybe an hour or two, maybe five minutes. I had to piss. How long did I usually go without using the john? Normally I got through the night. During the day every four or five hours. If sweating, longer. Well, I was sweating now but not the same kind. Dry sweat.

As I sat looking at the light in its cage beyond the cell, it blinked off. Either it had burned out or somebody had shut down the power. No, a feeble gleam bled indirectly into my space from the corridor bulb outside the room where they'd kept the machine gun and Belgian rifles. "Don't you go out on me too," I yelled at it.

I lay on the bunk. Try to think some good thoughts, I told myself. I pictured Blackie and me back in Montana when snow packed high around our cabin. We banked the fire and curled beneath goose-down quilts, each of us furnishing body warmth to the other. The wind would be talking. It would be saying, "I'm going to tear down your house and break your bones," but we had solid log shelter and each other to withstand it.

I pictured scenes I remembered. I'd driven the pickup out to repair a fence, and as I unrolled a length of barbed wire, I had a sensation of being watched. I turned to see a tawny cougar crouched in the prairie grass. He had amber eyes and was thinking of making a meal of me. I reached for my iron tamping bar, faced him, and stood ready. For an instant I felt we communicated as if our minds had merged. "You're not what I want" was his thought, and "I don't care for you either" was mine. He rose unhurriedly, coughed, and moved away, his tail lashing side to side through the dry grass.

I again sat up believing I'd heard something. I stood and looked at the ceiling. Pepe maybe. He could be cleaning up and had dropped his broom or part of a vacuum cleaner. Then again, maybe my mind had created the sound. I waited and heard nothing more. Back on the bunk.

Another scene. In Saigon where I drank rice wine and sat beside a petite Vietnamese girl who could not have been more than sixteen. Her golden silk gown shimmered in the sunny light of the outdoor café. She was demure and careful of her long red fingernails. When she turned away to speak to a bar girl at the next table, the purse slipped off her lap. My hand reached it before her fingers, and as I lifted it to give it back, I felt the weight. She tried to snatch the purse, but I broke her grip, opened it, and inside among lipstick, comb, and a gilded compact lay an American grenade. I removed the grenade, gave her the purse, and she fled, her golden gown flapping at her heels. That's what Nam was, screwing and being screwed.

I ate two dry handfuls of Wheaties and drank water. Afterwards I did forty push-ups. In time I could again work up to a hundred. I used to swim a mile in the Axapomimi River, and one warm spring day had found myself among a school of migrating shad that brushed by me in the water, a curtain of fleeting shapes that stroked my skin. For a time I'd wanted to be a fish, maybe a porpoise or blue marlin arching from rolling swells of a sunlit sea.

I again tried sleep but couldn't get comfortable on the bunk. I thought of Blackie and how we rode out over the land we'd leased and hoped to own. She knew how to give her body to the horse, to become one with it. She would let her hair down, and when we galloped the hair streamed behind her like a black scarf in the wind. Speed made her laugh, and she showed her perfect teeth.

God, what time and day was it? I ate another pastry and used the john. If I was going to die here, I wanted to leave Blackie a note. With my Old Pal pocketknife I could've scratched words into the wall. Not *Kilroy was here*, but something nice for Blackie. What would I say? *Sorry I messed us up, and I'm going to miss you.* I scraped my fingernails against the granite. In the shadowed cell I couldn't see that they'd left even a trace.

I thought of Montana wind. There was always wind. It moved over the prairie grass and sage like an invisible hand passing by and bent them at its will. I thought of mountains crowned with snow and a flock of cranes that landed in our pasture to move and peck about on long stiff legs. They had a stuffed-shirt awkwardness on land that fell away as they rose into a flapping grace against the cloud-laden sky.

The cell closing in on me. Compression. Near darkness. I felt I was losing it, causing rage and fear to build in my chest. I banged my forehead against the wall. It'd been that way for a time at Leavenworth until I worked myself into the foggy limbo of prison life. It'd been like submerging into the grayness of the underworld. Phantom shapes had moved around me, noise become muted, what was left of the heart had shrunk and dried up. Land of the walking dead.

I heard a thump. Sure God heard it. I stood at the cell door. I'd learned to listen in Nam. I had sent my hearing into the darkness, pushed it way out in the jungle, let it wind its way like a snake. I did so now. I willed it from the cell into the corridor and beyond to the spiral steps. I sent it up to the iron door.

Nothing. Maybe the thump hadn't come from upstairs or anywhere in the mansion but from outside. Workers might be digging with a backhoe. A heavy truck could've caused a rumble or a jackhammer breaking up concrete. If there were people laboring out there, I hadn't been abandoned. Somebody should see Ben's Chevy pickup, wonder about it, ask questions. Ben himself might come searching for it. He'd need his truck. Blackie would let him use the Caddy. He could drive to Wild Thorn, spot the pickup, and know I had to be somewhere around. He'd knock on the door and ask questions. He'd demand to know where I was and that the mansion and grounds be searched.

Christ, my mind was going. I went ahead and screamed. Loud and long until I had no more breath. I staggered around and bumped the wall, the bars, the bunk. I let down to my knees and sprawled face down on the floor. For a time I didn't move. Maybe a long time. How would I know? I pushed up and ate the last pastry, a chunk of pie, another handful of Wheaties, drank water, and settled on the bunk. This time I slept. It was easy. I let go and coasted down into the darkness that had no bottom. Like sinking underwater into a black river and drifting along with the languid current.

I moved up toward the surface but sank again. So this is the way it's going to end, I thought, just descending effortlessly until I finally reach bottom. No great pain or suffering. I felt ashamed I'd screamed. Not that shame made any difference. I wished I'd been braver, yet who was I impressing? Just me in the sweet drift of the black sea.

A faint noise descended into the sea. I didn't open my eyes. I wasn't going to be faked out again by my mind composing sounds to trick me. Yet I heard it a second time. The clang of iron. I swung my feet to the floor. Silence. Nothing. Then a faint chiming of the metal steps that became louder. I stood and looked toward the dimly lit corridor. A shadow approached and formed in the doorway. Its hand clicked the light switch.

"Who here?" it asked, and the voice belonged to Pepe.

"Yeah, me," I answered, my voice hoarse.

He shined a flashlight on me.

"Mr. LeBlanc, I never knew you down here," he said. "I let you out."

He crossed to the hook for the key, fitted it into the lock, and stood away to open the door. He'd slicked back his hair and sported a white tie and gray double-breasted suit, the pants baggy, maybe hand-me-downs from the St. Georges.

"I didn't know you here till Mr. Duncan call me, okay? I don't know nothing."

I pulled on my khakis. My wallet, Old Pal, and change were still in my pants pockets. I fitted my feet into my boots. I moved past Pepe to the corridor and slowed at the laundry room.

"You able to wash all the blood off Mr. Duncan's things?" I asked Pepe.

"Don't know nothing," he said, his eyes fleeting. *"Nada."*

I used the rail to haul myself up the steps to the first floor, where I headed for the front door. Pepe followed. The house was dusky, the curtains drawn at windows. When I had trouble opening the door, Pepe did it for me. I blinked into daylight.

"He never told me nothing," Pepe said.

I walked into the courtyard and freshness of morning air. Machinery was still parked about, but no men worked. Sure, Duncan would've let them go. I lifted my hands palms up and cupped them as if I could gather and hold the warm touch of the sun.

TWENTY-NINE

I looked toward the circular drive where I'd left Ben's pickup. It was gone, and I turned to Pepe as I scratched at my unshaved itching face. Pepe left the keys to the mansion inside on the ebony reception hall table but locked the front door by pulling it shut and testing it behind him. As he started to leave, I called him back.

"Why'd you do that with the keys?"

"Mr. Duncan tell me to."

"You got a car?"

"Piece of one."

"I need a ride."

"I in a hurry."

"Pepe, you carry a green card?"

"Sure," he said, yet glanced behind him as if jumpy somebody might be close and listening.

"Show me."

"I don't required to show you nothing."

"You don't have one. Now, you're going to drive me to the place where I'm staying whether you want to or not. And I'll give you twenty bucks."

His eyes shifted. He was considering his chances if he ran or had to fight me.

"I don't want no trouble."

"I don't either," I said. "Now get your car and let's move."

His Plymouth two-door vintage 1991 sedan had recently been given a purple paint job. The backseat held a suitcase, folded clothes, and a guitar.

"Stop at the stable," I told him as we passed between the gateposts, their lanterns unlit. I'd thought of the hunt whip. Pepe took the asphalt road outside the wall and down the slope. The weather vane on top the louvered spire pointed northeast. A gooseneck trailer had been backed to the throughway entrance, where Toby and two other men loaded horses.

"Where you taking them?" I asked.

"Charlottesville," Toby answered, leading the bay inside. "They been consigned."

It was like Duncan methodically to take care of business even in extreme situations. I reached for the keys to the Plymouth so Pepe couldn't drive off and leave me stranded. "Hey," he called as I walked to the tack room. Jeannie Bruce and Angus's hunt whips no longer hung from their wall fastenings. Duncan would've seen to that too.

"Maybe you shouldn't be doing what you doing," Pepe said when I got back to the car and gave him the keys.

"You about to stop me?" I asked. His pocked, swarthy face had turned threatening, and he might have a knife. I gave him the death stare I'd developed during my years at Leavenworth.

"Okay, I told you I don't want no trouble," he said, his dark eyes sliding away. He started the Plymouth and drove hunched forward and fast toward Cliffside. The Plymouth's engine sounded as if it could've used a new set of plugs. He hit the brakes hard as three wild dogs ran across the road and dodged among spruce pines. Pepe had swerved to miss them. He cursed Latino style.

"The family all cleared out?" I asked.

"They gone. Mr. Duncan paid off the workers and told them not to come back till he tell them."

"Where'd he go?"

"He never told me nothing except wait for his call. I been at a cousin's house in Hinton. Mr. St. George telephone where the keys. Told me to check out the basement."

"You meeting him?"

"I don't know where he's at. I going to Arizona. My sister in Nogales."

When we reached Ben's, I saw his pickup parked at the side of the house. Pepe stopped at the gate. I stepped out and handed him a twenty-dollar bill.

"I just do what he tell me and don't want no damn trouble," he said, turned the Plymouth around, and gunned away down the road. To remember his West Virginia license-plate number I repeated it aloud three times.

I crossed to the house, and as I climbed the steps to the porch, Ben pushed open the screen door. He'd been shaving, and he stood bare-chested, his face partly lathered. He held a towel and razor, not a safety but a straightedge, the blade open.

"Damn if you ain't sorry looking," he said. "And I hoped you was gone for good."

"Where's Blackie?"

"Don't know I need to tell you that."

"Ben, please."

He spat off the side of the porch before he answered.

"She lit out again. Said she just wanted to drive around a couple of days. I got a good mind to let you have a load of Number eights in your tail. What'd that St. George woman do, use you up and send you pack-ing? You look like hell. Least I got my truck back, no thanks to you. You had me fooled, Charley. I figured you might turn out to be worth something."

"You going to give me a chance to explain?"

"Not in this house. You stand right there and do your explaining."

Weaving and dizzy, I held to a porch post to steady myself while I told him where I'd been and what'd happened at Wild Thorn. As I talked he slowly closed the razor's blade into its ivory handle. He never took his pale blue eyes off me. He was scenting truth, his mind fingering my words. When I finished, he toweled his face.

"Me and Blackie came out to Wild Thorn looking for you," he said. "Saw my truck, the keys still in it. Banged on the house door. Nobody around anywhere. We figured you'd left with the St. George woman. No way we could know old man Duncan had you locked up in his basement. He don't look fit enough to pop the top off a soda-pop bottle. I'd like to lay my hands on that scrawny little sonofabitch."

"Blackie coming back?" I asked.

"She's still got her things here, so I reckon so. What you aim to do?"

"Clean up if you'll let me in the house and then visit District Attorney Sligh."

Ben opened the screen door for me. Nothing had been disturbed in my room. I showered, shaved, put on the clean khakis Blackie had washed, pressed, and laid out on the cot. I felt faint and wobbly for a second. When I walked into the kitchen, Ben had fixed me a sliced tomato sandwich and poured a glass of milk from the pitcher he kept cooling in his refrigerator.

"I've heard about that old jail out at Wild Thorn," he said. "Never had no idea it'd ever be used again. You can borrow my truck."

"Sure you can trust me?"

"I been studying on it," he said.

I drove to Cliffside and the courthouse, where for once enough cars had been parked at the curbs on all sides to fill most spaces. I circled until I found an empty slot, dropped a dime into the meter, and crossed the lawn among the waddling pigeons reluctant to move out of my way. I rode the creaky elevator to the second floor.

"Mr. Sligh's in court," Miss Minerva Lemon said, removing earphones she'd used for typing. She looked at me as if I'd tracked in dirt.

"I'll wait," I said and took the chair by the window. I wasn't about to ask her permission. Leaves of the white oak shifted in a breeze that also ruffled the flag a moment before it again fell limp. Pigeons flapped to the eaves. A brown mongrel dog ran across the lawn and looked up after them.

I tried not to keep eyeing the electric clock above Miss Minerva's desk. I stood twice to stretch, and both times she watched me. When I pulled out my pack of Camels to smoke, she frowned, and I stuck them back in my shirt pocket. I waited an hour and twenty minutes before District Attorney Sligh entered, brisk and dapper. He carried the briefcase that appeared too large for such a small man. His quick steps faltered when he caught sight of me.

"I heard you'd left us," he said in that deep oratorical voice that was much too loud for such a runt. I wondered whether he used that tone when he talked to his wife. His right index finger stroked both sides of his precisely trimmed miniature mustache.

"Need to talk to you," I said.

"Make an appointment with Miss Lemon for tomorrow. I've had quite a session in court. Man accused of rustling sheep. Just like the Old West. The jury has the case now."

"Murder's on my mind."

"What?" he asked as Miss Minerva looked up.

"Use your office?" I asked and indicated the door.

He hesitated, nodded, and I followed him inside. He shut the door after me and crossed around his desk to set the briefcase on top.

"All right, I'm listening," he said, still standing.

"I want to trade information. First I give you what I have and then you tell me a couple of things that I need to know. Can we agree on that?"

"You're in no position to bargain with the law," he said and pulled at his pants as he sat. His eyebrows rose as he waited for me to speak.

"You don't want to know who killed Aunt Jessie?"

"We think we do know that."

"Not Esmeralda."

"Oh? Whom are you nominating for the crime?"

"Do we have a deal?"

"I will listen."

"And I'm trusting you," I said and laid it out for him. I told him about Jeannie Bruce being Violette Slaughter, the hunt whip, and Duncan's last visit to Aunt Jessie's cabin. I didn't mention I'd been on the bed with Jeannie Bruce. Sligh's eyebrows lowered slowly, and the fingers of his left hand that had been tapping on the desk stilled.

"Now your evidence," he said.

"I saw the whip. Jeannie Bruce St. George admitted she'd hit Aunt Jessie with it. The blow hurt Aunt Jessie, addled her, and caused her to fall from her chair and hit her head on the hearth after Jeannie Bruce left the cabin. Duncan St. George rode over in the golf cart and strangled Aunt Jessie while she lay unconscious."

"That's absurd. Why would he?"

"You can check with him about that. He had his reasons."

"That's all you intend to tell me?"

"I'd say that's right much."

"You have the whip?"

"Forensics has the silver cap."

"I know what forensics does and doesn't have. Without the whip the cap can't be proved to belong to Mrs. St. George."

"Yeah, Shawnee County's so full of hunt whips."

"Watch it, Mr. LeBlanc. And Duncan St. George confessed to you?"

"He played with me in a manner that was a marginal confession."

"There's no such thing as a marginal confession. Either he did or he didn't. And if he denies killing Aunt Jessie, your testimony alone won't stand up. Any other witnesses to back up your story?"

"No."

"And you have nothing more for me?"

"Duncan did it."

"How did you know Aunt Jessie had been strangled? That determination hasn't been made public."

"I can't tell you that." I'd not give him Sheriff Sawyers. "You got to know Esmeralda had no motive for killing Aunt Jessie."

"A person in Esmeralda's condition doesn't need motive. She's not responsible for her actions."

"She's smarter than you think. She'd have to be to survive all these years here in Shawnee County. You believe she went to the cabin, carried a hunt whip, hit Aunt Jessie with it, and then choked her? In all her life here Esmeralda never hurt anybody or anything."

"Not conclusive," he said. "There's still the blood on her dress."

"Explained by her kneeling to help Aunt Jessie and leaving before Duncan reached the cabin. No jury would convict Esmeralda on the blood."

He turned from me a moment and looked at the wall and his framed University of Kentucky diplomas. What did he see—maybe the bountiful future he'd once envisioned gone and himself left stalled in the moldering courthouse of an impoverished county? Was there something in what I'd told him he might use to propel his career upward to a political position of a loftier order—state attorney general, a judgeship, the governor's office?

"Where are the St. Georges?" he asked.

"Out of the country by now's my guess. I can tell you when and if they're found you'll have a hard time bringing them back. And maybe even harder indicting and convicting them."

"You talk like a jailhouse lawyer," he said. "With your background any testimony you give would be torn to pieces by a good defense attorney. And where's this Pepe?"

"On the road. He mentioned Arizona. Probably a lie."

"You should've brought him in to confirm your story about being locked up."

"There's stuff left in that cell that'll confirm my story, and I can give you his license number. He'll be tough to track down if he makes it south of the border. Got paper and pencil?"

He handed me a pad and the fountain pen from his pocket. I wrote down the number and gave them back.

"I don't like the feel of any of this," Sligh said. His small clean fingers again tapped the desk. "Even if I were to convene a grand jury, there isn't enough here to bring in a true bill of indictment. I need one hell of a lot more than what you, a felon, have told me. And it will require an intensive investigation and perhaps years to bring the case to trial even if you're telling the truth, of which I am far from totally convinced."

"Could make your reputation."

"That's an insolent remark. I have my reputation."

"Sorry, Mr. Sligh, didn't mean to upset you. I heard you had political ambitions. Sometimes you can use what's at hand."

"My ambitions are none of your affair," he said and shot his cuffs. They had gold-set onyx links in them. "Now, what is it you want from me?"

"Where's Aunt Jessie's Bible?"

"In police custody."

"She kept her papers and a handwritten will in it. You know Bartholomew Asberry out at Rich Find?"

"I do. A good man."

"He'll back me up on that. Her land goes to Mt. Olivet Church. Maybe ask the sheriff if he's seen the will."

"What are you suggesting?"

"He might have overlooked it."

He stared at me and stroked his mustache. He knew what I meant. He had to know about Sheriff Lester's plan to leave office and take the job at Wild Thorn.

"I'll question Mr. Asberry. What else?"

"What did Esmeralda carry away bundled up when she ran from Aunt Jessie's cabin?"

He hesitated, coughed, and sat forward, his mousy mustache twitching under his nose.

"I don't see that information can compromise the state's case if ever we have one. What Esmeralda had in her possession was a doll, an antique possibly brought over to this country from Scotland by one of Aunt Jessie's forebears. The doll had on a newly sewn dress, and her hair had been replaced. The State Police found it cradled in a box at Esmeralda's mountain burrow. Several people from Mt. Olivet have seen the doll. They say Aunt Jessie kept it in a trunk at the foot of her bed."

"Aunt Jessie would want Esmeralda to have it," I said and remembered Leroy Spears had mentioned the doll and the trunk to me.

"It's up to the forensics to release it."

"And important to Esmeralda's welfare to possess it."

"I can't make that decision."

"Sure you can. Let me have that doll."

"You can't order me around."

"You want to help an innocent, bewildered, and frightened woman, you'll do it, Mr. Sligh."

He shifted uncomfortably.

"I'll look into it," he said.

THIRTY

I drove to Ben's hoping to see the Caddy, but Blackie'd not returned. Rattler lay in the shed where Ben sat on an upturned bucket dabbing grease to pack a wheel bearing of his Ford tractor. He laid the grease aside and stood to wipe his hands and listen as I gave him an account of my meeting with District Attorney Sligh.

"What's next?" Ben asked.

"Blackie's next," I said.

"Nothing to do but wait."

I waited. I tried lying on the cot. I swung on the porch swing. I walked around Ben's fence line. I chopped weeds in his garden. I sat by Laurel Creek and listened to its rocky flow and the pulsing insects of the pasture. I heard the hawk screech, and the dove's lament. I rehearsed what I'd say to Blackie if she allowed me to talk to her at all.

When she drove in at midafternoon, I was again on the cot and heard the car. I could've identified the Caddy's engine among a hundred others during a traffic jam. I stood at the window to watch her park at the side of the house. She stepped out, set on her Stetson, and tightened her belt, which had the Mexican silver buckle as well as a tumbleweed design tooled into the leather.

I walked out to meet her. She shied around me and entered the house. When I followed, she again shut her bedroom door in my face. I turned back to sit on the porch and wait. I smoked two cigarettes before she came out carrying her suitcase, her clothes bag, and the lever-action Winchester .30-30. She walked down the steps and across the lawn to the car. A second time I followed her.

"I'm prepared to beg," I said.

She opened the Caddy's trunk and wouldn't let me lift her suitcase up and in. She laid her clothes bag and Winchester across it. When she saw Ben edge out the screen door to the porch, she hurried to him. They talked a few minutes before they hugged and kissed. Ben was slow releasing her hand.

"This my car, right?" Blackie asked when she returned to the Caddy. "I mean registered in my name?"

"It is. The card's in the glove compartment."

She reached for the Winchester, lifted it, and levered a shell into the chamber. Using her good eye, she sighted the rifle at my forehead. A tan patch covered the other eye. I looked into the muzzle, saw its rifled grooves, and waited. Ben started down the porch steps toward us.

"I could happily use it on you," Blackie said but lowered the rifle, shucked the cartridge, caught it in the air, and fingered it. She thumbed down the hammer. "You not worth the price of a bullet."

Ben stopped in the yard.

"I'd like you to listen to me."

"Nope, I'm gone," she said. She reloaded the Winchester, laid it back in the trunk, slammed the lid, and slid behind the wheel. Before tucking her jeans into her boots, she set her Stetson aside on the seat.

"Where to?" I asked.

"Where the sun does shine and the cold's not mine," she said and fastened her seat belt.

"I'd like to go with you."

"Why would I want a poor, sorry thing like you along?"

"Blackie, the truth is you mean a lot to me."

"More than the rich bitch?"

"More than anyone."

She weighed me with that dark shiny eye that could see all the way through to the bone.

"You know I could've had that beautiful hunk named Angus," she said. "He was wanting a piece of me, and I was tempted but didn't follow through 'cause I thought you and me had something lasting going. I never called it by word, yet it was strong and I believed pretty good."

"I know what it was," I said.

"Yeah, I thought of shooting you, but I already killed one man and served time. That's a-plenty. Not wasting no more of my life on you or any man."

She started the engine.

"You'll need money," I said.

"I got the checkbook and credit card."

"You won't tell me where you're headed?"

"Once I settle in, Ben'll be the first to know."

She shifted to D and pulled off. I ran ahead to open the gate, stood aside, and watched her drive to the paved county road and bump over onto it. As she sped off, she honked the horn three times.

I stood feeling gutted. When I turned and walked to the house, Ben still waited in the yard.

"You crazy if you let that get away," he said. "Get down on your knees to her, boy. For a time you got to learn to walk on your knees."

I had no liquor. My last bottle lay in the Caddy's trunk, and that was a good thing 'cause I'd have gone on a full-throttle, commode-hugging bender. What I needed most was a means of transportation. Blackie and I had a joint account with the Bank of Chinook out in Montana. We were down to what I figured in my head to be about nineteen thousand dollars. Ben carried me to Sam's Sales, the dealer of secondhand cars in Cliffside, his shack of an office on a show lot paved with cinders that had fluttering red, white, and blue whirligigs twirling around stove wire fastened to poles. The gigs hummed and rattled.

For three thousand dollars I bought a 1992 Ford Ranger pickup with seventy-eight thousand miles on it. Sam, a beanpole of a man who wore a straw hat and carried a bamboo cane like a vaudeville hoofer, had cleaned it up, but I made out grains of powdered coal under the seat and in hard-to-reach crannies of the engine compartment.

"I swear 'fore God it was owned by an old Baptist preacher who never in his whole life made it up to the fifty-five-miles-an-hour speed limit," Sam said. He changed his grip on the cane as if it were a fencing sword and lightly tapped the hood.

"That preacher must've been handy with a pick and shovel," Ben said.

Still, the Ranger drove all right. It had six cylinders and a radio but no air. I didn't fret about air. Not having it was a kind of penance. I stopped at Peck's Store. The old man had a call for me. He now knew my business so well he no longer bothered to write down the number.

"Mr. Frampton on the line," he said. "Been trying to reach you two days."

Walt answered the phone. I heard his wife and her son's voice in the background. Family life. Walt deep in it now. And where was I? In the pit I'd dug for myself. Jeannie Bruce had left her brand on me all right.

"We have a compromise in the making with your brother Edward," Walt said. "He'll not agree to half but just might grudgingly revert to a quarter of what Bellerive brought. My feeling is he'll not move off that point even at the risk of having his reputation smirched by what you threatened to reveal about your father. I advise you to accept, assuming I can finish working it out."

"Okay," I said. "Take the dollars and run."

"You sound down in the mouth. It's still a lot of money."

"It's not the money."

"What then?"

"Walt, I don't feel like talking about that right now. I'm heading out of Shawnee County, and when I light somewhere, I'll ring your bell."

"It's been good seeing and talking to you, Charles. Maybe Mary Ellen, Jason, and I'll come out and visit you in Montana. You can teach us to ride."

"Sure, fine," I said and told him good-bye. When I started from the store, the phone rang, and Mr. Peck called me back. On the line was Miss Minerva Lemon.

"District Attorney Sligh wants you in his office," she said.

I drove to Cliffside and the courthouse. Most cars had vacated the parking spaces. The jury verdict on sheep rustling must've come in. Although I had a choice of spots and would soon be gone before they could haul me back for payment of a fine, I dropped a dime in the meter's slot.

Miss Minerva Lemon, sour as her name, buzzed me through to see Sligh. He stood, walked to a file cabinet, and slid open a bottom drawer. From inside he lifted a package wrapped in brown paper and bound by masking tape. He carried it to me.

I set the package on his desk to open it. The doll inside hung loose, her arms and legs floppy. The new dress Aunt Jessie had sewed for her was yellow with a white lace collar. Lids of the doll's button-blue eyes opened when I set her upright. The ringlets of brown hair must've been recently snipped from someone's head by Aunt Jessie, maybe a member of Mt. Olivet Church. They still felt soft and pliant.

"How'd you get it so fast from Charleston?" I asked.

"The State Police sent it down here in a patrol car coming this way. You'll need to sign for it. You'll also want to know no charges will be brought against Esmeralda whatever the outcome of further investigation. Dr. Joseph P. Fredrick at Huntington State has diagnosed her as unable to stand trial and recommends commitment. She'll remain a ward of the state. You can if you wish petition the court for her release into your custody. It'll be a lengthy and time-consuming procedure."

"I got time."

"You're carrying the doll to Esmeralda?"

"As soon as I can and then leaving Shawnee County."

"We'll want to know your whereabouts. This office will attempt to locate the St. Georges and question them and their servant Pepe. If what you've told me holds true, that may require some doing. Do you have an address where you can be reached?"

"Not yet. I'll let you know."

Like hell I would. The law was never again going to tangle me up in its boa-constrictor embrace. Aunt Jessie was gone. No way I could help her. As for Jeannie Bruce and Duncan, let them live out their anguish bound together. Each could be demon to the other.

"One more thing," Sligh said. "I suggested to Sheriff Lester that he search for the Bible, and he's found it. He tells me it had been misplaced in the property room."

"Isn't that something?" I said, thinking Shawnee County's police department's property room couldn't be much larger than a closet.

"Yes, something," Sligh said, his dainty little fingers nervously tapping at the desk.

"And Aunt Jessie's will?"

"Folded in the Bible and to be sent to probate. If there are no unforeseen complications, Mt. Olivet Church will receive all her property and worldly goods except for the doll. That was specifically consigned to Esmeralda."

I nodded, signed for it, but didn't thank him. I just wanted to be away from the law and those who supposedly served it. I rewrapped the doll, walked from his office down to the Ranger, and headed for Huntington.

While driving, I tried the radio. It worked maybe five minutes. Sam had cheated me, yet I wouldn't go back to accost him. I'd had enough hassles for a lifetime. Let me get away from man to the clean sight of a greening prairie that reached all the way to snow-capped mountains and the aerie of eagles.

At Huntington State I was immediately able to see Dr. Fredrick. His gray hair stuck up in rebellion at the back of his skull, and he had cut the knob of his chin shaving. I told him that since no charges were to be brought against Esmeralda, by rights she should be turned over to me, a kinsman.

"It's not that simple," he said. "Technically she's still under the supervision of Social Services. They won't release her until convinced her life will be bettered. Miles of red tape and a court order required."

"I know a good lawyer," I said.

"You'll need him. Now, Esmeralda is eating enough to sustain herself. Her blood count remains low, and she suffers occasional arrhythmia. She also still resists being touched. She has started brushing her hair for hours at a time. Nurse Adams gave her the brush. Esmeralda won't, however, open her eyes or face anyone. She turns away from all personal contact."

I showed and explained to him about the doll, and we walked over to Building 7, where Nurse Adams unlocked doors and led us through the ward to the one-way window outside of Esmeralda's room. She sat on her bed, her hands folded on her lap, her back to the window. Beside her lay the hairbrush.

"She keeps herself clean and is no trouble," Nurse Adams said. "The staff continue to be drawn to her. They never pass without looking in and speaking."

"Try the doll," Dr. Fredrick said to me.

He and Nurse Adams waited while I entered the room. Esmeralda didn't turn to me. I moved around in front of her. Her eyes stayed shut.

"Esmeralda, I've brought you something I think you'll like," I said.

She remained motionless. This woman gave birth to me, though I'd not known her and she could never mean to me what the lady who'd reared me had, but still was my mother, and maybe our genes would transmit between us their secret language. I hoped for that.

I unwrapped and set the doll not on her lap but the bed. Esmeralda didn't react. I touched her hands and then her cheek, yet got no response. I lifted her limp right hand and settled it on the doll. It remained there. I refolded the wrapping paper, backed away, and waited. Nothing. The eyes stayed shut, and she appeared lifeless.

When I left the room, Nurse Adams closed the door. She, Dr. Fredrick, and I stood outside watching. Esmeralda hadn't moved. We continued to wait, but after a time Dr. Fredrick shook his head and turned to leave, his body stooped, his shoulders rounded.

"Whoa," Nurse Adams said.

Dr. Fredrick crossed back to the window. Fingers of Esmeralda's right hand slowly felt along the length of the doll. The left hand crossed from her lap, slipped beneath the doll, and with both hands she gently lifted and held it against her breasts. She bent over and sheltered it. Her hair fell around the doll. Esmeralda began to rock slowly forward and back with the instinctive and universal motion of a woman tending to, comforting, and nursing a child.

"Definitely something here to build upon," Dr. Fredrick said to Nurse Adams and me. Nurse Adams was smiling, and I expected she would soon be passing the news along corridors of the ward.

Dr. Fredrick and I stood in sunshine outside Building 7. Inmates wearing bathrobes and slippers moved aimlessly across the yard, sat on benches, or stopped at the high white pickets of the fence to look out at a shaded side street. One man moaned quietly until an orderly walked to him and led him away.

"I want an open place with lots of grass, birds, and trees for her," I told Dr. Fredrick. "She's used to and needs space. You think you can line that up for me?"

"Facilities like that exist, though they're very expensive. My guess is it'll take a year or more before you can work out any transfer, if at all. In the meantime she'll be well cared for here."

"I'll phone once a week to ask about her and give you numbers where I can be notified of any change in her health or her status with the authorities," I said, thinking here was a good man and another NS#3. "Buy her anything she needs."

"Some will hate to see her go," he said.

I left Huntington State and drove to Shawnee County and Ben's.

Dusk was settling into the valley. I heard ravens calling on the ridge. I packed up my few belongings.

"You driving into the night?" Ben asked. He made me eat a bowl of the beef-and-biscuit stew he'd cooked. We walked out to the Ranger. No doubt about Ben. He was an NS#3 all the way to the bone and heart. The writer who'd argued these people would be bypassed by civilization and history had it wrong. The Bens of the world carried the rest of us on their backs.

"If you hear from Blackie, I'd like to know her whereabouts," I said.

"Only with her say-so," he said.

"By the way, Leroy Spears has a clipper ship I ordered. I want you to have it. It's paid for."

"I thank you, Charley. Leroy does good work."

"Is Aunt Jessie's grave still empty?"

"Reburied her while you were at Wild Thorn. Bartholomew Asberry preached a second service. Another big crowd."

"I'll stop by and like to pay for her tombstone if you'll take care of that for me," I said, and he nodded. We shook hands. He opened the gate for me to leave.

When I passed through Cliffside, the few lights still burned bravely against the closing darkness. Mt. Olivet appeared ghostly under the moon. There was enough of its glimmer for me to find Aunt Jessie's plot. The flowers people had laid over the humped-up grave nearly covered the moist, raw soil. I picked a few wild daisies along the fence to add my thanks.

I stood awhile. The moon laid a pale sheen over the cemetery, the valley, and the humped silhouettes of mountains. Whippoorwills called. A breeze stirred leaves of the sugar maple. This was not a bad place to lay the body down.

When I left Shawnee County and connected up with Interstate 77, I followed its winding course thinking of Blackie. I'd get things straight in Montana, most likely sell the horses, and track her down. I'd done lots of tracking. I had her license number, and canceled checks and credit-card bills would be flowing back. I knew she'd always wanted to live in Florida. With her I could adjust to la-la land. Take up fishing, buy a boat, maybe grow a few oranges. Have her beside me during the dark of night.

At Pax, West Virginia, another once-thriving coal town, I took the off-ramp to gas up with Blue Sunoco. Pax. Peace. Who'd given it that unlikely Latin name? The station sold groceries, soft drinks, and general merchandise. My headlights played on shiny blades of new garden shovels for sale propped against the outside wall, their price tags dangling and twisting in the breeze. I asked the gangly, long-faced youth behind the cash register if the store carried kneepads, meaning the kind Bartholomew and Tolliver Asberry wore at their diggings near Rich Find.

"Not worth stocking any longer, I reckon," he said. "Not many fellers working coal around here these days. You need 'em bad?"

"I could've used 'em," I said. "Appears I'll be on my knees a bunch in weeks to come."